BEF

S

FALLS

ALSO BY DYLAN YOUNG

The Silent Girls
Blood Runs Cold

BEFORE SHE FALLS

DYLAN YOUNG

bookouture

Published by Bookouture in 2018

An imprint of StoryFire Ltd.

Carmelite House
50 Victoria Embankment
London EC4Y 0DZ

www.bookouture.com

ISBN: 978-1-78681-620-7
eBook ISBN: 978-1-78681-619-1

PROLOGUE

SEPTEMBER

Depending on the tides, Louise Griffiths either walked the beach or up along the cliff path at least twice a week, rain or shine. She always parked in the Dunraven Bay car park and dressed accordingly. Today, the tide was in and so the beach was out of bounds. It was late September, the day cold and blustery, and Louise wore an anorak, hat and gloves. Toby, her energetic cocker, preferred the beach because the cliff top meant he'd have to stay on a lead. Louise had read lots of horror stories about dogs chasing birds and jumping off viaducts and mountainsides in pursuit. Southerndown Cliff was two hundred and ten feet high when you reached the top. It wasn't worth the risk. Toby would just have to wait until they reached the other side and the river mouth to run amok.

Unlike Toby, Louise preferred the cliff path. Though it flanked the Bristol Channel, this far around it was an almost west-facing coastline and open to the Atlantic. It made for a bracing stroll, and more often than not, Louise would stand at the very top and wonder at the view. To the south, she'd look out across the channel towards England. Below, at the bottom of the cliff, was the beach, though the rocky limestone shelf and the lack of sand barely qualified. Still, it made for a spectacular landscape that went a long way towards explaining why this spot was such a popular location.

The sharp easterly whipped up the surf and Louise took a handkerchief to her running nose before turning back towards the path to continue her walk, through the second car park at the top of the rise and out on to open common.

There was someone else approaching on the path and Toby looked up, his tail already in overdrive, ready to greet a fellow walker. A smile formed automatically on Louise's lips and her brain formulated a greeting: a mutual appreciation of nature and the weather that had become her standard gambit over the years. But it froze halfway as the girl came closer. No, *strode* closer, because there was a determination about this walker that, as she neared, seemed out of place. She would have seen Louise. There was no way of avoiding that, but there was no happy reciprocal smile on her face. As she neared, the girl put her hand up to her forehead and kept her face lowered so as not to make eye contact.

Louise was no psychiatrist, but she'd taught at a local comprehensive for almost fifteen years, so she knew when things, with girls especially, were wrong.

'Are you OK?' Louise asked.

The query triggered a reaction. The girl looked up briefly. Louise flinched and felt something, a mixture of shock and alarm, ripple through her. It wasn't only the girl's lost, hopeless expression but the large mark on her face that made Louise start. A dark stain like the curved rays of a black sun, obtrusive and obvious, designed to startle. The exchange of looks lasted the briefest of seconds before the girl passed by on a spur that left the main path and headed towards another viewpoint.

'Hello,' said Louise to the girl's back, her voice taut and urgent.

But the girl took no notice. She walked on to where the land began to fall away, where earth started to crumble.

'Hello?' Louise said again, but she got no further.

The girl hesitated, half turned and let out one shuddering sob before swinging back to face the sea and, without warning, running towards the edge of the cliff where she dropped, like a stone, into the void.

Something imploded inside Louise and she fell to her knees. Toby barked, unnerved by the strange emotions he sensed, but his voice was drowned out by another's.

Louise's anguished wail was lost amidst the sound of the gulls and carried off by the wind into an uncaring sky.

CHAPTER ONE

FEBRUARY – FIVE MONTHS LATER

SUNDAY

Detective Inspector Anna Gwynne watched her dog, Lexi, sprint away, plant both feet in a controlled skid and duck her head for the retrieve just as the ball she was aiming for hit a pebble and bounced. Lexi lost all footing and rolled. Twice. Whether through sheer luck or canine judgement, she then sprang upright and took the ball cleanly in the air as it bounced once again. Looking enormously pleased with herself, she performed a rolling shake of her torso to get rid of most of the sand and began trotting back towards her owner.

Anna shook her head, smiling. It made the muscles under her eyes bunch up. 'She's going to need another bath.'

Next to her, Ben Hawley grinned. 'Good pickup, Lexi. The old wipeout and snatch.'

Lexi trotted up to where they were standing and dropped the ball at Anna's feet before looking up at her entreatingly.

Anna tried chastisement. 'Your muzzle is more sand than fur.'

Lexi wagged her tail.

Anna pressed the end of an orange Chuckit launcher over the ball, picked it up and threw it forty yards towards the water. Lexi followed. They were west of Friars Point in the Old Harbour in Barry, near Cardiff. Boats had moored here since before the sixteenth century. With the tide out, a huge expanse of yellow sand made it a haven for dog walkers. Anna smiled. Even after two months of having Lexi in her life, it tickled her to think of herself as one of those. She'd finally taken the plunge just before Christmas and, with Ben's help, rescued Lexi, a brown Borador – a Border collie Lab mix – from a shelter near Bristol. Anna still didn't know why, out of all the dogs, she'd chosen Lexi. The easiest answer was that the dog, who'd sat calmly and watched with bright, intelligent eyes as Anna walked past her kennel, had chosen her.

Something in that appraising look had struck Anna instantly and the deal was done.

This time, Lexi took the ball in full flight as it bounced and, in contrast to the pile-up of moments before, ran a graceful arc before cantering back.

Anna's work phone beeped a message. Superintendent Mark Rainsford's name appeared in the text window. Anna frowned. Rainsford rarely texted on a weekend. It must be something important. She glanced at the message.

Take a look at this and we'll talk later.
https://tinyurl/coronercardf

Ben looked at her. She shrugged and handed him the Chuckit. He stepped away to give her some space and called the dog to him. Anna watched Lexi glance her way, as if asking permission.

'Go to Ben,' she said.

The dog complied. Lexi had bonded deeply with her and was startlingly intelligent. In a moment of stark self-awareness, Anna looked across at the two living creatures she cared most about in the world and shook her head, wondering what had brought on this sudden, and for her unusual, emotion.

Ben had been the significant other in her life for only a few months longer than she'd owned Lexi. Six months previously, Anna would have scoffed at the suggestion that within half a year she'd have a lover *and* a dog. And this feeling that now sprang up, this warmth, did so unbidden, leaving her a little hot and bothered. Emotions always did, mainly because they were not at all amenable to analysis and logical explanation: the twin disciplines she used to navigate through life. She stared at the brown dog with white-tipped paws and at the man with a quick smile and healer's hands. *Must be the ozone making me a little high*, she thought. She pressed the link Rainsford had texted over. It took her to a newsfeed.

Coroner demands action as inquest hears harrowing details of how Internet challenge caused suicide of 16-year-old girl

A coroner raised concerns yesterday about the increasing danger of children becoming entangled in an Internet challenge known as the Black Squid.

Kimberley Williams, 16, died after jumping off a cliff at a notorious suicide black spot in Southerndown, South Wales. After police examined Kimberley's social media and Internet activity, her family revealed she had been goaded into leaping by her involvement in a suicide game. In a statement read out to the court, Miss Williams' sister described how the teenager had become increasingly withdrawn after a recent break-up left her depressed and receiving counselling.

Responding to questions, pathologist Richard Murphy confirmed that Miss Williams died from multiple injuries as a result of the fall and that her face had been painted with the crude image of a black squid.

Dr Katia Piercy, a forensic psychologist, explained to the court that suicide games are thought to have begun as an elaborate hoax, with some children wishing to participate and use the narrative to explain their experiences of self-harm. However, in May of 2017, the Russian authorities, in the wake of some 130 deaths linked to online suicide challenge games, passed a law imposing a maximum of 6 years imprisonment for anyone caught inducing suicide in minors online. Dr Piercy explained that the game Kimberley Williams chose to participate in, known as the Black Squid, involved completing twenty tasks designed to psychologically channel vulnerable participants towards a final suicidal act.

Family members paid tribute to Miss Williams and described her as a bubbly member of the family. Her sister Vanessa said, 'Kimberley was my best friend. We all loved her to bits. She was an amazing person who got caught up in something really horrible.'

The coroner, Caroline Masters, said she would be writing a report to the chief medical officer as well as to the Chief Coroner for England and Wales. It will also be circulated to the Association of Police and Crime Commissioners.

Anna read it twice more and then rang Rainsford.

'Morning, Anna. What do you think?'

'How long have you known about this, sir?' It came out sharp, almost an accusation.

'I got a heads-up half an hour ago from a colleague in South Wales Police who knows about you and Shaw.'

Anna suppressed an ironic laugh.

You and Shaw.

Three little words that were the signpost to a minefield. Hector Shaw was a convicted serial killer whose own daughter Abbie had been a victim of the Black Squid. Anna, through her work as the operational lead of Avon and Somerset Constabulary's cold case squad, had needed to interview Shaw on more than one occasion. As a result, she had become embroiled in his complex case. Still, the thought that she'd become something of an expert on Shaw in other people's minds was no cause for celebration. Not in the slightest.

Yet it was the obvious answer to why Rainsford's contact might have told him. Any Black Squid-related search entry on HOLMES, the Home Office Large Major Enquiry System, would flag up Abbie Shaw, and by extension her notorious father. And, terrifying as it might seem, Anna's name was now inextricably linked to him. Shaw had targeted his victims because of their involvement as peddlers or administrators of the game. His killing spree had been a vengeful act, in the course of which he'd gleaned intelligence about other Black Squid victims. Intelligence he'd kept to himself until the last few months when he'd inexplicably chosen Anna as his conduit for revealing the burial sites of more than one of these victims.

Even so, Anna did not have the brief for investigating Black Squid deaths, so Rainsford's motivation in telling her about Kimberley Williams, especially as it was off their patch, intrigued her.

Operational bubbles were the reality of police work. You existed in your own, or at least your own force's, little world full of details and minutiae that meant sod all to anyone outside your team. Anna barely knew what was going on in the rest of Avon and Somerset. Her squad, South-West Major Crimes Review Task Force, was a regional unit investigating historical cold cases over three or sometimes four force areas. A suicide in an area outside the MCRTF's remit would not appear on their radar unless it had some kind of supra-regional significance, or unless someone savvy realised that there was an overlap. Kimberley Williams' death would need to tick both of those boxes. Shaw's past wasn't enough.

'So why have you sent me this, sir?'

The two long beats of silence answered Anna's question almost before Rainsford could.

'This report was in yesterday's papers. It would explain why I got a call from Whitmarsh this morning. He will have seen it, I'm sure.'

He.

And there it was. The big, lumbering elephant that stomped into the room whenever Rainsford mentioned Whitmarsh prison.

Hector Shaw.

Rainsford continued, 'George Calhoun, Whitmarsh's governor, says Shaw is bleating about meeting you but that there's no need to go to Whitmarsh. He says this one is much closer to home.'

This one. Another body?

'How close?'

'Bristol. He won't give us a location, of course.'

Anna snorted. Of course. He never did. Not revealing the actual location of a buried body was the only way Shaw could guarantee one of his little awaydays from prison. He'd already had a couple and 'enjoyed' Anna's company on both occasions.

'When?'

'Tomorrow… Anna? Are you OK with this?'

OK with watching another rotting corpse being dug up while Shaw stares at me with his eyes full of accusation? Why wouldn't I be?

'Yes, I'm fine with it,' she said, despite her true feelings.

'Good. We'll catch up tomorrow. I'll get on to Whitmarsh and get the ball rolling. Enjoy the rest of your weekend.'

She killed the call. Rainsford's sign-off might have come across as sardonic to someone who didn't know him. But he didn't do sarcasm. He'd meant it. Anna allowed herself a little ironic smile at that.

They both knew how dangerous Shaw was. His decision to suddenly cooperate after years of admitting nothing about his knowledge of the Black Squid deaths mystified police and prison authorities alike. And Rainsford was right. Shaw had probably seen the news and it would have upset him. Odd to think that a serial murderer might get upset, but Anna knew that anything to do with the Black Squid was highly likely to get under Shaw's skin. He'd killed at least six people in his hunt for the person he deemed responsible for his daughter's suicide. A suicide in which she, too, had drawn a facsimile of a black squid on her face before throwing herself under a train.

Shaw had conceded to Anna that he'd failed to find the twisted mind behind the sickening game. The published details of Kimberley's death would have rekindled the burning desire for vengeance that had driven him to kill in the first place. And it was that which scared her. Somewhere along the line, Shaw'd seen a way to use her as a tool, revealing the buried victims of the Black Squid to her periodically in order to keep the investigation alive. And though the discoveries had given closure to several families as a result, still Anna found his cat-and-mouse tactics repugnant. She could not say no to Rainsford since Shaw flatly refused to talk to anyone else. To that end she felt as trapped as a buzzing fly in a spider's web knowing that she had a moral and professional obligation to comply.

There were the obvious sniggering comments from colleagues whenever this was brought up, of course. Anna was a physically fit, attractive, young, female police officer. Why wouldn't Shaw show an unhealthy interest? Yet in all of her interactions with him, Anna had never sensed the slightest innuendo. Indeed, on more than one occasion he had reminded her that his daughter, had she lived, would have been around Anna's age.

But Anna doubted that Shaw would ever have discussed with his daughter any of the topics and details he'd revealed to her. Even now, she could hear his nasal voice describing how he'd tortured his victims into telling him what he wanted to know. Delivered always in a stone-cold, matter-of-fact way.

And now she was about to invite him into her life once again. The thought of what the working week might bring made her suddenly shiver.

She looked up and out over the expanse of sea and sand and inhaled deeply, savouring the moment and reminding herself that it wasn't Monday yet.

CHAPTER TWO

MONDAY

They'd agreed on Clifton Observatory in Bristol as the meeting point. This early in the morning it was eerily quiet. The school trips and tourists were yet to arrive, and sensible people who were not at work were all indoors. They were firmly on Avon and Somerset ground here, not more than seven miles from police HQ at Portishead, and they'd dispatched a team to Whitmarsh prison to fetch Hector Shaw in an escorted police van.

Anna had dressed warmly: puffer jacket, gloves and a woolly hat. Arctic plumes moving south across the county had plunged even the South-West into sub-zero temperatures. It had not snowed in Bristol but it was forecast as a significant risk. It wouldn't last because yet more incoming Atlantic storms to the west were set to blow away the cold. But at this time of year, in the heart of winter, even that was a poisoned chalice.

Rainsford sat in his car, phone to his ear, but Anna, too restless to stay seated, stood outside with the rest of her MCRTF squad, namely DCs Justin Holder and Ryia Khosa. Holder, mid-twenties but looking ten years younger, defied the cold with the arrogance of the young in an unbuttoned padded jacket. He walked forward to meet the arriving transport and pointed to a space behind a Network Rail van parked with its bonnet pointing towards the city. Khosa, a good head shorter than Holder, her face barely visible under the fur-lined hood of the heavy coat she wore, spoke in a muffled voice through the scarf wrapped tightly around her mouth.

'Bit different to the last time, ma'am.'

Anna nodded. She and Khosa had been in this situation before, the last time on a warm, muggy day in August in a park in Sussex. She'd known then that they'd have to indulge Shaw his 'expeditions' again but had not expected it to be in the middle of winter, like this. She felt he preferred the warmer months in order to make the most of getting out of prison, even for a day.

This demand, in the dead of winter, had a sense of urgency about it. Yet all he'd said, communicated to her through the governor of Whitmarsh, was that they needed to get access to the railway line near Leigh Woods. So here they were with two railway workers who'd brought keys to let them into the sealed-off access roads.

Holder came back to join the two female officers. 'We're following them in.'

'Do we know where we're going?' Khosa asked.

'He's told the driver it's a storage area somewhere down there, that's all,' Holder said.

'Typical,' Anna said. It was Shaw's way. Keeping information to the bare minimum so they had no option other than to follow his lead.

Anna and Khosa hurried back to their Focus, one of two pool cars allocated to the unit, and followed the convoy. It took them across the suspension bridge, spanning the gorge with the dirty-brown river below, and down along the A369 towards Somerset until they got to Ham Green. There they turned right, back towards the river along narrow lanes only wide enough for one vehicle, until they got to a gate where the railway workers got out and used their keys. The Ford sagged on its suspension as the passenger side tyre found a pothole, causing Khosa to curse and apologise in the same breath. She pointed at the satnav on the dashboard and muttered, 'None of these roads are on the map.'

She was right. The stoned tracks the Ford now navigated with such difficulty were Network Rail access roads used to gain entry to the railway for maintenance. Anna didn't know this line – the old Bristol to Portishead line from the main station in Temple Meads out to the flat estuary land and the port. It was still used for freight, and the rumour was that they were going to make it a metro link by the end of the decade. But for now, it was a rarely used and desolate stretch through cuttings adjacent to the river, looping in towards Ham Green where there had once been a station.

They drove slowly parallel to the line, the narrow lane widening abruptly into a large, cleared area on which chippings had been laid. Their tyres crunched on the stones as Khosa pulled in and Anna stared out of the windscreen. The actual railway line ran only ten yards away. To her right stood stacks of sleepers, some concrete and others older and wooden. Next to them stood a ten-foot-high mound of grey track ballast chippings. All in all, the space must have been the size of half a football field. Where the stoned parking area ended, bramble and dead fern made a natural barrier bordering the woods beyond. It was a desolate spot.

The Network Rail van had parked in front of them. Holder got out and spoke to the driver. A minute later, the van drove off and Holder stuck his head down to talk through the passenger side window to Anna.

'Not many people come down here, apparently.'

'What is this place?' Anna asked.

'They call it a sleeper depot. Somewhere to keep spare ballast and sleepers for essential repairs on the line when needed.'

Anna looked at all the parked cars now with their doors closed. There were cadaver dogs and handlers, ground radar contractors, Rainsford, of course, and uniformed support.

All waiting for her.

She pulled on some gloves and got out of the car. Half a dozen other car doors opened as if on cue. From the police Transit, two uniformed officers emerged. Anna knew that at least one of those in the escort vehicle would be armed. She walked across to the van just as the rear doors opened and out stepped Shaw. His hands were cuffed in front of him and he wore a heavy coat over his lurid prison garb of chequered yellow and green. It was the first time she'd seem him in an 'escape suit'. Someone in Whitmarsh, or even higher up in the Prison and Probation Service, must have decided that Shaw's jaunts were a significant security risk. The boiler suits were designed to easily identify and prevent the escape of prisoners assessed as flight risks while being escorted outside the prison.

Watching Shaw blinking into the light, Anna was reminded of a bewildered jester transported from some ancient court. But there was nothing funny about Shaw as he stared at the surroundings, taking in the bleak landscape until his eyes landed on Anna. There they stopped and watched her approach. The prison had given him a hat to wear and it hid his shaved head, but his skin looked pale behind the thick glasses that distorted the contour of his face and made his eyes look smaller than they were.

'Anna,' he said in his slow Mancunian drawl. 'Here we are again, eh?'

'Hector.' She used his name but didn't offer a smile.

'This is real witch's tit weather,' he said, shivering inside his coat.

'Maybe we should get on with it, then.'

'Good idea.' Shaw started walking along the stoned area, looking up towards the denuded trees lining the railway and bordering the fields beyond. Anna, watching him carefully, walked with him, the uniformed officer within arm's reach of Shaw and his gun-carrying colleague five yards behind.

'What are you looking for?' Anna asked.

'I reckon it's special. Needed a little bit of extra persuasion to tell me about this one did that shit-stain Krastev.'

Shaw hissed out the last two words of the sentence as if they were hawked up phlegm. Anna tried not to think about what it all implied and failed. Krastev, a vicious and sadistic criminal who had eluded capture in his native Bulgaria, Italy and Belgium by fleeing to the UK, had been embroiled in the Black Squid game and consequently Abbie Shaw's death. Hunted down and captured by Shaw, Krastev had paid the price of that involvement with his life. But not before Shaw had managed to extract a great deal of information. Anna knew that whatever it was they were searching for on this freezing Monday morning would have Krastev's bloody hands all over it. Such was the pattern. Shaw had already led them to more than one of Krastev's buried victims, but it was his emphasis on the word 'persuasion' that made Anna squirm. As well as information about Krastev's own murderous activities, Shaw had obtained links to other members of the Black Squid cell that Krastev had been a part of. Targeted by Shaw just as Krastev had been, the crime scene photos of their deaths showed that 'persuasion', in Shaw's hands, was a chapter straight out of the medieval torturer's handbook.

Shaw swivelled, scanning the horizon. 'He said something about a fence.'

They passed a pile of wooden sleepers and then another. On the other side of the track a thin strip of dead fern and grass ended in more trees. Sometimes, when Anna took the train, she'd look at these strips of land adjacent to the embankments and cuttings and wonder how many thousands of acres of dead space it all added up to. Though nothing more than a fleeting thought before, now she was here, at ground level, it came back to her vividly.

Shaw kept walking until finally he stopped, quite abruptly, and said, 'Here.'

Anna turned and followed Shaw's pointing finger across the storage yard, between another stack of sleepers, and the pile of dumped grey track ballast. Through the trees she saw the geometric pattern of a fence, at least seventeen feet tall, black-coated metal with sturdy poles sitting on a concrete base.

Anna turned back and called to Holder. 'Get the dogs searching this area.'

'Yes, ma'am.'

Anna dropped her voice. 'And find out what's behind that fence.'

She turned back to Shaw. He smiled. 'You're looking fit, Anna.'

The nearest uniformed officer raised an eyebrow. Anna ignored it. She took no offence from Shaw's words. She was fit and could hold her own in terms of endurance and physicality with anyone of her size and bigger. And she knew Shaw meant it in its truest sense, subtext-free.

'Life must be treating you well,' Shaw added.

'As well as,' she said.

'Unlike me, then,' Shaw said.

Anna frowned but Shaw didn't elaborate. Instead he sucked in the cold air and exhaled loudly.

A few flakes of snow drifted through the air, wafted away on the brisk wind that seemed to cut right through Anna's legs. The cadaver dogs were out of their van. She watched the handler give his instructions and saw the dogs start their work. Two springer spaniels with docked tails covered the ground like quicksilver.

Rainsford exited his car, his Crombie buttoned with the collar up around his ears. They'd agreed that he'd stay in the background so as not to antagonise Shaw. Much as she hated to admit it, Anna knew she was the link here and no one else. But Shaw looked across to where Rainsford stood, following Anna's gaze.

'Getting his hands dirty at last, eh, Anna?' Shaw said.

'You should go back to the van and wait,' she replied before walking away.

She watched the cadaver dogs working for ten minutes until one of them, its stumpy tail twitching, turned abruptly, sat on its haunches next to a pile of the wooden sleepers and began to bark loudly. Holder signalled to the Forensics team, a couple of whom came forward with a small grey box on wheels attached to a long handle they could use to trundle the ground radar equipment over the earth. Within minutes they had a tent set up, largely to protect their laptop from the worsening weather. Anna went over and stood near the tent until Holder emerged.

'It's a positive, ma'am. Radar's showing a definite disturbance here,' Holder said.

Anna nodded. If this was another body, another innocent victim to find justice for, it was up to CSI to do their bit.

There remained the possibility, never far from Anna's mind, that Shaw had been responsible for the killing and the burial in every case, and the narrative he'd invented to explain them all away was nothing more than manipulative lies. Though she had very little evidence to disprove this possibility, deep down in her core she did not believe he was lying to her. Yet today she'd already sensed something different about him. Less of the smug swagger of before.

Anna looked up at the grey sky and felt a snowflake brush her eyelashes. She turned and was walking back to where they were holding Shaw when Holder called to her. She looked back to see him standing next to another, taller stack of concrete sleepers. The cadaver dog handler was there next to the second dog, who'd parked herself on the ground, again barking loudly.

'Ma'am, a word,' Holder called out.

Anna crossed the space between them, rubbing her gloved hands together for a bit of warmth.

'What's wrong, Justin?'

'It's Zipper, ma'am, the second dog. Frank, here, thinks she's found something, too. In a different spot. He wants the radar guys to take another look.'

Anna, her face stiff from the cold, stared at Frank. She'd not worked with him before. An ex-police dog handler, he now worked for a private firm specialising in buried remains. Frank shrugged an apology. 'I'd put good money on it. Looks like it's under this lot.' He gestured towards the stacks of sleepers. There were four of them, each a pile of eight pallets with four sleepers on each palette.

'We'll need to move these,' he said.

'Justin, get back on to your Network Rail pals. I'll speak to Rainsford.' She waved at the superintendent, who immediately strode towards her.

'There's a problem, sir. Shaw only suggested there was one body, but the dogs have found something else in a second area,' she said.

'We need more manpower,' Rainsford said. 'I'll get on to it, and we'll need to discuss who'll be senior investigating officer.'

Anna nodded. 'These may simply be dead sheep, sir.' The cold was beginning to seep into her bones.

'He hasn't shown us any dead sheep before, has he?'

Anna shook her head.

'How is he? Shaw, I mean?'

'Difficult to say.'

'In what way?'

She shrugged and shivered. 'Something's off. Maybe it's Shaw. He seems... different. Angry as always, that's a given. But I can't quite put my finger what else there is yet.'

Rainsford didn't comment. Anna's instincts were not to be scoffed at. Though the superintendent had never talked about it, they both knew it was part of her make-up and a useful tool. So far, those instincts had served her well in her ability to clear cases and deal with Shaw.

Rainsford glanced across at the Transit van. 'Do you want me to tell him there's more than one?'

Anna shook her head. 'No point. He'll only talk to me.'

'OK.' He glanced around at the desolate surroundings. 'We'll set this whole area up as a crime scene. I'll talk to the crime scene manager and see what he thinks about moving those sleepers.'

Anna nodded. 'Shaw's reference point. The fence. Any idea what that is?'

Rainsford's eyes narrowed. 'It's the northern perimeter fence of Ryegrove.'

'But that's near Leigh Woods. I had no idea it stretched this far.' Anna turned to look back at the black fence.

'Let's hope it is just that. A reference point.' Rainsford sighed. 'You finish up here with Shaw and liaise with the CSM. First thing tomorrow we'll have a briefing. We need to discuss strategy.'

Anna nodded. She wanted to ask him what he meant by hoping the fence was 'just' a reference point but he already had his phone to his ear as he walked back to his car, leaving Anna alone to digest this new morsel of information. It bothered her enough to make her want to scratch the itch. She walked back to the tent and stood behind it out of the worst of the wind and punched 'Ryegrove Hospital' into a search engine on her phone. Up came a page posted on a local history site.

Ryegrove Hospital began life as a great house for a sugar plantation owner with a refinery in the city itself, but by the early twentieth century had been bought by Bristol Corporation and turned into an isolation hospital for typhoid and tuberculosis patients and later smallpox. After the Second World War, the National Health Service Act split the site into a geriatric unit and long-term institution for the mentally ill. A reallocation of services in 2000 saw a major redevelopment for the provision of much-needed mental health services. The geriatric unit was closed, and new builds led to the establishment of the Somerton medium secure unit and the Riverside low secure unit.

When she finished and looked up, Shaw was waiting.

She walked over to the van, got into the front, turned and spoke through the grille. 'We have one very likely spot,' Anna said.

Shaw's hands looked very cold in the cuffs. 'I saw the second dog indicate. There's something else here, isn't there?'

'We need to move the sleepers.'

'Krastev said only one,' Shaw said.

'We'll know for definite once Network Rail move their stuff.'

Shaw was shaking his head. 'You need to stop them, Anna.'

'Stop who?'

'The bastards who are still out there doing this.'

Anna searched his face. 'Doing what, Hector?'

'Trapping mixed-up kids. Getting inside their heads, tormenting them with their sick games.'

Anna searched his face. Shaw turned away to look at the activity through a rear window. 'Like that girl, Kimberley Williams. She had the Black Squid mark on her, just like Abbie.'

'I don't know all the details.'

Shaw turned back, his eyes blazing.

'Honestly, I do not know,' Anna said.

Shaw leaned forward. Though he was several safe feet away, the gesture made her want to move back. When he spoke, it was in a low whisper.

'Then find out. I can't stop these bastards, Anna. You have to.'

Anna glanced at the site and the crime scene tape already marking out areas where the dogs had indicated a find. 'We're going to need heavy machinery. It's all going to take time.'

Shaw smiled and eased back into his seat. His lips looked dry and cracked. 'You sending me back to my hole again, Anna?'

'I have no intention of freezing to death out here.'

Shaw nodded. 'You'll let me know what you find.'

Anna didn't answer as she started to get out of the van.

'And when you do, I'll help you even more.'

Beside her, the driver was staring, a look of distaste on his face. She hoped it was because of Shaw and not because he felt she was pandering to him. But she said nothing more as she exited the vehicle and walked away.

Anna sent Holder and Khosa back to HQ while she stayed, watching the forensic team do their dance, Shaw's words gnawing at her like an irritating splinter. They'd been right to assume that the report of Kimberley Williams' 'suicide' had got to him. It would have brought what had happened to his daughter bubbling to the surface all over again, and that was reason enough for him to be animated.

Yet Shaw's impassioned plea for her to 'stop these bastards' implied that, in Shaw's mind at least, the same perpetrators were involved. Anna considered that. Abbie's and Kimberley's deaths were sixteen years apart, but Shaw believed other bodies he'd shown her were Black Squid victims too. And this latest revelation threw up a list of unanswered questions that simmered in Anna's head.

Was it possible that there were others? Was Kimberley Williams the latest in a longer line? Could there be an active killer out there with sights on yet another vulnerable young life?

CHAPTER THREE

Beth Farlow waved at the security guard on duty behind the glass in reception at the end of a long shift. Everyone who came or left Ryegrove Hospital went through the same checks, like airport security. They weren't just screened for sharp objects; they weren't allowed phones, money, glass, computers, maps of the area, chewing gum or string. The guard, Jack, was busy checking a video display but he generally made time to talk to Beth, and she was always genuine in return.

At twenty-four, Beth was doing what she'd always wanted to as a staff nurse, and not even the repetitiveness of the security check could dampen her spirits. When she explained to people that she nursed in a secure mental health unit, it not only stopped conversations, it generally made people's faces twist in incredulity. Something about the way she looked, and her personality, made them think of paediatrics or a care home assistant when she said she was a nurse. But that was just her surface coating. Underneath the smile burned a bright and sharp commitment to mental health, the least glamorous of all the NHS services. Beth liked making a difference. As part of the Forensic Services division of the North Bristol NHS Trust, she worked providing care and treatment for a client group with learning disabilities and personality disorders, who displayed 'serious irresponsible behaviour' – which was a deliberately broad term. Her patients – she hated the word clients – were murderers and rapists and people whose views of the world, and of themselves, were very badly skewed.

She'd been lucky to get the job and even luckier to have found a room in a house in Severn Beach, shared with one of her old college mates, Dee, on the nursing degree course at the University of the West of England. It was way too far out of town, but it was quiet and cheap because the house – more a cottage if truth be told – had once been owned by Dee's grandmother. Beth took the train in and out of the city to work and cycled the final mile from Severn Beach station to the cottage on the edge of what once had been a farm.

She joked that it was keeping her fit.

From her cottage bedroom she could see the river and the Severn Crossing, and opposite the property was a wild wood. Because most of the traffic hissed by above them, it was surprisingly quiet, and two or three nights a week, she had the place to herself with Dee over at her boyfriend's.

It was almost six thirty when she got off the train. The station emptied quickly, and Beth walked outside, pulling on her gloves and reaching for the key to unlock her bike. If Dee was home and not sleeping, she'd come and pick Beth up, but today was not one of those days. Thank God it wasn't raining. She reached for the key to unlock the chain that held her bike to the rack. Her helmet was in the pannier on the back and she slid it on. People were hurrying to their cars or their homes. In ten minutes she'd be at the cottage: a nice warm meal, a little TV, bath and bed. She looked up at the road and the lights of the Severn Crossing in the distance and felt the little twinge of anxiety that had been her unwelcome companion these last few nights. Something about this final leg of the journey, one she'd made dozens of times, had begun to unnerve her. She wasn't even sure why.

Just get on with it, then, sensible Beth muttered. *It's keeping you fit, remember?*

On a dark and freezing February night, all Beth wanted to do, like everyone else, was get home. She shrugged and wished it wasn't quite so far and quite so cold and quite so winter dark.

CHAPTER FOUR

Anna got back to her ground-floor flat in Horfield after stopping off with a neighbour to pick up Lexi. The arrangement was easy and very convenient. Having a dog and walking it on the common brought Anna into contact with a whole community of like-minded people. One of them, a retired teacher by the name of Maggie, lived four doors down with her Labrador, Bruce, who'd made an instant connection with Lexi. On seeing Anna rushing back one evening desperate to walk the dog, Maggie offered to dog-sit on an ad hoc basis, which turned into every ad hoc weekday. Anna could not believe her luck and jumped at the chance. Lexi thrived on it and Maggie, a bluff and no-nonsense spinster, treated Lexi like her own child. The words 'Want to go to Maggie's?' triggered an instant pricking up of the ears and a look of absolute approval from the dog.

By eight thirty, after a shower and a heated-up bean casserole she'd made the week before, Anna was feeling a lot better and significantly warmer than she had done most of the day. A dense cold had seeped into her core in that forsaken burial ground adjacent to the railway line, and she suspected not all of it due to the sub-zero temperatures. It was as if the horror of whatever crimes had been committed there hung over the sheltered spot like a malign cloud.

She sat at the kitchen table, half a glass of Riesling at her elbow, Lexi stretched out in her basket, while Fleetwood Mac from her dad's vinyl collection played in the background. She checked her private phone for messages. One from Ben telling her he'd seen two cases of frostbitten fingers in people sleeping rough on the streets and asking her to remind him not to eat burned sausages ever again, and a couple from her sister, Kate, with photographs of her kids dressed in enough layers to get them to the South Pole and back.

And one more. This time from her mother. Never a big message sender, a WhatsApp from Sian Gwynne was noteworthy in itself. Anna and Kate had dragged their mother into the digital age with a gift of a simple, pared-down smartphone. Despite initial stubborn resistance, Sian was now able to send and receive images and emails as well as video calls. Even so, spontaneous texts were unusual, certainly with Anna as the recipient. Whatever warmth Sian had towards her children was generally reserved for Kate and her amazing family. Anna's relationship with her mother, in contrast, was one of polite tolerance. The message read, 'I hope your Christmas scarf is coming in handy in this cold weather. Looking forward to seeing you and Ben on the weekend.'

Anna sent a thumbs-up emoji in reply, but no words, telling herself as she texted not to analyse the subtext and failing. The reminder of the Christmas present was irritating, the reference to Ben even more so. Much to Anna's annoyance, Ben had immediately met with her mother's approval because he was male, and a doctor to boot. Sian Gwynne's vitriolic criticism of Anna's lifestyle choices found a great deal of ammunition in the fact that she was a detective – *what sort of a career is that for an intelligent woman with a good degree?* – and seemingly incapable of maintaining any kind of long-term relationship. But Anna knew, too, that the reason she found this so incredibly annoying said a lot more about her relationship with her mother than it did about Ben; a mere pawn in a pathetic psychological game.

She sipped her wine and put her phone on the table, dragging her thoughts away from her mother and back to the morning's search of the railway.

Shaw had seemed genuinely surprised the cadaver dog had scented a second possible corpse, and that bothered Anna a great deal. It wasn't that Shaw had the monopoly on buried bodies, but it meant he might not know as much as he said he did. She shook her head. This was a dangerous and unrewarding game to play. They weren't even sure if it was a body yet. But her intuition, a tool she'd learned in previous investigations to ignore at her own peril, was kicking in. Whatever awaited her in the cold earth between the woods and the river, it would not be pleasant. By ten thirty she was in bed and doing an impression of a foetus, relishing the warmth and wishing Ben was there as a human hot water bottle next to her.

She dreamed of desolate places and cold winds and of things moving beneath the ground. They had no faces or shapes, but they writhed in torment as above them someone disturbed the earth. She was there in the damp darkness with them, waiting for the light to break through. Waiting for a hand or a shovel to rupture their peace. And when it did, the scream erupting from the chambers oozed out of the earth like a black ghost.

Her work phone rang at 6.25 a.m., five minutes before she needed to get up, but twenty minutes after she'd woken. She recognised the voice as belonging to Chris Bradley, the crime scene manager.

'Sorry to wake you, ma'am, but you said you wanted to know.'

'I do,' Anna said, and sat up, wiping sleep from her eyes.

'It's a jackpot. We have two confirmed sets of remains. Both undoubtedly human.'

'Sounds like you're going to be busy, then.'

'You and me both, ma'am.'

She killed the call, threw on as many layers as she could get hold of and took Lexi out into the frozen street. The dog was happy enough to trot up and down the fifty yards Anna walked, relieving itself at a couple of lamp-posts. Anna wore gloves but in the pocket of her anorak had both a can of PAVA spray and an ASP telescopic baton. She carried them automatically, as commonplace to her as a watch or a purse. A couple of years before Shaw had entered her life, she'd have laughed at anyone paranoid enough to want to carry defensive weapons when walking their dog. But Anna wasn't anyone. No one had ever attacked her on this quiet street, but she'd been attacked once in a wood not too far from where she was now, all thanks to Shaw and his machinations. And the common, only a few yards away, could be a dark and dangerous place. As such, wariness of her surroundings was simply a question of being prepared for the next time.

It was still dark at seven thirty when Anna pulled into the crime scene she'd left yesterday afternoon. Lights were set up and the perimeter walled off by interlocking fencing. A separate cordon was in place for vehicles. There was only one way in and out, and a red-nosed uniformed constable watched her approach. She didn't know him and, having shown her warrant card, he took her details and noted them on the clipboard in his hand. This was the scene log, a record of everyone who would now attend and their reason for being there. It served as a stark reminder to Anna of how things could change in just a few hours. Three tents were set up and Anna made for the largest along a taped-off pathway. Inside, some foldable chairs and tables were dotted with equipment and an array of thermos flasks and plastic cups. A man in fetching white Tyvek waved to her: Chris Bradley, a rangy man in his mid-forties with thinning hair, and the designated crime scene manager.

'Morning,' he said, his voice croaky and dry-sounding.

'You've not had any sleep?'

'I'm off in an hour. Time enough to show you what we have.' He pointed towards a pile of packaged scene suits and overshoes. Anna dressed and followed Bradley out across the stoned ground towards a smaller tent. Bright halogen lamps illuminated a pit some four feet deep at the bottom of which was an array of exposed bones. They weren't the first she'd ever seen and, mercifully at this stage of decomposition, there was no flesh clinging to them and the smell was of cold earth and mould, not the cloying stench of decay. The bones were in disarray. The ribs canted, the long bones of the legs bent, the arms still half buried. Yellow-tipped markers and paper measuring tape lay next to some of the limb bones, waiting for photographs. But it was what lay in front of the ribs that drew Anna's attention. A white shape, domed, mostly still buried in the earth.

'What's that?' Anna asked.

Bradley looked at her and nodded. 'Exactly what you think it is.'

Anna frowned and looked towards the top of the ribcage, to a space where there should have been a head but where there was nothing. Her eyes jerked back to the dome. 'Is that the skull?'

Bradley nodded. 'It is. And there's no way it would have moved there through migration or vermin activity. This corpse was decapitated, and the head placed next to, or possibly on, the chest at the time of interment.'

'It would not have become detached on its own?'

'Gupta doesn't think so. Something about a crushed vertebra.'

Anna swallowed and tried to work out why the head would have become separated from a body. The experts would probably have an explanation, but it made for a grim few seconds of imaginings. She already knew that Gupta was the Home Office pathologist on this case and he would take great delight in providing a theory, she was sure.

Discipline brought her mind back to the here and now; she needed to know if there was anything solid at all to go on so her squad could get moving.

'Clothes?'

'Cotton-based products would all be gone in sixteen years. But there are remains of synthetic fibres – trainers most likely. But we have a belt buckle and what is likely a plastic wallet.'

Anna perked up. 'And?'

'Quite a bit of clay here, ma'am. Very damp. They've taken it to the lab without opening it. Hopefully we'll have something by the end of the morning.'

Anna nodded and followed Bradley out to the second smaller tent. In this one, the pit was shallower but in an earlier stage of investigation – some of the skull and the upper torso only exposed.

'At least this one has its head in the right place,' Bradley said.

'Is that a ring on the finger?' Anna pointed to a metallic band on the left fourth digit.

'Looks like it.'

A ring might mean a female but it was premature to assume anything yet. She turned to Bradley. 'So what's the plan?'

'We'd hope to get the bodies out by this afternoon. We could be lucky and find something here like we did with the first. Otherwise, identification will be the usual: we'll get ages and sex from the bones and then check against missing persons. Gupta took one look at the remains and knew there wasn't much for him.'

'OK, so my best bet is with the lab back at HQ and this wallet?'

Bradley nodded. 'They're already on it. Hopefully we'll have the contents open and inspected by nine. Gupta's contacted the unit at South Wales for an archaeologist and an anthropologist.'

'We need both?'

'Depends on what we find. Trouble is, once we find it, we don't want to be waiting. Better we have them on-site. Superintendent Rainsford wanted bells and whistles.'

'Can I have some images of the site as is?'

'I'll see to it.'

She thanked Bradley and walked out of the tent. The sun was now up but wouldn't reach this stretch of railway for hours, if at all, though Anna could see golden light caressing the tops of some of the taller trees on the rise. She picked her way across to the edge of the storage area and stared up at the black posts marking the perimeter of Ryegrove Hospital, pulled out her phone and dialled Holder.

'Justin, go straight to the labs and find out what you can about the wallet taken from one of the bodies last night.'

'It is bodies, then?' Holder said.

'Yes. Two. Bradley says the lab is already working on it. There's a briefing at nine. I need that information.'

'On my way, ma'am.'

CHAPTER FIVE

TUESDAY

The MCRTF team had a home on the second floor of Avon and Somerset Police HQ at Portishead. It was an open-plan room with four desks and a cubbyhole that Anna called her office. Every desk held a computer screen and file trays loaded with paper in various guises, and every wall had shelves stacked with labelled box files. Two of the desks were occupied. At the nearest one to Anna sat a young woman whose sleek short black hair and dark eyes had been well hidden by her outdoor gear at the site the day before. Khosa's competence as a detective constable was only exceeded by the size of her extended family. She had an aunt or uncle in almost every Midland town, and Anna wondered if Khosa's move to Bristol had in part been driven by her need for a little freedom. A change of hairstyle and some new clothes to go with a slimmer profile had not gone unnoticed over the past weeks. But most telling of all was how Khosa had given up ribbing Holder for his romantic escapades. Anna suspected Khosa had a partner and that glass houses and stones did not go together well.

Next to her sat Trisha Spedding, the team's civilian analyst. Early forties, she was older than Anna by over a decade and looked after herself and her teenage sons. Trisha was a sounding board for all things practical and a skilled organiser. Something Anna found invaluable. Talking to Trisha with his usual restrained congeniality,

Rainsford looked dapper in a grey suit, white shirt and a tie with some tiny repeating pattern, which, Anna suspected, only meant something to someone with military connections.

It was a little after 9.15 a.m. and Holder texted her to say he was on his way down from the lab. Pasted images of the crime scene with indicators for where the bodies had been found were up on the board. She contemplated these now, marking the fact there was a lot of blank space between. She hoped Forensics would have something she could add. On cue, the door opened, and Holder strode in, looking triumphant and waving some photocopied sheets of paper.

'Got him, ma'am. Photo ID in the shape of a CitizenCard.' Holder began sticking A4-sized photographs to the board.

'What's a CitizenCard?' Khosa asked.

Rainsford answered, moving closer to look at the images. 'Photo IDs that began in the late nineties, I think. In response to the No ID, No Sale campaign that tried to help retailers with age-restricted goods. They carried the Proof of Age Standards Scheme hologram.'

Khosa stood to join the superintendent and Anna. A brown stain covered one half of the image, blurring the face but still bearing the print that clearly read 'Under 16'.'

'In case you can't read it,' Holder explained, 'this belongs to a male, Jamie Carson, date of birth, 15 June 1986. The card was issued on 15 June 2000. Carson went missing on 8 August 2001.'

'Anything else in the wallet?'

Holder's mouth turned down. 'Not much. Some money. Couple of notes and a few coins.'

Anna turned to face the team. 'So we have a name we can run, assuming no one has deliberately planted someone else's wallet to confuse us. If Shaw's timeline is correct, and the remains are those to whom the wallet belongs, Jamie's body has been in the ground for almost seventeen years. That's a long time for his family to wonder what's happened to him.'

'Do we think that this is related to the death of Shaw's daughter?' Holder asked. 'Something to do with the Black Squid?'

A good question. One Anna knew she'd be asked. One she'd prepared for. 'We don't know anything about him yet, but he's the right age to be a Black Squid victim.' She ducked out of the room and into her office. When she emerged, she clutched a one-inch-thick file. 'I've been doing some homework just in case.'

Rainsford said nothing, but his eyebrows shifted up an inch.

On the board, Anna put up a photograph of a young girl. Big eyes heavily made-up with pink and grey eyeshadow and way too much eyeliner in an attempt to make her look older than the thirteen she'd been when the image was taken. Black hair with a pink fringe hung low over her brow. On a sweatshirt beneath were the words 'My Chemical Romance'.

'Abbie Shaw,' Anna said. 'Taken two months before she threw herself under a train just before Christmas in 2001. She was thirteen. It was her death that triggered her father's murderous, misguided vendetta.'

Next to Abbie's image, Anna posted a stylised black block-drawing of a squid. An arrow-shaped body above, two large eyes on the sides and, protruding from the front end at the bottom, eight arms and two tentacles curling menacingly. 'There wasn't much left of Abbie after she stepped out into the path of the London to Manchester express, but a crude version of this image was painted in black felt tip on her cheek.'

From her file, Anna took a CSI image with Sussex Police's logo stamped upon it. 'This is what we found at the end of last summer when Shaw took us to Sussex.' She pinned up a second image. A boy in school uniform, buck-toothed, smiling at the camera. 'Dental records and DNA confirmed this to be Daniel Litton, aged fourteen at the time he went missing.'

The silence in the room was almost palpable as Anna kept going, adding another sheet to the board. This one much more recent.

Post-mortem images taken from the site of Kimberley Williams' suicide. She was lying face down on the rocks. The part of her head that was visible had been roughly edited, masking out parts. Her eyes – what were left of them after the deceleration of hitting the stone 'beach' floor smashed them into unrecognisable mush – were taped over, as was what was left of her lower jaw. But on the skin of her cheek and on her nose a dark smudge was visible. 'I got these this morning from South Wales. This is Kimberley Williams, who died five months ago. She threw herself off a cliff.' Anna turned away from the board. 'Three of these are definitely linked. Abbie, Daniel and now Kimberley all left notes for their families.' Anna reached for the file once again. She did it quickly, so no one would notice how her hand was trembling.

Anger did that to her sometimes.

She removed one other image. One she'd manipulated on the computer that morning to show the three 'notes', each consisting of a crude facsimile of the black stylised image of the squid she'd already put up. One had a kiss in the shape of a cross beneath. One had 'Inky blackness, Mum. It's the only way. Soz' written on a Post-it note. The other showed nothing but the image of a squid.

'Jesus,' Holder said.

'If you haven't already, you'll need to read up about suicide games. The Black Squid isn't the only one. They're much more prevalent in Eastern Europe – 130 deaths, supposedly. Some in the USA. But essentially, they are the same. The classic one was the Blue Whale challenge. Up to fifty tasks designed to tire out the victim by making them wake up too early, watch horror films, self-harm, alienate themselves from support. All verifiable by photographic evidence. It sounds incredible, but these are already vulnerable individuals. There are some who think it's still a hoax that has perpetrated copycat acts. Kids can be very gullible.'

'But is there any evidence they didn't actually commit suicide?' Khosa asked.

'No,' Rainsford answered, drawing everyone's focus. 'But as it stands it remains against the law to aid, abet, counsel or procure the suicide of another. That carries a fourteen-year sentence.'

'I thought the CPS weren't that keen,' Khosa said.

'No one in their right mind in the crown prosecution service wants to stand in court and prosecute someone who's helped a terminally ill relative on to a plane to Dignitas,' Anna said. 'Public opinion in those cases is torn. But this is different. This is someone deliberately manipulating vulnerable kids into doing something because they think it's a game and ensuring they follow through with it. It's wrong, cowardly and very prosecutable.'

'We need to find if there's anything else linking these cases together,' Rainsford said. 'With Kimberley Williams' death it looks like this game may have resurfaced, but we need to be sure.' He turned away from the images.

It sounded to Anna as if Rainsford needed convincing. Shame they couldn't wheel Shaw in. He didn't need convincing. One look into his murderous eyes would tell Rainsford that.

'I've spoken to the chief superintendent and the assistant chief constable. Given DI Gwynne's links to Shaw and his extensive knowledge of this case, as well as his direct involvement because of his daughter, they want this squad to investigate Black Squid-related cases, in addition to and alongside the bodies found by Shaw.' Rainsford turned to Anna. 'Can I have a word?'

They went out into the corridor, away from prying ears. Rainsford dropped his voice and folded his arms. Never a good sign in Anna's book.

'I realise that this isn't strictly your usual remit, but we're facing a new round of budget reviews. With so many new cases, cold case squads are easy targets often seen as an expensive luxury.'

'But we've been successful, sir. Haven't we?'

'Spectacularly so. However, it'll do no harm if we can demonstrate a wider benefit. The Williams case has brought cybersuicide into the national awareness and I think I can rope in some help as a result. If this case can shed some light on what's happening elsewhere, the accountants will have a hard time cutting off our funding.'

Anna frowned.

Rainsford shrugged. 'It's a constant battle. I'll be the supervising officer, mainly for administrative purposes. I'll get someone over from South Wales Police to brief us on the Kimberley Williams case, too. It's better that I do the liaising. It'll free you up to do the ground work.'

Anna went back into the office to join the team, nursing a dull disquiet.

'What about the second body, ma'am?' Khosa asked.

'We'll know something later this afternoon, hopefully. We already know about Abbie and Daniel. I suggest we put our efforts into finding out about Jamie.'

Trisha, who'd been busy at her computer, spoke up. 'I've run the address found in the wallet. It's in Mangotsfield and is still registered to the Carsons. It doesn't look like they've moved.'

Anna nodded. 'Then that's where we should begin. My lucky day to be the one knocking on some family's door with the news they've been dreading for almost twenty years. Anybody fancy coming with me?'

Khosa and Holder looked at one another.

Anna fetched her coat from her office and slid it on before heading for the door. She paused. 'Toss a coin, you two. I'll be in the car. Whoever doesn't come rings the pathologist. I want to know when those bones are in the lab.'

CHAPTER SIX

Mangotsfield lay to the north-east of Bristol, on the Gloucestershire border. It had a medieval church and a manor house and an honourable mention in the *Domesday Book*. The village, originally housing miners and farmworkers, grew to absorb the surrounding hamlets. Despite the inevitable urban expansion, it had not quite shaken off its rural background. The Carsons lived in a house covered in cream-painted stucco on Charnhill Road. Two cars sat on a drive made of compressed concrete coloured to look like brick. A plastic hammer and chisel from a child's toy toolset lay abandoned in the porch. Khosa stood next to Anna as she rang the bell. She hadn't commented in the car whether the toss was lost or won. They both knew this was part of the job.

A shape appeared, blurry through the random pattern of the obscure glass pane in the porch door. The man who eventually opened it looked older than the sixty Anna knew him to be. Jamie's father, John Carson, had retired from the docks with back problems. From the look of his ample belly and the veins around his nose, it hadn't stopped him visiting the pub.

'Help you?'

Anna showed him her warrant card. 'Detective Inspector Gwynne, Mr Carson. This is Detective Constable Khosa. We're here about Jamie.'

John frowned and shook his head. 'Jamie don't live here anymore.'

Anna nodded. 'We know, Mr Carson. We're here with news about his disappearance.'

John's eyes were blue islands in a florid face. They narrowed now. It was difficult to judge his expression, but his lower jaw suddenly began to tremble. 'Come in,' he said, turning away and began to shout, 'Gill, Gill! There's police here. It's about Jamie.'

Anna followed with Khosa behind. John stood in the corridor, blocking off the rest of the house and ushering them into a front room full of lived-in furniture. A couple of sofas in brown leather, the cushions on the seats hollowed out from years of sitting. A wall-mounted TV sat above a cabinet full of DVDs. The carpet looked shabby with a couple of suspicious stains. In two corners sat piles of toys: cars, action figures, bits of Lego. More evidence of children.

From somewhere at the rear of the house came conversation, muted through the walls, the rise and fall of surprise and anxiety in equal measure. The Carsons appeared in the doorway together. Gill Carson was not tall, ample around the waist, and her straw-coloured blonde hair framed a round face without make-up. She wore jeans and a rugby shirt with the sleeves rolled up. Behind her stood a taller, thinner man.

'Mrs Carson,' Anna said. 'Sorry to intrude.' She looked up at the taller man and judged him at early thirties, his hair already starting to thin, his complexion pale but his arms, in the T-shirt he wore, defined from work or sport. 'And you must be Tom.'

Tom Carson nodded. Below him, a head appeared, dark-haired, wide-eyed, pulling at Gill's leg.

'Hello,' Khosa said.

The face pulled back, cowed.

'My grandson, Orlando.' Gill turned to her surviving son. 'Tom, put a video on for him in the playroom.' She turned to the little boy. 'Want to watch *Paw Patrol*?'

Orlando let out a delighted, 'Yeaaahhh,' and disappeared with his father.

'What's this about?' Gill asked. Colour had rushed to her cheeks and Anna knew this needed to be done swiftly.

Tom reappeared, and the Carsons once again crowded into the room. Gill and John on one settee, Tom in an armchair, which left the other settee for Anna and Khosa. But Anna chose to stand with her back to the window.

'There is no easy way to say this and so I'll get right to it. We've found some remains near the river at Leigh Woods. At present we've been unable to confirm identification, but we found Jamie's ID card inside a wallet with the victim.' She nodded at Khosa, who placed two photographs on the coffee table. One of the wallet after Forensics had frozen it and vacuum-dried it, and one of the CitizenCard. The Carsons leaned forward. Gill was the first to turn away, a sob catching in her voice, her hand unable to suppress it as it emerged, the first in a series ratcheting from her throat. Her husband put his arm around her, big hands squeezing her shoulder ineffectually.

'You said remains?' John asked, his blue eyes already angry.

'Whoever it is that we've found has been buried for a long time.'

'Do you want me… Do I need to see the body?'

Anna shook her head. 'Identification will need to be by dental records, maybe DNA. After this length of time there's nothing for you to see.'

John stared at Anna, but she knew he wasn't seeing her. The trembling in his lower jaw had become much more obvious. It was Tom who seemed the most able to take things in.

'These are Jamie's,' he said after a while. 'The wallet and the card. They are his.'

Khosa took her cue. She stood and said, 'Mr Carson, a cup of tea is usually good in these situations. Can you show me?'

John looked at her but didn't see her, then he blinked and stood up. 'The kitchen. It's at the back.'

Khosa helped Gill up. 'Come on.'

She didn't argue. Grief had rendered her compliant.

Anna waited until they'd gone and then said, 'I'm sorry to bring this to your door.'

Tom shrugged. 'It's not as if we weren't expecting it. But Mum… she's never quite accepted… It's hard.'

Anna nodded. 'If the remains are Jamie's, then I need to try and find out what happened.'

Tom nodded.

'You're living here?' Anna asked.

'Me and Laura, that's my partner. We're trying to save up for a place. You know how it is.'

'When Jamie went missing, there was an investigation, I know.'

Tom nodded. 'They came round, went through his stuff. But they thought he'd run away.'

'Did he have a reason to?'

Tom shook his head. 'Not from here. But Jamie had a hard time at school.'

'How so?'

'Wasn't into sport. Liked his music, but not the stuff I was into. Bit of a loner, to be honest.'

Anna nodded. 'Did he speak to you about things?'

'I was his brother. We didn't speak about anything serious. I was caught up in my own stuff.'

'Did he spend much time on the Internet?'

Tom shrugged. 'Not here. We had dial-up access and one computer. Dad was always on about the phone bill. Jamie used to go to an Internet café over in Fishponds.'

'Mobile phone?'

'Yeah. An old Nokia. We both had one. Pay as you go.'

'Was that ever found?'

Tom shook his head.

Anna put the block image of the black squid on the table. 'Does this mean anything to you?'

Tom stared, leaning in closer. He looked up at Anna, perplexed. 'Yeah, I mean I've seen it before.' He got up abruptly.

'Where are you going?'

'I won't be a minute.'

She heard his feet taking the stairs two at a time. He returned within two minutes carrying a file folder. 'This was Jamie's.' Tom opened the folder. Inside was a jumble of papers, postcard-sized photos of bands, cuttings, the odd ticket stub and a sketchbook. Tom took everything out and flicked through the pages. Doodles and sketches mostly until he got to a page towards the end. He stared at it momentarily before turning it around to show Anna. On it, sketched in dark ink, was an unmistakable image of a dark shape with eight arms and two tentacles.

Anna took the book. Jamie had also written 'Day 1' and 'silent running'.

Anna turned the page over. The same image, but this time with 'Day 11' and '4AM. Walk alone, count to thirty. Watch XRCST.'

'Did you show this to the police?'

'Yeah. They gave it back to us after a week. Said it didn't really help much.'

'Did he say anything to you before he went? Leave anything, a note?'

'Not really, only this.'

'This?'

Tom nodded and reached into the pile again to pull out one single sheet of A4 paper with the words: 'Gone to Ink.'

'The police thought it meant he'd gone to get a tattoo.'

Anna stared, her pulse ticking a little louder and quicker in her throat. The police would have sought to interpret these words, and a rebellious teen announcing he was off to get a tattoo would have fitted.

She turned back to the book and began flicking through the pages. She counted twenty squid images. On the last one, 'Day 20', Jamie had written 'terminal'.

'Can I take this?' she asked Tom.

'Yeah. What does it mean?'

'I can't be sure. Not yet.' She delivered the words automatically, wanting to be as truthful as she could. The original investigators had suggested naturally enough that ink could mean a tattoo. But it had a very different meaning in relation to Shaw and his daughter's death.

And coincidence, in Anna's book, was a very dirty word.

Her pulse ticked up another notch.

Tom nodded, happy to accept her lack of commitment. 'You think these remains are definitely Jamie's?'

'We can't say for definite. Not yet. But I'd say it's highly likely.'

Tom nodded and sighed. Even though he'd admitted to having expected the inevitable, now that it was here, it was an unwelcome guest. 'He was different, you know?'

Anna nodded. She did know. All too well.

'He wasn't like me. But he was my brother.'

Anna half turned away. 'Someone from Forensics will be along to take some swabs for DNA. It's belt and braces these days. They can do familial tests and match it with what's left of the remains. That way we'll be absolutely certain. But I think the chances are slim that this is someone else.'

Tom nodded. 'We had no idea he was doing this. That he felt like this.' He glanced down at the drawings.

Anna didn't say anything. This was murder by stealth and guile. But still murder.

CHAPTER SEVEN

Khosa took a call from Holder as they left the Carsons' house. A brief call, full of someone else talking and Khosa providing OKs. She finished the call and turned to Anna as they reached the car.

'Justin has some news about the second body. It's been moved to the mortuary as well. Gupta says we can take a look when we get back. Justin will meet us there.'

'You drive,' Anna said. 'I'll fill you in on what Tom Carson said.'

As Khosa headed south, Anna explained about the sketchbook.

'So definitely Black Squid-related,' Khosa said when Anna finished. 'Do you think there's a chance they pulled his phone records when he went missing?'

'There's a chance. But I doubt they'd have used text messaging in those days. More likely it'd be a chat room of some kind.'

'Internet records?'

'Maybe. But we don't even know if that Internet café in Fishponds still exists, let alone who their provider was. And then we'd need to try and find out when Jamie was there.'

'Worth checking though, ma'am.'

'It is. But I'm not hopeful.'

'What about the other victims we've connected? Daniel, Abbie?'

Anna didn't answer immediately. The police files on Daniel and Abbie were thin. But someone else had carried out an investigation into Abbie's death and found lots of answers. It would be an obvious and necessary step. First, they needed to find out who the other bones belonged to.

*

They'd built a new mortuary in Flax Bourton in 2009. It was an odd – some might say perverse – place for a mortuary: in a village five miles out from the centre of the city and nine from HQ at Portishead. But then the Avon Coroner's Court was in the same village. They'd built the mortuary with forensic capability at the back of the impressive stone listed building the coroner inherited from its previous incarnation as a magistrates' court. But the mortuary was very different, a modern yellow-brick and mustard-rendered building with special parking bays for the hearses. Anna thought it garish, but she supposed it didn't matter what she thought; the dead wouldn't care.

Inside in the autopsy suite, disinfectant and death mingled in a sickly perfume. There were white walls, high windows, stainless steel sinks and tables arranged around the edge of the room. Two of the tables were occupied with draped corpses awaiting their turn. But on a different two tables at the far end, the bones from the railway had been laid out on sterile drapes. Sunil Gupta, the Home Office pathologist, was a small, neat man in white wellies and blue scrubs, with a sort of jovial demeanour that sometimes grated with the setting. He looked up as Anna, Holder and Khosa, all suitably dressed in paper gowns and masks, entered.

'Over here, Inspector,' Gupta called.

Anna had been to many autopsies, and at least this time there was no flesh to cut through or gas to escape from a punctured and bloated abdomen. Gupta stood between the two tables. Next to him stood a tall, slight woman similarly dressed in the pathologist's uniform of scrubs and plastic apron.

It always worried Anna to see this garb. *What awful diseases can you catch from bones?* she wondered.

Gupta spoke as Anna approached. 'This is Detective Inspector Anna Gwynne and her team, DCs Khosa and Holder.' Gupta turned towards his colleague with gesturing hands. 'And this, ladies and gentleman is Dr Karen Brown, forensic osteologist. It is she who has answered our call.'

'I take it there was no soft tissue left, Dr Gupta?' Anna asked.

'Nothing for me to get my teeth into,' Gupta said and smiled at the way Khosa grimaced. 'Gallows humour,' he added. 'Should be taught as a required course in medical school.'

'You'd be head of department, then,' Anna said.

'And you, Inspector, would be my toughest assignment.'

'Shall we?' Brown spoke. Her accent was southern, but that's all Anna could glean through the mask. 'Firstly, we have the male. Young. Long bones not quite fully fused. The dental records have confirmed his identity as Jamie Carson, though we only have half a jaw to compare with.'

'We've been to see the family,' Anna said. 'Have you any idea about cause of death?'

Brown moved to the head of the table. Anna was glad to see the skull sitting where it should have been.

'If you look here' – she pointed towards the space between the top of the ribcage and the bottom of the skull – 'many of the cervical vertebrae are missing and those that aren't are severely damaged. Crushed and splintered, as was the bottom of the skull and mandible.' Brown held up the mottled bone and pointed, with an extendable metal pointer, towards a jagged hole. 'The *foramen magnum*. It's where the spinal cord runs down from the brain. Usually it's a smooth oval. But here you can see a piece of it is missing, the edges fractured. And the mandible and jaw are in pieces, here.' She pointed to an arrangement of bones on the drape. 'Some of them had teeth.'

'What could do that?' Holder asked.

'Severe trauma. Something that might have caused the head to swivel, severing the vertebra and rotating the head until it came off, probably crushing the lower jaw in the process.'

Khosa took a step away.

'There's a bucket over there.' Gupta pointed towards an adjacent table.

'I'm fine,' Khosa said. She didn't look it.

'It fits our pattern,' Anna said. 'Anything else?'

'No.' Brown shook her head. 'Otherwise remarkably clean.'

'Nothing from you, Dr Gupta?'

'Stomach contents? DNA stains? This is not *CSI Miami*, Inspector. All organic material has long been consumed by our friendly anaerobic bacteria or simply degraded into bugger all.'

Anna nodded. It was exactly as she thought.

'The body was near a railway track. If the head came off in some sort of major trauma, for example a train running over his neck, then the head would have had to be placed in the grave separately for us to have found it there?' she asked.

'Yes.' Brown nodded and then stepped towards the second set of bones. The team followed, sliding around the edge of the table until they could see. 'Now this one is quite different. Older, definitely. Height, I'd say around five five. And, judging from the pelvic differences, the broad sciatic notch, circular inlet, the flaring, this one is female. She has had some dental work and there was a ring on her finger. I think you noticed that at the site, am I right?'

'She wouldn't have missed that,' Gupta said.

Brown frowned.

'Cause of death?' Anna asked. She had no time for Gupta's frivolity.

'Can't help you there, I'm afraid. The hyoid bone wasn't intact.' Brown saw Holder frown. 'That's the thin bone above your Adam's apple. It is frequently crushed in strangulation. But here I can't tell if it was degradation or break.'

'So, it's possible she was strangled?' Holder asked.

'Possible, but I can't be definite. She does have evidence of a broken arm, though.' Brown pointed at the break in both bones of the forearm on the left side.

'What could that mean?'

'There's no sign of healing so it must have been just before or at the time of death. Could just about do for a defensive injury.' She looked up at Gupta for confirmation.

He nodded and said, 'She might have had her arm up to fend off something heavy.'

'So, no clues as to who this is?'

'Ah, that's not quite true.' Brown indicated a separate area where two items lay on a blue paper drape. 'The ring, awaiting transfer to the lab for analysis, and what appears to be a plastic card.'

Anna leaned in close. 'Is that an image I can see on it?'

Brown nodded. 'Looks like it might have been a photograph. It's now more or less a silhouette. There are also some traces of letters, but too faded for the naked eye. And they are not embossed so that suggests it's not a credit card. But there is a magnetic strip. If I had to guess I'd say that this was some kind of a swipe card.'

Anna nodded. 'A hotel door key, that sort of thing?'

Brown pursed her lips. 'Yes.' Then she added, 'The lab might be able to enhance the image.'

'Good.' Anna took out her phone and photographed the items. 'Why do you think this was left?'

'It was underneath the pelvis, a bit like the wallet from the other body. It's possible this might have been in the back pocket. Easily overlooked by someone doing a quick search.'

Anna frowned. 'Why do you say that?'

'No phone. No other ID. Just the ring and this card. The ring might have been hidden. Perhaps her hands were muddied or bloodied, who knows. And the card might have been totally unobtrusive in a back pocket.'

'Makes sense,' Holder said.

'Thanks. You've been really helpful,' Anna said.

'You never say that to me.' Gupta looked peeved.

'That's because getting information from you is like squeezing a desiccated lemon,' Anna said.

Gupta grinned. 'None taken, Inspector.'

CHAPTER EIGHT

Outside, Anna sent Holder back to HQ with an update for Rainsford and a message saying she would follow.

In the car, she told Khosa to head back out to the burial site next to the railway.

'What else is there to see, ma'am?'

'Not sure yet. I may know when I get there.'

It was an enigmatic answer but the best she could offer. They'd struck lucky with identifying Jamie Carson and Brown's confirmation that the second victim was an adult female. It was useful, but it also threw up more questions than answers. Could she, too, be a Black Squid victim? As far as Anna knew, all other victims had been teenagers. The ring, a thin band with a few stones, looked suspiciously like an engagement ring to Anna. And it had been on the right finger. Of course, an engaged woman could be depressed, even suicidal, but the broken bones in the forearm strongly suggested a violent act had been committed, not a suicide. Yet it was the card that threw her. Something, some link in the chain, was trying to forge itself, and her gut told her the site was where the answer lay. Too difficult to explain to Khosa, she simply fell into a contemplative silence. And Khosa knew her well enough not to question Anna's pensive moods when they came to call.

They parked in the cordoned-off area. The day was bright and cold. The tents were still set up but there was markedly less activity than previously. They signed in on the scene log and Bradley, the CSM, met them as they crossed the tape.

'Afternoon,' Bradley said. He looked cold under his Tyvek suit.

'You've found nothing else, I take it?'

'We've found a few things, ma'am. Bits of plastic, water bottles, broken cups, blown paper. I doubt any of it has anything to do with what went on here.'

Anna nodded. 'Network Rail?'

'This site has been used for storage for years. The wooden railway sleepers were here at the time of Carson's disappearance. But the concrete sleepers were dumped here sometime in 2009.'

'Right, so we know the second body has been here since then at least. She must have been here when they were put here.'

Bradley nodded.

Anna walked across to the tents. To where they'd found the second body. An area of some twenty square yards behind, including the tent perimeter, showed the stone chipping to be of a lighter colour than those surrounding it: a pale footprint of where the concrete sleepers had been stored, cordoned-off by markers. She stood at the edge and looked around. The trees seemed denser here. More overpowering.

'What is it, ma'am?' Khosa asked. She'd put on her outer clothing and her voice again emerged from a deep cavern of faux fur.

'Something, but…' Anna sighed and strode back to where they'd found Jamie and repeated the exercise while Khosa followed. The only noise was the walls of the thin Tyvek tent rippling in the keen wind. Anna looked at the railway and then walked behind the tent. From there, she could look the other way, across to the rising ground and the dark fence beyond.

She called over to Khosa. 'There, what do you see?'

'Trees and bushes, ma'am.'

'Further up.'

'A fence. That's Ryegrove, ma'am.'

Anna nodded, feeling the link slot into place. She turned away and began walking quickly back to the car.

'What, ma'am?' Khosa asked.

'I've just remembered. When Shaw first told me about this body, first said he had something else to show me, he mentioned that the victim he'd got this information from had used a phrase. The "monster house".'

Khosa turned her head towards the fence, her big eyes now a little wider.

Anna said, 'And what sort of security would they have there, Ryia?'

'High. There was razor wire on the top of that fence.'

'And inside?'

'Don't know, ma'am. I've never been.'

'Come on, let's get out of this cold.'

They went back to the car, sliding in, unbuttoning coats, removing headgear.

'OK,' Anna said, 'pretend you're a member of staff in Ryegrove. How do you think you'd get from one area to another?'

'Keys?'

'Keys.' Anna nodded. 'Big, metallic, jingly things that are heavy and difficult to carry. Secure units have had a lot of money spent to modernise them. Ryegrove certainly has. So maybe they've changed the locks.'

Khosa frowned. 'Changed them to…' Her lids fell and then opened wide with pained realisation. 'Electronic access cards. Ma'am, you're a genius.'

Five minutes later, they were heading back through the lanes towards the entrance to Ryegrove. A standard North Bristol NHS Trust sign signalled the entrance to a sprawling site. After thirty yards the common access road split. On the left were the old buildings, more Grade II-listed pennant stone like the coroner's court at Flax Bourton, now part of the University of the West of England's Applied Sciences faculty. But Khosa took the road to the right, to a grand façade where the old house had once stood. On either side of the sandstone, two new wings spread out in an arc. Two storeys of yellow brick and render with grey slate roofs and a steel and glass entrance. Extending out on both sides of the new build was the fence. Black-coated steel, seventeen feet high.

Khosa parked in one of the bays and they headed for the main entrance. The atrium inside was airy and manned by a glass-walled reception. There was no way in other than through a turnstile inside a curved entryway.

The security guard behind the glass wore a lanyard with a photo ID. The name read Jack Morris. He looked at Anna's warrant card and nodded. 'What can I do for you, Inspector?'

'HR, please.'

'They expecting you?'

'No.'

'It's easier if they come out to you, then,' he said with a nod towards the security access X-ray machines.

'Good idea.'

The guard picked up a telephone.

'One question: your badge, does it also work as a key?' Anna asked.

'Yep.' The guard hesitated and raised one eyebrow. 'You're not going to ask me if you could borrow it, are you?'

Anna snorted, 'No. Why, have you been asked?'

'Oh yes. That and a hundred weirder things. We get all sorts through here.'

'No. I don't want your badge. We'll be over here.' Anna pointed to some blue sofas.

They sat under some posters advertising an upcoming 'Friends of the Hospital' concert.

'They use their badges as key cards,' Anna said.

Khosa nodded. 'But our unknown corpse could not have worked here for years.'

'No. So that's another question we need to ask.'

Anna watched people come and go. It looked like a lot of people worked here. After a few minutes, a man, small, neat, with a hipster beard, appeared though the security door and walked over to them. He wore a shirt and jeans and the inevitable badge on a lanyard.

'Hi, I'm Ruben Childs, Human Resources. Can I help?'

'We're investigating a suspicious death, Mr Childs. So far, we have not identified the deceased. We have reason to believe there may be some link with the hospital.'

'Really?' Childs looked alarmed.

'Yes. But this is not recent. We're looking at prior to 2009. We wondered if you had anyone on file reported missing before that date?'

Childs frowned. He looked to be about the same age as Khosa. He would have been mid-teens in 2009.

'Wouldn't your lot know? I mean the police have records of missing persons?'

'We would, but it would help if we could narrow it down.'

Childs nodded. 'OK, I can have a look, talk to my colleagues.'

'Is there someone in the department who would have been around at the time?'

'There's Jocelyn Mitchell. She's the head of department. Been here for donkey's.'

'OK, good. So, we're looking for an adult female, possibly under forty, possibly linked to the hospital.'

'As a member of staff or a patient?'

The question threw Anna.

Khosa answered, 'Best to consider both.'

'OK,' said Childs. 'I'll speak to Jocelyn first.'

Anna glanced at her watch and gave him a card with her number on it. 'Ring us if you find something, please.'

Childs nodded again and turned back to the barriers separating reception from the rest of the hospital, heading back towards the security checks.

‘This place gives me the creeps,’ Khosa said, looking up at the exposed metal ducting and white corrugated ceiling and the solid wall of glass and steel.

‘Then let’s get out of here, Ryia, before they find us both out and invite us in.’

Khosa gave Anna a ‘speak for yourself’ look, but she was smiling as she followed her out.

CHAPTER NINE

Anna took the call from Jocelyn Mitchell as they left the western edge of the city en route to Portishead.

'Hello?'

'Inspector Gwynne. Jocelyn Mitchell. I'm the director of HR at Ryegrove.'

Anna threw Khosa a raised eyebrows glance.

'That was quick.'

'It wasn't difficult. When Ruben told me what you were after, all I had to do was pull the file. I already knew who you were talking about.'

'Really?'

'Absolutely. Alison Johnson went missing in 2001. She was a staff nurse and it made quite a splash at the time. Nurses who go missing, especially ones who work in secure units, generally do stir up quite a bit of interest. She disappeared into thin air.'

'Can you text me some details? Address, date of birth?'

'Certainly.' Mitchell sounded efficient.

'Are you the only one still working who's been there that long?'

'No. There are a few of us.'

'Could you make a list of those still there who would have come into contact with Alison?'

'No problem. I'll get that to you right away.'

'We'd appreciate it if you kept this confidential for the moment, Ms Mitchell.'

'Of course.'

Anna finished the call and replied to Khosa's questioning glance. 'It's a lead. A big one. We may have found out who the second corpse is.'

She dialled Trisha Spedding's number and gave her the details. There'd be a misper file. It was a good start. Anna could feel the tingle inside her. It was rare for a case to gain traction so quickly. Luck seemed to be with them so far. She wondered how long it would last.

CHAPTER TEN

Beth did some shopping in the minimart in Severn Beach. She was on a late shift that started at two and she'd have just enough time to get some essentials bought before she set off for work. It was early lunchtime and the weather was miserable, the air damp and cold with a murky fog that had rolled in overnight off the estuary. A mist that stubbornly refused to burn off in the weak winter sun.

She put her provisions in a backpack, wheeled out her bike and set off home. In the summer she'd use the Severn Way, parallel to the river, but in winter the path was far too dark at night, and even in daylight, too empty of visitors for comfort.

She stuck to the road.

As she curved right along Beach Road to the junction with Beach Avenue, the feeling hit her. The absolute conviction someone was watching her. She turned her head back to look. There was a bus stop in front of an abandoned amusement arcade and beyond that the embankment led up to the sea wall and the defences that kept the Bristol Channel out. But she saw no one.

So why did she feel so convinced? She didn't consider herself nervous. You didn't last long on nights in a medium secure unit if you let nerves get to you. Yet it wasn't the first time she'd felt this conviction. Her trips home in the dark after work had become notable for this unnameable anxiety she felt. It bothered her even more to think she was now feeling it in the daytime, too. And always it crept over her somewhere along this stretch, with the dark water of the channel just a few yards away. She was glad she hadn't experienced the feeling on the final stretch on Shaft Road, which was very narrow and very unlit at night. Dee's dad had fitted security lights to the cottage, which lit up like a beacon as soon as she got within twenty yards of the place, but before that stretched a hundred yards of darkness. Here, near the bus stop, at least there were lights and other people, in case.

In case of what exactly, Beth? she thought. But even though she dismissed the thought as nothing more than heebie-jeebies, she found herself pedalling just that little bit harder.

CHAPTER ELEVEN

The MCRTF office was busy when Anna and Khosa arrived back. Rainsford was at the whiteboard with two other people Anna had not met before. One was a woman. Small, dark hair, dark brown – almost black – eyes with no way of differentiating pupil from iris. Her mouth was wide, and her skin olive-tinged under black jeans and a white blouse. She would not have looked out of place on the streets of Milan or Madrid. The other, a man, was a little overweight, his paunch sagging over his belt, tie loose over an unfashionable, and unseasonal short-sleeved shirt. He had a full face with a small nose and unruly hair that looked as if no amount of combing could control the way it wanted to curl. She put him at around forty. His eyes locked on to Anna's, appraising and a little knowing. She felt at a slight disadvantage.

Rainsford spoke. 'OK. Introductions. Inspector Anna Gwynne and DC Ryia Khosa, this is Detective Sergeant Leah Cresci from South Wales Police. Sergeant Cresci's been involved with the investigation into Kimberley Williams' suicide and is on their task force looking at other Internet-related deaths.'

She shook Cresci's warm, dry hand. When she spoke it was a Cardiff accent that emerged. 'Nice to meet you, ma'am.'

Rainsford turned to the man. 'DS Phil Dawes is from our own Major Crimes Unit. He'll be liaising with Sergeant Cresci on this. Given Shaw's link to the Black Squid and his conviction that what we've found next to the railway tracks are Black Squid-related, it seems sensible to expand the remit. If there is a link and if there is still someone out there responsible for goading kids into suicide, this may provide us with a golden opportunity for a new line of investigation. Sergeant Dawes will be joining your squad, Anna. You remain the senior investigating officer.'

Dawes, too, held his hand out. Khosa shook it and then so did Anna. His eyes held hers, small but full of a hunter's intelligence.

Jamie Carson's photograph was posted up. Trisha appeared at Anna's elbow and handed her another black-and-white printed image, this one of a woman of about Anna's age, hair cut in a boyish pixie style, smiling for the camera. Anna stared at it and turned it over to read a handwritten line.

Alison Bridget Johnson, reported missing 9 August 2001.

She kept the photograph in her hand. 'OK. Shall we?' She pointed to Jamie's image. 'Jamie Carson was fifteen when he disappeared. He's been missing since 8 August 2001. I've spoken to his family, and Gupta's just confirmed dental records match. I also found a sketchbook at Carson's house with images of the black squid, and a likely timeline of instructions. The initial investigation was unaware of its significance. He also left a note with the words "Gone to Ink".'

The faces staring back at her reflected her own disgust. 'Jamie's brother told us he used an Internet café, which, according to Trisha's enquiries, no longer exists. We need to see if there is any record of who owned and ran it and if there's an IP address and ISP record, though we have no idea of the timings of Jamie's visits there so it's a shot in the dark.'

Holder nodded and wrote on a pad.

Anna pointed to Abbie's image. 'Abbie Shaw. Known victim. Unfortunately, most of what we know about her involvement with the Black Squid is in her father's head.'

'Can I help with that, ma'am?' Dawes asked.

Anna shook her head. 'He only speaks to me.'

Dawes frowned.

'Long story,' Anna said, 'and believe me I wish it wasn't true. But it is.' She turned back and pinned up the image Trisha had just given her. 'The second corpse. No confirmation of identity yet, but this is a strong candidate. Alison Johnson, missing since 9 August 2001 but last seen on 8 August 2001, the same day that Jamie Carson became a misper. Alison worked as a nurse at Ryegrove's secure unit. Trisha is pulling her misper files. We can't be sure this is her, but for now it's the best lead we have. We'll need to interview friends and family and colleagues at Ryegrove. Confirmation, as with Jamie Carson, will come from familial DNA and dental records.' She turned to Holder. 'Justin, check if copies of the dental records are on file already. Given that she was reported missing, the investigating team would probably have had copies made in anticipation. If so, get them over to Brown and Gupta right away.'

'What else makes you think it's her?' Dawes asked.

'Remains are the right age, the engagement ring fits the profile, and there's a magnetic strip key card like the ones that are used at Ryegrove. Forensics have both the ring and the key card as we speak.'

Rainsford nodded. A faint smile played over his lips. Anna took it as a sign he was pleased. 'Thanks, Anna. DS Cresci, could you fill us in on your side?'

Cresci stood on the other side of the board and addressed the team. She pressed a remote, and a TV screen in the corner lit up. She held herself upright, addressing them in an efficient, capable manner. 'I think you all know the background.' A photo of a girl with dark hair and acne-ravaged skin appeared on-screen. Her hair looked wild and windswept, and her face bore black marks and streaks. It looked like she'd been the victim of some insane face-painter, but it was the expression of abject misery that drew everyone's gaze. That would stay with the team long after Cresci had gone. 'Kimberley Williams threw herself off a cliff in Southerndown after painting her face with an image of a black squid.

Before she did, she took a photograph of herself and posted it on her Instagram account.'

'Was that image made public?'

'It was. We had her phone looked at. She was in communication through WhatsApp with a user known as Humboldt. For those of you who aren't aware, there is a type of sea creature known as a Humboldt squid. There are transcripts of communications between Kimberley and Humboldt. They run over several weeks and it's clear she was being groomed for some sort of final act.'

'Can we see those?'

She held up a cardboard file.

'So, you know who she was talking to?' Holder asked.

Cresci shook her head. It was a resigned gesture that told Anna she'd known the question was coming. 'That's where it becomes difficult. Our tech people have tried to trace Humboldt but he covered his tracks well. Most of us know WhatsApp, right? It's popular because it encrypts messages. Anyone can sign up, but the sign-up process uses a phone number for verification. These days you can sign up for a virtual phone number with a throwaway email address. There are apps that do this for you. Humboldt used a WhatsApp account that never revealed his ID.'

'Is that even legal?' Holder frowned.

'It is. But it's a huge security issue. Bottom line is that the WhatsApp account Humboldt used was completely untraceable.'

'So why did Kimberley get involved with Humboldt?' Khosa asked.

'She was unhappy. She'd broken up with a long-term boyfriend. Struggled in college. In fact, she was being medicated for depression. But she claimed they made her put on weight and so she stopped. Her Internet search history shows she spent a lot of time online looking at suicide websites. After she visited one site in particular, she stopped looking and that was when the WhatsApp relationship with Humboldt began. We've interviewed family and friends. They paint a picture of a bright girl striving and failing to compete academically and socially. There were issues around her skin condition, too, and she was undergoing treatment for that.'

Shades of Abbie Shaw there, Anna thought. From photos of Shaw's daughter, Anna knew she also struggled with her skin. It had sapped her confidence. One of many reasons she'd probably had a tough time at school and sought solace in online chat rooms. Just as Kimberley had done.

Rainsford spoke to Cresci. 'Thanks, Sergeant. The question is, does it link in with our supposed Black Squid cases? And if so, how? There's a significant time gap.'

Anna nodded. 'But this isn't the only case of late, am I right?'

Cresci shrugged. 'Sporadic reports from Holland and France. Three confirmed cases in the UK over the last two years. We've hit a roadblock with Kimberley and the Black Squid isn't the only game of this type. But with the coroner referring the case to the Association of Police and Crime Commissioners, it's made everyone sit up. One of the reasons I'm here, ma'am, is that when I typed Black Squid into HOLMES, Hector Shaw's name lit up.'

'Why do they keep calling it a game?' Khosa said, her distaste obvious.

Cresci said, 'Challenge would be better. Let me show you.'

The rest of the team sat around Khosa's table, which was the tidiest in the office. Cresci opened her file and laid out ten sheets of paper, each one covered in typed exchanges, some highlighted. 'Underlining indicates Humboldt.'

The first exchanges were brief and with warnings.

> *Welcome. If you enter the Black Squid's domain, you may never leave. Make sure you understand. We know you're in pain and the Black Squid can take that pain away. It is a challenge with the ultimate prize: no more pain and no more torment if you successfully complete it.*

I want to. I want to win the prize.

Good. But the Squid needs commitment. To know you are not a time-waster. The Squid knows that pain can be a release. Have you cut yourself before, Kimberley? Have you seen your own blood well up and felt the relief? It means your body is trying to help you cope by releasing its natural painkillers to soothe your soul. Let's soothe your soul now, Kimberley.

I'd like that. Will it hurt.

Yes, but afterwards you will thank the Squid.

OK.

Take a blade, or a needle if you have one. Carve the Squid's shape into your forearm. Be artistic. Don't be scared. You will feel so much better. And when it is done, hold your forearm up to your face and take a photo. Send it to me. That way we will see that you really mean what you say.

'For God's sake,' Dawes said. 'That's dated 15 July last year.'

Cresci nodded. 'Kimberley must have thought about it for a few days. She sent back the image a week later. There was a copy on her phone.' She turned back to the screen and pressed the remote again until she found the image she wanted. Kimberley Williams in her bathroom, a crude, bloody shape on her forearm, her face solemn and unhappy.

Cresci went back to the transcript. 'On 23 July, Humboldt accepts Kimberley's commitment.'

'This is sick,' Holder said.

'The exchanges continue. Humboldt manages to get inside her head,' Cresci said. 'He accesses her social media, knows who she's been talking to, knows what she's been saying. He's friendly to start with, then cajoling, then coercing. It's all designed to isolate and degrade and disorientate through sleep-deprivation and self-loathing. Until the last day. By this time the suicide prep is more or less complete.'

Anna's eyes had drifted to the top of the second page. Another entry.

> *Today, I want you to know how bad your life would be if it goes on like this. I want you to feel sick. Get up at 3.30 a.m. Drink water until you throw up. Then see how sick you might be by watching the whole of The Exorcist in a dark room alone.*

'*The Exorcist*,' Dawes said. 'With the rotating head and green vomit? Put me off carrots and peas for a month when I first saw it.'

But Anna was on her feet and on the way to her office. She came back with the sketchbook Tom Carson had given her, open at the page that said, 'Day 11' and '4AM. Walk alone, count to thirty. Watch XRCST.'

'Oh my God,' Khosa said. 'It's the same. Or virtually the same.'

'Maybe this stuff is common knowledge,' Holder said.

'A copycat?' Cresci suggested.

'Or the Black Squid has been asleep for all these years and has just woken up again,' Anna said.

'Long time to be asleep,' Dawes said. 'Unless it's been locked away somewhere.'

Anna tilted her head and nodded. She liked the way Dawes thought.

Cresci said, 'Whatever the reason, I can't help wondering how many more Kimberleys it has dangling on the end of its sick phone messages, playing its disgusting game.'

They spent an hour poring over more of the exchanges between Kimberley and Humboldt, asking questions, Cresci answering as best she could. The messages counted down to the last day, with clear instructions for how Kimberley was to proceed with her own death. It made for difficult reading.

Two coffees later, when they'd finished or were unable to stomach any more, Rainsford turned to Cresci. 'Thanks, Sergeant, you've been really helpful. As you can see, we're right at the beginning of all this on our end. Any suggestions?'

Cresci shrugged. 'Shaw seems to be the link here. It would probably make sense for me to interview him.'

Everyone turned to Anna. She repeated what she'd said to Dawes. 'You're welcome to try. Up to now he has refused to talk to anyone but me.'

'So I've heard,' Cresci said. There was no subtext. Just irritated regret. 'I assume that once both bodies are formally identified, you'll be interviewing him again, then?'

'Possibly,' Anna said, not wanting to agree to anything at this stage.

Cresci looked at her oddly but said nothing.

Rainsford nodded his approval. 'OK, we'll let Sergeant Cresci get back to Cardiff. Phil will be in touch with anything we find and, obviously, if anything new comes up in the Williams investigation, you'll let us know.'

Cresci did another round of shaking hands and Rainsford walked her out.

Once she'd gone, Anna got down to business. 'So, actions?'

'Chase up Alison Johnson's misper file and dig out what we can on Carson. Speak to remaining relatives and friends. Gee up the forensics, dental records, etc.,' Dawes said. 'I can rope in another DC from MCU for legwork if needed. And we've got two extra for the HOLMES team.'

Anna nodded. She felt suddenly fired up. They'd never had this much help before and having a couple of extra people inputting data into HOLMES would be a big boost for Trisha. 'Great. Justin, you work with Sergeant Dawes on Johnson. Trisha, see if you can get Jocelyn Mitchell. Tell her I'd like to set up a meeting with her tomorrow at Ryegrove. Ryia, I'll want you with me on that but before we do, we'd better go back to Mangotsfield and tell the Carsons the dental records confirm it's Jamie that we found. I'd rather do that in person.'

Everyone got up at once. There was a lot to do.

Though Cresci had gone, Anna couldn't help but dwell on what she'd told them about Kimberley. This was the destruction of a human being from a distance. A sick and twisted game with death as the prize.

CHAPTER TWELVE

Anna visited the Carsons and gave them the bad news. It was a harrowing fifteen minutes. Even though they'd been primed for sixteen years to the possibility, the extinguishing of all hope of seeing a son and a brother again was painful to deliver. She held back from mentioning the Black Squid at this stage. They'd need to be told, but Anna needed more evidence before letting the Carsons know their son might have been coerced into killing himself.

Back at HQ, Anna did some paperwork and wrote up a report for Rainsford on what they had so far. But the facts left lots of gaps to be filled in. The hows and the whys. Anna hated not knowing which direction this case was going to take her and the unknowns were stacking up. They were, for the moment, at the mercy of the pathologist and the forensic investigators, who had their own processes to follow to uncover how Jamie Carson and Alison Johnson – if it was Johnson – had died. They would come up with the goods, she was sure of it. But for now, they needed to wait for due process and start afresh the following day.

Anna called a halt at five thirty. It had been a busy day, and meetings with too many people drained her.

She found release in a gym off Gloucester Road, where she put her body through a bit of pain so that the endorphins could give her a boost. Afterwards, she sat in the car to cool down and answered the messages on her personal phone. The most important ones were from her sister Kate in relation to tomorrow evening.

Kate's little boy, Harry, was five on Wednesday and he was having a proper kids' party. But afterwards, once the children had gone to bed, Kate was planning a less frenetic celebration. Anna wanted to bring something, and Kate had suggested Ben. The resultant text exchange had been pithy to say the least. Kate would no doubt have all sorts of wine and great food. And both were absolutely vital to help Anna cope with her mother.

The truth was that Anna's qualms were all internal. She couldn't handle socialising for that long. Like most high-functioning introverts, Anna needed an entry and exit strategy for gatherings. 'Arrive acceptably late and leave early,' was her motto. That way she managed to avoid the twin horrors of boredom and excessive small talk that hung over every party and meeting she'd ever been to. Not that Harry's birthday party would be too arduous – it was family and she'd know everyone there. Still, one of her recurring nightmares was the thought of being buttonholed in a crowded room by a bore she didn't know.

That wasn't the only reason for her angst. When it came to her mother, Anna's tolerance scale was set to zero. There were a thousand reasons for this, and Anna had insight enough to acknowledge there was blame on both sides. Her mother dismissed Anna's introversion as nothing other than a mood problem she should and could 'snap out of'. She could never accept that one of her daughters could be anything other than the bubbly, outgoing, yummy mummy that Kate had grown into with such ease. It had not helped that her mother had forced her father to leave, and how during that silly and unnecessary hiatus in their marriage, he'd died alone of a heart attack. The blame Anna levelled was illogical and unfocused, but it caused friction. And friction could burn.

Sitting in the car, she sent a reply to Kate and then she phoned Ben.

'Hi,' she said.

'Hey. How are you?' She could hear noises in the background. A busy hum, the faint wail of sirens, a baby's cry. Ben was at work.

'Fine. Just on my way home to pick up Lexi. You?'

'Not bad. Averagely busy. Nothing major so far.'

'About tomorrow, umm… we could go in my car. Lexi's happy in the back.'

'You sure you don't want me to drive? You might want to have a drink.'

'I will undoubtedly want to have a drink, but I won't. I'll drive. Can you come over to mine by five?' She was picturing him in her head. In his scrubs, refusing to wear a stethoscope around his neck – an affectation he despised – probably studying an X-ray or some blood reports even as he spoke to her.

'No problem,' he said.

She hesitated, finally getting to the reason she'd rung. 'Ben, you don't have to come, you know that. They'd understand. I'd understand. It's a family thing.'

'I like Kate and the kids.'

'Who doesn't? But it won't be just Kate and the kids.'

'I'm coming. I like birthday parties. Even if all the use I'll be is as a deflector shield for you.'

She gave up then. Pleased and relieved. 'Well, then, you're a very nice deflector shield.'

'Oh please, you're making me blush.'

Anna laughed and felt a little flutter in her chest. Anyone who managed to make her laugh was worthy of her time. 'Right, I'd better go or Lexi will forget what I look like.'

'I doubt that applies to anyone with a pulse.'

'Was that meant to make me blush?'

'Did it?'

'Tomorrow,' said Anna, and she ended the call. Still smiling, she gunned the engine and drove off, knowing her cheeks were red.

CHAPTER THIRTEEN

WEDNESDAY

It was already two days since they'd found the bodies next to the railway tracks. Dawes and Holder were on their way to see Alison Johnson's ex-fiancé, now a married man with two kids. There was a good chance he might recognise the ring she was found wearing. Anna decided this was the most appropriate way to approach things because the alternative, interviewing Alison's parents, struck her as unnecessarily cruel given the paucity of their evidence. Gupta was still awaiting the dental records, and neither Rainsford nor Anna felt they had enough to go on to open up that raw wound. But they had someone she'd been engaged to. He, at least, had moved on. He would, she was certain, be upset, but if he could confirm it was Alison's ring, it would put them one step closer.

While Dawes and Holder set off to a school in Bath where Johnson's ex worked, Anna and Khosa were on their way back to Ryegrove after picking up copies of Alison Johnson's misper file from Trisha. Apart from the ring, the key card was the only other piece of firm evidence they had while they waited for forensic confirmation, and a link, tenuous though it was, to the hospital. If it was indeed Alison Johnson's body they'd found, she had worked at the unit. Anna's instinct was to try and learn as much as she could about their likely victim as soon as possible because she didn't fit the pattern that Shaw's other buried treasure – all potential Black Squid victims – seemed to fit. And that bothered Anna greatly.

February daylight barely oozed through a canopy of dense grey cloud above them. It felt almost as if the morning was going backwards as they took the lower road across the Cumberland Basin beneath the suspension bridge and up towards Leigh Woods.

Ryegrove was lit up this gloomy morning as Khosa parked in the same visitor spot as the day before.

Morris was once again on the front desk behind the glass barrier.

'We're expected,' Anna said, showing him her warrant card for the second time.

Morris consulted his clipboard. 'That you are, Inspector. Professional visit, it says here. Right, let's get you through security.'

Morris buzzed a door open and Anna and Khosa pushed through turnstiles that took them into an enclosed access way. They shed everything on the prohibited list, and Morris gave them lanyards and badges and led them to a corridor with a signpost that said 'Administration'. Childs was there to meet them. He opened another locked door with his key card, and two minutes later they were in a conference room. Both Anna and Khosa said yes to the offer of coffee, despite Childs's warning of, 'It's only instant.'

Anna long ago gave up being choosy while on the job. You never knew where your next cup of coffee would be coming from. On his way out, Childs almost collided with a tall, full-figured woman in skirt suit and tan tights coming in.

'Inspector Gwynne?' The woman looked between Khosa and Anna for some acknowledgement. She wore thick-rimmed glasses and wore another pair slung around her neck.

Anna stood. 'Ms Mitchell?'

Mitchell nodded. Anna introduced Khosa and they sat.

'Thanks for meeting us. What can you tell us about Alison Johnson?' Anna's question was simple, direct and, she hoped, uncontentious. So, she wasn't prepared for Mitchell's face to crumple and for a hand to come up to her mouth to hide a quivering lip.

'Sorry,' said Mitchell, waving her fingers in front of her face. 'It was an awful time, and this is bringing it all back. Ruben said this is a murder enquiry.'

Anna didn't answer. The misper file Anna'd read explained that Alison's disappearance hit the headlines in 2001. CCTV had shown her leaving Ryegrove in her car and turning right instead of left towards the city. ANPR picked the car up twice more heading south and it was later found in a car park on the outskirts of Glastonbury. Despite extensive searches and enquiries, no trace was ever found of her whereabouts and the file had remained open.

Khosa said, 'Strictly speaking, at this moment, we have a body which we're treating as a suspicious death.'

'Is it Alison?'

Anna answered. 'The truth is we don't know yet. This is only one line of enquiry. What was your impression of what happened to Alison?'

Mitchell sat back, shaking her head. 'It was a difficult time for us. Lots of strain on everyone because of the changes.'

'Changes?' Khosa asked.

'Over a two-year period, the old hospital, Ryegrove Asylum, was transformed into what you see today. The Trust spent a lot of money. But change isn't easy. We still had patients while the construction took place. It was a massive job trying to juggle security with the need for construction access. The sensible thing would have been to close the whole unit and move everyone out.'

'Why didn't they do that?'

'Move them to where?' Mitchell asked with a shrug. 'This unit is both medium and low secure. There wasn't another unit in the area that could have coped. So, we did instead.'

'Do you think that had anything to do with her disappearance?'

Mitchell shrugged. 'We did lose some staff who found the whole thing too much. Trying to provide a safe clinical environment on a building site is never easy.'

'You were going to give us a list of staff members who were employed at the time and who are still here,' Anna said.

Mitchell handed over a list of some thirty names. The door opened and Morris stuck his head in and looked at Khosa. 'Phone call for you. We're patching it through.' He nodded towards a phone on a small table near a water cooler. It rang a few seconds later and Khosa took the call while Anna studied the names. Mitchell had organised them into areas. Hotel services, clinical, administrative.

Khosa hardly said a word as whoever was on the other end of the phone spoke, but she drew Anna's attention when she heard the word 'sarge'.

Khosa came back all smiles but tight-lipped. Whatever Dawes had told her was not for sharing. Anna turned back to Mitchell.

'How well did you know Alison?'

'I didn't. Oh, I bumped into her now and again. Knew her to say hello to. Lots of people work here but you tend to bump into the same people. You know how it is. She was nice. A pretty girl. Looked after herself. Well liked.' Mitchell shook her head.

'What about her sickness record?' said Khosa.

Mitchell frowned. 'Good, as far as I know.'

'No spells off work?'

'None of note.'

Khosa nodded.

Anna knew where that question came from. Khosa was trying to find some link between Johnson and Carson and the Black Squid. She was fishing for any history of a chronic illness. Something that might have led to depression and involvement with the sort of websites the Squid fished in. But Mitchell simply looked blank.

Khosa tried a different tack. 'From this list you've given us, who would have come across Alison most frequently?'

'I did glance at it this morning and funnily enough there's hardly anyone left on the clinical side. Most have moved away or retired.'

'Were most of the people who worked with Alison older than her?' Khosa asked.

'Yes. And of course, mental health nurses can retire at fifty-five.'

Anna said, 'The search team spent most of their time over in Glastonbury, but I did pick up a statement from a Dr Martin King. The last person to speak to Alison here at Ryegrove the afternoon she went missing.'

'Oh, Dr King. Yes, he's still here. He's our head of clinical psychology on Somerton ward. That's in the medium secure unit. They were all part of the same multidisciplinary team.'

'Would it be possible to speak to him?'

'I'll talk to his secretary. And then there's our nurse manager, Monica Easterby. She's been here forever, but I know she's away at a conference today.'

'Thanks. And I'd like to take a look at the grounds. Is that possible?'

'Yes. They are pretty special. I'll get our chief of security to liaise.'

Mitchell left and Childs came back with coffee and biscuits. When he'd gone, Khosa explained about the phone call.

'Sergeant Dawes, ma'am. It's a definite yes on the ring. The ex even had a photograph of it and a receipt. As a memento, he said. Gupta's getting the dental records as we speak. Sarge said he'll call back at the lab so we should have some confirmation within an hour or two. If it's a yes, they'll head to Alison Johnson's parents in Redlands.'

Anna blew out air through puffed cheeks. 'We're going to have to take another look at the list of employees at the time Alison worked here. See if anyone's a nominal on the PNC.'

Khosa nodded. If someone had been convicted, cautioned or arrested at any time after Alison went missing, they'd be on the

Police National Computer database. They may not have been suspects at the time, but if they'd crawled out of the woodwork since, it would be worth looking at them again.

'But they found the car in Glastonbury. If it is her, she must have come back here another way,' Khosa pointed out.

Anna turned to look out of the window as three magpies flew up and settled in a tree across the car park outside. The collective term for a flock of the birds always stuck in her mind. A mischief of magpies felt suddenly appropriate. As if they were mocking her. 'I don't think she ever left here, Ryia. But someone made sure it looked like she did.'

The head of security wore a grey suit, a pale-coloured shirt and no tie. Terry Marshall – a big, competent-looking man with a small radio in a clip on his belt – took Anna and Khosa outside through hotel services and into a fenced-off yard. At the end of the yard stood a locked steel gate at least ten feet high. Marshall took out the radio and spoke to someone.

'Mel, gate four in the exercise yard, please. I have two professional visitors.' He turned and waved at a CCTV camera mounted above the gate. A buzz and a click followed, and Marshall pushed the gate open. Beyond, the grounds swept away with paths through the grassy hillocks and shrubbery.

'Do the patients come out here?'

'Some. We have programmes during the summer. In the low secure unit we have patients ready to step down into the community. They're allowed unsupervised access. Others help in the gardens. The medium secure patients are only allowed in here under supervision. There are 150 CCTV cameras here in Ryegrove.'

'Can we go to the furthest point?'

'Sure.' Marshall led the way, happy to give them the spiel. 'Jocelyn told me you were interested in the history of the site. The revamp was completed in 2004. Very expensive.'

'What was here before that?' Anna asked.

'Hedges, some fencing. But nothing as secure as this.'

'When did they start building this fence?'

'It took almost four years, so around 2000.'

The lawns ended, and the path entered a wider area, the trees bare, the ground leaf-strewn. The gravel path petered out into a narrower walkway descending through a birch copse. After twenty yards, the descent became steeper until the black-coated fence appeared at the bottom of the little wood.

Marshall stopped and pointed. 'There you go. That's where it ends.'

But Anna kept on walking, arms slightly out to balance herself as she negotiated the slippery leaves. Finally, she reached the fence and walked along its edge for another thirty yards, Marshall and Khosa a few steps behind.

'Are you looking for anything in particular?' Marshall asked.

'Yes. A view.'

She found it after stepping over a puddle and some discarded branches. She stood at the fence, the land beyond dipping to reveal the grey expanse of the storage yards and the three Tyvek tents in the distance. Beyond was the railway and a clutch of vehicles further up on the access road.

'My God is that where you found—'

Anna cut Marshall off. 'I'd be grateful if you kept it to yourself for now.'

'Has anyone ever escaped from Ryegrove?' Khosa asked.

Marshall's smile was dismissive. 'Not for years.'

Khosa picked up on it. 'When was the last time?'

'Nineteen ninety-nine, something like that. He didn't get far.'

'Is that why they built the fence?'

'Partly. And the kerfuffle over the attacks on the university campus next door.'

Anna asked, 'What kerfuffle?'

'Way before my time, but some young girls were attacked. Around the millennium. No one caught, but with this place being so close and the escape the year before, it was enough to trigger a multimillion-pound response.'

'Can you be more specific about dates?' Khosa asked.

Anna left her to it and walked on, seeking a little distance. Something was tripping an alert in her head. She sensed a significance here that could not be denied. This was the only spot along the whole of the perimeter fence where the railway and the burial site came into view. A clear line of sight. Above, the grey canopy of cloud was finally breaking up, allowing shafts of sunlight to angle down on to the tents below. If she'd been in any way open to omens, such a sight might have sent her into a quasi-spiritual spin. But Anna's brain was wired for logic and analysis. The sun was low and a little to her left. A lighting show for the stage on display. Because this was how she was beginning to see this set-up. As a composition. Had to be.

Anna took some photos with her phone but realised she'd need better images. 'I'm going to send back some techs to take better photographs,' Anna said when she rejoined the others.

'OK,' Marshall replied.

She was glad he hadn't baulked. Glad he could tell the difference between a statement and a request.

They walked back quickly. Mitchell was waiting for her.

'I haven't had any luck with Dr King, I'm afraid. He's tied up all day in sessions.'

Anna nodded. 'OK. We'll fix up an appointment and come back. You've been very helpful.'

Mitchell handed over an envelope. 'They're photocopies, I'm afraid. Here's the full list of staff and inmates at the time of Alison's disappearance.'

Khosa took it and they exited the way they came in. Anna's phone showed three missed calls from Dawes. Once in reception, she walked towards the other side of the atrium and rang him back.

'Ma'am,' he said by way of answer, 'Dr Gupta says the dental records confirm it's Alison Johnson. We're about to go to her parents.'

'Thanks, Phil.'

'So, are we officially calling this a murder enquiry now?'

'Was there ever any doubt? Neither Alison Johnson nor Jamie Carson could have buried themselves.'

'We'd better have vespers today, then, ma'am.'

Anna smiled. Vespers had been the colloquial term Anna's old boss always used for a late afternoon catch-up of the day's investigations.

'Four-ish. I have to be away tonight.'

'Anywhere nice?'

'Birthday party.'

Anna killed the call before Dawes could say more. She had the feeling he wanted to but she was not in the mood for small talk. A confirmed ID was real progress, but it was a bugger about King. It would have been nice to have crossed that 't' while they were at Ryegrove because… because she did not like being there. Something about the place made her nervous. All the fences and locked doors and not knowing what went on behind them. She was definitely with Khosa on that one. But one more thing needed to be ticked off. Back at reception, Morris nodded another tight-lipped acknowledgement.

'Mr Morris, you knew Alison Johnson, am I right?'

'The nurse who went missing? Yeah, I knew her. Said hello to her most mornings, like I do with lots of staff.'

'What was her disposition? Was she a quiet girl?'

Morris shook his jowly face. 'No. Exact opposite, in fact. Full of the joys of spring, she was. Lovely girl.' Morris frowned. 'Is that why you're here? Is all this about Alison?'

Anna kept her gaze steady, but Morris could read the signs and his shoulders slumped in genuine regret. 'Ah Christ. I knew it was bound to happen, but…'

'Did you see her the afternoon she left?'

Morris nodded. 'Like I said at the time, she was her usual cheery self. Maybe a little bit preoccupied, but too polite to not smile. It would have been rude. And she wasn't rude.'

'You said all this to the investigating officers?'

'I did.'

'Any idea what might have been preoccupying her?'

Morris shook his head. 'I've wondered that for sixteen years. Still haven't got a clue. It's all one big bloody mystery to me.'

CHAPTER FOURTEEN

Through the MCRTF office window Anna could see the afternoon had brightened but was quickly yielding to early evening murk with a forecast of lashing rain by ten that evening. She spent half an hour in her office, checking emails and reports and trying to get a handle on the operation to find Alison Johnson sixteen years before. It had been prolonged and thorough but ultimately fruitless. The search concentrated on Glastonbury for obvious reasons, but they'd also covered the hospital grounds. The search team had no reason to extend the parameters to the railway. But another fifty yards might have yielded a very different result. Her fiancé and other family members had been questioned and eliminated. No one knew why she might have gone to Glastonbury. Someone had postulated a carjacking and abduction theory, but it remained just that.

When Rainsford appeared shortly after 4 p.m., Anna left the tiny senior investigator's room and joined the team.

'Afternoon, ladies and gentlemen,' Anna said. 'This is a brief summary of today's events and an update on what we know so far. We now have both bodies identified from dental records. It seems highly likely Carson was an early victim of the Black Squid given the details in the notebook provided by his brother. We've referred to this as a "game" previously, but I think it's time we call it what it was: a grooming website designed to incite suicide in vulnerable victims.'

She turned to the TV screen. Trisha had loaded some images of Jamie Carson's drawings on to a disc. Anna now presented them as a slide show.

'This was what Jamie Carson drew in his book just before he died.'

'The word XCRST?' Rainsford asked.

'*The Exorcist.* It's the same as per the Kimberley Williams case. As is the getting up early, spending time alone in the dark, self-harming. It's a slow turning of the screw.'

Holder shook his head.

'What about the other historic cases?' Dawes asked. 'The kid from Sussex…' He paused, remembering the name.

'Daniel Litton,' Holder said.

'Yes, and Shaw's daughter?'

Anna replied, 'Sussex police have found no hard evidence other than Litton's mother confirming that he'd drawn a squid on his belly in ink. She thought it might have been an abortive attempt at a tattoo. And as for Abbie Shaw, I'll need to talk to her father about that.'

'But they are linked?' Khosa asked.

'The specific tasks leading up to deaths, the drawings and the notes all suggest so.' Anna turned back to the whiteboard. 'But that leaves us with lots of questions.'

Anna wrote on the board as she spoke. 'Does what happened sixteen years ago to these young people have any bearing on what happened to Kimberley Williams? If so, how and why? Is this one perpetrator or an organised group? And, more importantly, if they are linked, why the long gap between cases? And then there is the question of Alison Johnson. Murdered within sight of her place of work just yards from a Black Squid victim.'

'Do we think she's one too?'

'That's exactly what I intend to find out. You all know that the word coincidence has no place in any investigation I'm involved with.'

Dawes nodded. 'So, where do we start with her?'

'I've already asked Ryia to look through the employee lists for anyone who's now on the PNC.'

'I'm on that, ma'am.'

'Justin, go over the original investigation into Alison's disappearance. See if anything jumps out at you.'

Dawes stared at the board. 'If you want my opinion, the answer to all of this lies in Ryegrove.'

Anna agreed. 'The head of security there mentioned attacks on students at around the time the hospital underwent its rebuild. It might be worth digging up those reports.'

Dawes nodded. 'And a word with the contractor maybe. Especially if you say there were security issues.'

'Which brings us back to personnel,' Anna said. 'It's a nightmare visiting that place. Maybe we could get them to come to us? This Dr King, for example, and the nurse manager.' She paused, remembering the name. 'Monica Easterby.'

'I'll turn on the charm,' Dawes said. 'See if we can get them to spare an hour from their busy schedules.'

Anna looked up at Rainsford. 'There's little or no information on the digital footprint left by Jamie Carson. But I'd like some help with that, sir. Varga at Hi-Tech, if I can.'

'I'll speak to them.'

Anna had worked with Hi-Tech, Avon and Somerset's Digital Forensics Unit, before. Szandra Varga was a bright, no-nonsense data forensic investigator.

'Which leaves me needing to talk to Shaw.'

Dawes lifted his eyebrows. 'The offer's still on the table, ma'am, if you want me to—'

'No. It's OK, Phil. That's my job. What do we need to know?' She smiled and hoped it looked confident. Inside, she was full of dread.

'Everything he does,' Dawes said. 'From what I've read of his daughter's case, the Black Squid connection was glossed over as urban legend. She got marked down as a suicide full stop. What the hell does Shaw know that makes him so certain?'

And so murderously angry, Anna thought. 'He's never been happy to discuss his daughter before.'

Dawes shrugged. 'In my opinion, she is the key.'

Anna nodded, knowing he was right. Knowing, too, that her interview with Shaw was rapidly becoming as attractive a prospect as a root canal without anaesthetic.

'Anyone want to add anything?' she asked.

Trisha said, 'The CSM rang, ma'am. The archaeologist would like to speak to you. They've analysed soil samples. Wanted to show you something on-site.'

'OK, let's fix it up for tomorrow morning. I'll meet them there at nine. Right. Looks like there's enough to do.' Anna was conscious that she had not said when she'd go and see Shaw. There was no denying she needed to. But she didn't want to think about it now. It was almost four thirty and she needed to take some personal time to attend her nephew's birthday party. A promise was a promise.

The bodies had been buried beneath the earth next to the railway line for a long time. They could wait another day.

But even as she heard those thoughts manifest inside her head, Anna knew she was trying to reassure herself, assuage her own guilt. Someone had buried Alison Johnson to hide a crime. And that person might still be out there.

CHAPTER FIFTEEN

Ben had already picked up Lexi when Anna got back to her flat. She was met by a fur-covered bundle of exuberant joy as soon as she let herself in. Anna fell to her knees to hug the dog. Ben watched, leaning against the door frame, arms folded, a smile playing over his lips.

'You know something, you're lucky I'm not the jealous type…'

Anna sent him a disbelieving glare. 'We both know you got exactly the same treatment when you picked her up.'

Ben grinned. Anna stood and kissed him earnestly on the cheek. 'Thanks for doing this. I hope it won't be too much of an ordeal.'

'It won't be so shut up and go get changed out of your cop gear. You have the delightful aroma of stale police car about you.'

'I'll ignore that because I know deep down you don't mean it because you are a really nice man.'

'You've already said that once so please stop. You're ruining my reputation. Now why don't I take Lexi here out for a comfort break while you smarten yourself up.'

Anna squinted her eyes but didn't argue.

Anna's sister Kate lived in a nice new detached property a few miles north of Cardiff with her husband Rob and two children. A year and a bit younger, Kate was the exuberant extrovert to Anna's controlled coolness. She'd married a local boy who'd coped effortlessly with Kate's wild partying during their courtship. And even now, with two children and a mortgage to contend with, Kate still knew how to have a good time. Something Anna had struggled with for what seemed like forever.

Traffic over the Second Severn Crossing was busy with commuters heading back from Bristol towards the marginally cheaper housing on the Welsh side of the river. By six they'd arrived at the new stone farmhouse guarded with wrought-iron gates, today adorned with balloons. The front door was similarly decorated as were the hallway, stairs and almost everywhere else Anna cared to look. Birthday boy Harry had that slightly glazed expression that overtired children shared with Saturday-night drunks, while his little sister Elin, her party dress smeared with a variety of lurid foodstuffs, ran after her brother wherever he went, hooting like a train. They both ignored Anna and made beelines for Lexi, who seemed delighted with all the attention as her lead was grabbed and the children led her outside.

'They do love you really. It's just that you aren't furry enough and don't have a tail.' Kate, dressed in jeans tempered by heels and a flouncy top, grinned at Anna as she walked right past her to hug Ben before embracing her sister. Through the French doors, Anna watched Lexi fetching a ball, much to the delight of Harry and Elin, who were jumping up and down in excitement on the lit deck adjacent to the garden.

'Shouldn't they be wearing coats?' Anna asked.

'I've sent Rob's mum and dad on that mission,' Kate said. 'And, should they wish to accept it, best of luck to them since the kids are in super-fuelled "no to everything" mood.'

Outside, Rob's parents appeared and desperately tried to get outerwear on to the children. Two fit sixty-year-olds, smartly dressed and always upbeat as befitted the comfortable retirement they were enjoying after years of building up the haulage company Rob now ran.

Anna waved and got smiles and gestures of good-natured frustration in return.

'Mum?' Anna sent Kate a questioning glance.

'Kitchen, washing up.'

'What a surprise.' Anna composed an over-bright smile, grabbed Ben's arm and said, 'Come on, come and say hello.'

Sian Gwynne wore a sparkly top and dark trousers – all, Anna surmised, picked out by Kate. But the shoes that might have completed the birthday outfit had been abandoned in favour of polka-dot house slippers.

'Hi, Mum,' Anna called out.

'So, you've turned up then,' Sian said without turning around.

Anna, still smiling, gave her sister a pointed look.

'Evening, Mrs Gwynne,' Ben said.

This caused Sian to freeze mid-scrub. She turned quickly and, with majestic disregard for her carping remark of earlier, smiled warmly. 'Ben, how nice to see you.'

Ben walked across and embraced her.

'Mum, there's no need to do this now,' Kate said.

'Don't be silly. You'll have your hands full once the children stop playing with that dog. And someone better wipe its paws before it comes back in.'

'"It" is called Lexi,' Anna said.

Sian shook her head. 'Harry's already overexcited.'

'We do have a dishwasher, Mum,' Kate said.

'Ruins the glasses.'

Kate gave up with a little sigh of exasperation. Sian Gwynne was a woman with unshakable belief in doing things her way. It frustrated Kate, but it drove Anna to distraction. And there was no doubt she was getting worse with age. A widow for more than a decade, her grandchildren were now Sian's raison d'être. The children loved her but her inability to treat neither Anna nor Kate as adults was a source of some amusement between the sisters. Anna usually let the slings and arrows bounce off her armour, but Kate found the jousting increasingly difficult to handle.

'She's losing her filters,' was becoming Kate's favourite phrase. Anna was less ready to accept her mother's cattiness as a sign of anything other than her disdain for Anna's lifestyle. Something Sian made no bones about criticising whenever the opportunity arose.

'Busy at work, were you?' Sian asked, directing her question at Anna.

'Yes, as a matter of fact.'

'Something horrible?' Kate asked, her face lighting up with Schadenfreude.

Anna shook her head. 'Horrible enough. Some bodies found near a railway line next to a secure unit.'

'What's a secure unit?' Sian asked.

Ben answered. 'They used to call them mental hospitals. Or before that, asylums. Where they house the criminally insane.'

Sian frowned and stared at Ben as if he'd uttered some sort of curse before turning her horrified gaze on Anna. 'I hope you're not going near a place like that?'

'Erm, of course I am. I was there today. Their security is ten times more thorough than any airport—'

'You need to stay away from those places,' Sian said in a harsh whisper.

'What?'

'Mum, are you OK?' Kate stepped forward as Sian leaned on the sink and put her hand out to steady herself. But she shrugged off Kate's supporting arm and kept her gaze on Anna, shaking her head.

'I used to visit my aunty Mary in a place just like that. In *Talgarth*.' The word came out like a curse. Sian shook her head, her face suddenly pale. 'It terrified me. She terrified me. Sitting there, hunched over, like a shell of a real person. Like who she really was had all been sucked out of her.'

'You don't need to tell me, Mum,' Anna said, with a shrill giggle. 'You made me go with you, remember?'

'Talgarth?' Kate asked.

Sian squeezed her eyes shut. 'A terrible place. I hated going there.' She looked up, her eyes boring into Anna's. 'When you were small I was worried you might end up there, you know that?'

Anna knew her mouth was open. She forced it shut.

'You were so different from your sister. Your father said I was being stupid, but he hadn't seen Mary. We never talked about her. They just let her rot away.'

'Mum,' Kate said with urgent chastisement in her whispered tone, but she held up an open hand in appeasement towards Anna before taking her mother's arm. 'Leave the washing-up now. Let's go and sit down. And no more wine for now either.'

Ben leaned in and whispered to Anna, 'Go and see Lexi and the kids,' before following Kate through to a sitting room beyond.

Anna stood, rooted to the spot, wondering what had just happened and trying to work out how, in the space of two minutes, her mother had managed to both ruin the mood and throw another grenade into their family dynamics. She walked out into the hallway as Rob, her brother-in-law, came through the front door carrying a case of beers. He put them down and kissed Anna on both cheeks. Rob was big and burly with an easy-going temperament.

'Got a drink, Anna?' he asked when he'd given her a hug.

'Maybe later,' Anna said.

'What are you doing in here on your own?'

Being odd, I expect. The retort flashed into her mind, but she held it back. Rob wasn't her mother.

Instead, Anna pointed to the French doors. 'Watching your children freeze to death and waiting for social services to arrive.'

Rob nodded, grinning. 'Your fault for bringing that bloody dog.' But his eyes never left Anna's face. 'You OK? You look… distracted.'

'Do I?' She had a choice then. Burden Rob with a little bit of Gwynne baggage, or lie. She opted for the lie. 'Work, you know.'

'Hmm.' Rob wasn't buying it. 'Ben here?'

'Yes, he's talking to Mum.'

'And you aren't?'

'Dog comes first,' Anna said, letting Rob have her best jokey smile.

She was saved from more awkwardness by the French doors opening and Lexi bounding in with a tennis ball in her mouth and two squealing children in hot pursuit.

Anna took the ball from the dog. 'Right, you two. We have presents,' she said.

The next hour and a half were spent in convivial chaos with the children getting more and more tired while the adults tried to placate them with games and stories. By seven thirty, Elin had fallen asleep on the sofa, and birthday boy Harry, in Rob's father's arms, lay listening to a story, his lids getting heavier by the paragraph. Rob's mother carried Elin to bed, and his father took a surprisingly docile Harry up with the promise of another chapter as long as he got into his pyjamas.

Kate, Rob and Anna sat in the living room. Ben and Sian were in the kitchen, sitting around the table.

'Shall we go through and join them?' Kate said, smiling, waiting for Anna to say the obvious. But Anna didn't want to. She didn't want to be in the same room as her mother if she could help it. The barb that had been delivered a couple of hours before was still smarting. She was fed up of being a target. Fed up of being the patsy. Anna knew that Kate and Rob were looking at her, their expressions ones of anxious entreaty.

She was saved from continuing the embarrassing silence by Ben appearing in the doorway.

'Kate, your mum says she wants to go home. She's feeling a bit tired.'

Kate got up and headed for the kitchen, concern making her pout. Anna could hear their voices. Kate questioning, her mother's reassurances. Two minutes later Sian was in the hall and Anna went to say goodbye. Sian was all smiles.

'Lovely party. Harry must be exhausted. Thanks for the food and thank you for the chat, Ben.' She turned to Anna, her smile genuine. 'Lovely to see you, Anna. Don't work too hard, now. Is it Rob who's taking me home?'

'Yes, me again, I'm afraid.'

'Are you OK to drive?'

'Yes, I'm on the pretend beer. Low-alcohol stuff.'

Sian kissed Kate and then Anna and followed Rob out to his car. When she'd gone, Kate turned to Ben. 'Are you some kind of witch whisperer?'

Ben shook his head. 'Comportment.'

Kate frowned but then waved to her mother as the car drove out. When it had gone she shut the door and turned back to Ben. 'Say that again.'

'Let's go into the kitchen.' He turned away.

Kate threw Anna a glance, but all she could do was shrug.

Ben sat at the table. 'Comportment. It's a psychological term that applies to the appropriateness of certain behaviours in a given situation. I've had a long chat with your mum. I think she's comportment-challenged.'

'I could have told you that,' Anna said.

Ben nodded. 'I know. And I'm not trying to excuse it, but I don't think she has any insight either.' He looked at Kate. 'She is losing her filters, as you put it. It's like having a hair-trigger for anything that irritates her.'

'Why are you telling us things we already know?' Anna said.

'Because it can be a sign of something. How about her personality? Has that changed?'

Kate sighed. 'She has been getting a little tetchy lately. With me not the kids.'

Ben nodded.

'Come on, Ben, spit it out,' Anna said. 'You think she's losing it?'

'One way of putting it. Early-onset dementia can present like this.'

'Oh, come on. She more or less called me a lunatic. It's obvious she thinks I'm disturbed.'

Kate put her hand on Anna's arm. 'It wasn't a very nice thing to say, I have to admit.'

'Agreed.' Ben nodded. 'As I say, I'm not making excuses. I'm just suggesting there may be a reason why.'

'I'm the reason why,' Anna said.

'Don't say that,' Kate said.

Anna sighed. 'I know. It's all very well for me, I'll be swanning off and leaving you with the mess.'

'But she isn't a mess. Most of the time. She's great with the kids.'

'You're still happy to let her babysit?'

'Couple of hours in the daytime. She's fine… It's…'

'What?' Anna said.

'She's worse when you're around.'

'Thanks, Kate.'

'Anna, I know it's not your fault.'

Kate was right. Anna was her mother's kryptonite. But knowing it didn't help Anna's sour indictment. 'I can't believe that all these years she's been worried I might go off the rails.'

It seemed an open invitation for someone to make a flippant remark, defuse the tension, but neither Ben nor Kate did because it was so obviously true. Somehow it made things worse.

'Don't hate her, Anna,' Kate said.

'I'm trying not to,' was all Anna managed to say in reply.

CHAPTER SIXTEEN

THURSDAY

Anna got in to work early next morning. Trisha had left a note on her desk to remind her about the meeting with Dermot Keaton, the archaeologist. The team drifted in with waved greetings. When Trisha arrived at half eight Anna asked, 'What exactly did Keaton say when he rang?'

Trisha shrugged. 'Just that he had some findings you might be interested in.'

Anna was pondering exactly what that might be when her desk phone rang. She picked up and immediately recognised the receptionist's voice.

'Inspector Gwynne, we have a Mrs Easterby here in reception. Says she's a nurse manager from Ryegrove. Says you wanted to speak to her.'

'I'll be right down.'

Monica Easterby was a big woman who managed her girth with good clothes and no stretch fabrics. Her broad face was made up attractively to match her dark complexion. Late-fifties in a dark suit, she jangled with a variety of chunky metallic adornments as she walked – earrings, a bracelet and necklace all matching with some kind of African theme. Despite her size, she moved with surprising ease as Anna introduced herself and took her to an office used for informal interviews on the ground floor. She rang upstairs and got Holder to join her with two coffees. Always good to have someone to take notes if needed.

'Thanks for coming in so promptly,' Anna said.

Easterby smiled without showing her teeth. 'When Jocelyn told me… anything I can do to help, Inspector.'

Holder came into the room with a couple of mugs and sachets of sugar. Easterby took two.

Anna waited until the coffee was stirred and then asked, 'What is your memory of Alison Johnson's disappearance?'

'We were mystified. She was a very good nurse. Efficient, caring. She was engaged to a nice boy. There was no reason for her to have gone off. She left a big hole to fill. Of course, after nothing was found we all began to fear the worst. But I'm ashamed to say I'd almost forgotten about her until Jocelyn said you'd been asking questions.'

'I understand there was a great deal of disruption in the unit at the time.'

Easterby nodded. 'Made it easy for some of the patients to take advantage of the changed routines. Some of them were – how can I put it – less cooperative.'

'In what way?'

'They'd hide. Sometimes they'd slip through the net and head into the grounds.'

'Anyone actually get away?'

'No. Absolutely not. We were very careful about that.'

'What sort of patients did you have on the unit then?'

'A lot like we have now. The difference is that we're able to segregate properly these days. The old unit was not fit for purpose. Don't forget Ryegrove was once an isolation hospital for infectious diseases. We even had mixed wards.' Easterby shook her head. The noise her jewellery made reminded Anna of a wind chime. 'It's only twenty-five years since we started to shift care back into the community,' Easterby continued. 'They closed the Bankside asylum which was adjacent to Ryegrove and migrated the patients. We did have secure wards, both male and female, but it was nothing like it is now.'

'Did Alison work on the secure unit?'

'She did. And she was good at it.' Easterby smiled. 'You're going to ask me now if I remember anything suspicious and the answer is no. I can't even remember who she was working with directly. We tended to allocate nurses to patients, so they could establish a relationship. There's more than one usually. But I can check.'

'Thank you. They were working on the perimeter fence and the grounds at that time, were they?'

'Yes. The fence. seventeen feet all the way around.' Easterby's smile was wistful.

'Don't you approve?'

'Of course I do, but it does give a terrible impression. It always reminds me of the fences at zoos.'

Anna flipped over a couple of pages in her notebook until she found what she wanted. 'There's a point at the very edge of the grounds that overlooks the railway line. Have you ever seen that?'

'No. The railway line? Is that where you found Alison?'

'It is. Would she have known about this spot, do you think?'

Easterby shrugged. 'She would have been in the grounds with patients, obviously. Supervising. But I can't say if she ever went to that particular spot.'

Anna nodded. 'She would have had access.'

'Yes.'

'That spot is important, we think. Would anyone else know?' Anna asked.

'I'll ask around but there aren't many nurses left who were there with Alison at the time.'

'What about patients?'

'Oh yes, there are a few of those. That's the trouble with our work.' She sighed. 'One or two are probably never going to leave.'

'I'd need a list. We may also need to establish the whereabouts of those who were there at the time but who have now left. In case we need to interview any of them.'

Easterby nodded. 'See what I can do.'

When she'd gone, Anna stayed in reception with Holder. 'Fancy a little trip?' she asked.

Holder nodded, and Anna rang Trisha.

'Can you check with Keaton, the forensic archaeologist? See if he's on-site now?'

While they waited, Holder filled Anna in on what progress he'd made on the original Alison Johnson file. 'Looks pretty textbook, ma'am. The initial investigating officer made a risk assessment and, given the circumstances of her work and the area, the case was elevated into a major search due to significant risk of harm, and a local SIO was appointed. The fiancé was made the point of contact as they were living together, though there was close liaison with the parents. Digital seizure of computers and phones of those closest to her threw up nothing, but Alison's phone was never found. There was a strategised search of the area where the car was found abandoned as well as air support. Passive data on CCTV and ANPR showed nothing after the car entered Glastonbury. She was not seen by any surveillance.'

'That's because she wasn't there.'

'No, ma'am. There's been a couple of case reviews and, needless to say, both financial and proof of life enquiries showed nothing over the years.'

Anna nodded. This was standard procedure. If someone chose to disappear they often slipped up and left some crumbs. Loyalty cards, requests for passports or car rentals, typically.

'But they didn't search the grounds of the hospital or adjacent?'

'The grounds, yes. But it was a building site. They also searched changing rooms and lockers she may have used. Found nothing.'

'Media?'

'Used early and extensively.'

'Last person interviews?'

'That was the security officers at Ryegrove, ma'am. Jack Morris is on that list. And a Dr King.'

Trisha rang back. 'Dr Keaton is on-site and waiting for you, ma'am.'

Anna got up and grabbed her coat. 'Tell him we're on our way.'

They took the fleet Ford Escort. Holder drove; Anna stared out of the window at passing traffic while her brain sifted what intelligence they'd gathered for indigestible lumps. So far, there were few, if any.

Keaton met them outside a support unit vehicle with 'Dept of Forensic Investigation, University of Wales, Cardiff' written on the side of it. He was as tall as Holder but at least twenty years older. He handed out overshoes but said they didn't need to put on the Tyvek suits. He took them across to the tent where they'd found Alison.

'Obviously, we took samples as we dug down and we've had some analysis back already.' He stepped inside the tent and pointed to the large stones beneath them, adjacent to the excavation. 'You can see there's a difference in colour here.'

Anna followed his finger. The large stone chippings were all grey, but some seemed lighter than others.

'In this area directly adjacent to the grave, some of the stones are lighter and match those we took off the surface to the actual grave. This pale colour is the result of bleaching.'

'Bleaching?'

'Yes. Whoever put the body here poured bleach first and then' – he pointed to another stone smudged a darker, brown colour – 'poured diesel over that.'

'Why?' Holder asked.

'My bet is to mask the smell in case of a dog search.'

'Would that work?'

'I don't know. But whoever did this may have hoped it would. It's possible in the early stages it might have. But it didn't fool the cadaver dogs. The penetration was only to a few centimetres. Consistent with someone pouring it on after the burial.'

'What about the other site?'

'It's the same. Diesel and bleach.'

'Could imply the same perpetrator,' Holder said.

He was right. Anna looked at Keaton. 'Were these graves dug the same way? Same tools?'

'I would say the same tools. Some cleaving of the smaller stones is consistent with a mattock – a double-ended tool with a pick one side and an adze on the other. The same sort of cleaving damage is seen in both, but this one, the one containing Alison, is much shallower by some three feet.'

'Why?' Holder asked.

'Maybe it was done in a hurry,' Keaton suggested.

Anna was beginning to like this man. He was willing to suggest answers rather than hedge and retreat behind science, like Gupta so often did.

'You can tell by simply examining the soil?'

Keaton nodded.

Anna walked out of the tent and, skirting the first site, walked to the edge, looking across the divide to the Ryegrove fence. She turned her head back. 'Has anyone asked you to look over there?'

Keaton joined her. 'Where?'

'At the fence. This side of it.'

'No, no one.'

'OK, then I'm asking now.'

'What am I looking for, exactly?'

'I have no idea. But I'd be grateful if you'd cast an eye. That fence overlooks this site and I think that's highly significant. Is there more than a sightline? Some physical link perhaps?'

Keaton nodded. 'OK. I'll take a look.'

Anna held out her hand. 'You've been extremely helpful, Dr Keaton. I'm much obliged.'

Back in the car, Holder looked a little perplexed.

'Come on, Justin, what's wrong?'

'Nothing, ma'am. It's just it wasn't exactly vital, all that stuff, was it?'

'No, but useful. Come on, what's the take-home?'

'Whoever buried them wanted to mask his crimes?'

'Yes, they did. And?'

Holder looked blank.

'What about Alison's grave being shallower?'

'Could mean they were running out of time?'

'Exactly. Or had to do it quickly. In either case it sounds like her death was not as planned as Jamie's.'

Holder nodded, concentrating, trying to follow her thinking.

'So?' Anna waited, probing gently.

Holder sighed. 'No, I'm not seeing it.'

'If it wasn't planned then it probably was not directly Black Squid-related. All of those deaths have been orchestrated, the victims well aware of what they were meant to do. Alison also had a broken arm. A defensive injury. She didn't want to die out there. And her killer needed to get rid of the body quickly. Probably before it was noticed she was missing. That means within a few hours of her leaving work. What time did her fiancé report her missing?'

'Seven the following morning.'

'So now we have a working time frame, too.'

Holder nodded. 'Where to now, ma'am?'

'Back to HQ. I'd like you to call in on the lab. See if they're getting anywhere with the key card we found. Is there a logo or an image of some kind that'll confirm where it's from? I want you to make Alison Johnson your specialist subject on this one, Justin.'

'I can do that.'

Anna smiled. She knew he would. Already an idea was marinating in her head. Anna liked patterns. Her brain found them unbidden, and there was no doubt the Black Squid deaths all followed one. But Alison Johnson did not fit that pattern. She glanced across at Holder. He still looked like a kid from the sixth form on work experience, though she knew he was mid-twenties. He was conscientious and ambitious, and she could trust him to get a handle on the dead nurse. What she didn't say was how she would have given him everything in her bank account to swap that specialist subject with the one that had become hers.

The idea, unfounded, but making all her antenna twitch, was though Alison's death might not be directly Black Squid-related, it was tied up with that sordid game in some way she could not yet fathom. And it meant she was going to have to invoke her specialist subject very soon if she was going to get anywhere.

Hector Shaw loomed on her horizon like a dark stain she wished she could scrub out.

CHAPTER SEVENTEEN

It was quiet when Anna got back to the office. Trisha only had eyes for her computer screen, busy with the nuts and bolts of the investigation. Dawes remained out and about. Anna took the opportunity to peruse Abbie Shaw's file once more. She'd read through this many times over the last few months, trying to familiarise herself with the case in an attempt at understanding what made Shaw do the terrible things he had done.

There were several images of Abbie in the file, including four post-mortem which Anna had looked at once and then put back in the buff envelope that housed them knowing that she didn't ever want to look at them again. The others were in a transparent folder. But the one that sat on top, the one she always brought to mind, was of Abbie just a few weeks before her death. The same one she'd put up on the board in the squad room.

She'd been a small girl – a factor, so the reports said, that might have contributed to the bullying she'd suffered at school. But Anna also saw an attractive face which would, with time, have blossomed. She wore glasses to correct her short-sightedness, like her father. For some reason this image was imprinted on Anna's brain. It was how she thought of Abbie. The investigating team had pieced together Abbie's last movements from witness reports and CCTV. Those movements and the subsequent enquiry were all in the file and Anna had read it so many times she almost knew it off by heart.

In December 2001, just a few weeks after her thirteenth birthday, Abbie caught the 192 bus from Manchester to Hazel Grove at

7.30 p.m. CCTV confirmed she got off at the stop near Crowcroft Park, crossed the A6 and entered Cayton Street, a dead end between a nursery and a breaker's yard and vehicle service centre. At the end of Cayton Street, a refuse bin placed against the brick wall suggested Abbie had climbed up and over the iron railings, using the overhanging branches to hold on to. On the other side, beyond a few yards of overgrown wasteland, was the main Manchester to London railway line. At 8.05 p.m., Abbie stepped out from the darkness of the bushes into the path of the Stockport-bound train doing 75 mph. The driver did not see her, and her body, what was left of it, stayed at the edge of the tracks until a slower train picked her out two hours later.

Abbie's mother had been almost impossible to arouse when the police went to call. She'd consumed the best part of a bottle of vodka and two of Chardonnay. She had not been aware Abbie had left earlier that evening and was convinced the police were mistaken and Abbie was asleep upstairs. Her screams, on finding her daughter was not in her bed, were heard two streets away. Abbie's mother asked the police to contact Shaw and declined to do so herself. When asked why, she said she was scared of how he might react.

As it turned out she had excellent grounds for those fears.

Unlike his estranged wife, Shaw did not scream. The police report detailing the account said only that he became extremely quiet and still, listened carefully to what they had to say and then asked if they wanted him to identify the body. The SIO at the time counselled against it, but Shaw insisted. Anna often wondered if that one regrettable, weak moment on the part of the SIO might have thrown the switch in Shaw's head that led to the maelstrom that followed.

She skimmed the reports of the digital seizures in the case. They'd found Abbie's phone, damaged from the train impact. Calls and messaging did not reveal anything suggesting criminal behaviour, and her computer and ISP history had no clues other than a tendency for her Internet searches to dwell on MSN chat rooms and support groups for 'acne sufferers', 'flirting with older men' and 'school blues'. Two of Abbie's friends admitted they frequented Internet cafés in order to surf beyond the reach of prying parental eyes. Not one of them suggested that Abbie was suicidal, but she had admitted to feeling a need for 'finding an answer to all the shit'. There'd been reports of name-calling in school, and one of her friends, a boy, had been hospitalised after being attacked for wearing the wrong kind of trainers.

On her computer screen, she'd left the Post-it note for her mother. It said, 'Inky blackness, Mum. It's the only way. Soz.'

Again, the police did not interpret this as anything other than a slanted hint at the dark depression that must have consumed Abbie. They looked and were critical of her dysfunctional family arrangement. An estranged father living on the other side of the city, an alcoholic mother, a lonely child with little or no guidance to hand. But someone guided her to a spot on an alleyway off the A6 with access to a high-speed train line. The report suggested she'd done her own research. The Black Squid, on the other hand, remained in the deep waters, out of sight and out of mind.

But not to Shaw. He wouldn't accept that his daughter planned this act alone. When what was left of her was buried in the ground, he set about finding out the truth. His job as a network analyst at GCHQ gave him all the tools he needed, and posing as a troubled teen, he stalked the chat rooms and put together his own investigation. One that led to him tracking down some so-called 'administrators' of the Black Squid. By that time, months after his daughter's death and consumed by silent rage, Shaw's mind had slipped into psychopathy. He killed six people, including his wife, before police stopped him. And yet from Anna's dealings with him, she knew he felt there was unfinished business. A consuming regret at not having reached all the people to blame for Abbie's death. A fact Kimberley Williams' recent death had now confirmed.

It was Holder's beaming face around the edge of her door that interrupted these troubling thoughts.

'OK, I'm guessing either you've won on a scratch card or your visit to the lab was worth it?'

Holder held up a piece of paper. 'It's not a scratch card, ma'am.' He walked in with Khosa in tow and placed the paper on Anna's desk. Blown up front and back images of the key card found on the female body, the faint outline of the image stamped upon it still unrecognisable, and next to it a passport-sized photograph of a woman with blonde hair and a zigzag parting.

'This is the photo of Alison on the personnel file.' Holder produced a smaller cut-out version of the image. 'This is the same photo resized proportionately.' He slid the cut-out image on to the image of the key card front. It matched the silhouette perfectly.

'Bingo,' Anna said.

Holder smiled, but it was the bemused grin of a child realising they were in the wrong classroom. 'I don't get it, ma'am. We've already had confirmation that the body is Alison Johnson's. Why is this important?'

Anna explained, 'Why would you have your key card in your back pocket, Justin?'

'Because, you left it there?'

'Why wouldn't you have put it away?'

'Because you were in a hurry?'

'Exactly. Alison had finished work. She'd have a purse. She'd have put the card away unless she was in a hurry and slid it into her pocket without thinking.'

'You think whatever happened was immediately after she left work that evening?'

'Now I do.' Anna looked out into the office as Dawes entered with four cups of tea. She stood to greet him.

'When did you get back?'

'Over an hour ago,' Dawes explained. 'Dropped the construction company employee list off with Trisha and went in search of Parky. You know Parky? Dave Parker? Been here longer than most. Still a sergeant like me but can't bring himself to retire. Thought I'd pick his brains about those attacks on students around the time the Ryegrove fence was being worked on. He remembers it all right. Some break-ins, petty theft and a couple of girls scared by seeing someone loitering. Nothing came of it.'

'What's his take?' Holder asked.

'Very non-PC. He reckons there were a lot of outside workers on the Ryegrove project. Bound to be a couple of bad 'uns in amongst them – his words. They did some enquiries but there was no hard evidence, so it fizzled out. It was like once they'd made their presence felt, it scared the buggers off.'

'And the construction company?' Anna asked.

'They weren't that forthcoming when I rang so I went up there. Big offices on the industrial park up Swindon way. They were much more helpful with me cluttering up their reception than they were on the phone. Young lady by the name of Lauren printed off a list. Reminded me of that Beyoncé, she did.'

Anna saw Holder and Khosa hide a smile. Dawes was entertaining.

'Anything come up?'

'I'm still checking the names, ma'am. Lots of workers with similar surnames. It's taking forever to run them through the PNC.'

Trisha got up from her desk and walked towards them. 'I've just come across one name, ma'am. I haven't run it yet, but it rang a bell with me because I've seen it before. I mean, I think it's the same spelling, but you never know just from a name.'

'Who, Trisha?' Anna asked.

Trisha held up a piece of paper. 'Mihai Petran.'

Anna looked at the name, highlighted in fluorescent yellow, and felt a little spurt of electricity firing off in her synapses. At the edge of her vision, both Holder's and Khosa's heads snapped up.

'Please tell me this company, erm... Casperson, have images of their workers on file?'

'I'll get on to them.' Trisha hurried away.

Dawes looked bemused. 'Sounds like this bloke's significant.'

'Oh, he is. Very significant. If he's the same Mihai Petran I think he is.'

'So how does he fit in?'

Khosa answered with barely disguised distaste. 'Petran is the identity stolen by Boyen Krastev, a Bulgarian lowlife on Europol's red list for years. Wanted in Belgium, Italy and the Netherlands for abduction, sexual assault and drug-trafficking offences. According to the Border Agency, he'd never entered the UK.'

'He nicked Petran's ID?' Dawes' eyebrows shot up.

Anna nodded. 'Krastev is also the man who told Shaw about Jamie Carson's body before Shaw killed him. His contention was that he'd tracked Krastev down in the hunt for his daughter's killer.'

Dawes sat down, a frown darkening his expression. 'Really?'

Anna nodded. 'Krastev was a facilitator, part of the Black Squid cell. Shaw's victims were all members of that cell. And knowing what he did to them, if they knew anything at all they would have told Shaw.'

'And you believe him?' Dawes scepticism tilted the end of his question up half an octave.

'Yes, strangely, I do. He's not trying to hide anything he did. It's Shaw who led us to Jamie Carson, remember.'

Dawes sipped his tea before saying, casually, 'Course, we have considered the possibility that Shaw's a manipulative speck of filth and that he could have buried both these bodies...'

Anna nodded. 'But now we have Krastev in the picture. He was working at Ryegrove at the time Jamie Carson and Alison Johnson went missing. He was also, according to Shaw, involved in Daniel Litton's apparent suicide. So I'm still inclined to believe Shaw's version of events. Krastev is up to his neck in all of this. Unless anyone can come up with a better explanation?'

No one answered.

Anna looked at the silhouette of Alison on the key card. 'Then it definitely looks like I'm going to have to ask Hector Shaw some questions a little sooner than I'd hoped.'

CHAPTER EIGHTEEN

Oscar Louden was unpopular with his teachers and unpopular with his peers. He was apart from the herd, shunned and isolated. And the herd, with the feckless cruelty of youth, made no bones about making sure he knew it. Rat boy, Mouse, Tosscar – he learned to laugh at the names they called him, joining in to survive. He despised them and gradually learned to despise himself.

The bullying began with texts and Facebook messages. Later, Instagram and Snapchat. They excluded him from anything they could. Oscar, at thirteen, began feigning illness so he didn't have to go to school. But his parents, naive and unsophisticated, stalwarts of the local church, would stand for no nonsense. His father even made sure he wore an old blazer to school. A blazer his father had worn with pride. Though a blazer was a part of the uniform, it wasn't the exact same colour and nothing like the modern, tight-cut style that all the other boys wore. Oscar wore it like a red rag, and every day got snubbed and jeered at and told to cut his own throat so the world could be rid of 'one more effing loser'.

His teachers knew what was happening. But they also knew that any intervention on their part might lead to an escalation. And so it continued on a slow burn, eating into Oscar's fragile teen psyche. He felt alone, unwanted and a freak. Small for his age and a little awkward, Oscar the tosser.

Tosscar Louden.

He found places in school to hide during lunch and break. Never went anywhere near the toilets. Took sandwiches to avoid the refectory. Rainy days were the worst. Then his tormentors would hunt in packs. Seeking him out for 'special' attention. His only solace was the online communities of like-minded victims, and Oscar was a member of many. MindHelp was one he liked. The forums there were easy to access, and he scanned them often. Eating disorders, fashion and pop culture, gender issues – the people there all seemed to have some sort of pain, like he did. He didn't talk to his parents about it. His was not that sort of family. He preferred to hide his shame. He had some friends, but they, like him, were weak in the face of the ferocious vindictiveness that had somehow snowballed. School was a nightmare Oscar endured. It became a game amongst his tormentors to find new ways to humiliate him.

Worse were the threats of what they might do next. They'd already ripped his clothes, stuck his head down the toilet, put ice down his shirt. Vickers, the ringleader of the boys who'd decided to make Oscar's life hell, had posted a Facebook message with an image of someone on fire running from a burning building with the line, 'Barbecue for hamster-boy?'

It had received 200 thumbs up likes.

The school knew some of what was going on, but there were others, his classmates, who seemed to get a sickening thrill of knowing he was a victim. That was the part he could not understand. The way people laughed at his discomfort. The way they giggled when he sometimes couldn't stop the tears. The way some teachers looked at him when he turned up to class looking bedraggled from yet another dousing in the boy's toilet. Where he'd hoped for sympathy, he'd found derision.

But then, when he was fourteen, he'd found The Answer Files. A site offering ways out for those at the end of their tether. It was there he'd come across the Black Squid. He'd read about it on other sites but never knew how it worked. But on The Answer Files there'd been a link to a simple questionnaire.

> Do you want help to end the misery?
>
> Does no one else care?
>
> Play the only game that offers real answers.
>
> Interested? Post your email here. You'll get a message and chance to send your phone number. If accepted, the game starts immediately.

The email message asked for details of how he was feeling and why. He had no trouble answering that. In fact, he'd written an essay. He'd opened up, given of himself, said more than he had to anyone else. Three days later, when he'd believed the game was just another anonymous joke, he'd received a WhatsApp message.

> *Welcome, Oscar. If you enter the Black Squid's domain, you may never leave. Make sure you understand. We know you are in pain and the Black Squid can take that pain away. It is a challenge with the ultimate prize of no more pain and no more torment if you successfully complete it. Rest assured that you are amongst friends. We understand what you are going through. We have the answers.*

He'd carved the shape of the squid into his forearm and posted the image on the WhatsApp link he'd been sent. It hurt, but it had felt good, too. Like he was finally doing something about a hopeless situation. Two little ticks showed him that the Black Squid had seen it. He'd progressed through the first five days easily, given them access to his contacts and all his photos. Now he was into the real game, the twenty-challenge game.

Things were progressing well.

At last, Oscar had found a way to beat his tormentors.

CHAPTER NINETEEN

FRIDAY

Whitmarsh was one of eight high security prisons in the country that housed category A inmates who posed a danger to the public. After a spell in Rampton Hospital following his conviction, and despite the viciousness of his crimes, Shaw had been deemed of sound mind and he was transferred to Whitmarsh to spend the rest of his sentence at Her Majesty's pleasure. The shabby interview room at the prison was a place Anna had become depressingly familiar with, but still she found the wait disquieting. Previously, Shaw had always been in the room waiting for her whenever she'd visited. Not today.

It was Dawes' first visit to Whitmarsh and he looked around at the grey walls and the bolted-down furniture and wrinkled his nose.

'There's no ventilation in here,' he said. 'Smells like a squirrel's armpit.'

'I'll take your word for that, Sergeant.'

Finally, a door clanged open and Shaw appeared, handcuffed, flanked by two prison officers. When they had him seated and shackled to the floor, one prison officer exited. The other sat at the back of the room, his face composed and blank.

Shaw sat and looked from Anna to Dawes and back again. He leaned back in his chair and said, 'Who's your minder, Anna?'

'This is Sergeant Dawes, Hector. He's helping me with the case.'

'Good listener, is he?'

'The sergeant works in major crimes. He has a lot of experience.'

Shaw nodded slowly. Anna read it as tacit acceptance and she frowned. This, too, struck her as unusual. Shaw's intolerance of other police officers had been a feature of their relationship. She looked at him carefully. He'd lost weight and his eyes looked puffy from lack of sleep. 'Are you well, Hector?'

Shaw tilted his head. 'No, I'm not. Doc says I'm anaemic. They're running tests.'

'I'm sorry to hear that.'

'If you are, you're in the minority.'

'Hector, we're here to talk to you about Abbie.'

Shaw's eyes narrowed. The last time she'd mentioned Abbie to him, it hadn't been well accepted. A throwaway remark by the officer she'd been with, a DI called Becker from Sussex police, resulted in Shaw, despite his handcuffs, knocking the man over and trying, unsuccessfully on that occasion, to bite the man's neck.

'Why?' he said.

'The body we uncovered from the shallow grave you took us to belongs to a boy called Jamie Carson. We now believe he, too, was a Black Squid victim. He left drawings and a message which, though not meaning much to the investigators at the time, suggests to me that he'd been targeted.'

Shaw watched her, unmoving as she continued.

'We believe Krastev had a role to play in all three victims so far. Abbie included.'

Shaw frowned. 'I already told you that.'

Anna nodded.

Shaw's eyes narrowed further. 'But there's something else, isn't there?'

Dawes shifted in his seat. Whether it was surprise at Shaw's sharpness, or some too tight boxer shorts, it didn't matter. Shaw threw him a glance and then smiled. 'You need to work on your poker face, Sergeant.'

'Krastev, masquerading as Petran, was working on the reconstruction of Ryegrove – a medium secure unit adjacent to the spot you took us to, set back from the railway line.'

Shaw looked away and let out a snigger before looking back. '*Chudovishtna kushta.*'

'What?' Dawes said.

'It means monster house in Bulgarian,' Anna said, but she kept her gaze on Shaw. 'We're trying to piece together exactly what Krastev's role might have been in what happened to Jamie Carson.'

The smile slid from Shaw's face like egg off a greasy plate. 'He called himself a facilitator. He was supposed to help with the final act. Make it easy for the victims. But I didn't believe him. I think these kids went along with it but at the end, the very end, I think Krastev did the pushing.'

Dawes sat up. 'You think he killed Carson?'

'Carson, Abbie and others. They were just kids who found themselves alone with a monster in a place none of them should ever have been. I made him tell me what he did to those kids before they topped themselves. I made him tell me what he did to Abbie.'

Anna glared at Shaw. 'There's nothing in the report—'

'That's because there wasn't enough of her left for the pathologist to find the evidence. But I knew.'

'Jesus,' Dawes said.

Shaw sent him a slow, reptilian look. 'He wasn't there. Never fucking is.'

'You never reported this,' Anna said.

'Come on, Anna. Who's going to believe me, the rabid killer?'

'I do,' she said.

'This Krastev, he's the Black Squid, then?' Dawes said.

'No. He was nothing more than a blunt instrument. Someone else did the planning. Someone much brighter than Krastev. Someone who covered his tracks.'

'The others… your other victims, they didn't tell you who it was?'

'No. They didn't know. If they had, they'd have told me and he'd be dead now, too. And there'd be no more kids throwing themselves under trains or off cliffs.'

Anna sat forward. 'You're sure these recent cases are linked?'

Shaw nodded. 'Yeah. He's just found a different way, a better way. For a start, there's no Krastev anymore. But technology's better. And this bastard is smart.'

Anna wanted to get back to Abbie. 'So you think the Black Squid arranged for Abbie to meet Krastev at Cayton Street and he assisted her—'

'He killed her.'

'And killed her there.'

Shaw's mouth became an ugly slash in his face. 'She was confused. Just a messed-up kid. These bastards knew that.'

Dawes said, 'None of this helps us with Alison Johnson.'

Shaw's eyes widened. 'She the other body, is she?'

Dawes looked momentarily stricken but Anna shook her head and said, 'I was going to tell you. She doesn't fit the profile. Older, a nurse in the unit—'

'So, she's a break in the pattern?'

Anna nodded, astonished again at how quickly Shaw could follow her own reasoning. She remembered their meeting in Sussex when Shaw first mentioned Krastev's reference to the monster house. Something he'd said then. 'You said Krastev was reluctant to tell you about Jamie Carson and where he was buried. That he needed a lot of persuading. Why do you think that was?'

'He was hiding something. Something he was prepared to suffer pain for rather than tell me. Wouldn't even sing when I chucked the first shovel full of soil on the plastic sheets I'd wrapped him in.'

Anna grimaced. Shaw spoke about his murders so casually. 'Why?'

'Maybe because he was more scared of telling me than he was of what I'd do to him. That's a powerful fear, don't you think?'

Anna held Shaw's gaze. The colour in his irises seemed to move like oil. As with everything he said, it hid a subtext. Something too obscure to read.

'What happened to Krastev?' Dawes asked.

'I let him sleep on it. Under six feet of earth. Unfortunately, when I dug him up the next day, his heart had given out. Maybe something to do with all the bleeding he did. Never got a chance to finish his story.' Shaw grinned. 'But I had enough to be getting on with.'

'And you can't think of any reason why he'd kill a nurse?' Dawes said.

'I can think of several. The bastard was an animal. But it's not what's important.'

Dawes took offence. 'Her relatives think it is.'

Anna kicked him under the table. 'What do you mean, Hector?'

'You should be asking different questions. Like why was Krastev working at a medium secure unit? Was that by chance? Or was it where he could be close to someone? Someone he liked and admired maybe.'

Shaw's gaze, fixed on Anna, was unflinching. She, in turn, searched his face for any sign of mischief, but found none. Shaw believed nothing happened coincidentally. It mirrored her own thinking. The answer to what took place next to the railway line lay across the waste ground in Ryegrove. Dawes pushed his chair back. Ready to go.

Shaw said, 'Let's let the sergeant go, Anna. I want a quiet word.'

Dawes immediately sat down again, but Anna said, 'I'll meet you in reception.'

Dawes threw her a quizzical glance. She returned it with a single nod.

When Dawes had gone, Shaw leaned forward and steepled his hands. 'You've heard all that crap about parents. You know, how they should never have to bury their children? It's a modern indulgence. Three hundred years ago you'd name all your children the same, knowing at least half of them would die.'

His tone caused Anna to frown. It wasn't like Shaw to talk about his emotions. She waited for him to continue.

'You lost your father early, right? I know it left a black hole. Losing Abbie left a bigger hole in me.'

'Hector—'

Shaw held up his hands to stop her. 'I'm not well. I'm bleeding from somewhere, the doc thinks. Probably bowel. I'm going to get tests. But the point is I'm going to ask you to promise me something. If you find out who was running Krastev, who the real sickness is behind all of this, you'll tell me.'

'You know I can't give you information that's part of an ongoing—'

Shaw did the same hand gesture and gave her a vulpine smile. 'We both know that's bullshit, Anna. It's never bothered you before. I can give you more details of what Krastev said. But I need a promise. I need to know that if you find out who really killed my daughter, you'll tell me, or you leave now, and I'll bleed to death slowly not knowing. But you'll have my blood on your conscience.'

Anna did not let her gaze drop because she knew it was what Shaw wanted.

'Why?' she said. 'Why are you so desperate to know?'

'Because if you tell me, I know the bastard will get what's coming. I trust you to make the arsehole burn.'

It sounded plausible. She tried, for a moment, to put herself in Shaw's place. Festering away in prison knowing her daughter's killer was out there. Free to think about what he'd done. Free to plan. Free to do it again. It would have torn her apart.

'OK. If I find anything, I'll let you know.'

He sat back then, his whole body slumping as if talking to her had required a great effort.

'When are the tests?'

'A few days. They don't tell me much. A scan, maybe stuff a camera up my colon. I'll know when they give me the crap that makes you shit through a needle to clear everything out. But I'll spend the time thinking about what Krastev told me and I'll give it to you. That's our deal, Anna.'

'What will you do, email me?'

Shaw smiled. 'You know we don't have access to email, Anna.'

'That's never stopped you before.'

The smile widened. Anna had received several anonymous emails over a period of months. From the content, she had little doubt that the sender was Shaw, utilising his network of contacts within and outside the prison to get the messages to her.

'I suggest we keep this all above board.' Shaw looked at her under his hooded lids. 'Come back to see me when you have something.'

She waited while they took him back to his cell, wondering what the doctors might find.

There was no death sentence in the UK. But perhaps, in Shaw's case, nature was going to administer its own version.

CHAPTER TWENTY

They ate in the car in transit to Portishead, stopping off in a service station for something on the go. Anna had almost finished her beetroot and feta wrap before they hit the motorway, popping in the last mouthful as Dawes pulled out into traffic. He, meanwhile, proceeded to munch his way through a small tub of sausage rolls, his shirt and trousers slowly accumulating a crumb mountain.

Dawes talked as he ate. 'I know you and Shaw have got history, ma'am, but he's a creepy bastard all the same.'

'A creepy bastard who knows an awful lot about this stuff.'

Dawes munched for a while and then said, 'Couldn't have been easy to lose a daughter like that, though. Got a boy and a girl coming up to that age myself. Kelly'll be moving up to the comp next year. She thinks she's eighteen now. God knows what she'll be like in a year's time.'

Anna inclined her head. Sometimes empathy chose awkward moments to bloom. 'It's not an excuse for what he did, but it is a big part of the reason.'

Dawes signalled and pulled out into the fast lane. 'Don't mind me asking, ma'am, and you don't have to answer, but why did he want to see you on his own?'

Anna knew Dawes wasn't prying. She might have taken offence. She knew a lot of fellow female officers who would. But Anna knew concern when she saw it.

'He wants to seal our deal,' Anna explained. 'He'll tell me what he knows about Krastev so long as I promise to tell him who is really behind the Black Squid killings.'

'And you don't have a problem with that?'

'I didn't say I'd do it.'

Dawes sent her a swift, appraising glance, wanting to see what sort of expression she wore as she delivered the line. He seemed satisfied with her neutrality and flipped his gaze back to the road without comment. It was a fleeting moment but one that left Anna again questioning her relationship with Shaw. She was a police officer and that gave her ways and means of dealing with criminals. You could be frugal with the truth when circumstances demanded and there didn't always need to be a code of honesty on your part. After all, most criminals lied through their teeth. But Shaw was different. He hadn't lied to her once. Yes, he'd been manipulative in the extreme, but she couldn't remember him ever telling her a frank lie. And that put her own integrity on the line.

Szandra Varga was waiting for Anna and Dawes in the office at Portishead when they got back. Her great strength was understanding that not everyone was as IT-literate as the digital forensic bods she worked with day to day. Varga wore her dark hair cut short and had an accent from somewhere east of Germany. She was sitting at Khosa's desk, with Khosa sitting next to her and Holder watching the screen from behind.

Dawes had never met her, so Anna made the introductions. Khosa filled them in on how she'd asked Varga to explain how Jamie Carson and Abbie Shaw might have accessed chat rooms.

'Szandra was just showing us how things have changed online since the noughties.'

'These are archived web pages from the millennium,' Varga said.

On the screen were garish, simple screenshots of sites, often with white backgrounds and line by line comments from users with anonymised usernames. No video, no flash colours, no images.

Varga said, 'MSN tended to supervise their chat rooms, but other live messenger services did not. Microsoft had Internet Relay Chat extensions before MSN. But ICQ, a play on the words "I seek you", required no registration. By 2001 there were 100 million users.'

Dawes said, 'So what you're saying is it isn't going to be easy finding what these kids were doing online back in 2001?'

Varga said, 'It will be very difficult. We have contacted the owners of the Internet cafés your victims frequented. These are very old ISP records and, as you will imagine, thousands of hours of searches and contacts. We don't have usernames. We don't have URLs.'

'OK.' Anna bit back her disappointment. 'What about today? The new Black Squid stuff. Surely there's some technical way of finding out who and where this game is coming from and who's behind it now? I mean it's 2018, for God's sake.'

Varga swung around to face them. 'I have looked through all the digital evidence provided by DS Cresci from Kimberley Williams. They have been thorough. As already explained, the WhatsApp user known as Humboldt who gave instructions did not have an ID. There are several verification sites he could have used to do this.' She turned back to the screen and her fingers typed. Up came a site. She pressed return and a list of six numbers appeared: two next to a Canadian flag, two next to a US flag and two next to a Union Jack. In a blue box next to the number it read, 'Read SMS.' Varga used the capped end of a ballpoint to indicate one UK number. 'This is the number you use for your WhatsApp application. Verification is by text message. The verification is received on the site. You punch this code into your mobile and that's it. You can now use the messenger service on your phone without revealing your own number. My guess is the user would also use a different or disposable SIM and even a separate phone. Possibly stolen.'

'So how do we find him?' Dawes asked.

Varga shrugged. 'Not through digital forensics, I am afraid.'

*

Rainsford was away and so Anna decided there'd be no vespers that afternoon. She let the team get on with their tasks while she wrote up her interview with Shaw. Krastev seemed to be at the heart of everything and yet they knew very little about him. While he was masquerading as Petran, he'd been on the watch list of three force areas for sexual harassment, theft and petty crime. She asked Trisha to pull up his record, nursing a vague frustration that Varga had not been able to help. What with that and the visit to Shaw, it was shaping up into a maddening day.

But at 4.45 p.m., Khosa stuck her head around the door looking animated.

'Monica Easterby's rung. She's dug out the personnel report on Alison Johnson. I think something happened on the day she went missing, ma'am.'

CHAPTER TWENTY-ONE

Anna beckoned Khosa into her tiny office. 'What personnel report?'

'Some sort of internal document for their own files. I suppose if someone stopped turning up for work, there'd be a bit of paperwork. Anyway, a name came up. Colin Norcott. He was a patient in Ryegrove after being convicted of two counts of manslaughter. Killed two people but was judged to have diminished responsibility.' Khosa looked down at her notes. 'Easterby says the nursing reports indicate Norcott had become very agitated and anxious that evening. Alison spent several hours with him and eventually he calmed down.'

'She spent time with him alone?'

Khosa cocked her head. 'I asked the same question. There probably would have been video surveillance. Someone would have been watching. But there was no audio.'

'Is there still a tape?'

'Unlikely.'

'Do we know why this Norcott became so agitated?'

'No, ma'am. And when he found out Alison was missing, he refused to speak about it. '

'Where's Norcott now?'

'He was discharged back to the community nineteen months ago.'

'If he was one of the last people to see Alison the day she went missing, we need to speak to him. I'd like to know why he was so agitated. Why he asked for her.'

'Yes, ma'am. Easterby suggested we also speak to another nurse called Beth Farlow. She was Norcott's allocated nurse therapist prior to his release. Probably the one closest to him. She knew him better than most. I've tried contacting her but she's not on duty today. Easterby says she's on early shift on Monday.'

'Good,' Anna said.

'Trisha's pulled some notes together on Norcott, ma'am.' Khosa handed over a plastic folder containing several sheets of paper.

'Good work, Ryia.' Anna grinned. It was late in the day, but the DC had used a lot of initiative and Anna felt a little zing of anticipation. At last something positive in the case. 'Ring Easterby back. Tell her we'll be in early on Monday and we'll want the same room she gave us use of last time. We'll need to see this Beth Farlow and we might as well try and see the doctor, King. And no excuses. Either he comes to us or we bring him back here.'

Khosa nodded. Anna looked at the shiny blue plastic folder on her desk. 'Right, Mr Norcott. What do you have to say for yourself?'

Five thirty came and went and the rest of the team drifted away to Friday evening activities and social commitments. They left with waves or, in Dawes' case, a head thrust around the door and a quick goodbye.

No one asked what she was doing for the weekend. That was chit-chat. Anna thought it was overrated and her team knew that. But she hardly noticed the polite farewells as she buried herself in Norcott's file. It made for uneasy reading.

Gradually, using the psychiatric reports, police notebooks and the court testimony from social workers, witnesses and teachers, Anna pieced together Norcott's story into a digestible narrative. As she read, and the separate bits of information solidified into a genuine horror story, she couldn't help but recall her mother's voice letting slip those non sequiturs about her aunt locked away in an asylum.

In 1990, Colin Norcott, aged six, moved with his parents and sister Sara, aged four, to a smallholding in West Wales. The kind of move dreamed about by so many city dwellers overwhelmed by the dust and diesel fumes of an urban existence, whose only exposure to open space and greenery come from Sunday league football or caravan parks in the summer. Bolstered by a windfall from the sale of his parents' house – a tiny terrace on the edge of London's Zone 1 that fetched a ridiculous price – Peter Norcott took the plunge. He walked away from his portering job at St Thomas', upped sticks and took the family west to a smallholding in rural Carmarthenshire. Peter and Tina Norcott became landscape gardeners and seemingly threw themselves into the local culture. She volunteered in the community shop, he offered to drive patients to hospital on weekends. They both took lessons in conversational Welsh, all the better to integrate themselves in the county with the highest percentage of Welsh speakers in the country.

The Norcott children had adapted seamlessly, feeding chickens and collecting eggs as if they'd been born to it. Colin would spend hours in the fields of the family's twenty acres, making dens in the woods with his sister or, equally often, on his own. Their nearest neighbours, the Morgans, had children of about the same age and the four grew up together. Anna imagined it like some sort of Blyton plot. They'd attend the same schools and hang out together during the long school holidays, play hide and seek in centuries-old woodlands, explore the hedgerows of the Morgan farm, herd sheep and cattle.

School reports suggested a different story when it came to academia, however. Colin struggled in a system that remained geared towards the vocations and was yet to appreciate the skill set of computer literacy. Because that was Colin's forte. Computer games. Given a degree of freedom most other children never experienced in a lifetime, reports of his lack of progress delivered by stony-faced teachers during parent–teacher evenings went unheeded. Peter and Tina Norcott wanted to give their children an unfettered lifestyle as befitted born-again hippies.

The young Colin would became an easy target for abuse. His school attendance record looked like a slice of Swiss cheese and he'd clearly evaded conflict by bunking off. According to one psychiatrist, Colin became fascinated by if not obsessed with a role-playing game in which the action was dictated by the player typing instructions into a dialogue box. He made his characters – the Knight, the Damsel, the Knave, the Executioner – do his bidding. With the game, he could make things happen in his world without speaking, remotely, with a simple line of instruction. He found this orchestration fascinating.

Ultimately, it was a fascination that would lead to the deaths of two people.

What changed Colin's life in one dread and fateful strike was a white Ford Transit with the words 'Mastip Engineering' emblazoned on its side.

Peter Norcott had taken Sara to fetch firelighters and charcoals from the Texaco garage four miles from where they lived. April brought with it the first real stretch of dry warm weather, and as an avid barbecuer, it was all the invitation Peter needed. That day, a Saturday, he promised the kids they could have hot dogs. Colin latched on to the promise and would not let his father forget.

At the garage, Peter filled up his old Subaru with diesel and put the briquettes in the boot with the firelighters. Traffic was light, but a white van was hammering down the hill towards him and Peter decided to let it pass before he pulled out. A manoeuvre he'd probably performed hundreds of times. It was an easy exit from the garage with good clear views of the A-road right and left. There was no reason to assume this time would be different. Except that this time, fate chose to deliver to Edward Bolton, the driver of the white van, a juicy cholesterol-laden clot to the brain just as the van accelerated down the hill towards the garage. The sales assistant, driven by some odd sense of foreboding to glance out into the forecourt, reported seeing Peter look at the van and then look the other way, checking for traffic to make sure he could pull out once the van had passed. He didn't notice, therefore, when the van began to veer towards them at seventy and hit them side-on. Both Norcotts and Bolton died at the scene, as did four sheep in the trailer parked at the pumps behind.

One of the firemen later said it looked a lot like an explosion in a jam factory.

According to the psychiatric report, the death of her soulmate hit Tina Norcott hard. The smallholding quickly changed from dream playground to sapping burden. But it was Colin who suffered the most. The outer veneer of self-absorption and solitude gave the impression his response was cold and undemonstrative. But underneath, Colin's world had shattered. With his sister and father gone, and his mother consumed with grief and worry, Colin became a ship without a rudder.

The community did what it could, but the fragile thread of Colin's stability snapped in the instant the Ford crumpled the cabin of the Subaru. Colin and his mother tried but his mother's need to talk it out was anathema to the already withdrawn boy. His school attendance, always patchy, fell to an all-time low.

Tina and Colin's relationship likely ended the day Colin admitted he had insisted on the barbecue. In therapy, Colin explained how his mother withdrew from him after that and made him sleep in the barn. She found solace in Xanax and the wild mushrooms she'd pick from the damp forest and dried in jars. It went some way to explain her use of harvested mushrooms on the pizza she begrudgingly cooked for him one evening.

She'd picked what she claimed were horse mushrooms. But forensic analysis of the remains of what Colin had eaten showed the flakes to be dried liberty cap. Unfortunately, Mrs Norcott did not see the effect the hallucinogenic had on Colin. At least not in the short time she stayed awake before a double dose of sedative washed down with the second half of a bottle of red kicked in.

About two hours after Tina fell asleep, mouth open, on the sofa, Colin, already confused and withdrawing into his own world, became lost in a psilocin-induced dream. He walked calmly over to the Morgan farmhouse and murdered Hywel Morgan and his daughter Carys after finding them in the barn tending to a sick cow.

As Anna read the factual description provided by the police notebook of the officer who'd responded to the call, she quickly understood the reason why Colin had been judged as insane.

> *I met Mrs Morgan in the yard. Unable to reach her husband and daughter by phone, she'd assumed they were out in the fields, but with darkness approaching, she'd sensed something was wrong and decided to look in the barn.*
>
> *Mrs Morgan became hysterical when we asked about the barn. She refused to accompany us. The door was open, and I entered. Mrs Morgan had switched the light on and it was well lit. There were two bodies in a stall. I also found Colin Norcott daubing the wooden walls with what appeared to be blood.*

With the office now empty, Anna removed the crime scene photos from a plastic sleeve. She teased them apart carefully with her index finger, not wanting to touch them more than she had to, knowing she was breathing through her mouth, feeling her scalp contract. She'd seen statements from the SIO after the trial, thanking his officers for their professionalism in the case. One where they'd been exposed to some of the worst scenes he could ever remember experiencing.

Anna looked at those scenes now and knew exactly why the SIO felt the need to express his gratitude and acknowledgement. Colin had used what was hanging in the Morgan's barn to kill his victims. Old tools like a hoe, a scythe, a pitchfork, adding in a few more delicate instruments from a toolbox for good measure. He'd trussed Carys and her father up with bailing twine and dragged them over to one side, leaving a slick of purple blood mixed with hay and cow shit over the floor. Mr Morgan still had a screwdriver poking out of his ear. The post-mortem said Colin used it first on Carys. The same post-mortem also showed that something had been rammed into both Morgans' brains through their ears using that screwdriver.

A message written on a piece of paper. The names of his dead father and sister.

There was no doubt in the defence barrister's mind Colin had suffered a psychotic episode exacerbated by the hallucinogenic effects of the mushrooms. Though the effect was theoretically reversible, Colin never quite returned to normal.

Mrs Norcott was never prosecuted.

Anna couldn't help thinking justice had not been served well there.

CHAPTER TWENTY-TWO

Anna picked Lexi up from Maggie a little after six thirty that evening and took her into the park. The clouds had cleared to leave a starlit sky, and frost was already glittering on the pavement. While Lexi sniffed at the same trees she always sniffed at, Anna phoned Ben. His shift started at seven. This was a good time to catch him.

'Hi, you on the way in?'

'I am. How are you?'

'Cold. But Lexi needed to get out.'

'How was your day? Productive?'

'Progressively weird.'

'Looking forward to hearing all about it.'

Anna smiled at the in-joke. They shared an unwritten rule. Neither of them talked about work when they were together. Not usually.

'Gritters are out,' Ben said. 'They're forecasting some isolated showers and black ice.'

'Oh dear.'

'Orthopaedics will be busy. Let's just hope it'll be slips and falls and not traffic accidents. The one good thing is that it's Saturday tomorrow, there'll be no morning commute. Who knows? We may be in luck.'

'I'll keep my fingers crossed. What do you fancy tomorrow night? Indian? Or there's that fusion place we could try on Figgie Street.'

'I'm easy.'

'I know. Why do you think I keep inviting you over?'

'You should know better than to distract a person while he's driving.'

'I'm cold and I need to think warm thoughts.'

'Happy to provide those free of charge.'

Lexi saw an oncoming boxer called Rimi and bounded over to say hello. Anna caught the eye of Rimi's owner. She seemed untroubled by the exuberant display, so Anna kept talking to Ben.

'I have one favour to ask. Sunday, you'll be delighted to know I've been excused of my lunch commitments, so I wondered if you fancied a trip to Talgarth, weather permitting?'

'That's the place your mother talked about. Where your great-aunt was hospitalised?'

One of the many things she liked about Ben was that he was an excellent listener.

'Yes. I don't know why, but having it mentioned has triggered all sorts of strange memories. I need to lay that ghost to rest.' She didn't add how her visits to Ryegrove had stirred up those vague recollections even more.

'OK. We know Lexi loves a road trip.'

'Shouldn't take more than an hour and a half to get there.'

'Good. Right, I'm at the hospital. I'll see you tomorrow.'

'Hope it's a quiet night for you.'

'It's Friday. It won't be.'

Anna ended the call. Ben didn't have to do night shifts, but the pay was good and he could pick and choose where and when. He'd be the senior emergency doctor there this evening. She also knew he relished the challenge.

Lexi and Rimi had spotted a pug and were giving it the olfactory once-over in very unladylike ways. Anna called Lexi back and headed for the flat, some leftover pasta and a glass of wine. She went to bed early and tried not to think about Colin Norcott.

*

On Saturday morning, Anna took Lexi to Leigh Woods. Ben had been right about the weather. It had rained briefly just before dawn and the roads were slick in places. Anna took her time and stayed off the smaller streets. Leigh Woods wasn't one of their usual haunts, and an excited Lexi found the new range of smells fascinating. But Anna had not gone simply to offer Lexi new ground to explore. Once they'd finished walking, Anna drove the extra few miles to the crime scene. If she'd judged Keaton correctly, she had a feeling he'd still be working the site. Seeing his black VW Golf in the parking area brought a satisfied smile to her lips. Lexi, nicely tired from her walk, was happy to flop on the back seat while Anna sought out the forensic archaeologist. The tents were empty, but on a hunch, Anna walked to where she could look across to Ryegrove's fence. It paid off. Across the scrubby divide, someone in a white Tyvek suit was hunched over, inspecting the ground. She hailed Keaton. He walked back so he could be within shouting distance.

'Ah, Inspector Gwynne. Your timing is spectacular. Walk north for forty yards and you'll come to a slight depression. Follow it down to where it crosses a ditch. You'll have to scramble under the chain link where it's at its lowest. I've put some boards down. Once you're over, follow your nose.'

She did as instructed and found herself in an overgrown patch of clumped rushes and fern and briar. The faintest line of a path led upwards. In summer, she surmised, none of this would have been visible. She emerged twenty yards from where she'd seen Keaton. He was waiting for her.

'Did you make that path?' she asked.

'I did not. It's old and unused, but this time of year you can see what it once was.'

'Animal origin?'

Keaton shook his head. 'Doubt it. What would make a path like that? No sheep here. No cattle either. Deer might. Badgers too. But I've yet to meet a badger who can pull up a buried and anchored chain-link fence.'

Anna liked Keaton's dry sense of humour. It was an acquired taste, but experts who knew their stuff could get away with sarcasm so long as it wasn't targeted at her. And she sensed nothing of that with Keaton.

'I, however, got a wet foot the first time I tried the ditch,' he added.

'Sorry about that.'

'Don't be, it was worth it. Come on.'

Anna caught Keaton's grin. It was still five degrees below freezing. The sun, low in the south, would not reach this spot for hours yet. The cold, she realised, was locking up Keaton's facial muscles.

'How long have you been out here?'

'First light. I found the path late yesterday afternoon. Didn't want to attempt following it in the dark. I came back early.'

They'd reached the fence. It stood above them, seventeen feet tall. Imposing and impenetrable. Keaton read Anna's thoughts.

'Looks solid, doesn't it?' He pointed to concrete footings where the posts were buried and at ground level where the bottom edge of the fence sat, firmly fixed with metal staples. 'They used machines for this. Small diggers, I suspect.'

'No gaps then?'

'None. But you don't always need gaps to get through barriers.'

'Don't you?'

'Follow me.' Keaton walked around the edge of the fence to where it started to curve up and away. Above her now, trees were visible beyond in the little copse at the edge of Ryegrove's grounds. 'They had to reinforce the bank here.' Anna followed his finger to a point where large grey stones sat in a flat triangle as part of the canted bank. 'Notice anything peculiar?'

Anna had gloves on, but the cold was seeping in and making the tips of her fingers ache. She scanned the bank twice before she saw it. Nothing much other than a slight outward bulge in the edge of the stoned area. A bulge where the stones looked smaller.

Keaton grinned when he saw her point. 'Exactly. Smaller stones in an outward extension of the edge there.'

'What does it mean?'

'Come and have a look.'

Keaton stepped over the rough ground to where he'd been working. Some stones had been removed from the top of the slight bulge and lay in a pile on the ground. A black plastic pipe, nine inches in diameter, protruded from the stones. Keaton handed Anna a long stick and pointed to the pipe. 'Go on, give it a poke.'

Anna did, surprised by how far in the stick went, almost two feet before she met with a solid resistance that resonated when the stick struck it.

'What's that?'

'I'd say it was some sort of wooden barrier.'

'As in?'

'As in a cover.'

'Why would you want a cov—'

Realisation stopped her from finishing the sentence. Keaton was grinning like a child.

Anna said, 'It's bloody tunnel.'

'Yep. That's what my money's on, too. The pipe is a dummy.'

Anna gave a little yelp before saying, 'This is fantastic, Dermot.'

Keaton, despite the cold, was grinning. 'We need to get some proper excavating equipment down here. We'll remove the stones manually, but in case we need to dig into the bank, we ought to have some oomph to hand. It may be just an abandoned drain, but then why put a pipe there?'

'Is that what made you suspicious?'

'Drainage pipes aren't unusual, but there'd have been a lot of concrete around when they were building the fence, so why not set it properly?'

Anna nodded. *Why indeed?*

'And there's more.' Keaton started walking to his right, to the remains of a rusting, barbed-wire fence. Grass had grown around the bottom strand, and in a couple of places the posts had rotted. 'That's the original perimeter fence for the sanatorium, where they kept the polio and TB cases before it became university property.' He stepped around a piece of solidified concrete spill and pointed to the ground and a faint line in the vegetation.

'Another path?' Anna said.

'Exactly.'

'Wow, Christmas and birthday rolled into one. I'll talk to the CSM, make sure we extend the crime scene perimeter on this side.' Anna peered beyond the rusting barbed wire to the renovated university buildings beyond. When she turned back, Keaton was watching her. His lips were a dirty aubergine colour from the cold.

'What?' she said.

'I was only wondering what made you think there might be something here?'

It was a good question. From here, below the fence, they were looking up at the point where someone inside Ryegrove could stand and see the railway.

'Everything seems to come back to this spot. There had to be something here.'

'Intuition?'

Anna nodded. 'Gift or curse, you can take your pick.'

Ben arrived at six thirty on Saturday night. He'd slept but not enough. Anna knew a Friday-night shift wiped him out for a good twenty-four hours so they ate early. The fusion menu turned out to be a little heavy on the spices, but since they both loved hot food, the surprise was a pleasant one. By nine thirty, they were back in the flat with this season's Scandi thriller on the box. But Ben's lids had drooped, and he'd finally thrown in the towel after jerking awake from momentarily drifting off the second time in ten minutes.

'Sorry,' he'd croaked.

'Hey, don't apologise.' Anna kissed him gently on the cheek. 'Go to bed. I'll wait until they set fire to another tramp in the name of entertainment and then I'll join you.'

Lexi looked up from her basket as Ben stood up, her tail thumping gently. Ben went over and ruffled the fur on her head before retiring. Anna stayed until the end of the episode and then climbed into bed, tired after her early start, relishing the warmth Ben brought and the smell of his aftershave. He was a neat sleeper and having him in her bed was no hardship. By tomorrow morning he'd be refreshed and then… who knew what might happen?

But in truth she did. A nice thought to go to sleep to.

CHAPTER TWENTY-THREE

SUNDAY

Beth Farlow was doing her laundry. She'd stripped the bed, had a full load on in the washing machine and was now in her bedroom, shaking out fresh sheets. She loved the feel of a clean bed. Her housemate, Dee, was out at her parents' and not due back until later that evening, so it gave her the whole afternoon to get chores done uninterrupted.

It was as she fitted a new cover on the duvet that she glanced out of the window, across the lane and into the patch of woodland opposite. Something there caught her eye. Something familiar and yet so totally incongruous that for a moment all she could do was stand and stare. It was small. So small that she walked to the window and had to peer across to try and make it out. The wind howled up the estuary, making the naked branches judder and sway. In the summer, some workmen had come and dug out the gutter and filled in a few potholes. They'd trimmed the worst of the vegetation back, but a wet summer had accelerated growth again.

Beth's eyes were drawn to a gorse bush a couple of feet in from the very edge of the road. Something snagged on the branches, dancing and snapping in the wind. A white shape, angled, slightly elongated and asymmetrical with an oval enlargement at one end. It was thin and light; that was obvious from the way the wind made it gyrate around the point of its snagging. A piece of paper, undoubtedly. But its shape was what had caught her eye. It reminded her strongly of something. So strongly that she threw the duvet, half out of its cover, down on the bed and went downstairs. She pulled on a puffer jacket and, still in slippers, opened the front door and stood in the doorway, looking across to the bush she'd seen from the bedroom.

Yes, it was still there.

Beth stepped out, put her hand on the gate and pushed it open. She'd taken one step out on to the road when a fresh gust caught her and made her turn her back into it, tilting her head and her face away from its bitter edge. When she turned back, the piece of paper was gone, ripped from its position and carried away by a gust. Frustrated, Beth turned up and down to see if she could catch sight of it, but it was gone.

CHAPTER TWENTY-FOUR

When Anna awoke on Sunday, Ben was watching her. She smiled and said, 'Do you want to go to the shower first or me?'

He returned her smile and threw off the covers.

Later, physically satiated but ravenously hungry, Anna ate Ben's cooked full English with gusto. She wondered, as she often did on Sunday mornings, if all that training in anatomy was what made Ben good at making love. He certainly knew which of her buttons to press.

'Penny for them?' Ben asked, eyebrows arched.

'They'd cost a lot more than that.'

'Intriguing.'

'All complimentary, rest assured.'

'So, Talgarth,' Ben said.

'We don't have to.'

'Oh, but we do. I've told Lexi we're going now.'

Anna glanced at the dog sitting next to Ben, salivating, waiting for the next illicit titbit to come her way. 'At this moment that dog would just about do anything for another bit of bacon rind. If you said we're going to the moon, she'd believe you.'

Ben glanced at Lexi, who let her eyes stray away from the edge of his plate to his face for a moment. Anna read total adoration written there. 'Right, come on, we can be there by ten if we get our skates on.' He got up and cleared their plates. Anna grabbed his hand.

'Thanks for breakfast. It's nice having you here.'

'You're as bad as the bloody dog,' he said and ruffled her hair.

CHAPTER TWENTY-FIVE

Nine miles away, Beth hurried back inside, feeling the cold bite, her fingers tingling, chiding herself for what she'd just done. Imagination could be a strange beast. Because by the time she got back to the duvet, that was how she'd rationalised her actions.

Imagination.

There was no other explanation for it. None at all. Because there was no way that piece of paper could have been what she'd thought it was. For a start, the patient, her patient, the one responsible for making the little origami shapes that had looked exactly like what she'd seen in the bush, was no longer her patient.

For a moment she wondered if one of the shapes he'd given her as a keepsake had somehow been blown out of her bedroom. But that was silly. They were in her wardrobe in a box.

Weren't they?

On impulse, smiling and shaking her head as if she couldn't believe she was actually doing this, she knew she needed to check. He'd made three for her, each one a different size and each one a perfect little representation of a human with a concave face and pointy arms and legs. She ran up to her bedroom, removed eight pairs of shoes and took out the storage box from the rear of her wardrobe. Inside was an old photo album of her grandmother's, a few letters and postcards and a file folder held shut by an elastic band. Inside were three small and delicate paper people, flattened by their confinement but still amazingly intricate. She unfolded one, the one with red lips to indicate a woman that the patient had said was her. Inside, perfectly positioned behind the folded-up face, were letters. H, t, e and b. Her name written backwards.

Satisfied now that some quirk of weather had not blown them away – *really, Beth? A wind that could open the wardrobe, upend a box and unclip a file?* – she shook her head, put the box back and got back to the business of making her bed. She didn't look out of the window for another ten minutes.

Because of that she didn't see the shape moving in the woods, in the shadows of the trees and branches. That same shape had pinned the golem to the gorse bush and then hidden to see if she'd respond.

She had.

And by doing so she'd confirmed once and for all that *this* was the cottage she lived in.

CHAPTER TWENTY-SIX

They drove over the bridge and paid a toll for the privilege. It was Sunday-morning quiet. They'd taken Ben's car because it had a bigger boot for Lexi to spread out in. Sometimes she'd sit up and look at them with her head resting between the headrests of the back seat. Cute enough to elicit a human response. A 'Will you look at that face,' or 'Hello, gorgeous.' The words didn't matter, it was all about the tone. For the most part, she seemed happy to lie down, as chilled as usual.

Ben drove. Anna was content to let the radio provide background noise while Ben chatted. But her responses became shorter and increasingly monosyllabic until Ben turned to her with a look that didn't need speech or embellishment. He knew her well. They were tuned to the same emotional station, and in that moment, Anna sensed how lucky she was – and not for the first time. Understanding was not to be sniffed at.

'You're thinking about your mother, aren't you?' Ben said.

Anna shrugged.

'The way she is, what she says, it's classic disinhibition. Remember what I said about comportment? When it starts to fail, it gets hard to see yourself as others do. It can come across as being rude and harsh. It's especially common in frontotemporal dementia.'

Anna listened without speaking. This morning Ben had been her lover. Now he was being her friend and, because it was his nature, a doctor. He'd seen her mother, heard her outburst but not mentioned it since. Not until now.

'Is it that obvious?'

'Pretty much. I think the clue is in the abandoned mental hospital we're about to visit.'

She toyed with the idea of telling him it was becoming a habit. Shaw had taken her to a similar sort of place in North Wales, were they'd found Krastev's body. But that was work; this was personal. Very personal.

It took them an hour and a half, turning north at Junction 24 off the M4, up through Raglan and on across open countryside. They'd built sanatoriums away from centres of population. Deliberately, for obvious reasons. Even Ryegrove was positioned across the river from Bristol city centre. Yet Anna had forgotten how empty parts of Wales could be. When they arrived at the village of Talgarth, Ben turned off and parked near a nature reserve. He'd downloaded a map and followed it in, walking along a back road that wound around the perimeter of the old hospital and around to the front.

Talgarth asylum was solidly built of grey stone, had two storeys and a clock tower; all boarded up, fenced off and abandoned. Haunted house material. One look made Anna shiver.

'Now I remember,' she said.

They'd come alone. Her and her mother. Never Kate and never her father. She could not understand why. But looking up at the gates, memory of those boring Sunday afternoon journeys was suddenly vivid. Her mother driving, Anna listening to Aunty Mary's story. Of how she was quiet – like Anna – and how she was indulged by her own parents, allowed to withdraw and kept away from other people because she was different. Always checking things over and over, off in her own little world. And of how Sian was convinced that had Mary's parents been firmer, stricter, the odd little girl might have blossomed. Sian blamed her grandmother. Smothering and weak. Didn't everyone have problems? You worked through them. Got on with it. And now here was poor Mary having electrodes attached to her head every day and drugged to the eyeballs.

They'd drive up and park and sign in with the nurse on reception. Sian had been often and didn't need to be shown up to Mary's room. Anna would go, seeing people dressed in gowns and in wheelchairs, some of them human statues, others moving like snakes, dancing to a tune no one else heard. She knew now that those movements, those writhing distortions, had a big and terrifying name: choreoathetoid. Nothing but a side effect of the drugs the patients needed to keep their brains docile. But at the time terrifying to a little girl.

But not as much as Aunt Mary was.

She'd sit in her chair, eyes open, half hunched forward, her hair hanging, mouth drooling. Catatonic was the word her mother used. Sian would sit and talk and make Anna sit, too. And the monologue would be carping and some of it – most of it – spoken for Anna's benefit. At the time, she hadn't realised why she had to go. But now, standing outside the gates of the huge asylum, she understood.

The visits hadn't been for Mary or Sian. They'd been for Anna. A warning. That was why her father never went. Her mother actively discouraged him because her agenda did not include the man who might have seen what she was doing and stopped her. And Kate would have been simply an encumbrance. Kate needed no encouragement or warning to be normal. Kate would have jabbered all the way there and all the way back and demanded to know why Aunty Mary was dribbling. Why she'd sometimes be talking to someone only she could see. Kate would have been an unnecessary distraction because these visits had purpose. Sian wanted Anna, her quiet, withdrawn daughter, to see what might happen if she didn't snap out of it and start being normal.

Anna shuddered.

She felt a pressure on her arm and looked down to see Ben's hand.

'You OK?'

Anna nodded. 'I don't even know why Mary was here. If she even had a diagnosis.'

'Sometimes there wasn't a diagnosis. Strange and inexplicable behaviour was enough in these old asylums. And once patients were institutionalised, it could become very difficult for them to leave. They'd use insulin therapy to induce a coma sometimes, then medicate when the patient came around.'

Anna shivered.

'Let's walk.' Ben touched her arm. 'If we don't, Lexi will explode.'

They did walk. Around the perimeter of the huge complex. And as they did, Anna opened up and talked about her visits and her mother. Half a mile from the car on their return leg, she'd finished vomiting all the poison up.

'Ignorance is a dangerous thing, but it's even worse when it's driven by love,' Ben said.

'Is that supposed to make me feel better?'

'Why, do you feel bad?'

'Yes. I'm almost thirty and I've just realised my mother thinks I'm mentally ill. Has probably always thought that.'

'Some people struggle with difference.'

'Is that what I am? Different?'

'You know you are. It's what makes you… special.'

'Wow. Different and special. Should I wear a bell?'

She was angling for a fight, but Ben simply grinned. 'Oh, and let's not forget feisty.'

He stepped away to avoid her half-hearted blow. He was right. Her difference even had a label, given to her through psychometric testing during her time at university: INTJ.

Introversion. Intuition. Thinking. Judgement.

Big words that Ben had distilled down to the bone. *'Yep, that's you. An idealistic cynic who takes nothing at face value.'*

'Seeing her aunt like that must have been awful for your mother,' Ben said.

Anna shook her head and rolled her eyes. 'Don't you have anything bad to say about anyone?'

'I have a list.'

'I bet it's a short one.'

'I'm not making excuses for your mother's behaviour, Anna, but you survived and proved her wrong. She probably has a hard time reconciling that. And now it's set up a conflict in a mind that doesn't know what's appropriate.'

'What if she's right, though?'

Ben gave her a scrunched-up smile. 'Where's all this coming from, Anna? The case in Ryegrove?'

Anna shrugged. 'Maybe. Something happened there, Ben, something bad.'

'Isn't that what you do? Catch the bad guys?'

'I try.'

'So, what's different about this one?'

'I don't know. According to my mother, I'm just a hop and a skip away from being there myself.'

'I can see she's upset you.'

Nothing new there, thought Anna. She paused and turned to him. 'I hate you having to deal with my baggage.'

'It's nice to know you have some because you know I do. Up to now I thought you were a superbeing. Flawless in all senses of the word. Difficult to live up to that.'

'Flaw-full, more like.'

'No, I've had a very close look. OK, there is a little naevus in the shape of New Zealand under your left breast, but on the whole...'

Lexi, caught up by a rabbit hole, looked up to see if they were following and noting their lack of progress decided to bound towards them at full tilt. She made an impressive sight, ears back, tail up, full of the sheer enjoyment of running.

Ben kneeled down and held out his arms. 'Come on, girl!'

Lexi decided not to slow down until it was too late and cannoned into him, sending him sprawling on the rough grass, much to his delight. 'Whoa, high tackle,' he said grabbing at the dog and pulling her to him. She responded by attempting to lick his face while he half-heartedly covered it up.

'Lexi, stop it,' Anna said. 'That's my job.' She held out a hand and helped Ben to his feet. He stood, closer than he needed, and didn't let go of her hand, his expression suddenly serious.

'Your mother's conflicted, probably always has been. But she's going to need your help. My guess is she thought she was helping you by bringing you here.'

'It didn't help.' She looked around. 'I can't believe I blocked it out. But being here now gives me the willies.'

'Then perhaps it did help. Perhaps it gave you a strong self-preservation mechanism. A determination to be yourself whatever the cost.'

'Cost?'

'Try not to hate her, Anna. Right or wrong, she thought she was helping.'

Anna looked away to stop him seeing the tears suddenly stinging her eyes. He was right. About everything. Her mother had so many fixed ideas about the world. It had driven Anna away and, ultimately, her father. And Anna did try not to hate. She tried very hard. If not for her own sake, then for Kate's. When she turned back, Ben was on his knees next to a sitting Lexi, his arm around the dog, who was watching her curiously as Ben whispered in her ear.

'Tell Anna she isn't that little girl anymore. Tell her she's all grown up now. Tell her she's very clever and the bad men who have done all those bad things ought to watch out because she's coming for them. And they better be scared. Very scared.'

Anna used the flattened tips of three fingers to wipe her eyes. She was smiling as she reached into her pocket and threw Lexi a biscuit. The dog caught it in mid-air, pulverising it with three crunches.

'And what does the doctor want as his reward for being my therapist?' Anna said as Ben brushed dirt from his knees.

'How about a pub lunch somewhere dog-friendly?'

'I think we could stretch to that.'

'Right. You google the pubs, I'll drive.'

CHAPTER TWENTY-SEVEN

MONDAY

By nine thirty on Monday morning, the whole of the MCRTF were on the Ryegrove site. Anna dispatched Khosa and Holder to talk to Keaton and they'd now involved Terry Marshall, Ryegrove's head of security. If Keaton was right, if what he'd found did lead to some sort of access way under the fence – and Anna had no doubt it would – they were going to need to get inside the hospital grounds and Marshall would need to establish a reasonable cordon. She was also sure he wasn't looking forward to that. In the meantime, Anna and Dawes were 'inside digging out', as Dawes so aptly put it when he'd explained to the DCs why they needed to dress up warm while he and the boss would be nice and cosy with lots of NHS cups of tea to keep them perky.

Anna wasn't sure about the tea, but the familiar conference room they'd adopted as a makeshift interview room was certainly warm. Monica Easterby met them at reception and ushered them through after the usual security checks. Someone had put silver flasks of hot water on a tray together with sachets of coffee and teabags and, much to Dawes' delight, a whole plateful of digestive biscuits. Between enthusiastic munches, he sounded Anna out.

'Is it me, ma'am, or do you think this is all a bit of a dog's dinner?'

'In what way?'

'I'm just having a hard time linking a series of Internet-related deaths *à la* this bloody Black Squid, which is what brought us to the bodies in the first place, to this.' Dawes waved a hand towards the walls and windows. 'I mean, I can't see anyone incarcerated here being capable of all that.'

Anna nodded. Dawes' presence on the squad had come out of Rainsford's hope that there might be a line of investigation that would help them understand the Black Squid deaths. That the information they were obtaining might uncover an existing threat to vulnerable kids. Digging about at the perimeter fence of a mental institution seemed a bit of stretch.

'I know what you're saying, Sergeant. But the fact is that Alison Johnson's murder must fit into this picture somehow. We know that Jamie Carson's "suicide" had the Black Squid's ink all over it. Alison's body is in the same place, she disappeared on the same date and now Keaton's found something odd about the fence. She's an inconvenience in this investigation but one that I think we need to pursue because I firmly believe it will throw up some answers to what was going on here. So, we keep at it.'

Dawes nodded, still sceptical but satisfied for now, it seemed, with what Anna had to say. He'd eaten two biscuits and drunk a cup of tea by the time the door opened and Easterby introduced Beth Farlow, dressed in the blue Ryegrove nursing uniform. Anna's initial impression was of a slight, athletic girl with a combination of short dark hair, good skin and large eyes that made you want to look twice and then look back again.

Dawes said, 'Cup of tea?'

Beth declined but Anna watched her relax. Tea meant she was being treated as a colleague here and Dawes knew it too.

'Miss Farlow, are you happy for me to call you Beth?' Anna asked.

'I'd prefer it.'

The smile accompanying this little confirmation was bright and open. Anna couldn't place the accent, except to know it wasn't local.

'OK. So, Beth, I'm not sure how much Mrs Easterby has told you, but we're here to ask you specifically about Colin Norcott.'

Beth nodded. 'That's what she said.' She looked suddenly troubled. 'Is he all right? Has something happened?'

'No. Not as far as we know. And what I'm about to tell you should remain confidential. We're investigating a serious crime which may or may not involve this unit. How long have you been here, Beth?'

'Four years. I qualified in 2013, did a year of non-forensic and then came here.'

Dawes nodded. 'But you were involved in the treatment of Colin Norcott, we understand.'

'Yes. I was part of the team handling his transition.'

'You got to know him well?'

'Yes, I'd say so.'

'Good,' Anna said. 'Did he ever mention the name Alison Johnson to you?'

Beth frowned. 'No. I know the name, of course, from what Mrs Easterby told me.'

Dawes said, 'Then you'll know she was a nurse who worked in this unit sixteen years ago. She went missing on 8 August 2001. We found her body buried near the railway line outside the hospital a week ago.'

Beth's eyes widened in horror. 'Do you think Colin—'

'We're trying to ascertain Alison's movements on the night she disappeared,' Anna said firmly. She needed Beth Farlow to be open. Accusing Norcott of anything at this stage might put the barriers up. She knew how fond some health professionals could get of their patients. Dawes took up the baton, his tone gentle but with just enough urgency to convey the seriousness of what they were about.

'On the day, or rather the evening, Alison went missing, she was working, just like you are now. She had a connection with Norcott.

You knew him well, I understand. Was he prone to agitation? Episodes of instability?'

Beth frowned, pondering the question. 'Not really. But you have to remember he'd been here a long time. He could get anxious. Anyone who's been in a place like this as long as Colin had would feel anxious about things.'

'Such as?'

'Moving back into the community, for example. He had anxiety over that.'

'Nothing else? Was he frightened of anything specific? Birds, the colour blue, that sort of stuff?'

Beth smiled. 'Are you asking me if he was mad, Sergeant? I get asked that a lot by people once they know I work here.'

'The courts thought he was.'

'Diminished responsibility can mean lots of things. He was here under a section 37. The court decided that he was mentally ill and needed the sort of treatment he wouldn't get in prison. That applies to a lot of our patients. Colin had served his time and responded to therapy, and the tribunal thought he was ready to leave. But his anxieties were natural. The process of leaving here is a gradual one once a patient is deemed ready. We don't simply open the doors and send them on their way. None of our patients would cope with that.'

'And you know nothing about what happened between Norc— uh Colin and Alison Johnson the day she went missing?'

'No, I didn't say that. We knew about Alison. Of course, we did.'

'What do you know?'

'I know it was the day Colin stopped talking.'

Dawes had a notebook open on the desk. He stopped writing. 'What?'

'Didn't you know?' Beth looked genuinely puzzled. When neither of the detectives answered, she supplied the explanation. 'It's well documented in his notes. He was never very forthcoming apparently, but that day, the day Alison Johnson went missing, was the last day anyone heard Colin speak for years. Selective mutism is a known symptom in some cases of schizophrenia but that didn't apply to Colin.'

'So why did he do it?'

'We never found out.'

'How did you communicate?'

'He wrote things down. Short sentences, words, nods. It's no different from having someone with a speech impediment. And towards the end he got a lot better. He'd talk to me.'

'Do you know why he stopped talking?'

Beth shrugged. 'It's tied up with anxiety disorders. But you'd better ask the consultants that.'

'Pretend I'm a worried relative. Explain it to me.'

'Colin was very traumatised by what happened. When he was convicted, I mean. He didn't speak much when he first came here and that got worse after Alison Johnson went missing. He was improving when I first met him. But he made real progress in the eighteen months prior to his release.'

'So, he did start to talk?'

'A little. But he would still write things down more. On a pad. Basics, like shopping lists. Things he wanted to know. Answers when he wanted to give them.'

'Did he respond to everyone or you alone?'

Beth shrugged. 'You needed to gain his trust. Become one of his golems.'

'Gollums?' Dawes asked. 'Like in *The Hobbit*?'

'Golem,' Beth said in a way that suggested it was an assumption she'd had to correct many times before. 'It's one of the ways Colin found to communicate. He made origami images of people he trusted. Once he did, you knew he'd let you in. He'd make them out of paper and write your name inside the head.' Beth smiled. 'It would be there when you unfolded it. He knew exactly where to write on a blank piece of paper so that it ended up hidden. Very skilful. As for communication, as I say mostly he'd write on a pad, but for important things, personal things, he'd write the question or the answer inside a golem.'

'And this all started when Alison went missing?' Dawes asked.

'The golems, yes. That's what I was told.'

Golems, thought Anna. *Just like he was trying to do with Carys and Hywel Morgan. Change them into his dead father and his sister by ramming a message into their brains through their ears using a screwdriver.* It surely didn't take a degree in forensic psychiatry to work that out. Beth must have caught the look of distaste creeping over her face.

'And yes, I do know what he did to his victims, but it was decided that his golems were an appropriate coping mechanism. Attempts were made through cognitive behaviour therapy to modify this compulsion, but it failed. He became very good at procuring materials. Toilet paper, tissues, envelopes. So, the team opted for moulding it into something positive.'

Anna nodded. 'And you never felt threatened by him?'

Beth let out a tiny snort modified by a slow and deliberate shake of her head. It struck Anna as odd and exaggerated. As if her question had triggered a reflex response Beth found it necessary to embellish.

Is it so as not to let something show?

Beth said, 'No, never. Colin… I know what he did was horrible but once we moved him from Somerton to Riverside, from medium to low security, he started to respond very quickly. I honestly don't think he poses a risk to anyone and never did. Except for that one psychotic episode.'

'The mushrooms?' Anna asked

'Colin's mother has a lot to answer for.'

'She was never charged.'

'She claimed it was an accident.'

'Did Colin ever mention her?'

'Yes. He made golems of her. Inside he'd write the words, "I forgive you." She was all the family Colin had left.'

'Did she ever visit?'

'Not in the time I knew him.' Her face spoke volumes.

'You didn't like her?' Dawes asked.

'I know you must have read up on Colin's file, so you must know what it was like for him after his father and sister were killed.'

Anna suspected Dawes had also read what she had about the deteriorating relationships between mother and son. But it would do no harm to be reminded of some of the detail. To that end, Dawes obliged.

'Remind us,' he said.

'His mother blamed him for the accident and refused to talk to him afterwards. She refused to have him in the house. Made him sleep in a barn. Communication was through notes. To many people, myself included, it looked like she'd tried to poison him. The mushrooms were just a continuation of that persecution.'

'I also read that Colin was computer savvy.'

'Before he was admitted here Colin was very computer savvy. It was suggested that because of his isolation, the lines between reality and his virtual existence blurred. It was all taken away for many years. But he took to it very easily when it was reintroduced. Patients who are rehabilitated into the community have orientation in information technology. He's bright.'

'You sound almost fond of him,' Anna said.

Something unreadable passed over Beth's face. 'It's not unprofessional to feel sympathy for your patients,' she said.

'Do you keep in touch?'

'It's frowned upon. Someone in the community will now be supervising his care.'

They thanked her for her time. Anna gave her a card. 'If anything occurs to you, anything at all, please give me a ring.'

'I think about Colin, about what happened to him, a lot,' she said as she left.

When she'd gone, Dawes got up and tested the water in the flasks. 'Top-up?' he asked. 'Just about hot enough.'

Anna waited until the tea was brought before pressing Dawes. 'Well?'

'Norcott sounds complicated. But in my book, once a nutter always a nutter, under the right circumstances.'

CHAPTER TWENTY-EIGHT

The tea was tepid and Anna took only three gulps to empty the cup. Dawes was reaching for a biscuit when the door opened and a tall man with swept-back silvering hair poked his head in.

'Am I in the right place?'

'That depends,' Dawes said.

'Are you the police officers?'

'We are.'

The man smiled and remained, for a moment, just a head with a slightly crooked, gap-toothed smile. The body that followed was long in blue chinos and a well-worn jacket, a tieless chambray shirt beneath. 'Martin King. I'm one of the consultants here.'

Dawes stood and shook the offered hand. Anna followed suit.

King's smile seemed a permanent fixture. 'Is that tea I spy?'

'It is,' Dawes said. 'Water's not very hot.'

'Port in a storm and all that, eh?'

Dawes made to get up, but Anna put a hand out to grab his jacket forcefully under the table.

'By all means,' Anna said.

King walked over to the tea tray and Dawes shot Anna a glance. She responded with the slightest shake of her head. King was used to being a dominant figure at Ryegrove. She didn't want to pander to it. Even though they were on his turf, she needed to establish some ground rules. The first was that they were not here for his benefit.

King kept up a cheerful monologue as he made the tea.

'Not the best teabags, I'm afraid. We joke that these are sweepings off the factory floor.' He gave them another grin. 'Nonsense of course, but one takes one's laughs where one gets them in a place like this.' He stirred in some sugar and came back to the desk where he lowered himself into the chair.

'Dr King,' Dawes said, 'we'll get straight to it. Did Mrs Easterby explain why we needed to see you?'

'All I know is it has something to do with Alison Johnson.'

'It does.'

'May I ask why you're interested?'

'New information has come to light.'

'Really?'

'We think we've found her body,' Anna said.

The cup King was returning to the table clattered against the wood, spilling tea in a brown pool. 'Really? Where? I mean… how?'

'We're not at liberty to tell you that, sir,' Dawes said. 'But we're here to try and understand what might have happened to Alison. We know, for instance, that she came to see you on the afternoon of her last shift here.'

All the fun had left King's expression. Now it hardened into dull horror. 'She did.'

'Can you tell us why?'

'It was an informal report on a patient called Colin Norcott. Alison was one of his key therapists and he'd become quite attached to her.'

'Can you tell us what the report was about?'

'Norcott had asked to see her. He'd become agitated and anxious.'

'Did Alison say why?'

'No. She didn't know why. It was often difficult to tell with Norcott.'

Anna watched the little brown puddle of tea inch towards the edge of the table and his trousers beneath. King didn't seem to notice. 'Were they common, these anxiety attacks?'

'Occasional rather than common. Norcott was very disturbed, but we were having some success with medication. It's so often trial and error in these cases.'

Dawes was frowning. 'Hang on, you're saying you have no idea what triggered these anxiety attacks?'

King inclined his head. 'What I am saying is that they were multifactorial. Sometimes it was his food or the sound of a barking dog. He would multiply these small things, dwell on them.'

'We understand he never spoke to anyone for years after Alison disappeared. In fact, only started to speak again shortly before his release.'

'Yes. Norcott chose to close off his world. As I said he was close to Alison, and her going missing represented another abandonment. Given the loss of his father and sister and his mother's estrangement, it was a regrettable, but in his case an understandable, reaction.'

'You're about to get a wet leg, Dr King.' Anna nodded at the tea.

King moved back and used a serviette to mop up the spilled tea.

Dawes said, 'We understand the unit was undergoing renovations at the time. Building work that caused a lot of disruption.'

'It was a testing time,' King said.

'Is it possible Norcott could have got out?'

King stopped mopping up the tea and frowned at Dawes. 'That's a surprisingly difficult question to answer. We now have a total lockdown policy overnight, but prior to that, and certainly at the time of the renovations, patients had communal areas. I won't lie to you, we did have some issues. Corridors were blocked off but not always as securely as we liked and there were a few "blips" as our head of security liked to call them. Patients wandering off into areas they should never have been in. But everyone was always accounted for eventually.'

'When you say patients were unaccounted for, how long are you taking about?'

'Oh, not for more than a couple of hours. Someone might have wandered into the garden when they should have been in art class, that sort of thing...' King stopped. 'You're not suggesting Colin Norcott had anything to do with Alison's disappearance, are you?'

Dawes said, 'Norcott is no longer a patient here. How do you feel about that?'

King, who seemed to have lost his composure at the veiled suggestion Norcott may have been responsible, took a moment to answer. When he eventually did, the words were carefully chosen. 'The review panel makes decisions on release.'

'Perhaps they do. But I'm asking for your opinion.'

'I was not in favour. My own opinion is that Norcott continues to pose a significant risk both to himself and to the public. My peers did not agree with me.'

Anna said, 'What about Alison, did she agree?'

'I really couldn't say. Obviously, she was not here when the decision was made.'

Dawes asked a few more questions. Mainly about Alison Johnson's demeanour on the day she disappeared. King had little to say about that. Anna watched him. He chose his words carefully.

After ten minutes more of exchanges, they thanked King, and Dawes advised him that he might need to answer more questions.

'Any time,' was King's earnest reply before he stood and left.

Anna turned to Dawes. 'Impression?'

'Cold fish. But he was rattled by the news. No doubt about that.'

'Who wouldn't be?'

'His answers were the same as what I read in the report. Careful and... what's the word... circumspect?'

Anna nodded. 'We shouldn't be surprised. He's protecting the unit.'

Places like Ryegrove were always wary of bad press. It was no accident that so many of them existed on sites previously occupied by hospitals and asylums. It was difficult to object to establishing units on sites already utilised for such things. But when it came to building new units, resistance from the local community was always vehement. There'd been a significant attempt over the last few years to educate the general public as to the safety of such places. Unprecedented access had been given to documentary crews, but even so views could become entrenched. Anna recalled King's use of the word 'blip'. One too many of those and the press fallout would be something to behold. She suspected Ryegrove would not want that to happen, even when it had taken place almost twenty years ago.

CHAPTER TWENTY-NINE

Beth Farlow waited inside the main reception area on the inside of the security barriers. She should have gone back to work but she'd seen Dr King go into the interview room and she didn't think speaking to him would do any harm. Her own interview had unnerved her for a reason she could not quite explain. No, that wasn't true. There was a reason for her disquiet, but she didn't feel she could share it with the officers. The man, the sergeant, seemed nice enough, but the inspector, the way her eyes seemed to see right through her. Beth shrugged. How come the police made her feel guilty even though she hadn't done anything wrong? And could she really be guilty by omission if that omission had no real solid basis anyway?

She mulled over all of this in her mind until, at last, King emerged from the room. As one of the senior consultants, he'd lectured to the nurses, both from a clinical standpoint and in terms of patient and staff safety. His was a familiar face. But today that face looked drawn and anxious as he stood outside the seminar room, stooping as he gathered himself. Beth hesitated and was on the point of abandoning her plan when he looked up and saw her watching him. He straightened and waved a greeting. Beth returned it and smiled, and that was enough for King to slide across the space towards her.

'Dr King, sorry to bother you.'

King looked at her face and let his eyes drop to her badge. 'Beth, isn't it? Did I see you come out of the Spanish Inquisition earlier?'

'Yes. They wanted to know about Colin Norcott. Something to do with Alison Johnson.'

'Same here. Though you, of course, would have no knowledge of Alison.'

'No. But it's Colin I wanted to ask you about. I mean, am I OK to discuss his case with them?'

'In what sense? Patient confidentiality?'

'Well, yes, I suppose.'

'If there is anything pertinent, it would be best to cooperate. The police have a job to do.'

'Thank you. I don't think there's anything bad. I mean everything I told them would be common knowledge on the unit. Colin didn't tell me any secrets. If he had, I'd have revealed them at the case conferences.'

'Of course.' King nodded approval.

'It's just that, for some reason, Colin's been in my thoughts lately. It's spooky, in a way.'

'Oh, and what's brought that on?'

'Sometimes I see his paper golems. At least I think I do. I thought I saw one yesterday stuck on a bush. But it wasn't. At least I don't think it was.'

'The mind can play tricks on us, Beth. Perhaps having been warned by Monica Easterby you were going to be questioned about him, subconsciously you've raised his ghost.'

King's words were reassuring. Beth smiled.

'You did a very good job with Norcott,' King added. 'There was a time when we never thought he'd get over his paranoia.'

'Thank you.'

'Don't worry, all this will pass. Poor Alison. And no matter how they try and swing this, I am sure they won't manage to implicate Norcott.'

'Implicate him? But he was a patient here at the time, wasn't he?'

King nodded. 'The police like nothing more than to mould the evidence around a suspect. If the cap fits and all that.'

'Surely not,' Beth said with horror.

King nodded sagely. 'I suspect it will not be the last time you or I will meet the cool and calculating Inspector Gwynne. Don't forget, if you're worried about anything my door is always open.'

Inspector Gwynne emerged from the interview room. Beth caught her sharp eyes focusing in on the two of them in the reception area and, in sheer panic, sent a wave. The nod she got from Gwynne by return was less than effusive. And though King helped by sending his own affable goodbye by raising one hand, it left Beth feeling exposed and somehow caught out.

She turned away and hurried back to her duties, wondering again why being in the presence of the police made her so inexplicably uncomfortable when she had absolutely nothing to hide. It made her wonder, too, what sort of duplicitous personality you had to possess to believe you could get away with anything.

CHAPTER THIRTY

Vespers on Monday afternoon saw the team once again seated in the office with Rainsford standing at the back, arms folded, leg bent at the knee with his foot against the wall behind like some angular bird.

Anna stood. 'I suggest we go around the room. I know we've all had a busy Monday. I think a quick catch-up would be in order. We'll start with Ryia and Justin.'

Khosa began. 'We spent most of the day with Dr Keaton. The exploration of the false drainage pipe revealed a wooden reinforced shaft. Most of the wood is rotten but basically the shaft runs for fourteen feet under the fence where it then becomes vertical. We've had good cooperation from Ryegrove and set up a thirty-square-yard perimeter around the area inside the fence where the shaft emerges. The opening is covered by a metal sheet and then six inches of dirt and leaf mould. No one's used it for years. Keaton thinks a simple covering of leaves would have camouflaged it and made it easy for opening up.'

'A quick escape route from Ryegrove,' Anna said.

'I wonder what they called it – Tom, Dick or Harry?' Dawes said.

Everyone turned to him. He returned their stares with incredulity. '*The Great Escape*? The World War II movie with Steve McQueen bouncing the baseball against the wall in solitary? It's what they named the tunnels the POWs dug.'

The vacant stares he received made him shake his head. 'Bloody hell. I must be getting old. My dad made me watch that sodding film every Easter bank holiday for ten years. It's a classic.'

At the back Rainsford snorted. Anna decided to forgive Dawes the interruption then and there. Anyone who could make Rainsford laugh deserved a medal.

'So, Keaton doesn't think it's new?' Anna said.

'No,' Holder replied. 'The weathering on the stones is the same as all the others in that reinforced bank. He reckons it was put in at the time of construction.'

'It might explain the incursions on to the university site,' Dawes said. 'The question is who was getting out and why?'

'We must assume it involves Krastev,' Anna said. 'He was working on the fence construction. I can't believe that's a coincidence. Sergeant Dawes is right. If Krastev dug that tunnel, who was he helping to get out?'

'Norcott?' Dawes said.

Quickly, Anna filled the others in on how their interviews had gone.

'But did Norcott know Krastev? That's what I'd like to know,' Holder said as she finished.

'Exactly what we need to find out. The more we learn about Ryegrove, the more I see Krastev's claw marks all over Alison Johnson's death. The real question is who else's? We know all about Krastev's link to Shaw and that he was up to his neck in Black Squid deaths as a facilitator. The fact that he was working at Ryegrove brings the Black Squid into the frame with certainty. But he would not have been acting alone. Breaching Ryegrove's security was a big risk. We need to establish a link between Krastev and Norcott one way or the other. Because if it isn't Norcott, then who?'

Her team waited for her to give directions. She knew what she wanted them to do. They were still fishing and there were lots of lines to reel in. She also knew her role was to go after the big killer carp lurking in the depths.

'Our priority for now,' Anna said, 'is to find Norcott and bring him in for questioning. But we can't take anything for granted. Ryia and Trisha, I need you to keep looking at Krastev. Find out why he was working there and what links he had to anyone at Ryegrove, or links to any of our victims. Keep an open mind.'

Khosa and Trisha both nodded.

'Justin, I want you with Phil. Find Norcott. He hasn't actually done anything wrong so we can't go in all guns blazing, but his was a conditional discharge, so it shouldn't be difficult…' Anna tailed off, seeing the sheepish look on Holder's face.

'We're already on it, ma'am. Sarge thought you might want this. I've done a bit of digging but it doesn't look good. Norcott was discharged to Kingmere House, a supported living placement off the Gloucester Road. His conditions of discharge were regular supervision by a psychiatrist and a social worker. He moved out of Kingmere into his own place after nine months with supervision.'

'With what?' asked Khosa. 'I mean, where did he get money?'

'Section 37 patients get their allowance in hospital,' Dawes said. 'After a lot of years, it builds up.'

'But then,' Holder continued, 'he transferred out of the area. He said he was going back to his mother's place in Wales.'

'And?'

'And when I asked about the paperwork, it all went a bit quiet.'

Dawes shook his head. 'Quiet is an understatement. The probation service's national Mental Health Casework Section have Norcott on their list. They're the ones who have an overview of offenders like him. Local key workers report to them. They knew that Norcott moved. They knew where he'd gone but hadn't heard from the local community health team down there in the sticks. They were apologetic but admitted they had eight vacancies in their casework team in London.'

Holder added the final flourish. 'I've rung the local team in Wales, ma'am. They deny ever having been contacted. They didn't know anything about Norcott coming back to their patch.'

'So, no one actually knows where he is?' Khosa said, eyes wide with shock.

Dawes threw up his hands.

Anna sensed what they were all thinking. They'd all read headlines about released patients who'd gone on to reoffend, sometimes with homicidal outcomes, only to hear about hard-pressed services failing to provide appropriate care plans, or treatment, or monitoring.

'What do you suggest?' Anna asked.

'We go down to his mother's place in Wales. Take a look,' Dawes said, his lips tight.

Anna nodded. 'OK. And I need to chase up Shaw. I think he's holding something back. He's promised to let me have what he knows about Krastev's link to his daughter's death.' She didn't add *If I keep him in the loop*, because she knew what Dawes would say.

He said it anyway.

'He's just stringing you along, ma'am, you know that.'

'Maybe. But I'll take what I can get from Shaw. He's proved very useful in the past. Besides, Farlow told us Colin Norcott, before his incarceration, was a computer geek and I hardly need to tell you the Black Squid challenge is still goading kids into suicide. Quite apart from finding out who killed and decapitated Jamie Carson, and who probably killed Alison Johnson too, I would very much like to put a permanent spoke in this Black Squid's wheel. And no one knows more about them than Shaw.'

CHAPTER THIRTY-ONE

It had been sixteen days since Oscar first connected with the Black Squid. But something had happened the day before. Something amazing. During his last lesson – English and *The Mayor of Casterbridge* – the head of year, Mrs Gibbons, interrupted the class and called him out. She told him to bring his things. He heard Vickers sniggering as he left.

Mrs Gibbons made small talk, explaining how the headmaster, Mr Smithson, decided to finally call in his parents for a little 'chat'. They went to the head's office. His mother and father were there, sitting, small like him and very flushed, both of them. His mother turned to him when he walked in. She looked on the verge of tears. His father didn't say anything, but his head dropped as Mr Smithson made Oscar come in and sit. He listened as Smithson explained the reason for the meeting. About how they felt that the situation had escalated to such an extent they'd felt obliged to intervene. He'd explained everything to Oscar's parents and everyone agreed the best course of action was for Oscar to move to a different school. Marston Comprehensive were happy to take him if he felt willing to go. It would be a big change and a chance for a fresh start. A new uniform, too. Smithson tried to make it sound exciting, but Oscar could tell this was meant for his parents. For them to understand.

Oscar did not object. Though the thought of a new school terrified him, things could not be worse than they were now.

In the car on the way home, his mother asked in a hoarse whisper, 'Oh, Oscar, why didn't you tell us?'

'I did, I told you about the blazer.'

Mr Louden kept driving. Kept his eyes front. Oscar thought he might be trembling.

'You don't have to wear the blazer anymore. Does he, Simon?'

Mr Louden didn't answer.

'The new school doesn't have blazers in the uniform. So, he won't have to wear it, will he.' She spoke with restrained patience. But it was a statement this time, not a question.

Mr Louden finally responded. And when he did, it was with an undercurrent of barely restrained fury. 'What is the matter with that school? Did you see those children? The girls with skirts up to their backsides. Boys with their shirts hanging out. We'd have been hauled up—'

'Shut up about you and your old school,' Mrs Louden snapped. 'This is about Oscar and Oscar's school.'

'I used to wear a blazer with pride,' Mr Louden said. 'We should have chosen the church school. This wouldn't have happened—'

'For goodness' sake, will you please give it a rest!'

They argued. Oscar tuned them out. It didn't matter. No more Vickers at school. Oh, there'd be the usual stuff on Facebook and texts, but that didn't matter as much. He could unfriend them. In the car, he pulled down his sleeves in an unconscious movement to hide the scars on his forearms.

He felt relaxed. More than he had in months. That night, he turned his phone off and had the best night's sleep he'd had in a long time.

CHAPTER THIRTY-TWO

TUESDAY

After no more than five miles on the A48 at the end of the M4, Holder's satnav took him and Dawes away from major roads, north and then east into the West Wales countryside, through a landscape of rolling hills and planted pine forest dotted with small farms and villages either huddled in the gullies or perched on the sloping hillsides.

'Just as well we have a nice lady to tell us where to turn,' Dawes said, pointing to a sign that read Abergorlech. 'I mean, how do you even start to say that? Might as well just clear your throat and spit.'

Holder threw him a look.

'What?' Dawes said.

'I wouldn't say that in from of Inspector Gwynne. You now she's a native.'

Dawes tutted. 'You millennials. So touchy. Besides, my grandmother was Welsh I'll have you know.'

They'd been in the car for two hours and Dawes' unending supply of stories and jokes had kept Holder entertained, apart from a half-hour gap when the sergeant did an impression of a nodding dog as he slumbered in the passenger seat.

Now, with just a mile or so to go to Norcott's mother's smallholding, Dawes was very much awake, taking in the scenery as Holder negotiated the narrow lanes with their denuded winter hedgerows on either side. The roads were damp and dotted with puddles from overnight rain, which, judging from the lowering skies, looked likely to return at any moment. They drove past fields, some empty and overgrown with rushes and grass, others containing forlorn-looking sheep. They passed a turning marked by a large milk churn on a raised stone table and the words 'Nant Isaf' painted in white upon the pewter grey metal.

'No idea what it means,' Dawes said, 'but if I remember rightly, that's the Morgan farm.'

'The one where Norcott killed the father and daughter?'

'The very same. The boss told me what it meant but I'm buggered if I can remember.'

'Something to do with a stream or river,' Holder said, remembering DI Gwynne's words.

'Show-off. Right, come on, let's get this over with.'

There was no gate guarding the entrance to Honeygrove Farm, just a handwritten curlicue sign stuck on a broken gate. Holder wondered how enamoured the locals had been by the Norcotts changing the name of the property from the original Welsh to something as kitsch as this. Holder swung the car in and they bounced sixty yards along the rutted track to a stoned yard and a low cottage. The walls and roof looked badly in need of maintenance. A blue Range Rover stood parked to the side. Out of it stepped a portly man in a corduroy jacket and plaid tie above some raspberry trousers. What little hair was left on his head was far too long and combed over in a poor attempt at shielding the shiny pate beneath. He stood expectantly with a business-like toothless grin.

Dawes was first out of the car, and the balding man approached him with hand outstretched. 'Huw Selby of Selby and Richardson.'

Dawes shook with his right hand. He already had his warrant card open in the other. Selby peered at it and grinned. 'You found the place, then?'

'We did.'

'Good, good. I've opened the front and back doors.' He jangled some keys. 'The outbuildings have no locks. If you could pull the doors closed after you leave, I'll be along later to lock up properly when you've finished. Probably about four, before it gets dark.'

Holder exited the car and stretched skywards to ease out the kinks.

'So, you've had no interested buyers?' Dawes said to Selby.

'Place has been empty for two years. We've received no instruction to sell. Property like this needs a bit of work and imagination.'

'Colin Norcott's the owner?'

'He is. Mrs Norcott died intestate. He is next of kin. I can put you in touch with his solicitor if you want.'

'And he has never been to visit?'

'Colin Norcott has never contacted us for keys.' He handed over a card. 'I'll be on my mobile if you need me. We have an auction at two. If you'll excuse me.'

Dawes nodded. Selby climbed into his car and drove off, leaving the two policemen staring at the ramshackle buildings where Norcott grew up. The weather had not improved on their journey west and the low cloud and damp air lent a deep chill to the surroundings.

'Get the torch from the boot, Justin. I doubt there'll be electricity here.'

Holder rejoined Dawes at the front door. 'This is where, in the films, the senior of two policemen about to enter the old abandoned house searching for signs of a known murderer turns to his junior colleague and says, "You take the outbuildings and I'll do the inside."'

'OK,' said Holder a little too quickly.

'Those are films, Justin. I am not going anywhere alone. We stick together on this one, like chewing gum on a shoe.'

'What am I, Sarge, the chewing gum or the shoe?'

'Juicy fruit or spearmint, take your pick.'

Dawes stepped towards the front door, knocked and called out, 'Colin, it's the police. We need a quick word. It's just the two of us come all the way from Bristol, OK?'

No answer. Dawes swung the door open and the damp mustiness of abandonment hit them both immediately. For some reason, it seemed colder inside the building than it was outside. Dried leaves littered the hallway, brought in or blown in during one of Selby's visits, no doubt. Off the hall stood a step and two doors before the corridor ended in a better-lit space, which Holder assumed was the kitchen.

They swept the downstairs first, wearing latex gloves and covers for their feet. Mrs Norcott had been a hoarder. The nearest door off the hallway led to a poky little room piled with stacks of magazines and boxes. In the corner, three large bin bags full of empty bottles clinked when Holder kicked one gently with his foot. The label on the bottle of the topmost read 'Value Blend' with a yellow £1.50 price label stuck on it. Holder picked up a copy of *Take a Break* from 2009. Colin's mother liked to imagine hobnobbing with the stars as she sipped on her cheap red of an evening, obviously. On the wall, in the top corner, a large, dark and ugly stain was spreading over the wallpaper. Some sort of back mould, creeping in to stake a claim over the unwanted building. Holder found himself wondering if whoever did buy it, assuming Colin Norcott ever sold, would bulldoze the place and start again. That's what he would do, he decided.

The middle room had an ancient TV, an electric fire and a reasonably clear table. Mrs Norcott's shape was imprinted in the seat and back of an old armchair with flowery covers mottled with stains. Best not to know or ask what the stains were, Holder concluded. Dawes left him to it and went into the kitchen. Holder didn't stay in the middle room alone. There was something about the place, something unpleasant that had nothing to do with the lingering smell of decrepitude. Water was still running through the kitchen taps when Holder tried them. Piles of unopened correspondence lay on the small table. Through the grimy windows, an unkempt backyard showed three low sheds.

'Come on, let's do upstairs,' Dawes ordered.

Mrs Norcott had been found when someone noticed she'd not been to collect her *Take a Break* from the community shop for a week. A neighbour called, saw the flies coating the inside of the bedroom window and called the police. They took Mrs Norcott's decaying body away, but Holder knew, from his time in uniform, the smell took a lot longer to go. There was nothing left of it now, but Holder still thought he could catch a whiff of a sickly sweetness as he mounted the stairs. As if some of Mrs Norcott's decay had seeped into the very walls.

The first floor was as deserted as the ground floor had been.

They came back downstairs to the back door which, swollen from rain, scraped on the stone floor when Dawes tried to open it. The noise spooked a couple of crows in a nearby tree and they took flight in raucous protest.

A concrete path led through the overgrown garden to the outbuildings beyond. The two on the left were low wooden huts with sloping roofs and a facing wall of chicken wire. Inside one was a smaller building, the coop itself where the chickens nested. Holder pulled on the door to the first and it came off at the hinges. The inner space was empty, the wooden shelves which had once provided support for chickens now broken and sagging. The second building had suffered the same fate from the same incessant weather. That left only the bigger, more substantial barn with half-timbered stone walls.

Dawes stood for a moment, his hand on the bar holding the hinged doors closed and called out again. 'Colin. It's the police.'

Only the drip of water from the eaves answered Dawes' question.

He lifted up the bar and pulled the door open. It swung with surprising ease, making Holder wonder if the hinges had been oiled in the recent past. Inside was gloomy, with only one window high up. As their eyes adjusted to the poor light, helped by Dawes opening the second of the big doors, Holder saw that whatever animals had once occupied this space had long gone to make room for just the one animal. An obviously human one. One side of the room had once been stalls or byres and these showed clear evidence of occupation. In one was a Primus stove with stacked tins of food; in another a camp bed, torches and an oil lamp. Holder saw a newspaper half hidden under the camp bed. He stooped and slid it out.

'Sarge,' Holder said. 'Look at this?'

Dawes leaned over and read the date. 'Tenth of October 2017. The bugger's been living here, obviously.'

'Well, he was four months ago anyway.'

On the little table next to the bed lay a stack of unopened cardboard packets. Holder read the labels and waved them at Dawes. He read out, 'Paroxetine and fluoxetine.'

'Looks like he's stopped taking his tablets and flown the coop,' muttered Dawes as he started picking up the books to look at their titles. Holder moved on to the next stall. It was the DC's sudden cessation of movement that drew Dawes' attention. He spun and saw Holder standing and staring.

'Justin?' Dawes said.

'You'd better come and look at this, Sarge.'

Dawes joined Holder. The adjacent stall was not empty but what it contained was too difficult to comprehend for a moment and both men could only stare. Someone had whitewashed the far wall to make a canvas and used it to paint a crude image. Three black figures with no faces stood against a cross-hatch of black lines. Either side of them was greenery. The only other colour in the image was a red smudge on a double black line between two of the figures. But it wasn't only the image that kept Holder staring. Beneath the sketch, hundreds if not thousands of bits of paper had been stacked, one on top of the other, to form an untidy, leaning pile, wider at the bottom, tapering off as it rose towards the sketch.

'What the bloody hell is this, Justin?' Dawes asked. 'Art class? And what are all these scrunched-up bits of paper?'

'They aren't scrunched up,' Holder said. He picked one off the pile and held it up for Dawes to see the shape. It was intricate and carefully constructed, with pointed limbs and a flattened face. 'They're golems,' Holder said.

Dawes stared at him, but Holder hadn't finished. 'And I know what that is, too.' He nodded towards the sketch. 'It's the fence at Ryegrove.'

'Right,' said Dawes, 'take some snaps and then get on the phone, Justin. I know someone who'll want to see this.'

CHAPTER THIRTY-THREE

Anna toyed with not going to see Shaw at all. His promise of giving her some more 'special information' about Krastev and his link to Abbie's death smacked of more Shaw-style manipulation. Dawes was right about that. She could have made her excuses, insisted that he send her what he knew by letter. But now that they'd found the tunnel under the fence, she'd decided, reluctantly, to quiz him again. See if he'd been hiding anything else from them.

Anna went alone. She didn't have to, but it would be a lot less hassle and would spare the other members of the team the simmering indignation she'd seen in everyone who accompanied her. Holder and Dawes both seemed to simply provoke Shaw. Khosa, on the other hand, could not stand being near him. For her it was like a fear of snakes.

Shaw's smug, goading persona did that to everyone. Of course, Anna remained naturally wary. But she realised, as Shaw was led into the poky, soulless interview room at Whitmarsh prison to meet her yet again, that she was not scared of him. He'd attacked people across the desk separating them, this very table, yet, as unpredictable as he was, she was certain he had no desire to harm her. What Anna saw was a man driven by deep anger and a need for vengeance.

'Must be starting to feel like a home from home for you, this room, Anna?' Shaw said in his slow, Mancunian drawl as he settled himself on the plastic chair.

Anna didn't grace this with a reply. Shaw's bravado felt slightly desperate for once and she quickly analysed that impression. He was paler, thinner even than when she'd last seen him. He'd lost fat from his face, and his eyes, behind the thick lenses of his glasses, looked puffy and red, though they'd lost none of their calculated cunning. Shaw held some folded sheets of paper in his hands. He placed them on the desk and covered them with his hands.

'Is that it?'

Shaw nodded.

'Why didn't you give the original investigators this information?'

'Because they didn't want to know. Besides, they weren't you, Anna.' He gave her one of his slow blinks.

'I'm looking forward to reading it.'

'The governor gave me some shitty paper to write on but denied my request for access to a computer. For checking dates.' Shaw's smile told her that he had not expected anything less. 'Didn't matter.' He tapped his temple. 'It's all up here anyway.' He made no effort to hand the sheets over. 'How about I give you the gist once you've told me what you and the team have found, eh?'

Shaw possessed no bargaining power here, not really. They both knew she could have the prison guards take the papers from him at any time. But they'd struck a deal and the sensible thing to do was not antagonise him. Anna had a feeling, too, that Shaw might retain certain vital bits of his story for just these sorts of situations. And then there was the tunnel.

'OK,' Anna said. 'We've confirmed Krastev worked as part of the construction crew contracted to build the upgrade to the secure unit at Ryegrove Hospital in Bristol. It's the fence you can see from the spot you took us to on the railway line. The second body was a nurse who worked at Ryegrove. So far we've found no link between her and Krastev.'

Shaw frowned. 'Krastev got his kicks from watching kids kill themselves and helping them take the final reluctant step. "I am only facilitator." That's what he said to me. As if it justified the bastard's actions. But someone told him what to do.' Shaw's lids dropped as if he was remembering something unpleasant. 'Just like they told the Black Squid administrators what to do.'

'The administrators?'

'The bastards who manipulated the kids. The scum I killed. They weren't all meant to die. I made mistakes, got too angry. But they weren't the real monster behind the Black Squid, we both know that.'

Anna sat up. The reports she'd read of Shaw's victims indicated he'd tracked them down. They were all different but shared one common feature of having dabbled in chat rooms, grooming victims for the Black Squid game. It was assumed they were part of a network. 'Are you saying the administrators were being made to do what they did, too?'

Shaw nodded. 'They were only halfway up the food chain. The Black Squid is the real apex predator here.'

'I don't follow.'

'Krastev was a sick bastard. He did what he did because he liked to. But the others I got to were just sad shits the Black Squid got its tentacles around and squeezed. It's how the Squid works. It finds you online, somewhere you really shouldn't be, and sucks you in. Maybe it makes you admit your weaknesses, then it starts to manipulate you. Being online should carry a government health warning, you know that?'

Anna nodded, letting him have some space. Eventually he continued.

'Once the Squid has one of these sad bastards on the hook, they become an administrator in the game. The Squid makes them do the dirty work. Sets them targets. A kill score. And it's easy for these creeps because it isn't real. It's play-acting. Their stage is suicide chat sites. They pretend to be someone who's been through it all, or a caring doctor, or another teenager in pain. Before you know it they've suckered in another vulnerable victim like Abbie. And once that victim trusts the administrator, they make them feel like there is no way out of the "game" but to end life itself. And all the while the real killer is once-removed, watching, manipulating with his fucking tentacles.'

'Then we're talking coercion, blackmailing people to be groomers. But why?'

Shaw gave her a slow blink. 'I know people think I'm an evil bastard, but *this* bastard has no conscience. It's killing by remote control. For the exhilaration. The sheer evil thrill of it.'

'So even after what you did to the administrators, you were no closer to the Black Squid himself?'

'Oh, I was. The administrators knew nothing, but Krastev did and he gave up the last site at Bristol very reluctantly. That's why I know it's important. He was desperate not to tell me about it. It's where the answer lies, Anna.'

Shaw unfolded the papers under his fingers. 'Three addresses for more buried treasure. One in Leicester, one in Devon and one in Cheshire, in the Wirral. Krastev liked to move about.'

Anna took the sheets and glanced at the handwritten locations. 'Is that it?'

Shaw stared at her, amused by her reaction. 'No need to be sniffy. I was going to make you go on three trips with me. Of course, if you prefer that?' He grinned and then let it fade away. 'Fact is, I might not be here to go with you.'

There it was again. The uncharacteristic gloom.

But he wasn't finished. 'When they looked at Abbie's case, they were clueless. In those days, digital forensics were like cave paintings to most coppers. And chat rooms had better anonymity than Swiss bank accounts. It's worse today with all the bloody social media companies bleating about freedom of speech and data protection.'

'So I've been told,' Anna said, remembering Varga's concise assessment.

'But when Abbie was killed the Black Squid had rules for the administrators. Verification is what it was all about. In the days before Snapchat and social footprints, that was Krastev's "job".'

Shaw made quotation marks in the air with his fingers. 'These days there'd be no need for him. He'd be a waste of space. Today you can get proof of action in an instant. Like that poor kid who took a selfie of herself before she jumped off that cliff. The Squid wants that. He gets a kick from knowing the victim has a mother and a father and brother or a sister. If one of them saw that image they'd have to live with it the rest of their lives. I have to live with what Krastev told me about Abbie. It's the last thing I think of when I go to sleep and the first thing when I wake up.' Shaw's focus drifted off towards some inner memory. When he looked up, his expression was solemn, his eyes black coals in his pale, anaemic face.

'You've got a chance to stop this, Anna. You can get rid of this stinking piece of shit before someone else treads in it. He's frightened of the one thing he has no control over. That one little mistake he's made that he thinks no one is looking for. Something he and Krastev couldn't hide behind their computer screens. They think they're invisible. But they aren't. I'd say you need to ask yourself three key questions. Why those railway tracks? Why has there been a gap in the Black Squid killings? And what was Krastev doing at Ryegrove?'

'We've found a tunnel under the fence. My guess is that Krastev was responsible for that. That's why I came here, Hector. To see if you knew—'

Shaw shook his head. 'I'm not doing well, Anna. I can see it in your eyes, too. No one's said it yet but perhaps it's the big "C" eating away at my marrow. I'm relying on you to finish the job that I started. I fucked up. Make sure you don't. And do I feel sorry for what I did? No. Rabid dogs need to be put down before they infect another. When you get to the Black Squid, remember that.'

Anna did remember that. Remembered it more than anything he'd said as she drove back to Bristol.

The rabies virus caused hydrophobia in its victims. Despite horrible thirst, any attempt at drinking, or even the suggestion of drinking, caused excruciating spasms in the throat and larynx. A slow strangulation. Enough to drive most infected mammals *mad.*

That word haunted Anna. Was it what Shaw was implying here? That the Black Squid was mad? Or simply bad?

She'd met several criminals whose humanity had long since packed a suitcase and gone on extended leave. These were the people who could no more empathise with their victims as recite the words to 'Supercalifragilisticexpialidocious' in Latin. She'd come face to face with the 'bad' on more than one occasion. People who genuinely wore a cloak of evil.

But then the general public, and often her colleagues in the force, needed to believe that criminals, especially those involved in heinous crimes, were in some way unhinged, in order to explain away how anyone could behave in that way. In Anna's experience though, true madness was rare, and most serious and violent crimes had their roots in pettiness and heightened emotions and the red mist of sudden loss of temper.

But there were exceptions.

And she had no doubt in her mind that some criminals she'd dealt with were not normal. Were indeed perhaps a little *mad.*

The word brought her up short once again as her thoughts ricocheted in a new direction.

Was that what the thinking had been with Aunty Mary? Anna knew this little bit of mental gymnastics paid no heed to logic, but she could not help herself from wondering if these were the terms of reference those around her had applied to poor Mary. The same thinking that her mother had perhaps applied to her unconventional daughter. Was that what was behind the disinhibited words her mother threw out like emotional grenades these days? This insight, pushing through the thin wrapping of denial Anna'd used to paper over their relationship, suddenly stuck its reptilian snout into the air and flicked a forked tongue. It made Anna think. It made her pause to wonder if, had she been born a generation before, her childhood social awkwardness, her need to be alone in her own head, her lack of warmth towards others might have led to a label and a misconstrued diagnosis with ECT as the only ultimate treatment.

She knew how irrational all this was and yet her memories of the frightened, broken, mumbling woman Aunt Mary became, alone and abandoned in Talgarth asylum, played out like a Dickensian scene in her head. Mary's drug-addled brain rendered her unable to articulate her fears and thoughts. Had Anna, even as a frightened child, seen herself reflected in those terrified eyes?

Her work phone's tone dragged her back to the moment. Dawes' voice was a most welcome intrusion.

'Ma'am, we're at the Norcott place in Wales. House is empty. My guess is he's off his meds.'

'Based on what?'

'Based on the twenty unopened boxes of happy pills in the barn. He's been here, all right, but preferred the barn to the house.'

Anna remembered Beth Farlow's words. *'His mother blamed him for the accident and refused to talk to him afterwards. She refused to have him in the house. Made him sleep in a barn.'*

'There's a newspaper here from four months ago,' Dawes said. 'I reckon he's been in the wind since then. And there's some other stuff here, ma'am.'

'Like what?'

'I'm sending you a photo. We've only just got a signal and that's after driving five miles back towards the main road. Should be coming through now.'

'OK. It's not through yet. I'll ring you after I've seen it.'

CHAPTER THIRTY-FOUR

Anna pulled into a service station and waited impatiently for the image to load, glad of something solid to concentrate on and drag her mind out from the dark alleys she'd been wandering down. She peered at the image as it appeared, hearing her heart beat a little louder in her own ears. Though the lighting in the barn wasn't brilliant, there was enough for her to see what had animated Dawes and Holder, and the extent of Norcott's obsession. She rang Dawes back immediately.

'I don't think there's any doubt that this is the perimeter fence at Ryegrove. Is it worth us getting Forensics down to Wales?'

'Don't see any point, ma'am. We know it's him. If you really want to test the matted hair on the sleeping bag to prove it, go for it.'

'No, you're right. And he hasn't done anything wrong.'

'Yet,' said Dawes.

'Have you got some samples of these golems?'

'A plastic bag full. Thought we'd drop in with the neighbours on the way back. Stop in the local post office, or a shop if there is one. Ask around. See if anyone's seen him.'

'Good idea.'

'I think the answer'll be no, but no harm in trying since we're here. Shame the bloody sheep can't talk. There's enough of 'em.'

'OK. It's well after three now. Don't bother coming back here. We'll have a briefing at eight thirty tomorrow morning.'

She sent copies to Trisha and asked her to get some eight by tens printed off as she drove back to HQ on autopilot, her mind elsewhere – peering through the fence in Ryegrove, wondering what it was everyone had seen.

As soon as she got to the office she logged on to her PC, opened a search engine and typed 'golem'. She got 7.5 million results but opted for a Talmudic legend site to begin her reading.

> The word golem derives from a mention in Psalms 139 15-16. The Hebrew word has been translated as meaning 'unformed substance'. A soulless body. Some religious sources believe it is possible to create such a creature using rabbinic instructions on a clay model in the shape of a man. The details have appeared in several texts and do vary.
>
> The first involves walking around the body and mouthing incantations.
>
> The second involves writing the letters aleph, mem and tav on its forehead.
>
> The third is to write the name of God or another soul on a parchment and place it inside the being's mouth, or arm, or head.

There was more. A great deal more. Golems appeared in legend and literature over the centuries. The most famous was the Golem of Prague, fashioned from clay and brought to life by a sixteenth-century rabbi to protect his people from anti-Semitic persecution. Yet it was the basic concept that interested Anna. It did go some way to explain how, in his delusional state, Norcott had killed the Morgans and then tried to reanimate them in the form of his own dead father and sister. Explained but in no way excused. Norcott was clearly a troubled individual. But was he capable of the kind of sickening manipulations the Black Squid was using? Or even capable of murdering his nurse therapist, Alison Johnson?

With her computer still open, she began to type up a report on her visit to Shaw. It brought her mind back to trying to answer his questions.

Why those railway tracks? With the discovery of the tunnel under the fence and the fact that it had a view of the railway tracks, the answer to Shaw's question wasn't difficult. From those railway tracks, the fence was visible and, more importantly, vice versa. She went out to the office and looked at the images Trisha had now posted of Norcott's sketch. Three dark figures standing against a fence, their faces blanked out. Why no faces? The answer came to her easily. Because they were facing away from whoever had seen this scene. Facing outwards, towards the two black lines in the sketch representing the railway tracks. She let the natural flow of ideas come, questions searching for answers. Why would anyone want to stand at the fence and look at the railway unless... unless something was happening there. Jamie Carson and Alison Johnson were buried there. There was a strong possibility that they had also died there. Was what Norcott had drawn an interpretation of that? Were these three figures observers? If so, what exactly were they looking at? She peered more closely. One figure was larger, taller than the other two, who looked to be of about the same height. It was nonsense, she realised, to ascribe too much detail to a scrawled sketch on a barn wall and yet the difference was notable. An adult and two children? Anna stood for a while longer and then went back to her office and turned again to her report.

The second of Shaw's posed questions was much more difficult to answer.

Why had there been such a gap in between the Black Squid killings? She considered this. Perhaps there had been no gap. Perhaps there'd been sporadic deaths that no one had found the link to. All reported as suicides... but then the Squid insisted on a trademark. The tentacled beast drawn somewhere on the person. And the drawings and references to the Squid found in each victim's belongings were obvious links in retrospect. Surely such a finding would have come to light. The second answer, therefore, was that there had been a hiatus. One which had now come to an end. But if so, why?

The third question was the most difficult of all. What was Krastev hiding? On the surface, not much since Shaw had been able to get the location of Jamie's body from him. Anna winced at the thought of exactly how this information had been obtained but consoled herself by remembering that Krastev was a killer and did not merit much in the way of sympathy. Was it Alison Johnson he'd been reluctant to give up? Or was there something else, as Shaw seemed so certain of? She sighed. Though Krastev was becoming a major person of interest, they knew so very little about him.

She sat pondering these questions and getting nowhere. It was four thirty when Khosa stuck her head in the door, holding a steaming mug of tea.

'Thanks, Ryia.'

Khosa put the mug down on the desk. 'How was it, ma'am? With Shaw, I mean.'

Anna handed over Shaw's file containing the few thin sheets of paper he'd written addresses on together with her report and the questions he'd posed. She waited while Khosa scanned them.

Why those railway tracks?

Why has there been a gap in the Black Squid killings?

And what was Krastev doing at Ryegrove?

'Those are three very good questions.'

'Aren't they just.'

'We've not got very far searching Krastev in the databases. A couple of force areas, erm, West Mids and the Met, wanted to speak to him about some complaints made. Sexual harassment claims. He'd come on to some girls in pubs and turned nasty. The only other thing of note was a traffic stop. He was picked up by our lot on a routine check while he was working in Ryegrove. The vehicle he was driving was not his, but he claimed to have permission. He had insurance and a licence and nothing came of it, so I presume he did have that permission.'

Anna nodded. 'Do we know where he lived?'

'Registered to a house in Bedminster. The landlord let out five rooms. We're tracing the other names.'

'Thanks, Ryia.'

Khosa handed back the file. 'We'll keep looking, obviously.'

'We'll be having an early briefing tomorrow morning. Be nice if we can have it by then.'

'Yes, ma'am. Anything else?'

Although she thought it, she didn't add one of her dad's old sayings that popped unbidden into her head: occasionally, when the water is so muddy you can't see the bottom, the best thing you can do is walk away and let things settle.

CHAPTER THIRTY-FIVE

Beth Farlow sat on the train on her way back to Severn Beach, her mind still full of work. Her shift at Ryegrove had been a difficult one. One of her patients, a schizotypal called Preece, had spiralled out of control. They were trying to change his meds and it hadn't worked.

Transitional phases, the doctors called them. Beth had gone to help when the alarm went off until the allocated 'Control and Restraint' nurses got there. The patient had stripped naked, his hands covered in his own faeces, the 'paint' he'd used to daub disgusting words on the walls.

They had restrained him, but she still had the smell in her nose. Had done all afternoon. All her clothes would need to go into the washing machine when she got home. She was very good at getting smells out of her clothes. Went through bottles of Febreze like it was going out of fashion.

It was dark outside the train windows. Another miserable, wet winter's evening. Around her, fellow commuters read papers or stared at their phones, eye contact banned for the duration of the journey. Her own phone buzzed to signal a message. There were a couple of birthdays looming. She'd half agreed to go to a party on Saturday. One of the other nurses was getting engaged and Beth was hoping to stay with a friend in town. Negotiations were ongoing.

She glanced at the screen. It wasn't a number she recognised. She opened the Text.

Careful of the police. They're maggots. They'll trick you and think nothing of ruining your career. I've seen it happen. When it does you'll have to face them and the authorities alone. Your colleagues will run for the hills. Plead ignorance. Take comfort in knowing there's someone watching over you.

Beth looked at the number again and then, reflexively, looked up at the faces around her. No one was looking. Everyone was still buried in their digital lives or the printed news. She read the message again, trying to interpret it. Obviously, it was about Norcott. On the surface it seemed a friendly enough piece of advice. No more than reinforcing the angst she'd felt herself after the interview with the DI, Gwynne. But that last sentence in the message:

... there's someone watching over you.

It bothered her for some reason that she couldn't quite explain. She looked up again, seeing no one watching, but feeling something cold slither over her skin.

Maybe she'd take a taxi back to the cottage this evening.

CHAPTER THIRTY-SIX

Anna picked up Lexi from Maggie's and, having walked her, ate something and then spent a couple of hours in front of the TV, letting the mindless images bathe her brain. She did this deliberately, Lexi at her side, one hand in the dog's fur, stroking and kneading it. She knew doing this released all sorts of goodies in both of their brains. Neuropeptides like oxytocin and serotonin to reinforce the bonds. It was soothing and relaxing.

Shaw's questions plagued her, but she didn't want her mind to contemplate them directly. Instead she flopped and petted the dog and watched people cooking and pretending that knowing how to make a culinary foam was the most important skill in the world. All the while hoping that this distraction might open the door and let in an idea or thought that might give the case the kick-start it so badly needed.

Krastev, she felt, was the key, even though his exact link to Ryegrove was yet to be established. Once it was, they'd have something, she felt sure of it. A connection that would tie the Black Squid to Ryegrove and then, possibly, to Alison Johnson. It was important she did that, and quickly. Dawes' frustration at not having any new intel to report back to Rainsford and Cresci was something she sensed, rather than him voicing it directly. And Shaw's reminder that the Squid remained active and hidden, with the potential for God alone knew how many more kids to fall prey, made their lack of progress all the more frustrating.

She drank her customary glass of wine and spoke to Ben for half an hour, wishing he was there with her because touching him was almost as good for her as touching Lexi. She told him that and he laughed. His laugh always made her feel better.

She went to bed with the water still too muddy to see anything but knowing something was moving about in there, something important. Something that she'd read or heard that day or the day before but which she couldn't quite interpret. She sensed it, could almost reach it, like a line from a song, or a haunting riff; frustratingly familiar but needing the next line to give it context and harden it into memory. She lay in bed searching for the link and not finding it, letting it fade into nothing as she fell asleep.

CHAPTER THIRTY-SEVEN

Oscar's mother wanted to take him into town to get some new clothes for his new school in the morning. Marston pupils wore a green jumper with a logo. Mr Louden was obviously disgusted but didn't say anything.

Oscar checked his phone just before he turned off the light. Saw the little red number next to his WhatsApp logo. Opened it up.

The Black Squid had messaged him.

> *Day 16. You are nearing the end of your journey. You may have doubts, but they are just whispers in the dark. Don't forget how much I've been helping you. There is only one way out for you. We both know your problems won't go away unless you finish the challenge. Your life will never get better unless you end this. Your tormentors will never go away. Think of that release, Oscar. Believe in me.*

Oscar continued scrolling.

> *We must keep going. Do not ignore me. If you don't reply, we'll tell everyone your secrets, your weaknesses. Being different is a curse, Oscar. No one will understand.*

He remembered the screens that had flashed up when he'd joined the Black Squid. Access to his contacts. Access to his camera. He'd agreed to all of it because not doing so meant he could not get in. He realised now how stupid he'd been. He tried to think what people would say if they didn't just think he was different, but knew how miserable he'd felt. The wounds from their taunting were still fresh. How much worse might that taunting be when they knew how much he despised them and how much more he despised not being one of them.

Oscar threw the phone down on the bed and then threw himself after it, burying his face in the pillow, feeling his cheeks burn with humiliation.

He felt the phone buzz next to his thigh. He picked it up. Another message.

Wait until midnight. Leave the house and follow the instructions you will be sent. Be ready. Do not let the world see you falter.

CHAPTER THIRTY-EIGHT

Beth had a bath and hurried to dress in warm pyjamas and a thick dressing gown. The cottage was usually cosy and warm, but tonight, as she crossed the landing to her bedroom, she felt an unaccustomed chill. It was an old building and prone to draughts, and Beth had to admit to being a cold person. Her mother, of course, put the blame firmly on the fact that her daughter was way too thin, though Beth preferred to use the word slim. Yet this chilliness was much worse than normal. Was there snow on the way? she wondered. She found some woolly socks and put them on just to be safe.

She was in the middle of drying her hair when she felt a waft of air caress her cheek. Draughts were one thing, but she'd never felt an actual breeze in the cottage.

The waft came again. This time strong enough to move a tissue on her dressing table. Beth frowned.

She'd left the bedroom window on the latch, open just a smidgen for the fresh air. Yet what she'd just felt suggested something more than an open window. Maybe she'd left the bathroom window open, too, and it was drawing a through flow of air. She crossed the landing and looked in, but all was secure, the bathroom mirrors still steamy. She stood in the doorway, hearing the wind buffeting the walls and making the old place shudder. It sounded almost like something trying to force its way in.

Could it be that she'd left a window open downstairs? Had Dee? Her housemate had left for her boyfriend's as Beth was running her bath. Maybe she hadn't shut a latch properly and the wind had done the rest.

Beth hurried downstairs. The draught was much stronger at ground level. She glanced at the front door.

Locked.

She turned in the passage, entered the small kitchen and started.

The back door was open; the plastic beaded string that slid the blind shut on the single upper door pane dancing wildly in the gusting wind.

'Jesus,' she said under her breath. Dee must have left it unlocked. Or not even closed it properly. She'd done it before but not in a wind like this. Beth didn't bother with the light. She simply walked the four steps across to the door and shut it.

It was when she turned around that she realised there was something in the room. Something roughly the size and shape of a man but much wider and thicker, standing in the shadows next to the fridge. Beth stumbled back against the wall, a grunt of fear escaping her mouth as her hand groped for the wall switch. She flicked it on and in the first few seconds of harsh white light, her eyes took in the layers of clothes and the unkempt hair and matted beard and she knew who this was.

Colin Norcott was standing four feet away from her, holding a paper golem in his hand.

CHAPTER THIRTY-NINE

WEDNESDAY

Anna slept well. A dreamless, restful sleep for once.

She got up at six thirty, walked Lexi and fed her. Then she fed herself, showered and brushed her teeth, loading the toothpaste as she always did, three minutes of brushing wired into the electric handle – and there it was. Suddenly, like flicking a channel and seeing a single frozen frame from a familiar movie and knowing it for what it was in an instant.

Krastev's link to Ryegrove.

It was too early to ring anyone, but not too early to text.

She sent Khosa a message, dressed and set off for HQ.

She wasn't the first one in for a change. Khosa was already at her desk, looking busy. Dawes and Holder were loitering outside her office, the sergeant holding a cardboard box as if it contained something alive. The two male detectives followed Anna in and Dawes put the box on the desk.

'I hope they're fresh eggs from your trip to the country,' Anna said.

'No, ma'am. Guess again.' Dawes peeled back the cardboard. Inside were dozens, if not hundreds, of small paper figures.

'Golems,' Anna said.

Holder nodded. 'We got nothing questioning the neighbours and the staff in the local shops. Last sighting was at least three months ago. He'd started wearing lots of clothes. And I mean lots of clothes. He'd grown his hair and a beard. The whole mountain-man thing. But that's it. No one has seen him lately. We spoke to the local nick. They haven't seen him either.'

'So much for shared intelligence,' Anna muttered.

She reached in and removed two of the paper golems. The folding was intricate. The legs were splayed, like a frog's. At the end of the appendages the paper was flattened out into spear-shaped feet and hands. The torso was thin, the head a shallow bowl surrounded by the 'hair' that looked more like a folded cowl.

'How long do you think it takes him to make one of these?' Anna said, holding one of the figures up to the light.

Dawes shrugged. 'He's made thousands. He could probably fold one up in a few minutes.'

Anna placed the paper figure on the desk on its back and slowly began to unfold the paper. It wasn't particularly thick, but she was careful not to tear anything. Gradually, it opened out. There was nothing inside. At least nothing physical. Dawes and Holder were leaning over, staring avidly and it was Holder who noted the small marks. 'What are those?'

'It's a word, isn't it?' Dawes said.

Holder said, 'I see an "I" an "L" and an "A"—'

'Ali,' Anna said abruptly. 'Ali for Alison written backwards.'

They each took another golem and began unfolding. It was a random sample. Even so, two sets of letters predominated: ila was one, the other Hteb.

'Beth.' Dawes said.

Holder was the first to find the third. Just one letter, a 'K' with a tiny crown drawn above it. A jagged crown.

'King,' Anna said once she saw it.

They stopped what they were doing and looked at each other. Dawes broke the silence. 'Bloody hell.'

Khosa appeared at the door, stared at the desk littered with paper but decided not to comment. There was a strange light in her eyes. 'Regarding your early morning text, ma'am. I think we've got something.'

Holder and Dawes looked expectantly at Khosa but Anna stood and said, 'We'll do this as a team. Justin, go and get the super.'

They trooped out. Trisha was standing at the whiteboard; Khosa joined her just as Rainsford walked into the room with Holder and took up his customary position at the back.

Khosa wrote the word 'KRASTEV' on the board before pivoting to speak to the others.

'At the time he was working at Ryegrove, Krastev got stopped in a routine traffic check and was found to be driving someone else's car.' Khosa glanced at Anna. 'This morning DI Gwynne suggested I run a check on the car's owner.'

The others all glanced at Anna. 'A hunch,' she said.

'Ah, one of those,' Holder said. He turned to Khosa and they both grinned.

'So, what did you find?' Dawes asked.

'It checked out,' Khosa said. 'The loan of the car was genuine.' She turned back to the board and wrote a name as she spoke it out loud. 'The owner was a Joshua Dorell. A twenty-eight-year-old from North Devon. He confirmed that they were friends and had given his permission for Krastev, aka Mihai Petran, to use the car.'

Anna waited. From the glint in Khosa's eye, she clearly wasn't finished yet. 'I gave the name to Trisha, who ran a search on Dorell. He had no record at the time. But the name rang a Trisha bell. She'd seen it on a patient list from the time of Alison Johnson's disappearance. A Miranda Dorell, twenty-seven, and the sister of Joshua.'

Anna smiled and gave Trisha a little nod of acknowledgement. This was good teamwork.

'Why was she in Ryegrove?' Holder asked.

'Long history of very disturbed behaviour,' Khosa explained. 'Detained at Ryegrove indefinitely for stabbing her ex foster-mother nine times in 1999 but was deemed fit for discharge after just three years and released in 2002. The official diagnosis was schizo-affective disorder. Two years later she was readmitted after stabbing two teenagers and attempting to decapitate one.'

'Where is she now?' Anna asked.

'I'm still on that, ma'am. Following trial, she was admitted to Broadmoor and then the Becton secure unit in Greenwich – part of Oxleas NHS Trust. I'm in the process of contacting them now.'

'Nice hunch, ma'am,' Holder said.

Dawes looked bemused. 'You get these often, ma'am?'

Anna shrugged. 'I have my moments, Phil.'

He stared at her with his head at an angle before exhaling. 'I'm impressed. So we can definitely link Krastev with this Dorell woman through her brother.'

'I think it's safe to assume that,' Anna said.

'So there's Norcott and his weird paper golems and now a class A nutcase in this girl Dorell.' Holder shook his head.

'But neither sounds capable of being the Black Squid,' Dawes said.

Anna bit back a rejoinder. She felt like telling Dawes to shut up, that she knew all of this, and him reminding her of it didn't help. Better they work with what they had. She turned to Trisha. 'Can we pull up Norcott's sketch on the monitor?'

Trisha went back to her desk and, a minute later, the large flat screen TV next to the whiteboard flickered into life and filled with the sketch Norcott had made on his barn wall.

'That's the fence,' Khosa said. 'A hundred per cent.'

Anna nodded. 'Then it all comes back to Ryegrove, doesn't it? Why did Norcott draw that sketch on his barn wall? And why is he writing those three names inside his golem dolls?'

'Are you getting the feeling someone isn't telling us something, ma'am?' Dawes said.

'Couldn't have put it better myself. I think I'd like to speak to King and Beth Farlow again.'

'Shall I get them in, ma'am?' Holder said.

'No. Let's go to them. Keep them on their toes.' She turned to Trisha. 'Chase up the secure unit in Greenwich. I want to know if Miranda Dorell is still there, and see if you can get an address for the brother.'

'What about Norcott?' Dawes said.

'Have a word with Dyfed-Powys Police. Say we're interested in finding him. Just in case he comes up on their radar.'

Holder nodded.

'Once that's done, we go back to Ryegrove.'

CHAPTER FORTY

Oscar woke up late, relieved himself and climbed back under the duvet. It was after eight in the morning. His mother usually dragged him out of bed at a quarter to… and then he remembered. He wasn't going to school that day. Wasn't going to that school ever again. A rush of relief and gratitude washed over him. His mother hadn't called because they'd given him three days off to prepare. They were meant to be going in to get a new uniform today. But there was no rush. He could stay in bed all morning knowing Vickers wouldn't be hounding him. Wouldn't be threatening to set him on fire. He smiled under the covers.

Then he remembered the Black Squid and last night's task.

His mood evaporated in an instant.

His phone was on the small bedside table, turned off for the night. He reached for it, switched it on, waited for the screen to light up.

He flicked back to the home screen, dreading a little red indicator on the WhatsApp logo.

There was none.

Oscar sat up, wondering if this was just another little bit of torment. Letting him stew.

He remembered the cold and dark of the night before, what they'd made him do in the early hours when the streets were empty. The Squid had wanted him to experience a high place. Know what it felt like to be inches from death

The church was on Alberston's Street. His parents' church. He didn't think of it as his own. Didn't think of religion as having any meaning for him. It had never helped. But he'd spent many hours bored stiff in that church. He knew all the secret places. Knew where the door to the tower was. Knew where the vicar kept the key. He'd gone in, climbed the tower in the gloomy dark and sat with his legs dangling over a parapet in the belfry. It was high but not high enough, he thought, to guarantee a swift end if he fell. Around him, the church had creaked and groaned, the wind had whistled. Shapes moved in the dark below. In the graveyard. Probably cats or foxes. Nocturnal hunters on the prowl. But from where Oscar was sitting, they looked like spectres drifting between the stones, taunting him, inviting him to join them. He sat, terrified, until the cold became too much to bear. He'd shot a grainy video of himself and posted it, as the squid demanded.

Previously, he'd had a message as soon as he posted his evidence. But not this morning. Today, the Squid was wanting him to contemplate his fate. He toyed, just for a moment, with telling his mother what was happening. But he soon pushed it from his mind. She wouldn't understand; only they did.

His mother shouted to him from the kitchen. Had he forgotten they were going into town?

He had. Oscar got up. He'd pretend all was well and wait for the message to come.

CHAPTER FORTY-ONE

They took two cars to Ryegrove through a filthy wet morning. Anna wanted to interview Beth Farlow and Dr King at the same time. She and Khosa would take Farlow; Holder and Dawes, King. They arrived at a little before nine, when the atrium was full of support staff on their way into work. Morris was on duty in reception. Anna flashed him her badge.

'I'd like to see Mrs Easterby, please.'

Morris nodded and picked up a phone. Anna was glad to see a sense of urgency. Ten minutes later, an anxious-looking Monica Easterby appeared in reception. They spoke through the metal grille in the porter's sealed unit.

'We'd like to speak to Beth Farlow and Dr King again, Mrs Easterby. And we'd like to do that now.'

Easterby's moon-shaped face stared back blankly.

'We can do it quietly here if you can give us a couple of rooms. Alternatively, we can do it all at the station—'

'But they're not here.' Easterby's words cut Anna off mid-vent.

'What?'

'I mean, they should be here. When I heard you were in reception, I thought… I don't know what I thought. I mean, Dr King has a team meeting at nine fifteen, and Beth should have been on at seven thirty. I thought you'd come to say… I don't know what exactly.' Easterby shook her head. She looked suddenly uncomfortable

Dawes exchanged a glance with Anna.

'I can't remember the last time either of them was off,' Easterby said.

'You've tried contacting them?' Anna said.

'No joy. Phones are ringing but no response.'

'We'll need their phone numbers and addresses.'

Easterby's eyes widened. 'You don't think anything's happened?'

'Like what?' Anna asked.

'I don't know. Your men at the fence, digging. The bodies on the railway line. I don't know.'

'Neither do I. But we'll find out. If you can get us those addresses and numbers, please.'

Easterby nodded and hurried away, her voluminous clothes rustling, the beads and bangles jangling.

Anna joined the others. 'Neither of them has turned up for work today.'

'Done a bunk?' Holder asked, not expecting an answer.

'What do we know about King?'

Khosa stepped up. 'Divorced, lives alone. Children grown up.'

'And Farlow?'

'Single, sharing a house with a female colleague, I think.'

Holder said, 'What are you thinking, ma'am?'

'I'm thinking about Norcott's paper golems. The ones you brought back from Wales with Beth and K written inside their heads—'

'And now they're both missing,' Holder finished off the sentence.

'Oh, Christ,' Dawes said. 'You think this is Norcott's doing?'

Anna started walking towards the exit, fear galvanising her. 'Once we get the numbers and addresses, we'll split up. Ryia, we'll go to Farlow's, you two go to King's place. And let's get on to the phone companies. If their handsets are ringing, we should be able to locate them.'

'What about Norcott?' Dawes said.

'From what you've told me, he isn't going to be easy to find. But let's get the word out. See if any patrols have spotted anyone hanging around here. Someone with a beard, unkempt hair, lots of layers of clothes.'

Dawes nodded. 'I'll get some help from MCU for that.'

Easterby was back in reception. Holder went across to meet her and came back with the numbers and addresses. King's in Clifton; Beth Farlow's somewhere in Severn Beach.

'Keep me informed,' Anna said to Dawes as they reached their cars.

He nodded. Holder was already on the phone to the service provider to try locating King's phone, and Khosa was doing the same for Farlow's. They left in a convoy, Dawes veering up and across the bridge while Anna took the low road along the gorge out towards the estuary.

She had a bad, anxious feeling about this. What had King and Farlow discussed after their interviews? There was probably only one answer, and that was Colin Norcott. She crossed the river at the Cumberland Basin and drove out under the high cliffs of the gorge, speeding past the traffic, the suspension bridge high above them. Next to her, Khosa was listening and nodding, throwing in the odd affirmation until, at last, she put her hand over the mouthpiece. 'The phone's at the subscriber's address, ma'am.'

'OK. Then why isn't she picking up?'

Khosa had no answer. They were on the outskirts of Shirehampton when Khosa's phone rang again. It was Holder on speaker.

'Right, King's apartment is a ground-floor flat in Clifton Park. Big Georgian place. Bugger to heat, I expect. Anyway, his car's not here, so the neighbour said. We've looked through the front window and it looks unoccupied. No answer to the doorbell either.'

'What about his phone, Justin?' Anna asked.

'Right, they've located it within a half-mile radius of Severn Beach railway station. They couldn't be more specific.'

Khosa's head snapped up, her eyes locking on Anna's face. She'd worked on the MCRTF long enough to abandon the notion of coincidence. 'OK. You two follow us over to Severn Beach.'

'On the way, ma'am.'

Anna exchanged a glance with Khosa. Neither of them spoke but Anna pushed her foot down a little harder on the accelerator. Outside, the rain battered the windscreen and Anna upped the speed to maximum.

'This is all we need,' she muttered.

CHAPTER FORTY-TWO

Beth Farlow's address was not easy to find. The satnav seemed to run out of ideas the further away from the station they travelled. But Khosa finally spotted Shaft Road, the sign half hidden behind an overgrown bramble. As Anna negotiated the narrow, rutted lane, Khosa spoke for the both of them.

'What the hell is she doing living all the way out here?'

But they both knew the answer. Austerity remained the reality for a huge number of people. Young people especially. Anna and Khosa both knew the cost of renting a place closer to the city. Even so, this was taking an 'out-of-town' existence to the extreme.

The lane curved back towards the estuary as the few houses at the town end petered out.

'Looks like there are only properties on this left side, ma'am. It's just woodland on the other.'

'What number was it?'

'Number 2.'

Anna drove slowly, trying to find a number on a door or a gate. There were gaps between the houses. Some of them were lanes leading to properties behind, others nothing but patches of low trees or bushes. 'There,' she said, finding a number 14 on a gatepost. 'Can't be far from here.' She drove on, finally coming to a point in the narrow lane where the hedgerow was cut back and a pull-in created. She parked and got out. Khosa followed.

'Think we should hang on for the others, ma'am?'

'Why should we wait?'

Khosa looked back up the deserted lane and at the wild ground opposite. 'Don't know. It's a bit isolated, that's all.'

'Come on. Bring your ASP if it'll make you feel any better.'

They walked out into the lane, Khosa with her hood on, Anna with her collar up. Number 2 stood right at the end. Anna could see nothing that might have passed for number 1. There was no car outside the house, nor in the narrow driveway. A porch stood out on the side of the house, but a front door faced the road, accessed by a moss-covered path. Anna assumed not many people used this way in, but it was where she headed. Khosa stood a little way back on the drive as Anna knocked. Three times. After the third time she headed instead for the other door.

The porch had some tidily arranged wellies and an umbrella in a cauldron stand. There was a bell. She tried it with no response.

'OK, let's take a look around. You go around the back, I'll take the front windows.'

Khosa, ASP extended and clutched in her right hand, walked slowly around to the rear of the property. Anna watched. No immediate call from Khosa. OK, so no one lurking. She moved quickly along the little cracked concrete path at the front. There were two windows either side of the door. On the left the curtains were drawn. However, they were open on the one on the right. Through the glass she spied a settee, armchair, TV and not much else. She rubbed away grime for a better view. It didn't help. Anna stood back on the soggy lawn and looked up. Above, on the first floor, the windows mimicked those on the ground floor in their arrangement. She was wondering if there might be a ladder when Khosa's urgent shout reached her.

'Ma'am!'

Anna ran around. Khosa was standing on the threshold of a back door. This one very much ajar.

'It swung open when I pushed it with my foot, ma'am,' Khosa said.

Anna used the back of a knuckle to knock. 'Police. Anybody home?'

No sound in reply. Anna pushed the door inwards with her foot. The hinges groaned in response, but it swung open to reveal a small kitchen beyond. It was clean and tidy, with a few dishes stacked neatly on a sink, and a table with two chairs to the side with two mugs on it.

Two mugs.

'Hello. Is there anyone here?' Anna called out. She didn't wait for a reply this time but stepped in, inhaling, taking in the smell of laundry and an air freshener, relieved that there was nothing else. But as she moved into the room, there was something… something faint. Something coppery.

Opposite, a door led through to another room. Anna stepped towards it. The door was open but only by a crack. Not wide enough to see beyond. She reached into her pocket and slid on some blue neoprene gloves, pushed the door open with one finger. This one creaked much more than the back door. But the noise was forgotten in the moment of reveal. A sun room, tacked on to the rear of the cottage, south-facing to catch the rays. She took in the flowery upholstered settee and armchair, a stack of magazines in a wire rack on the floor next to the settee. But then her eyes were drawn to something that should not have been there. Protruding between the rack and the settee was a shoed foot. In the second before she stepped further into the room, Anna realised the smell was stronger in here. A metallic butcher shop smell.

'Shit,' Anna said and stepped around the door.

He was lying face down in front of the settee wearing a waxed jacket and jeans, head turned to one side. Skin pale, a pool of congealed blood in a halo around his head.

'Is that…' Khosa said from behind her.

'King, yes.' Anna kneeled, put her finger to his throat, felt a pulse. Her touch must have woken him because he groaned and tried to lift his head. The blood came with it with a sickening, sucking sound.

'Stay there,' Anna ordered. 'Ryia, get an ambulance and Forensics out here.'

'Wha-where…' King was mumbling.

'Lie still. Don't move,' Anna ordered. 'You've been hurt.'

'Beth… Beth?' King said and then squeezed his eyes shut. It looked like he was drifting in and out of consciousness.

Anna threw Khosa a glance. 'As soon as the other two arrive, clear the rooms above and the garden.'

Khosa was already on the phone, but she heard Anna's order and nodded.

Anna remained kneeling, wondering if she should cover King with a blanket but decided not to. She wondered about moving him, but he seemed stable. He did not respond when she called his name a second time. And head injuries were best left to the professionals. Anna was also very aware of not wanting to contaminate the scene any more than she had already. She looked around. In the opposite corner an upturned side table, a picture frame face down, fragments of glass on the adjacent floor. There'd been a struggle. Not much of one, but definitely a disturbance. Through the picture window, the trees in the cottage garden beyond were swaying wildly in the wind.

What she would have given at that moment to have been standing there when whatever took place in this room had happened. But it was wishful thinking. They'd missed the boat and now they were going to have to play catch-up.

CHAPTER FORTY-THREE

King was drifting in and out of consciousness, disorientated and unable to answer questions properly. When the ambulance arrived, Anna sent Khosa with him to the hospital with instructions to ring her if and when King was well enough to talk. Dawes and Holder went back to HQ to chase up the hunt for any Norcott sightings, but Anna took the fleet car and retraced her steps to Ryegrove. There was something she wanted to ask Monica Easterby that had got lost in the morning's excitement.

Morris was still on duty in reception. At Anna's request, he rang through for Easterby. She did Anna the courtesy of coming out through security, and the two of them found some chairs to sit on around the little tables scattered through reception. Easterby looked anxious. 'Well?'

'No sign of Beth Farlow, but we have found Dr King.'

'Found?'

Anna nodded. 'He was at Farlow's house, semi-conscious. It looks like he's been attacked.' This wasn't the kind of information she'd normally volunteer in an investigation. But it had occurred to her on the way over to Ryegrove that Easterby might know more than she was letting on.

'Oh my God.' Easterby's voice emerged muffled through the hand suddenly clamped over her mouth. 'Is Dr King OK?'

'I'd be grateful if this all remained between the two of us,' Anna said. 'We don't know how badly injured Dr King is and we don't know what went on.'

'Is this tied up with what happened to Alison Johnson?'

'Good question. Do you remember a patient called Miranda Dorell? She was in the unit at about the same time as Colin Norcott. The only information I have from her police records is that she was sectioned after stabbing her ex foster-mother, released from here and then readmitted for reoffending.'

Easterby frowned and dipped her chin to make three more. 'It rings a bell, vaguely. What's Miranda Dorell got to do with Dr King being attacked?'

'The honest answer is I don't know, but her name has come up. Her and her brother's.'

'I'd like to help. Sounds like she'd have been sectioned from the courts.'

'That's what our records show.'

Easterby stood up. 'Give me fifteen minutes. I'll see what I can find.'

She hurried away, back through security, surprisingly light on her feet.

Anna sat and watched. Saw the doors close and the building swallow the senior nurse up into its secret innards like a huge whale, suddenly glad it wasn't her and that she was sitting this side of the security barrier, nursing a dull anxiety from not knowing what the hell was going on in this case. But knowing, too, her disquiet was not all work-related. There was something else, something that had grown like Topsy ever since she first walked through the doors of Ryegrove. No, not strictly true. Grown since her mother's outburst at Harry's birthday party. The same anxiety that triggered the visit to Talgarth and which circled like a patient predator around her subconscious. Though Ben had given her his professional opinion on her paranoia, it had not eliminated it. And now, here she was again being spooked by her proximity to the monster house.

Interesting word, monster. She'd looked it up more than once, trying to peer beneath the obvious. Monsters weren't just huge, ugly and frightening imaginary creatures. There were more nuanced meanings. Museums and medical laboratories harboured monsters in jars. Mutations, creatures that were beyond the scale of normality.

And wasn't Ryegrove and even Whitmarsh, where Shaw was being kept, just like these laboratories full of specimens in jars? Weren't they repositories for society's mutations? Perhaps it was just being here that made Anna uncomfortable. Or perhaps it was the memory of Shaw saying how alike he and Anna were. Suggesting they weren't all that different. His words oozed into her mind like blood from a wound.

'We both want the same thing, you and me. We want to be left alone to wander around inside ourselves. But the world won't let us, will it? The world is full of meddling arseholes. Never mind all that "the evil that men do" bullshit. It's arseholes and cockroaches and us. Me and you, Anna. We work things out and then do something about it. We either wipe the world's arse or step on the fucking cockroaches.'

Mind games. Gone but not forgotten. Because he was right.

She headed a team of people who respected her, wanted to be in her company, and yet here she was as happy, if not happier, being on her own. What did that make her? Antisocial? Hiding her isolation behind her 'process' for working things out? But it was a fine line between contemplation and wandering down a rabbit hole in your own head so deep you might never come back out.

More often than not, she stopped these thoughts in their tracks. But now, in the monster house, she let them run. How close had she been to her mother getting her seen by a child psychiatrist simply because she had not conformed to a type? Norcott hadn't conformed and his mother had struggled to understand him. Anna's father ensured her mother's overwrought imagination had never taken hold. He'd reined in her judgemental tendencies. But with that thought came the rider: how close to ending up like Norcott had Anna been? Was she, the slightly weird daughter, the reason her parents' marriage had broken up?

She knew guilt when it reared its bulging head. With Anna and Kate at university and out of the nest, their parents' simmering resentment, kept in check for the girls' sake, finally boiled over into a need for separation. At least it was how her mother had explained it. Anna recalled hearing it, trite and practised, initially thinking it was a joke. But this was her mother talking, so it could not have been. Sian Gwynne didn't do humour.

In a flash of insight Anna realised that her relationship with her mother, never warm, had turned positively polar from the moment her parents had separated. She'd assumed it all stemmed from her own disapproval of what her mother did to her father. But that, she now realised, was too simplistic an explanation. It went much deeper. When her father died, there'd been no one to act as a cushion for her mother's disapproval, and there was nowhere for their relationship to go but south. And all because Sian kept wondering if Anna was going to end up in a place like this.

Jesus.

Did it bother her?

No, it did not bother her.

Then why was she thinking about it now?

Anna shook her head.

It's this place. What it stands for.

Easterby appeared at the security doors clutching a laptop.

'I've got the transcripts on a thumb drive,' she explained, sitting again, this time opening the laptop on the table between them. 'Everyone who's detained under a 37—'

'That's the section order?'

'Correct. Used by the courts when an offender needs to go to hospital instead of prison. All of our medium secure clients are also section 41, considered to be a risk to the general public. They all get an automatic First Tier Tribunal after six months of being here. And if they haven't applied themselves in the meantime, at least one automatically three years later. It can happen every six months if the patient or relatives are keen.'

'What happens at a tribunal?'

'Typically, there's a judge, a QC usually, a medical member and a layperson. They assess the detention order and can uphold it or direct a discharge. Evidence is usually heard from a doctor, nurse therapists, etc. They're looking at compliance, drug efficacy, rehabilitation progress, that sort of thing.'

Anna nodded and waited while Easterby punched keys. 'The Miranda Dorell you mentioned was admitted in1999 and discharged in 2002. Diagnosis of schizo-affective disorder—'

'Which is what, exactly?'

'A very unpleasant mix of bipolar mood disorder and schizophrenic symptoms simultaneously. Delusions and hallucinations can occur during a manic phase and they can be particularly difficult to control.'

'And you say she was discharged early?'

Easterby turned the screen around for Anna to see. She read the tribunal heading.

> Miranda Dorell v NBHT
> DATE: 16 June 2002
> CHAIR: Anthony Worral QC

A name on the panel caught her eye as Easterby provided further clarification. 'The tribunal found in favour of discharge. The final decision is always with the Home Office, but they didn't object here.'

> Panel consists of Chair, Clinical Director William Thomson, supervising clinician to the appellant, Dr Martin King. Senior administrator, Simon Cosby.

So King knew Miranda Dorell. Hardly surprising, though, given his remit.

Anna said, 'She attacked and stabbed her foster-mother. Is it usual that someone who did something that bad would be released so quickly?'

'It's not unknown. If she responded to treatment and was deemed to be stable . Obviously, it was thought she was delusional at the time of the attack. But at the time of the tribunal, not so.'

'But equally delusional when she attacked someone else two years later?'

Easterby's response was a blank stare.

'You didn't know?'

She shook her head.

'In 2004 she stabbed some teenagers in an unprovoked assault that ended up in her being admitted to Broadmoor.'

'I had no idea,' Easterby said in a horrified whisper.

'Is there a tribunal transcript for Norcott?' Anna asked.

Easterby's fingers clicked the keyboard again, and another identical heading appeared.

Colin Norcott v NBHT
DATE: 20 February 2015
CHAIR: Celia Landsbury QC

Anna scanned the panel. King's name was not on it.

'What happens when someone is directed for discharge?'

'Protocol needs to be followed. Discharge is a phased process. First to a low secure unit; in Ryegrove's case it's a different ward. There's supervised and unsupervised leave from the unit, restrictions associated with discharge, such as a curfew, for example. There'd be regular supervision as well as rehabilitation in a community setting. It's quite a process.'

Anna nodded. 'And despite all of that, Colin Norcott is out there wandering around with no one knowing where the hell he is, Dr King is in hospital and one of your nurses is now missing.' She took out some keys from her coat pocket and unclipped a key ring which doubled as a thumb drive. 'Can I have copies of these two transcripts, please?'

Easterby hesitated, but only for a moment. Keys clicked on the keyboard, she removed her own thumb drive and carried on speaking even as she plugged Anna's USB drive in. 'Strictly speaking, I probably shouldn't. But under the circumstances…'

'I appreciate it,' Anna said.

CHAPTER FORTY-FOUR

Anna left Ryegrove, but instead of heading back across the river, she turned right, yet again, along the winding lanes towards the crime scene at the railway line. She parked and signed in but was disappointed not to see Keaton's car in its usual spot. The Tyvek tents were still up and there were people working inside them. But it was not the graves that interested her.

She walked across the uneven stones. Some of them moved with her weight and she took it carefully. It would be easy to twist an ankle here. The wind howled in but, for the moment, the rain held off. She got to the spot where Keaton had marked out a safe path across the scrubland to Ryegrove's fence. The wooden boards across the worst of the mud at the bottom of the ditch shook and shuddered as she crossed and walked up towards the fence. The site was deserted, and she stood alone a few yards from the perimeter, staring at the excavated tunnel. Beyond, in the grounds of Ryegrove, more police tape cordoned off the area where the tunnel emerged. Behind that, some temporary fencing had been arranged to prevent any of Ryegrove's inmates taking an unscheduled awayday afforded by Keaton's spadework.

The day was fast slipping away, and the February light was bleeding out. Anna stood and turned to look back at the railway, imagining herself as one of the three people Norcott depicted in his sketch, wondering what they could see, what they were waiting for. Everything she'd come across in the case brought her back to this point. Krastev's work on the perimeter fence. The burial sites within view, one of them by Krastev's own admission a Black Squid victim. Norcott, a patient at Ryegrove, who'd drawn an image of this very spot. The second victim, Alison Johnson, the nurse who treated Norcott.

So, what was this place's secret?

The wind buffeted her. The polar plumes had retreated back east, and it was the Atlantic's turn to show its strength on a south-westerly gale. The chill gusts that suddenly caught the lapel of her coat were reminder enough that a storm was coming. It made her turn her head suddenly, and for a moment she thought she saw movement behind her in the grounds. She swivelled, peering into the deepening gloom, but there was no one there.

Her phone, when it rang, was a welcome jolt of reality.

'Ma'am.' Khosa's voice on the line. 'The doctors say Dr King is well enough to talk.'

'Right. I'm on my way.'

Anna didn't look round as she negotiated the path back to her car. On an afternoon like this there were too many shadows to be certain of anything and she didn't trust her imagination in as godforsaken a place as this.

King was in Southmead – the nearest hospital to Severn Beach. Still shiny and new from a 2014 revamp, the A and E now took everything the old Frenchay Hospital used to handle, complete with helipad. But it was to the Emergency Department Observation Unit that Anna and Khosa went. They'd done scans on King and were waiting for results, wanting to ensure there was no fracture under the swelling haematoma on his left temple.

He was sitting up, bandages on his arms, butterfly stitches over cuts on his forehead and a sterile dressing taped over the left side of his face.

'Dr King,' Anna said, 'how are you?'

‘I’ve been better.’ King’s voice was hoarse.

Anna dragged up a chair and sat. She didn’t want King constantly looking up. Better to be on the same level. It made interviewees much more relaxed. ‘Can you tell us what happened?’

King’s hands fluttered up off the covers and then back down again. ‘Difficult to know where to start.’

Anna waited.

King sighed and continued, ‘After we spoke at Ryegrove, Beth talked to me. She wanted to know if you’d asked me the same questions. She was curious about Norcott. She’s young and at the time I thought she was simply being anxious when she told me that Norcott still had an effect on her. What happened to him, his strange behaviour, his fixations. I said my door was open if she ever needed to talk. I had no idea…’ He shook his head as his words dried up.

‘No idea about what?’

‘She said that sometimes she still believed she saw his golems, his paper dolls. She thought she’d even seen one last week.’

‘Where?’

‘In the lane outside her house. But she wasn’t sure. She even laughed about it.’ King’s lips were trembling. ‘It played on my mind. I made some calls and found out Norcott had left Bristol and gone back to Wales. I rang Beth. I wanted to reassure her. But she didn’t sound reassured. She said she felt like someone was following her. Watching her. She thought she’d seen someone in the wasteland opposite her house. I suggested she rang you, but she said it was just being alone in the house that was doing it. I said I’d go around.’

Anna watched King’s face, looking for the subtext. If there was any, he was good at hiding it.

‘Oh, I know what you’re thinking. I’m a middle-aged divorcee and Beth Farlow is a young, attractive, impressionable girl. I have a daughter of my own, Inspector. I’ve fielded phone calls like this before and I know things are always better face to face over a cup of tea. So, I went. I drove out there. I had no idea she lived in such an out-of-the-way place. It may only be a mile from a train station, but it might as well be on the other side of the moon.'

Khosa had her phone out, recording everything. 'What time was this, exactly?'

'Yesterday evening at around eight fifteen.' King reached for some water with a shaky hand, took a sip and returned the plastic beaker to the bedside table. 'I knew there was something wrong when she opened the door. She looked terrified, really terrified. She had every right to be because Norcott was waiting behind that same door. She tried to warn me, mouthing words, but then he emerged with a knife at her throat and dragged her in. Threatened to kill her if I didn't come in too. What choice did I have?'

'He spoke to you?'

'Oh, yes, he spoke. At least he uttered words, though not many of them were coherent.'

Khosa said, 'I thought he didn't speak.'

'His choice while he was in Ryegrove until the last few months. Even then he didn't speak much. But he was speaking last night. The better word would perhaps be babbling.' King looked from Khosa to Anna. 'He kept saying he wanted his sister back.'

'Jesus,' Khosa said. She'd read the case files too.

'What happened in the house?' Anna said.

'I tried to talk to him but he was clearly delusional. I doubt he'd taken any medication for weeks if not months. He wasn't listening, probably couldn't hear what I was saying, not properly. Beth was terrified. At one stage he let her sit down and began pacing, still holding the knife. Some of the things he said made a strange kind of sense. He'd been camping out in the woods, watching Beth for several days if not weeks. He told us that much. But the rest of it… I couldn't see any good way out of the situation. Foolishly, I tried to overpower him.'

'Is that when you were struck?'

King nodded. 'He had the knife. I tried to use a cushion to deflect it, but he caught my arm. I must have stumbled and then he hit me with something.' King's fingers strayed to his temple. 'I must have lost consciousness. I have no idea how long for.'

'Have you any idea where he's taken her?' Khosa asked.

King, his face suddenly miserable, shook his head. 'If I had to guess, I'd say the woods opposite. Where Beth thought she'd seen him.'

Anna turned to Khosa. 'I know it's late, but let's get things moving.'

'The storm is coming in, ma'am. They say there's a big risk of flooding due to the high tides—'

'All the more reason to get people out there now.' Anna held Khosa's gaze.

They both knew that in an unlit and wild area like the wasteland on Shaft Road, night-time searches were useless. They'd get a POLSA, a specialist Police Search Advisory team, in at first light, yet that was hours away.

'What about a chopper, ma'am?'

'Worth a try. Speak to Sergeant Dawes. He can get the super on it.' A helicopter could deploy thermal imaging and its Nightsun if necessary. If they could get one up.

Khosa picked up her phone and left the room. Anna put hers on the bed to continue recording.

Something she'd read or heard about Norcott niggled. 'Were you surprised to see Norcott? The way he was, I mean?'

King snorted. 'You're asking me if I thought we should have released him when we did? The answer is no. I was against it. But there were others who felt he'd responded to treatment and he seemed to do well in transition.'

'But you were not convinced?'

'The Trust puts the unit under a great deal of pressure, Inspector. We don't have enough beds. It's very tempting to take whatever positives we can in order to move patients through the system a little faster. Sometimes such pressure can be overwhelming and directives from pen-pushers asking us to reduce our average length of stay to some ridiculous number don't help.'

'So you had doubts.'

'Let's say I nursed a healthy scepticism. His mother didn't want him back. But her death seemed to be a turning point for him, I'll admit that.'

Anna picked up her phone, paused the recording, and pulled up the image Dawes had sent her of Norcott's sketch on the barn wall at his mother's smallholding. 'We found this at Norcott's home in Wales.'

King peered at it and then sent Anna a blank stare.

'You don't recognise it? The location?'

King shook his head.

Anna found another image, this time taken from inside the perimeter fence at Ryegrove. The shape of the background landscape and trees were very similar.

'Ah,' King said. 'I see.'

'Have you any idea why he's drawn this?'

'No.'

'We've found evidence of an access way at this point. A tunnel under the fence and into the grounds.'

King frowned. 'Really?'

'It's possible one of the construction workers might have built it in order to continue a relationship with a patient. Someone you might well have known. A Miranda Dorell.'

King nodded and uttered another acknowledging, 'Ah.'

'You remember her?'

'Of course. How could I forget? We were pilloried for allowing her early release before she reoffended.'

'You were involved in securing that early release, I understand?'

'Not only me. There's a process.'

'I know, a tribunal.'

'Exactly. It's sometimes difficult for people outside mental health to understand the tribunal's role is to assess the mental state of the patient at the time of the tribunal. Not at the time of offending, which, by definition, can be very different.'

King's explanation had the tinge of a lecture about it.

'What was she like, Miranda Dorell?'

'Troubled, young and in denial. It was not her first episode but, as is so often the case, once we found the right combination of drugs, she responded well.'

'Was there any family support?'

King thought for a moment. 'Not from the parents. Her manic phases were too extreme. She attacked her mother, if I remember rightly. But apart from that she'd do outrageous things and sometimes, even though there's a pathological cause, the fallout can be too great.'

'What do you mean?'

'She stole and got into drugs. Got into pornography at an early age, too. Was a party animal. Too much for her middle-class parents, I fear. But she and her brother were close.'

'Did you meet him?'

'Briefly. He supported her during the tribunals, along with her solicitor, of course.' King's pale face frowned. 'Why do you ask?'

Anna chose not to answer his question but continued with one of her own. 'Did you ever see her near the fence? Did you ever see her talking to any of the construction workers?'

'No. Not that I can recall.' King sighed and squeezed his eyes shut, his fingers straying to the bandage on his head.

'Are you OK?'

'Pounding headache.'

'Of course. We can talk about this when you're feeling a little better.'

'Sorry, Inspector.'

Anna moved her chair back but before turning away said, 'Did Norcott give you any inkling of why he was stalking Beth Farlow?'

'No. As I told you, he was not rational. I think I'm lucky to have got away with just a concussion.'

'Does the term the Black Squid mean anything to you?'

King frowned. 'Nothing more than what I've read in the paper. Something to do with a spate of teenage suicides, isn't it?'

Anna nodded. 'I don't suppose you came across anyone involved with it at Ryegrove?'

'Space Invaders and Candy Crush are all we allow, Inspector. And then only under supervision when patients are ready for release.'

Anna nodded. 'One final thing. You said you parked outside Beth's house?'

'Yes.' King frowned. 'Is my car not there?'

'No. Do you have your keys?'

King's frown deepened. He shook his head. 'I'd assumed you'd taken them.'

In the corridor outside, Khosa was still on the phone. She waved at Anna to wait. After some nods and yesses, she rang off. They walked out of the hospital together.

'OK, that's done. Sergeant Dawes is trying to get air support. What do you make of it, ma'am? King's story, I mean.'

'I want to go back to Beth Farlow's house. Where are Justin and Phil?'

'They say they've made some progress with tracking Norcott's movements.'

'Good. Tell them to meet us at Severn Beach. We also need to find King's car.'

CHAPTER FORTY-FIVE

Two hours later, Anna sat in Beth Farlow's kitchen with her team, viewing CCTV footage from the railway station in Severn Beach on a laptop Holder had brought. They watched a bearded man wrapped in too many coats with a beanie hat pulled tight on his head, walking through the ticket barrier alone. It looked like he was the sort of individual other people would not want to be too close to.

Dawes sat next to her. 'That's him we reckon,' he said. 'We sent a copy to Dyfed-Powys Police and they sent one of their lot out to the local shopkeeper in Wales we'd spoken to. She said it's what Norcott looked like the last time she saw him.'

'When is this footage from?' Anna asked.

'Two weeks ago. But we've found some from a month ago as well. We think we may have picked him up on a walkway going the other way towards Gordano.'

'Means he's been here a while,' Holder said.

Anna squeezed her eyes shut. Holder was stating the obvious and for half a second, she felt like screaming. But she recognised that feeling for what it was. The frustration of not having seen something in a case, not having prevented it from happening, was sometimes overwhelming. It made no sense to feel guilty about it, but since when did sense have any place in investigating crime? Especially crimes involving perpetrators who were off the scale in terms of their mental well-being.

A bit like you, then, Anna.

The thought, sly and unwelcome, arrived in her mother's voice. She trod on it and stood up, walked to the window. Outside, in the yard and the garden, CSI were doing a search under rigged lights. Although she couldn't see them, across the lane, ten uniformed officers were also searching along the road for evidence. Above she could hear the clatter of helicopter blades, waxing and waning. But it was dark and windy and pretty hopeless on the ground given the thickness of the undergrowth. They were all hoping the chopper might pick up Norcott or Farlow's heat signature in the woodland, but there'd been nothing and she knew they'd have to call things off soon. The flight commander had warned her they had enough fuel for about ten more minutes. That was fifteen minutes ago. They were still up there, reluctant, she supposed, to give it up. But even as she stood there staring out, she heard the engine noise get louder and then begin to fade as the helicopter departed.

The space left by the sound was quickly filled by the moaning wind.

Holder's phone rang. He walked into the corridor to take the call and came back two minutes later. 'That was the search coordinator, ma'am. They've found King's car at the end of Shaft Road.'

'How far away?'

'Half a mile.'

'Right. Let's go—'

Holder stopped her. 'There's nothing there, ma'am. The doors have been left wide open, as well as the boot. No sign of anyone. Looks like it's been abandoned. They're getting a Forensics team down there now, but conditions are really bad.'

Anna opened the back door and stepped around the corner of the cottage to peer into the road. The uniformed officers, all wrapped up against the weather, were walking back to their vehicles. She wanted to shout at them, tell them to keep at it. Car headlights lit up the narrow lane, showing the open land opposite as a dense, black, unlit void.

Dawes joined her, shouting to be heard above the whipping wind.

'Not much else they can do tonight, ma'am.'

'I've got a torch in the car,' Anna said.

'Ma'am, that's just asking for trouble. Night-time searches only work with air support, we both know that. You'd be lost in there within five minutes. I've spoken to the POLSA. He's promised to get things moving at first light.'

She'd already decided on the search parameters with the team. Between the cottage and the M4 Second Severn Crossing arching out over the river sprawled the patch of woodland and scrub, bisected to the east by the M49 feeder road between the M5 and M4.

Having the car found abandoned half a mile away simply reinforced the need to search the area. It was not a large patch but singularly wild and not often visited because of its proximity to the motorways. There were much nicer areas in which to walk where the constant roar and buzz of traffic did not accost your ears. But it also meant a quiet and undisturbed hiding place. Dawes was right. Things would be much easier in daylight. But at 10 a.m. there was a high tide and the forecast wasn't good, with a red alert out for local flooding.

Frustration gnawed at Anna. Dawes put his hand on her arm and motioned her back inside, shutting the door after him.

'I know it sounds useless,' Dawes said, 'but I suggest the best thing we can do now is all go home and get some rest.'

No one stood.

'Come on, I know she's out there somewhere but sitting here is doing no good at all.'

Anna looked at Dawes as if he'd suddenly grown horns. But he was right. If the POLSA knew she was contemplating venturing out herself, he'd have her up on a disciplinary charge. 'OK,' she said. 'Let's pick it up first thing. Briefing at eight at HQ. We'll all be better after some sleep.'

She registered some nods of agreement, but she wondered if, like her, it was tinged with guilt. They were all going home to warm beds. That was a luxury Beth Farlow would not have. Might never have again. That realisation did not bode well for a good night's rest.

CHAPTER FORTY-SIX

Anna followed the others out and back to HQ, where she picked up her own car. It was after ten when she got home via Maggie's. Lexi was, as always, overjoyed to see her. In the flat, Anna let the dog out into the dark garden to snuffle around and relieve herself while she checked her phone. Four missed calls. Two from her sister Kate and two from Ben.

Kate answered on the third ring. 'Hi, Anna.'

Anna smiled, amazed as always how her sister managed to infuse sympathy and sincerity into just two words with enviable ease.

'Hi, Kate. Sorry it's so late.'

'You sound tired.'

'A bit. Little ones OK?'

'They're fine. They both missed you on Sunday.'

'Really?'

'Yes. They were worried about the row you had with Grandma. They asked me if you were ever coming back.'

'Was it that obvious?'

'I said you'd be here as usual next Sunday.' Kate hesitated before adding, 'You will be, won't you?'

'Of course I will. You know I will. Mum does an excellent job of pressing my buttons, that's all.'

'She can't help it.'

'I took Ben with me up to Talgarth,' Anna said quickly.

'Why?'

'Because I didn't want to go there alone.'

'But why go there at all?'

'To remember.' Anna paused and then said, 'I don't think she ever took you, did she?'

'She said I was too young.'

'She didn't take you because in her twisted way of thinking, you didn't need to see. You didn't need to be warned that unless you started to behave in a way she considered normal, this was what was in store.'

'Mum told you that?'

'I don't know. I've probably blocked out the memory. But what other reason could there have been? I was what, eight? It was not the sort of place you'd take an eight-year-old unless you wanted to scare the crap out of them.' Anna tried desperately to recall the long journeys in the car but some safety mechanism in her brain had blanked them out. 'You heard her. You know what she's thinking.'

'She doesn't mean any of it, Anna.'

'Yes, she does. Of course she does. That's the bloody point. All these years of put-downs and disapproval, and all the while she's managed to keep the ugly truth locked away. But now the genie's well and truly out of the bottle and she can't help herself. Can't hide it. I was, I am, the little freak a whisker away from being locked up.' She caught herself, knowing how this sounded. Years of bottled-up resentment released in a tirade poor Kate was having to listen to. But what she wasn't expecting was the single, miserable sob that came down the line from her sister.

'Kate?'

'Oh, Anna. She's still Mum.'

Something was missing from the end of that sentence and Anna's mind supplied it effortlessly. *For now, at least.*

But this was Kate she was talking to, and she'd never be that blunt.

'I didn't mean to upset you,' Anna said.

Kate sniffed. 'You haven't. It's the truth and we both know it. But I see her more than you do. I've seen her change. She worries over nothing. But she worries more than anything over you when she sees the kind of thing you're dealing with in the news. She does care, Anna.'

'I know she does.' The words slipped out before Anna could stop them because they were true. Ignorance was no defence in the eyes of the law, but in the twisted dynamics of family relationships it was the cause of much strife. If she wanted to, Anna could abandon her mother. Hurl back her ridiculous, meaningless, bigoted nonsense and walk away. But to do so would mean changing her relationship with Kate, and that she was not prepared to do. Anna was not very good at compromise, but the threat of losing Kate and her kids in the crossfire was incentive enough.

'Look after yourself, babes,' Kate said. 'And remember I'm on speed dial on that phone of yours. I put it in myself.'

'Don't worry,' she said to Kate. 'I know exactly where that number is. I'll see you Sunday.'

Lexi had come in from the garden to where Anna was sitting and began nuzzling her free hand. Anna buried her fingers in the warm fur as her work phone buzzed on the table in front of her.

Anna put down one phone and picked up the other. It was Khosa.

'Ryia, what's up?'

'Just to say they've released Dr King, ma'am. Scans were negative. They were happy with his obs. He insisted on going home and one of the patrol cars dropped him off.'

'Good. We'll let him rest and pick up with him tomorrow. Thanks for letting me know.'

'It is OK to leave him on his own, isn't it, ma'am?' Khosa asked.

'So long as the medics think it is.'

'I meant protection-wise.'

'Why? Norcott's attack wasn't premeditated. He wasn't looking for King. Why would he be looking for him again, now? Besides,

Norcott's abducted Beth and disappeared into the wilderness. King will be fine.'

'They've upped the flood warning along the estuary, too, ma'am. I thought you ought to know that.'

'What time is high tide again?'

'Ten tomorrow morning.'

The door to the garden stood ajar after Lexi's entrance. As if to emphasise Khosa's warning, a gust of wind threw it back to clatter against the wall. Anna got up quickly, pushed it shut and locked it.

'Looks like we're in for a rough day tomorrow, Ryia. Get some sleep.'

'You too, ma'am.'

But sleep was something Anna knew would not come easily that night. She was physically exhausted, but her head was buzzing. She didn't want wine, not this evening. But she did need to speak to Ben. Needed his voice inside her head for a while so it could calm the thoughts that tossed and foamed like the sea in the weather footage of the Cornish coast she'd seen on the late news.

'Hello.' Though it was after ten thirty by now, Ben's voice was not sleepy. His hello brimmed with amused delight and anticipation as always.

'You're not asleep, then.'

'Not unless this is a shared lucid dream in which case we're both unconscious.' He paused for effect before adding, 'You OK?'

'Not really.'

He knew what she was working on. Knew it was, in his words, a 'bastard'.

'Just work?'

Anna smiled. Ben was probably the most emotionally intelligent person she knew. 'Don't probe into my psyche, Dr Hawley.'

'It's a psyche well worth probing into. Let me guess: Mummy dearest?'

'Indirectly. Kate was worried I would never want to go to hers while my mother was there ever again. It's such a waste of time and energy.'

'Emotions, you mean?'

'Feelings, maternal respect, upsetting the kids. It's so… exhausting.'

'What's brought all this on? Is it Ryegrove?'

'Maybe. I've been wondering what it might be like on one of the wards. Demonstrating how well adjusted I am to a team of therapists. I couldn't think of anything worse.'

She waited for one of Ben's pithy rejoinders, but none came. Instead, he was understanding. 'We know it's your specialist subject but not everyone does rational, Anna.'

She thought of Norcott staying silent for years, folding paper golems by way of communication. All completely irrational and yet there must have been some sort of reasoning going on in his warped brain. Knowing what that was would explain a great number of things. Anna dragged her thoughts back to the moment.

'What about you? Your shift go OK?'

'An alcoholic with bleeding oesophageal varices managed to redecorate a whole cubicle in projectile vomit. So yes, sublime is the word I was searching for.'

'Still on for Friday? That Spanish place?'

'Fingers crossed. Tapas and a decent Rioja, oh yes. I've heard good things. I have the whole weekend pencilled in with Lexi and you. Mainly Lexi, but if you happen to pop your head around the door, I'll be there.'

'Good to know,' Anna said.

'And I'm here on the end of the phone if you need me.'

'OK. Lexi sends her love.'

'I know she does. I'm sending some back telepathically.'

'Lucky dog.'

'She is, isn't she?'

'See you Friday.' Anna killed the call. She did it wistfully, full of admiration for the way Ben was able to ease her burdens without really trying.

She made it to bed at eleven and found some restless sleep a little before midnight. Four and a half hours later she was wide awake, listening to the rain batter the window and the wind conducting the trees in a hissing symphony in the park not forty yards away.

The storm was growing in strength. She lay in bed, hearing it rage and cursing it until the numbers on her bedside clock got to five thirty when she got up, dressed and took Lexi outside to see what teeth the gale had. She came back in ten minutes later, dried the dog and then threw her wet clothes into the laundry before showering. At six thirty, her work phone rang. She didn't recognise the number immediately, though something about it seemed terribly familiar.

'Gwynne,' she said.

'Inspector, this is George Calhoun. I know it's early, I took a chance you'd be up.'

'I am.'

'Courtesy call. Shaw collapsed during the night. We had him on a watch list, given his recent poor health. He's in hospital. Thought you'd want to know in case you planned on visiting. He is no longer here.'

Anna's pulse thrummed in her ears. 'Where is he?'

'Worcester Royal. Acute medical unit. They're doing tests.'

'How bad?'

'He's not dead. Not yet.'

'He told me they thought it might be cancer.'

'It might be. They're trying to find it. Anyway, thought you ought to know.'

'Thanks.'

Anna put the phone down and stirred her coffee, trying to analyse what she was feeling. She finally plumped for unsettled. Most of it stemmed from what was in front of her – the unknown. But a morsel of it came from Calhoun's matter-of-fact news. She sat staring at the swirling clouds the milk made in the dark liquid in front of her, knowing it was probably as murky outside in the storm. The POLSA would not get going for another hour at least. She didn't envy them their task and, much as she would have loved to get her hands dirty, there was no point in volunteering to get out there in the undergrowth herself. The rest of the team would be at the office at eight. They'd need half an hour or so to pick up on any queries they'd sent out last night. She could, if she wanted to, push the briefing back to nine thirty. That meant she had two hours to get to Worcester and back.

She'd never make it. But she'd give it a bloody good go.

CHAPTER FORTY-SEVEN

THURSDAY

Beth Farlow was struggling to breathe. She couldn't move. Her legs and arms were frozen. She couldn't see. She knew she was inside a building, but water was slopping around her feet. She could hear it and feel the cold seeping into her, sense it rising slowly over her ankles. Though her hearing was severely compromised, the force of the hammering wind was making something rattle behind her.

And then she thought of Colin Norcott.

She tried to scream but all that emerged was a stifled, high-pitched moan that filled the dark space and was whisked away by the howling gale.

CHAPTER FORTY-EIGHT

Anna dropped Lexi off at six forty-five with huge apologies that were immediately dismissed out of hand by the saintly Maggie and headed up the M5. It was a dark, wet, filthy morning. Spray turned the journey into an exercise in concentration. She made it to Worcester a little after eight.

Shaw was in bed in a single room on an acute medical ward, looking grey and subdued. One arm was bandaged and had a saline drip running into it; the other was chained to the metal frame of the bed. A white wire snaked up from his ears to an outlet on the wall behind him. In the corner, a prison officer sat on a chair, reading the *Daily Mirror*. Anna showed him her warrant card. He got up and left the room. Shaw took out the earbuds. Under the bright ceiling lights, his lips were pale and his skin waxy.

'Good of you to come, Anna.'

'I said I'd tell you what we found.'

'At eight o'clock in the morning? You must have left early. Must have had a sense of urgency. You worried I'm not going to make it to next week?' Shaw's hollow-cheeked grin had an anorexic look about it.

Exactly that, Anna thought. She'd never admit to concern over Shaw. Didn't need to because it wasn't true. But she did harbour an odd sense of duty. She'd made a promise and she wasn't going to be the one to renege on it. Anna shrugged and gave him a bluff answer. 'It was either now or not at all. Do they know what's wrong with you?'

Shaw shook his head. 'Anaemia of unknown origin. I'm due a transfusion any minute, then there's an MRI scan.' He held up his chained wrist. 'They'll have to take these off. That'll be fun watching them sweat.'

'I'm here because I keep my promises, Hector.'

'I know you do. That's what I like about you, Anna.'

'We're in the middle of a search. I don't have much time.'

Shaw nodded. 'I'm all ears.'

She told him about Norcott and his sketch of the fence with the railway beyond and the tunnel beneath. And about King and the missing Beth Farlow. How Krastev was linked through the Dorells.'

'So Norcott attacked King and has taken Farlow?'

'Yes.'

'What about this Dorell woman?'

'We're on it. I take it Dorell means nothing to you?'

Shaw shook his head slowly. 'Krastev never mentioned her. Can I see the sketch Norcott made?'

Anna saw no harm in it. She had the image Dawes had sent her on her phone and held it up for him to see. He leaned forward on the bed, but Anna stayed out of his reach. Even so, she could smell him, and he had the stench of sickness about him; she watched his face harden in concentration.

'Do you know who these three are?'

Anna's turn to shrug. 'You asked me what Krastev was hiding, why he didn't want to give up Ryegrove. I think he built the tunnel to get in to see the girl. It could be Krastev in the sketch. The other two could be the Dorells. It all fits.'

'What about the background? The lines and the black mound and the red area?'

'It's where we found the body. The black mound could be one of the piles of sleepers. The red… that might be Jamie Carson or even Alison Johnson.'

Shaw hadn't taken his eyes off the phone. 'The dark mound is curved. Railway sleepers are square.'

'It's all I have. Norcott is the only one who really knows.'

Shaw looked up at her and blinked, slowly. 'True. Him and the people in his sketch. They'd know.'

'As I said, we're tracing the Dorells. The girl's been in and out of institutions, so it shouldn't be too difficult. And Krastev... well, we can't ask him anything, can we.'

'Not unless you've got a medium on the books in Avon and Somerset.'

Anna ignored him. 'Bottom line, we're no further forward in finding the Black Squid, or who killed Alison Johnson. But the Dorells must be involved if they were anything to do with Krastev. Obviously, we'd like to talk to Norcott, too. He drew the fence. He probably knew there was a tunnel.'

'You like him for the murder of your nurse?'

'Maybe.'

'Or maybe he's just a pawn in the game. A shame you can't find him, isn't it?'

Anna saw the look on Shaw's face. She'd seen it before. He was planting a seed.

The door to the room opened and two nurses entered, followed by the guard. One of the nurses clutched a blood bag.

'Ah, breakfast,' Shaw said, grinning. But Anna could see it took an effort.

She took her leave.

'Don't be a stranger,' Shaw called after her.

She thought about wishing him well but held back. Shaw was a killer, and though their relationship was essentially symbiotic, her concern for his well-being was the same she'd have for anyone. Though Shaw had a place in her life, it was not in her heart.

CHAPTER FORTY-NINE

The journey back from Worcester was just as difficult, except that the light was a little better. Even so, Anna kept her headlights on. But the further south she went, the worse the weather got. As she neared Bristol, the urge to bypass HQ and go straight to the search site at Beth Farlow's cottage was almost overwhelming. Her stomach felt gripey and empty and she realised she hadn't eaten properly or drunk anything yet today. Ben would have given her one of his looks. The one that said, 'You can't do anything about what's around the corner, but you can make damn sure you meet it with an appropriate blood sugar level.' Thinking of Ben released a little of the tension in her nerves which, after seeing Shaw, felt as taut as piano wire. She took a breath and steered the car towards Portishead.

Everyone in the office looked up as she walked in. She dumped her battered briefcase in her fishbowl room, glanced at her watch and noted it was almost ten. When she walked back out into the office, Trisha handed her a cup of tea.

'You are a lifesaver,' Anna said and sipped. It tasted hot and sweet and wonderful. Her team was waiting expectantly.

'Thanks for being patient.'

Rainsford was already there. He knew she'd arrived. The office radar was working well.

'Apologies for being late but I had to make a little trip this morning to Worcester. Hector Shaw has been admitted to hospital after collapsing in Whitmarsh. He's about to receive a blood transfusion and a battery of tests.'

No one spoke, and she realised she ought to give them a reason as to why she'd gone. Distorted integrity and a misguided sense of duty would not cut the mustard here. 'Shaw's unwell. I don't know how serious his situation is but I felt obliged, in the light of our new findings, to interview him once more.'

'Before he croaks,' said Dawes nodding.

'But despite showing him Norcott's sketch, he was unable to help us interpret it. He denies ever having heard of Miranda Dorell. He agrees with me that the larger figure could well be Krastev, but otherwise had nothing new to contribute.'

'Is he actually dying?' Holder asked.

'I don't know. Nobody seems to. He's having tests and he looks bloody awful, let's put it that way. Anyway, when we look at all the information we've gathered from Shaw, Norcott's sketch, King's assault and now Beth Farlow, everything seems to revolve around something that happened at Ryegrove around the time Alison Johnson went missing. Something that's triggered a reaction culminating in the events of yesterday. What's the latest on the search?'

Dawes spoke up. 'They're combing the woodland. The POLSA has thirty men searching. But it's a big area and it widens the further north they go. The biggest obstacle is the weather. There have already been reports of flooding in the estuary. Even made the news with waves crashing over the sea defences. They reckon there might be some local evacuations by mid-afternoon.'

Anna shook her head. 'He must be there somewhere. He has no car. We would have known if he'd tried to leave by train or bus.'

'We've circulated his photograph to transport police. There's been no report of any sightings,' Khosa said.

'OK. OK. Let's look at what else we've got. I need to understand how Krastev and the Dorells fit into this picture. If they do at all.'

Khosa got up from her seat and handed out a blue plastic folder. 'Trisha's collated what information we have, including CSI images of the bodies, and the fence and Justin and Sarge's visit to Wales.'

Anna nodded. There were now too many photos to stick on the whiteboard and they were effectively being issued a murder book.

Khosa continued, 'At the back are two photographs, the most recent we could find of the Dorells. Both taken at their last court appearances, so a little out of date.'

'How so?' Holder asked.

'Joshua Dorell came out of prison after serving three years of a four-year sentence seventeen months ago. His sister, Miranda, was already out on licence from having spent four years at the Becton unit in Greenwich.'

'She's out again?' Anna looked at the photographs. The similarity between the siblings was striking. Miranda's image showed an attractive, wild-eyed, dark-haired girl with a frighteningly lost expression, taken as she stared at a police camera. Joshua had an equally full mouth and heavy lids. But his was a much more defiant stare. Behind those images were more of an older Miranda, this time made up, posing on a bed with her breasts on show. Behind that was another of a poorly lit room and a girl doing the splits in front of a silver pole.

'So, she's no Sunday school teacher, then?' Dawes said.

Khosa nodded, 'Pole dancing, online sex chat. She's done a bit of everything when the mood takes her.'

'Isn't that the point?' Anna asked. 'She's bipolar.'

'You're right, ma'am,' Khosa replied. "Her behaviour seems to see-saw, but even when she's been stable, she's been a bit of a wild child.'

'Child?' Dawes said. 'She must be knocking on forty.'

'What's her background?' Anna said.

'That's where it becomes even more interesting. Parents were well off. Their father was an academic, a lecturer in politics. Their mother was an artist and a poet. When the children were four and five, the Dorells moved to a commune in Devon. The children were home-schooled, but effectively allowed to run wild. They travelled in a converted bus. Moved with a group of other New

Age travellers. The type that pitch up on a farmer's land and squat there until they're evicted. When they were in their early teens, their parents both died of CO_2 poisoning in a friend's van. The Dorell children were asleep in their own bus at the time.'

Dawes made a face; it echoed Anna's thoughts. It could not have been an easy time for the Dorell children.

'What happened to them?'

'They went into care and a series of foster homes, none of which lasted very long. Miranda was luckier than Joshua. He stayed in residential homes mostly until he was eighteen.'

'And then?'

'They had money. Their mother was independently wealthy. Old money. The Dorells inherited that when they came of age.'

'Don't tell me,' said Dawes. 'Blew it all on a Ferrari and some decrepit pile in the countryside.'

'No. At least Joshua didn't. He went into drugs. Designer drugs. Synthetic opiates, MDMA, Spice, you name it. He was a talented chemist. His sister, meanwhile, seemed to be his main product tester. Unfortunately, the drugs didn't help with her psychoses much.'

'Off the rails?' Holder asked.

Khosa shook her head. It made her dark hair bounce. 'Not so much off as never actually on. She's been sectioned three times. One of her manic phases led to her brother being arrested and a search of the premises subsequently led to his arrest and conviction. And Miranda's online presence leaned heavily in the sadomasochistic direction.'

'Is that where Krastev comes into the picture?' Holder said.

'That would be my guess,' Anna said. 'Krastev either met Miranda Dorell while he worked on the hospital construction or knew her and her brother beforehand. Well enough to borrow Joshua Dorell's car, we know that. The tunnel under the fence was for Krastev to get access to Miranda possibly. Or for her brother to get her out.'

'They sound like a lovely pair,' Dawes said.

'They're also the key to the Black Squid connection. They must be if they had anything to do with Krastev. So where are they now?' Anna asked.

Khosa sighed. 'Not at the address she'd given to her community case worker. That lasted a week before she flew the nest.'

'First Norcott and now this charmer. Care in the community at its bloody best,' Dawes said.

Anna stared at the images in the folder. 'And we have no idea where they are, the Dorells?'

Khosa answered, 'None, ma'am. We're checking bank records, trying to find credit card details. See if transactions flag up somewhere. But they're both anti-establishment. I think it's unlikely we'll find them that way.'

'Could they be abroad?'

'I'm checking with the Border Agency. We'll know if they've used a passport.'

'You've done well, Ryia,' Anna said. 'One question. Were they about the same height? The Dorell siblings?'

Ryia checked her notes. 'Yes, Joshua an inch taller than Miranda. Why are you asking?'

Anna shrugged. 'Norcott's sketch. The smaller figures are roughly the same height. I know I'm fishing but it's possible it's them.'

'And the third?' Holder asked.

'Krastev?' Anna said, but she heard the upward lilt in her voice. A question rather than a statement. There were still far too many of those and far too few answers. Still no idea about what happened to Alison Johnson, the nurse whose death set them on this tortuous path in the first place. 'Right. Trisha, let's double-check on any properties linked to the Dorells. Just in case. But in the meantime, I think we should get down to Severn Beach while we still can. Norcott's been in that area for weeks hiding out. Someone must have seen him. I need to talk to the CSM at the cottage. See if they've found anything useful.'

'Don't you believe King?' Holder asked.

'I've got no reason to disbelieve him. But he was unconscious for a lot of the time. I'm hoping a forensic workup might tell us a bit more about what actually happened.'

CHAPTER FIFTY

The police tape across Shaft Road thirty yards either side of Beth Farlow's cottage bowed alarmingly in the wind screaming in off the estuary. They'd sent some uniforms to check on Beth's housemate, Dee. She expressed utter astonishment on hearing what had happened and had never heard of Norcott. She'd wanted to come back and help search. But the cottage was a crime scene. Dee would have to stay with her boyfriend until this was all over.

Khosa parked behind a big police Transit and she and Anna got out to be met by a gale. Rain whipped at Anna's face and she pulled her coat about her and ran, head down, towards the cottage. Dawes and Holder suggested calling in the few shops on Beach Road to talk to shopkeepers. On a day like today it was unlikely they'd get much from passers-by, but shopkeepers were fixed assets when it came to regular foot traffic past the door. And Norcott had to have been in their vicinity on his way to the train station.

Inside the cottage, they were still searching. Tyvek-clad CSI had taken over the lounge where King was found but they'd cleared the tiny kitchen. Khosa's phone rang and she stepped back out to take the call in the hallway. In the kitchen, Anna spoke to Chris Bradley, the same CSM who'd run the initial investigation at the burial site. It was no surprise to find him there. She'd asked for him.

'Anything?'

'We have found more blood and it isn't King's. We're running a match for Beth Farlow as we speak.'

The back door opened and another man entered, shrugging off a heavy jacket soaked from the rain. He hung it over the sink and blew into his hands. Jerry Lambton was the duty POLSA and Anna had never seen him look so unhappy.

'You know they've shut both bridges,' he said by way of introduction.

Anna didn't but was well aware of its significance. Highways England often shut the old Severn Bridge to high-sided vehicles when the weather got rough, but she couldn't remember the last time the Second Severn Crossing had been closed as well.

'To all traffic?' Bradley asked.

Lambton nodded and wiped rain from his face. 'It's crap out there. Visibility is terrible. The wind drives the rain like needles into your face. And there's a high risk of falling trees. My people don't want to stop, but I'm giving it another hour maximum. If it stays like this, I'm calling it off.'

Anna didn't protest. She knew the searchers needed no motivation to do their job, and any whining from her would just seem churlish.

Someone called to Bradley and he turned away to speak.

'They've seen no sign of any kind of occupation in the woods?' Anna asked Lambton.

The POLSA shook his head. 'Anything not bolted down has been ripped to shreds in this wind. There's a denser copse to the east. My guess is stuff'll get piled up there for inspection when this thing finally dies out.'

Anna stared at him.

Lambton sighed. 'You don't need to say it. I know. Sod's effing law.'

Bradley came back to her elbow. 'That was Ryegrove. They have Farlow's blood type on record.'

'And?'

'The samples we found in the lounge aren't King's or Farlow's.'

'What?'

Bradley nodded. 'We're trying to get them to dig into Norcott's file now.'

'Why would it be Norcott's blood?'

Bradley shrugged. 'I don't know.'

Anna blew out air. Something clattered over the roof outside. Two seconds later the sound of smashing stone met their ears. 'Another tile,' Bradley said. 'They've been coming off all morning in dribs and drabs.'

'They said there might be some structural damage.' Lambton turned and reached for his coat. He pulled his sleeve up to look at his watch. 'We were hoping to keep going until dark, but I can't see it happening. I'll keep them at it as long as I can but, like I say, I give it an hour tops.'

'Thanks,' Anna said.

Khosa joined Anna in the kitchen. 'Justin sent me a video, ma'am. They're standing just off the high street looking towards the beach.' She held out the phone and played the footage. The noise was a clattering mix of flapping clothes and howling wind. But the film showed waves crashing over a wall and cascading down an access road. Two cars parked on that road had seawater covering their bumpers.

'He says they're trying to speak to people but most of the shopkeepers are too busy piling up sandbags to care.'

'Shit,' said Anna. 'Shit, shit, shit.'

An hour crawled by. Then another. Anna shadowed Bradley, letting him show her where they'd found the extra blood next to the sofa, not far from where King was lying when they found him.

'Maybe Farlow panicked when she saw what happened to King. Maybe she and Norcott fought.'

Anna nodded. But it did not sit comfortably with her.

When confirmation came through that the blood was indeed the same type as Norcott's, Anna grabbed her coat and walked outside into the small garden behind the cottage, much to Khosa's alarm.

'Stay here,' Anna ordered. 'Get the others back here. See if they can pick up something for us to eat. I'm just going across the road.'

Anna opened the door and stepped out into the tempest, buttoning her coat, feeling her trouser leg cling wetly to the flesh of her shin in an instant. An umbrella was out of the question. She pulled up an ineffective collar and walked around the corner into the full force of the wind. It almost knocked her backwards. Leaning into it, she stepped out into the lane, her foot splashing in two inches of water. Further along, where the lane ended, towards the estuary side, the water was deeper already. Thankfully, Bradley had already moved King's car back to HQ for further testing.

Anna crossed over to the edge of the open land, bushes and naked branches doing a mad dance as the chaotic wind tried its best to rip them out at the roots. It was impossible to hear anyone speak, almost impossible to think, but think she did as she rocked back and forth, trying to keep her balance, staring off into the undergrowth.

They were assuming that Norcott had come out of this wilderness. Had hidden and probably watched Beth come and go. But something was bothering her. It was February. The frosts had come and gone, and this storm was a wet monster clattering in from the Atlantic. Horrible, but not freezing. Not like the Beast from the East. Nevertheless, camping out at this time of year was asking for trouble. She thought back to Dawes' report of the smallholding in Wales. Norcott had set up in a barn. He liked structures, four walls.

She'd told Lambton this and they'd noted a couple of abandoned buildings, one an old pumping station, and gone there first to search. But they'd found nothing bar some empty cans and a few condoms. Anna couldn't quite imagine settling down for a night of passion in a damp and dirty building, but then she wasn't sixteen and half out of her head on cannabis and cider.

She was still standing there when Holder drove up and parked. He and Dawes got out, waved a plastic bag at her and hurried into the cottage. Anna, wind-assisted, followed them in. The Forensics team was busy packing up.

'Finished?' she asked Bradley.

'Not quite, but we've been told to get out, ma'am. They've already evacuated a couple of campsites near the beach. Though why the hell anyone would want to be here in a caravan in February astounds me. Anyway, we need to get out and I suggest you do too.'

As if on cue, the door swung open and Lambton appeared, looking like he'd just stepped off a trawler in the North Sea. 'That's it, I'm afraid. We're bailing. See what it's like tomorrow. We've already had a couple of narrow escapes from falling branches and I can't risk it.'

He stood, seeking approval. Anna nodded, feeling frustrated and empty.

'Have you eaten?'

Lambton shook his head. Dawes put a selection of sandwiches, some crisps and four bottles of water on the kitchen table. Lambton ran the tap and washed some mugs. They ate and watched the cottage empty around them until, finally, they were the only five left. Anna filled Dawes and Holder in on the blood sample testing, and in return, Dawes told her about their canvassing.

'One newsagent says he remembered seeing someone who could have been Norcott. The streets were pretty dead, that's why he remembers – it was New Year's Day.'

'But he didn't see where he came from?'

'No.' Dawes bit down on a cheese and tomato sandwich. 'Just this shape going past the window in a hundred layers of clothes.'

'I really hope he isn't out there with her,' Khosa said. 'Not in this.'

Holder said, 'You'd think a storm like this might flush anyone out.'

Dawes sent his mouthful of sandwich down with a swig of water and pushed himself off the sink, where he'd been leaning, swivelled and looked out of the window. 'It's gone half three and the light is beginning to fade already. I don't know about you, but I don't fancy being stuck here all night. Mrs Dawes might have something to say about that as it's my turn to take Lucy to football. It'll be indoors tonight, though it's more likely to be water polo by the looks of it. And there was a lot of water on Beach Road as we drove out, so I don't think we should hang about, ma'am.'

'You're right,' Anna said. And he was. There was no point loitering. Whatever secrets this cottage harboured would remain hidden unless the crime lab could tease something out of their samples. But someone in the town had seen Norcott and she couldn't let it lie. She turned to Lambton. 'What sort of car have you got?'

'Long wheelbase Land Rover.'

She looked at the others. 'You three take the cars back to HQ. Stay away from the beach. Sergeant Lambton can run me back into the village. I'd like a word with your shopkeeper. Which one was it?'

Holder said, 'McCreedie's, the mini-market.'

Dawes gave Holder his keys. 'There you go, Justin.'

Holder frowned. 'Aren't you coming, Sarge?'

'Nah. I'd like another word with the newsagent myself.'

'What about Lucy's football?'

'It's called off.'

'But you said—'

Dawes cut Holder off. 'Executive decision.'

Anna shook her head. 'There's no need to chaperone me, Phil.'

Dawes ignored her. 'Go on, you two, off you go.'

Khosa and Holder left. Dawes finished off the crisps while Lambton put on his coat.

'Thanks,' Anna said softly.

'It's a bugger of an afternoon to be out alone, ma'am.'

The Land Rover smelled of oil and wet clothes. Lambton drove, and at first the road took them away from the beach, but then it turned at forty-five degrees, heading back towards the river. Halfway along Beach Road, there was a foot of water. When they got to the point where the road curved closest to the estuary, Anna could see waves pluming over the sea defences and the water was up to the bonnet.

'Well over three feet, I reckon,' Lambton said.

'It'll cope, will it?' Dawes asked.

The look Lambton sent him was answer enough. 'If it gets any deeper, you better lift your feet. It'll let water in, but then, when we're on drier land, just open the doors and it'll drain away.

Dawes sent Anna a look of great disgust. It made her smile.

Ahead of them, a fire engine was clearly visible where houses began in a strip between the street and the sea. A fireman in full regalia was waving them forward.

'Keep going,' Anna said. 'We'll plead ignorance.'

Anna watched the sea furiously battering the defences to her right as they drove. To their left, some people outside their red-brick houses were staring nervously up at the grey water spewing up over the walls. They'd piled sandbags against their front doors, where dirty brown water was lapping. The light was fading badly now. The water looked thick and silted. Scummy foam danced on the surface near the low wall of a little park nearby. They neared the junction with Beach Avenue branching east. Anna looked left. The further back up the avenue she looked, the less water there was, but ahead, on Beach Road, the main street leading to the railway station, the houses between road and estuary were under four feet of river. Immediately on her right, a lane ran off to some steps up to the sea wall. Only the top half of a bus stop showed above the lapping water, and a sorry-looking cluster of buildings surrounded by chain-link fencing that had once been Severn Beach's amusement arcade was now a repository for flotsam. More of the foam she'd noticed earlier had coagulated against the fence. Lapping waves shifted it up and down, lathering it against the wire. And then they were past, and Dawes was pointing towards the blue and yellow McCreedie's sign.

'There it is, ma'am.'

Anna didn't answer.

'Ma'am?' Dawes said, noting the thousand-yard stare consuming the inspector. 'Ma'am, are you all right?'

'Back up,' Anna said to Lambton.

'What?'

'Back up. Back up to the bus stop!'

Lambton threw the car into gear and began to reverse, sending a wave of water up the road. Anna, in the back seat, craned her neck, staring out into the pelting rain and the afternoon gloom. Lambton stopped ten yards from the stop.

'There,' Anna said. 'Up against the fence. Can you see them?'

'See what?' Dawes peered across Lambton's chest to where Anna was pointing. 'All I can see is floating rubbish.'

'Reverse up the avenue,' she said. 'Where there's less water.'

Lambton turned in his seat and manoeuvred the four-by-four up Beach Avenue, slowly at first and then, as the water shallowed, gathering speed. When it was a foot deep, he stopped. 'This OK for you?'

But Anna didn't answer. She opened the door and, shoes off, stepped out into the cold and wet storm.

'Ma'am?' Dawes said with more than a bit of impatient incredulity in his voice.

'I need to see it close up. Stay here.'

Ten steps and a foot deeper in, Anna heard the passenger door of the Land Rover open and turned to see Dawes exiting, powerful pencil torch in hand.

'Don't say anything,' he said, shouting over the wind as they waded towards the bus stop.

There were people in the street behind them, staring, wondering, Anna had no doubt, just what the hell these two mad coppers were doing. She could feel the road under her feet, feel the water's winter cold sucking heat from the skin inside her trousers. By the time they reached the submerged bus stop, the water was up to her waist.

'Three and a half feet, I reckon,' Dawes said. Or rather screeched over the howling wind.

But Anna didn't stop to acknowledge him. She kept walking and almost stumbled against something solid. A kerb in all probability. She would have fallen if it hadn't been for Dawes' clutching hand on her forearm. As it was, the lunge she took let the water up to her chest and the wind turned it instantly into a clammy hand over her heart.

'I bloody well hope this is going to be worth it, ma'am,' Dawes yelled.

Anna grabbed the torch. The chain-link fence was just yards away and she waded towards it. The white flotsam bobbed and danced in the grey foam. She put her fingers through, trying to catch some of it. It took three attempts before she managed to pull something through with fingers that didn't want to cooperate and held it up in the fading light. It flapped and jerked in the bitter wind until she put her hand behind it, letting the gale flatten it against her shaky palm, steadying herself with a broad stance. She flicked on the torch and lit up the flimsy scrap.

'Jesus,' Dawes said. Not loud, but with such feeling that Anna heard him clearly.

In her palm, wet and mangled though it was, sat one of Norcott's golems.

CHAPTER FIFTY-ONE

Anna turned back to the foam, eyes squinting through the gloom and the wind and the driven rain. Now that she looked, there were more of the golems, some half submerged, more bobbing up against the chain link. Dozens of them. Shivering, she looked through the gaps in the chain link at the buildings beyond. A concrete shed with a corrugated shutter for a door sat squarely in the middle of the small compound. Above it, rattling in the wind, a rainbow sign in a childish font read 'Amusements'. Next to it a white painted burger stand. Solid-looking, made of metal. Everything looked sealed up and nailed down, and the fence stretching above them had been topped with barbed wire.

'We need to get in there.' Anna started wading around the edge of the fencing.

'Ma'am!' yelled Dawes. 'We need equipment.'

Anna turned back. 'Look at the water, Phil. There isn't time.'

Dawes nodded, though it could simply have been his head shaking from the cold. It was very gloomy now; what little light was left in the day seemed to be getting sucked out of it by the battering wind. They edged their way along, behind the bus shelter to where the fence took a right angle to run back towards the sea wall. Anna's knee banged against something solid. A wall. Concrete by the feel of it, but not tall, two feet at the most. She climbed up and held on to the fence. Inching her way along, her fingers grasping the chain link for balance, she peered in at the decrepit buildings. The concrete shed beneath the 'Amusements' sign sat in the middle of the compound but next to it, nearest to her, was another low building. Some sort of windowless storage facility made of the same white painted metal as the burger bar. Between it and the amusement arcade was a narrow space. In this space, something moved; flapping and clattering.

'There.' Anna pointed and shone the torch into the gap. The beam picked up the cut edge of a corrugated metal sheet snapping in the wind.

'Is that a window?' Dawes asked.

'Maybe,' Anna said. She inched along another foot until she was in the middle of a span of fence between two supporting posts. Here the fence sagged a little. She gripped the top edge beneath the barbed wire and yanked it down. The metal bent. Dawes saw what she was doing and lent his weight. The metal bent a lot more, leaving a fish mouth gap of three feet between chain link and barbed wire.

Standing on the wall, the water was only thigh-deep. With difficulty, Anna managed to get a knee on the edge of the fence. Dawes had his hand above, holding the barbed wire up as far as he could. There was only one way for Anna to breach the gap they'd made and that was by putting both knees across the metal, swivelling precariously and trying to pivot to face the other way. The fence with Anna's weight upon it wobbled madly, but she used Dawes as her solid prop and managed to drop down into the compound. The water splashed up over her chest and Anna caught her breath, bobbing on her toes and sucking in air.

'You all right?' Dawes yelled.

'Fine,' Anna lied.

She turned and pushed towards the shed. It was obvious someone had pulled the sheet away from the wooden frame of a small window and left it loose to be buffeted by the wind. Something splashed in the water behind her. She looked back to see Dawes floundering. He'd landed almost up to his neck, but he righted himself and waved her on.

Bloody idiot, she thought. *Bloody wonderful, loyal bloody idiot.*

Then she was at the window, pulling back the metal with one hand to peer in. Another layer obscured her view. Something soft and sopping barred the way. Someone had nailed up a sleeping bag as insulation. She ripped it out and shone in the torch. The beam bounced across graffiti-strewn walls and a layer of murky water. Things floated and bobbed. Food cartons, cans, plastic milk containers. But at the far wall something was not floating. Something pale that made Anna's breath catch in her throat and made her heart stutter.

The pale thing was unmoving. A featureless face above the water, tilted forward, glistening strangely, its chin covered by the brown river.

Beth Farlow.

CHAPTER FIFTY-TWO

Anna screamed back at Dawes.

'She's here!' She turned back and yelled into the room. 'Beth! Beth!'

No movement. No acknowledgement. Anna looked at the window. It wasn't big. A two-foot square. Too small for Dawes, but not for her.

'I need a leg-up,' Anna said when Dawes was next to her. 'Keep this bloody flap open.'

Dawes leaned against it.

She turned, stepped on Dawes' knee, reached up and grabbed for the roof of the adjacent storage shed, hiked herself up and reached back with her foot until her shin slid backwards over the rim of the window and down into the dark wet interior of the amusement arcade. Dawes handed her the torch and Anna waded across. There were things in the water. Some solid, some softer. Some that didn't move when she touched them. She dared not think what they might be. She was shivering from cold and filled with terrifying disgust at the dark and the squalor of this terrible place.

'Beth,' she called out. 'Beth.'

The taped-up head was just above the water. The torch beam picked out silver duct tape across her mouth and her nose and her eyes. Anna reached for the skin at her throat.

'Be there. Be there,' she muttered, and her trembling wet fingers searched for a pulse.

She pressed and then pressed again. She felt nothing, but then, the face moved slightly and, astonishingly, Beth moaned.

Anna stared wildly at the tape. Someone had tried to cover her face, smother it. But there was a section, just over the corner of her mouth, that was not covered. A half-inch slit through which, somehow, Beth had managed to breathe.

'She's alive!' Anna screamed towards Dawes. She ripped at the tape to make the slit bigger and then felt for the chair under the dark water and the tape strapping Beth to it. She started to drag the chair back towards the window. As she moved she made waves, and on those waves bobbed Norcott's golems. Hundreds of them, dancing and weaving in the room.

'Phil!' Anna shouted. 'We need to get her out now.'

There was no reply. Dawes wasn't there.

'Phil? Where the hell are you?' She heard the little girl in her own voice. Pleading, terrified. 'Phil!'

Light filled the dark space of the window. Two new faces. Lambton's, she knew. The other she didn't. But it had a big yellow fireman's helmet above it and she had never felt so pleased in all her life to see that iconic shape.

'Can she stand?' the fireman asked.

'She's on a chair. Tied… or maybe taped,' Anna replied, her voice stuttering from the cold.

'Right,' the fireman said. 'I'll reach in and lift her up; you'll have to cut the ties from your side.'

'I'll try,' she said, teeth chattering.

'I'm not going to be able to put my head through, just my arms.' He handed through a knife. 'Wrap the wrist strap around your arm. You need to lift the chair and I'll grab the back and hoist it.'

The water helped, providing a degree of welcome buoyancy. But the higher she lifted, the heavier Beth got. She could feel her muscles shaking, the cold sapping her energy. The fireman's fingers were scrabbling for purchase but then his elbows flexed and the chair came up as forearms were levered against the window frame in an exaggerated bicep curl. Anna grabbed the knife.

There was no cord to cut. Only tape. Despite Anna's numb and trembling fingers, the black blade sliced through it with slick ease.

'I've got her,' the fireman said, lifting the body. 'I've got her.'

The chair splashed into the water and the fireman pulled Beth out through the gap, leaving Anna alone in the arcade. Lambton's face appeared. 'Ambulance is here. Just reach through, ma'am. We'll pull you out.'

Hands plucked her out of the water, up through the window and out into the compound. It wasn't dark there anymore. The fire engine had pulled up and its headlights and Lambton's search-lights lit up the sorry little square. There were blue lights flashing everywhere. She turned towards the bowed metal where they'd scrambled through, but Dawes and Lambton pulled her back and pointed straight ahead.

The fire brigade had cut a hole in the fence behind the bus stop. No need for any more climbing. Just as well because she didn't think she could manage it. Energy seemed to be leeching from her. She didn't even argue when someone put an arm round her waist as she stumbled and splashed out through the rising tide.

CHAPTER FIFTY-THREE

Lambton helped her into the Land Rover. It felt wonderful to be out of the screaming wind.

Dawes got into the passenger seat. He looked grey, his eyes sunken, his lips purple. He was soaked.

'You look terrible,' she said, though her bottom jaw had given up working properly.

'I wouldn't recommend a selfie just at this moment either, ma'am.'

Anna tried to smile but her facial muscles seemed to be made of cardboard all of a sudden. 'Thanks for... for coming with me.'

The driver's door opened and Lambton got in. He nodded towards an ambulance further up the road. 'She's barely conscious. They're taking her to Southmead.'

'We... should go... too,' Anna said, trembling with each forced word.

'No,' Lambton said. 'Your DC, Holder, is going there. We're going straight to HQ. We're all hypothermic. You two need to get out of your clothes now. I've got towels and blankets in the back.'

Anna's hands were shaking badly as she peeled off her clothes. She felt lethargic and desperately tired. Lambton kept up a stream of talk from the front. 'She's been in the water for a long time but if she was responding to your voice, that's good. Very good. They'll probably stick her on cardiopulmonary bypass and warm her blood like central heating. Slow and steady. Safest way, by all accounts.'

Anna was only half listening. She had a blanket over her shoulders, now down to her bra and taking off her trousers. She kicked them off and rubbed a towel over her skin with fumbling hands before wrapping another two blankets around herself. Warm air from the heaters was pumping in, but still she shivered and kept on shivering until they arrived at HQ, blue lights flashing.

Lambton drove them around to the sports hall. Khosa met them and took Anna to the female changing room. It was warm and dry and Khosa plied her with hot tea. Half an hour later, a quarter of an hour after she'd stopped shivering and the tingling had all gone from her toes and fingers, Anna took a shower, trying not to think about Beth Farlow strapped to a chair, feeling the cold muddy waters of the Bristol Channel rise all around her, waiting for a slow and inevitable death. But her insides churned at the thought. Gradually, as she dried herself, horror turned to a simmering anger. Someone taped Beth Farlow to that chair and left her there.

Norcott, ill though he may have been, had a lot to answer for.

Khosa lent Anna some joggers, a hoodie and trainers and, an hour after leaving the flooded amusement arcade, the two women plus Dawes sat in the MCRTF office drinking more tea. Rainsford was away in Cardiff at a meeting and decided to stay the night rather than risk the long journey up and around through Gloucester – the only way back to Bristol now both Severn Crossings were closed. All the other staff had long gone home to batten down the hatches. Dawes spoke to his wife and then Khosa got Holder on speakerphone from the hospital at Southmead.

'Is there any point us coming over there, Justin?' Khosa asked.

'Not really. They've got her in intensive care on a bypass machine. She had a Glasgow coma score of eight. They tell me that's pretty bad. But her heart was still OK, which they said was amazing.'

Lambton had hung around until he was sure Dawes and Anna were OK. He'd explained to them how sometimes severe hypothermia could send victims into heart failure.

'They're not letting us anywhere near, ma'am,' Holder said. 'We're going to leave a uniform here overnight.'

'Thanks, Justin. No point you hanging around either. Go home.'

'How about you, ma'am?'

'Yes, me too. Our priority will be to find Norcott, but no one can do anything in this weather. It's meant to blow over by the early hours. We'll pick up where we left off tomorrow morning.'

'The docs said another hour and she'd have probably died from cardiac arrest if she hadn't drowned,' Holder said. 'You made a good call, ma'am.'

'I'll drink to that, Justin.' Dawes raised his second mug of tea. 'Now let's all try to head home.'

Later, Anna sat on the floor of her living room with Lexi next to her, amazed that it was still only ten, nursing a glass of wine and listening to one of her dad's old vinyls. When Ben turned up, he smelled of antiseptic from having washed his hands a hundred times. It was a clean, good smell. She wrapped her arms around him, buried her head into his shoulder and just let him hold her.

'Want to talk about it?'

'Not now,' she murmured into his neck. 'Maybe never.' She moved his hands to the bare skin under the too large hoodie Khosa'd sourced for her. His touch was smooth, his hands soft, thumbs sliding over her ribcage to her breasts easily. She turned her head to look up at him. 'Thanks for being here.'

'This is no hardship, Anna.'

She pushed away and pulled off the hoodie, used a thumb to slide down the baggy jogging bottoms. She had no idea why she wanted to do this, but suddenly it felt like shedding the day's horrors. Ben looked at her, bemused but not displeased. She came back to him as naked as the day she came into the world and pressed herself against him, wanting to forget the cold caress of the dirty water and only feel his good clean hands upon her. She didn't question it. The irony of Anna Gwynne – who usually needed no one and nothing – needing Ben Hawley more than anything she'd ever needed before.

'We'll talk tomorrow,' she said. It emerged as a croak.

The bedroom was warm. An hour later, when they'd finished, Anna let Ben spoon her into sleep, both of them tired from their day's work and their evening activities.

They slept well.

But it was Beth Farlow Anna first thought of when she awoke the next morning, her mind struggling to imagine the horror she'd been through, the terrible hours of freezing loneliness as the waters rose and the storm raged. How on earth had she managed to breathe through that tiny slit in the tape? It was so far beyond normal human experience that Anna's imagination simply gave up. Which was something Beth Farlow had not done. And with that realisation Anna came fully awake, buoyed by a new and steely determination.

Beth had survived against all the odds. Trussed up and left for dead by some monster.

Now that monster needed to be brought to book.

CHAPTER FIFTY-FOUR

FRIDAY

She was making coffee when her work phone buzzed. She took the call in a half-whisper, her voice still croaky from sleep.

'Justin, what's up?'

'It's the hospital, ma'am. I left them my number. Beth Farlow is awake and asking for you.'

Anna left Ben in charge of Lexi. He was on a late shift, beginning at ten that morning and finishing at eight. Then he'd be off over the weekend. They were both looking forward to it.

Anna showered and dressed in record time and was out of the door fifteen minutes after Holder's call.

She met him in Southmead's swish new reception area that was more like an airport than a hospital. Holder was sitting on one of the green-and-black upholstered seats in front of the Costa outlet. He held out a cup.

'Cappuccino.'

'Justin, you are a gem.' Anna gulped the coffee down as they walked.

'She's still in ICU, but off the bypass machine.'

Having never been to the ICU, Anna followed Holder, who explained, 'It's a maze here. She's in pod B, bed 15.'

Anna sent him a look.

'I know. It's big. Forty-six beds.'

They were individual rooms, too, with floor to ceiling glass walls on the corridors. Through the open blinds, Beth Farlow looked like a lost child in the middle of the big bed and the banks of equipment. One of the nursing sisters escorted them from reception and spoke to them cheerfully.

'She's doing brilliantly. Core temp is back up to normal but we're giving her some IV antibiotics because she'd cut her leg and floodwater isn't the cleanest.'

Anna could have said she knew that. But she kept quiet and walked in with Holder behind her, the nurse hovering in the doorway. Beth's eyebrows went up and her mouth crumpled with emotion. She reached a hand out and Anna took it, only to be pulled into an awkward hug by the girl on the bed.

'I heard it was you who found me,' Beth whispered. 'Thank you.'

Anna didn't say anything. Returning the hug, she guessed, was enough. She pulled back to see Beth's mouth trembling. 'Have you got him?'

'Norcott? No not—'

'Colin? Where is Colin?'

Anna searched Beth's face. Norcott's name had triggered confused concern. Not the sort of reaction you'd expect from mentioning a kidnapper and torturer. She'd used his first name twice. Victims, especially those involved in violent crimes, hardly ever used their attacker's first name. Alarms were going off in Anna's head.

'Where is Colin?' Beth asked again, the words broken, her voice high.

Anna grabbed her hand again and squeezed it. 'Beth, I need you to tell me exactly what happened, OK? Can you do that?'

Beth looked terrified, gasping short little breaths. Finally, she nodded and squeezed her eyes shut. Anna handed her a tissue. Beth took it in the hand not taped up to an IV line and dabbed her face. After several more gasps, she finally spoke. 'Colin came to the cottage. There was a draught, it woke me up. The back door was open and he'd walked in. I nearly died of fright there and then, but there he was, talking normally. I was never scared of him when he was on the unit. I knew they'd kept him there far too long because of his refusal to talk. He'd told me he'd been watching me. Waiting for…' She inhaled a stuttering sob.

'Waiting for what, Beth?'

'For the right time to speak.' She buried her face in a tissue.

Anna waited. Beth was still in shock. The words she was speaking were disjointed, fragments of a bigger story. Eventually she continued in a low whisper, still staring at the tissue held an inch from her face. 'All this time he'd been hiding in the abandoned amusement arcade just so he could watch me. He'd travel into the city. Walk up to the Downs, across the open common, where he could look across the estuary towards the opposite bank. To the railway line on the edge of Leigh Woods. Waiting for someone to find out.'

'Find what out?'

Beth seemed lost in reflection. 'I can just imagine him on the train. People staring, avoiding him and his weird clothes and funny haircut. They'd assume he smelled, but he didn't. He was always clean. He told me he got fresh clothes every week from a Sally Army drop-in at Easton or the Methodist centre at Lawrence Hill. He wasn't a danger to anyone.'

'What was he waiting for someone to find, Beth?' Anna said, more forcefully now.

Beth's head snapped around. 'The bodies. He knew about the bodies.'

'Exactly what did he tell you?'

Beth's eyes searched Anna's, as if she was looking for something solid to focus on. 'He told me what he saw. All those years ago when they were building the new unit. He liked to go out into the garden alone. In those days there was no lockdown – there'd be communal TV and games rooms. But he found a way to go out into the gardens when everyone else was busy. He liked doing that, liked being alone. One evening, it must have been summer, he saw people at the fence. Four people. One of them disappeared into the woods and then came up on the outside of the fence and walked away. He knew it was wrong, so he hid and watched. The other three stood at the fence and looked out towards the railway line. The man that left met with someone else. Colin couldn't see the detail clearly from where he was hiding, but whoever was at the railway looked small. Younger. And he was pleading. But Colin said his hands were tied. Then the man took him into the bushes and the others watched a train come. Colin didn't know what happened after that, but the man came back up to the fence afterwards and that was when Colin ran away. That was when he called for Alison, the nurse he trusted most. She came to see him, and he told her. She made him promise not to say anything until she talked to someone about it. It was the last time he ever saw her. But he kept his promise.'

'Was that when he stopped talking?'

Beth nodded.

'Norcott drew a sketch of those people at the fence. Who were they, Beth?'

'He only knew two of them. One, a girl he called Miranda. But the other…' Beth's hand came up to her face once more to stifle another sob. 'The other one was Dr King.'

Anna's insides seemed to fall through the chair she was on. 'King?'

Beth was shaking her head. 'Colin had only just stopped telling me all of this when the doorbell rang. I didn't know who it was. I thought it might have been you.' Her voice became airy and hopeless. 'I opened the door. It was Dr King. He must have been watching the cottage because as soon as he saw my face, he knew. He must have known. He pushed me over and just barged in. He hit Colin. Hit him and then injected him in the leg.'

'What with?'

'I don't know. But if I had to guess, I'd say haloperidol. It's what we'd use to calm an aggressive patient. I tried to stop him but…' She shook her head again. 'He made Colin tell him what he'd told me and more. Where he'd been hiding. Who he'd spoken to.' She stopped, her mouth widening in a grimace as she fought back the tears again.

Anna turned to Holder, who was staring at Beth in astonished horror. She spoke in a low, commanding voice. 'Ring Sergeant Dawes and then both of you get over to King's place now.'

Holder nodded and left the room.

Beth dropped her head down, sobbing again.

Anna pressed her. 'What happened then, Beth? It's important I know.'

Beth looked up, her eyes ragged and raw. 'Dr King tied us up. Colin was… he was bleeding but unconscious. Dr King wrapped him up in bin bags and put him in the boot of his car. Then he taped me up and put me in the back seat and waited until it was really late. He parked at the back of the amusement arcade. It's February. There's never anyone around. He'd tied me up and put tape over my mouth. Colin was out of it, wrapped up in those plastic bags. Then Dr King took me to into the arcade. Colin had been living there. Dr King made him tell and took his keys. There was a padlocked back door…' Beth faltered, her head down. It took three deep breaths before she could continue. 'Then he brought Colin in. He had another syringe. I watched him inject Colin in the foot and then in the leg. Lots of times. He left Colin on the floor and wrapped tape around my head. I couldn't breathe. I thought I'd choke. He just left us. And then… then the storm came.' Beth finally lost it. Hung her head and sobbed.

The nurse came into the room, sat on the bed next to Beth and put her arm around her, looking at Anna accusingly. 'I think you ought to stop now.'

But Anna barely registered what the nurse said. She was sucking in air slowly, raggedly, listening to it, not looking at the bed anymore but at a piece of equipment on the wall, fighting to stay in control of herself as she remembered the cold, wet tomb she'd waded through the previous evening and the large, solid object she'd had to push away with her feet to get to Beth.

'Inspector?'

Anna looked at the nurse and nodded.

Then she was up on her feet and hurrying out, pulling her phone from her coat pocket and dialling Khosa's number. When the DC answered, Anna didn't bother to return the cheery greeting or answer the query as to her well-being. 'I want the Underwater Search Unit to Severn Beach now. Tell them they're to search the flooded amusement arcade and tell them they're looking for a body.'

'Do we know whose, ma'am?'

'Yes. Colin Norcott's.'

CHAPTER FIFTY-FIVE

It was a twenty-minute drive from Southmead to Portishead along the M5 and Anna negotiated it with her mind fizzing and her face hot. She hated being lied to. And King had lied to her. Worse, he'd seen how interested they'd been in Beth and used what she'd told him to his advantage. Left her trussed up in a dingy prison to die frightened and alone.

Anger threatened to overwhelm her. She recognised it for what it was and knew she needed to be careful. Anger was sometimes necessary. But, like any weapon, it needed to be aimed and used with skill.

Dawes rang when she was halfway to HQ.

'We've missed him, ma'am. He's buggered off.'

Anna slammed her palm against the wheel. 'Shit.'

'I know. We'll get the place properly searched but my guess is he's flown.'

'Justin's told you what Beth said?'

'Most of it.'

'How could we have let this bastard slip through our fingers?'

'Norcott knew all along—'

'No, we can't blame Norcott for this. I've read his files. King was on his case, literally, for years. I think he deliberately kept Norcott at Ryegrove, trod on any hope he had of release by cooking up damning psychiatric reports. He had power over Norcott until he got shifted to a different section where he couldn't have so much influence. We can't blame Norcott for being scared of King.' Anna heard the disgust spilling out of cracks in her speech. Dawes could hear it too.

'You OK, ma'am?'

'No, I am bloody well not. You and Justin get over to HQ and we'll go over everything we've got.' Dawes ended the call before she could add, 'And everything we sodding missed.'

Trisha and Khosa were already in the office when Anna arrived. They both sent her encouraging little smiles, but they were not what she needed this morning. She didn't need sympathy. She needed them to be on top of their game.

'Before either of you ask, I'm fine. Justin and Phil are on the way in and we'll go through everything that's happened then. In the meantime, I have to speak to the POLSA. Trisha, have you heard anything from Superintendent Rainsford?'

'Both bridges are open this morning and he's on the way back from Cardiff but snarled up on the motorway after an earlier accident.'

Anna nodded. She caught Khosa's eye. 'I've got your joggers in the wash. Get them back to you in a day or two.'

'No need, ma'am.'

'Thanks for last night.'

Khosa shook her head.

In her office, Anna rang Lambton's number. The extraneous noise on the call told her he was outside.

'Good to hear your voice, Inspector.'

'How's it going?'

'Slow. We have a lot of branches and trees down. It's making the going tough.'

'You got my message about the amusement arcade?'

'The Underwater Search Unit? They're on it. They've been inundated, as you can imagine, and were out until midnight but should be with us by ten.'

'Is there still a lot of water?'

'I drove through this morning. It's a mess but there's less than there was. Probably no more than three feet around the building you were in last night.'

Three feet sounded deep enough.

'OK. I'm aiming to get over there at some point.'

'I'll let USU know. You OK, ma'am?'

There it was again. The sympathetic concern that irritated her so. A little spurt of anger threatened to spike her response, but she bit it back. Lambton had driven her and Dawes to HQ last night in record time. 'Yes, I am. And thanks for your help.'

'It's me who should be thanking you for finding that nurse. If we'd have missed her, I would not have been able to live with myself.'

Anna ended the call, turned to her computer and began writing up her report on last night. Beth would need to be reinterviewed but since what would follow today was a consequence of what she'd learned at the side of Beth's hospital bed, she needed to put on record her observation of her state of mind as well as the words she'd spoken. It all needed to be put into HOLMES and, in her experience, there was no time like the present. She opened the recording app on her phone and typed as she listened back.

She kept on writing exactly what Beth Farlow had told her until movement in the outer office announced Dawes and Holder's return. Anna joined them and exchanged a nod with Dawes, who reciprocated. No need for words. They'd shared the experience and that was enough. Tea was rustled up and a little banter about how much damage the storm had actually caused rippled around the room, but Anna didn't let it run on. She called for everyone's attention, skipping over the previous evening, knowing that everyone in this room, like everyone in the whole building, knew exactly what had happened. They were part of it. But they hadn't heard Beth Farlow's statement. Not all of it. And so, Anna laid it all out.

'If Norcott is to be believed, then it's likely King, the Dorell siblings and Krastev were in this together. They were the figures in Norcott's sketch.'

'By this, what do you mean exactly?' Dawes said.

'I mean the Black Squid deaths. My guess is Norcott witnessed something and, from what Beth Farlow told me, it wasn't exactly a suicide. Norcott said the victim on those railway tracks – and we can assume this is Jamie Carson – was not a willing participant.'

'If he was dragged out and chucked under a train then it sounds more like a bloody sacrifice,' Dawes said.

Anna nodded. Trisha's face was white. Khosa and Holder both looked like something had died under their desks. 'My own feeling is that Jamie, and the others like him, were coerced into going to their suicide spot, but once there Krastev made absolutely sure they carried out the final act.'

'Then it's not suicide. It's murder,' Khosa said.

Anna nodded. 'Kimberley Williams jumped, we know that. In her case it must have been coercion. The act confirmed by social media. So the modus has changed. But at the beginning Krastev was the facilitator. He was there to make sure the victims did what they were supposed to do. In both Carson's case and, I suspect, Abbie Shaw's.'

'Jesus.' Holder let his head drop.

'It would be good to talk to Norcott,' Khosa said.

Anna nodded. This was the one part of Beth's story she hadn't told them. But they deserved to know. 'I doubt that's going to be possible. The Underwater Search Unit is back in the amusement arcade. Beth said King left Norcott trussed up on the floor there. And while I was wading through it… I felt something on the floor. Something heavy that I couldn't move. We'll know for definite within a couple of hours, I expect.'

They all looked at her. No one said anything. Trisha excused herself. It wasn't the first time the civilian analyst had done so. Anna suspected it would not be the last.

'I'd like to be alone with King for ten minutes when we find the bastard,' Dawes said thickly.

Join the queue, Anna thought. *It'll be a long one with me at the front.*

'Finding him is our top priority,' she said instead.

'We've got a search team and Forensics at his place now, ma'am. I've asked them to check for a passport. But I've already alerted the Border Agency. Question is, do we go to the press?'

'I need to talk to Superintendent Rainsford about that,' Anna said. 'But let's involve transport police, too. Get them some images of King.'

Holder said, 'Do you think he'll run or hide?'

'God knows,' Dawes said.

'But it still leaves us with the Dorells.' Anna stared at the two figures on the screen. They were still unformed shadows in this mess and she had no clear picture of their role.

Khosa stood up with a notepad. 'I did speak to Joshua Dorell's probation officer. The day after his licence expiry date he disappeared. The supervising officer said Dorell texted him and said he was going off the grid and added several other words which were best forgotten.'

'What do you make of it?'

'It coincides with his sister's disappearance. Joshua Dorell's PO said he was always talking about the road. Going back on the road. My guess is that they've headed back to their roots, ma'am. We've traced his bank statements. Five months ago, the day after his licence expiry date, Joshua Dorell withdrew £25,000 from his account. Since then there's been nothing.'

'If they've dived back into one of those New Age communes, we might never find them,' Dawes muttered.

He was right, but they needed to use what they had. 'OK, there's enough to do. I'm going back to Severn Beach.'

Holder said, 'Need any company, ma'am?'

'No. Stay here and find King.'

'You sure, ma'am?' Holder held her gaze.

'Very.'

She left them to it, grateful for Holder's concern and dismissing it as unnecessary. But as she came in on Green lane over the M49 again and found herself once more on Beach Avenue where she'd exited Lambton's Land Rover shoeless the night before, the memory of that cold brown water made her shiver. Much of the flooding had drained away, leaving a brown slick in its wake. As if some huge slimy serpent had slithered this way. At the junction in front of the bus stop, the water was only a couple of feet deep. Several police vehicles were parked out of the water, and Anna recognised Lambton's Land Rover immediately. She walked across, showed the duty uniform her warrant card and stood at the edge of the floodwater. Lambton was in waders next to the bus stop. He saw her and came over.

'They're in there now, ma'am,' he said.

They'd opened the shutters on the amusement arcade. Two black-rubber-suited men stood in the compound. Another two were inside the arcade on their knees, the water up to their necks. They were dragging something out. She heard shouts and someone went to fetch a black plastic sheet. The two men outside joined the two inside and manhandled something heavy out through the compound and up Beach Avenue. When it was free of the water, they covered it in the plastic, passing the point where Anna was standing, to where the water ended. There they put their burden down.

Lambton walked over and spoke to the USU men. When he came back, his face was grim.

'It's a body, ma'am. Male. Too much bloating and clothing to make out much else.'

'They'll take it to Gupta?'

'Yeah. He'll have it by midday, probably.'

It. Colin Norcott wasn't an it, and yet she could not blame Lambton for his words. They couldn't be sure until someone ID'd the body. But she had no real reason to doubt it was Norcott. And she was glad she'd come because there would be no one else to mourn him with Beth in the hospital and his mother long since dead. She felt she owed Norcott for no reason other than the fact that his life had taken the wrong fork for the sake of a barbecue and some dodgy mushrooms.

No one deserved that.

Anna nodded. She turned, got back in her car and drove away.

She'd left her work phone in the car. It had already been on silent for the visit to Beth but now she heard it buzz incessantly. She picked it up and saw five missed calls from Rainsford. She put the car in gear and called him back.

'Anna, where the hell have you been?' The question was curt, but more anxious than angry.

'Sorry, sir. I've only now seen your calls. I've just watched them take a body out of the amusement arcade at Severn Beach.'

He said nothing for a couple of seconds. 'Where are you now?'

'On the way back.'

'My office as soon as you get here.'

Rainsford's door was along the corridor from the office they shared as the MCRTF. He sat behind his tidy desk with a framed photo of his family in pride of place and a corkboard with monthly target graphs on the wall behind. 'Sergeant Dawes has filled me in. You've had a rough couple of days,' he said by way of greeting.

'Why have I got the feeling that today isn't going to get any better?'

'I don't suppose you've seen or heard the news?'

'No. We've had enough of our own.'

Rainsford nodded. 'I recorded this for you.' He pointed a remote towards the TV on his wall. *BBC Breakfast*, the news bulletin.

A familiar TV studio filled the screen. The female presenter gave the camera an earnest look. 'Police have confirmed reports that a convicted murderer has escaped from custody while being treated in an NHS hospital.'

A different image appeared. A man, balding, heavy-lidded eyes staring defiantly back at the world.

'Hector Shaw was serving an indeterminate life sentence for the murder of six people when he absconded from Worcester Royal Hospital, where he was being treated after collapsing in prison. Maggie Whitehead has the details.'

The scene shifted to a different part of the studio. A curved desk, two women. 'Thank you, Helen. With me is Detective Superintendent Jackie Peterson from Worcestershire Constabulary. Superintendent Peterson, could you tell us about this very worrying incident?'

Peterson was dressed soberly in a jacket and blouse, blonde hair to her shoulders. 'Yesterday afternoon between three thirty and four, we were contacted by prison guards who were escorting a prisoner for HMP Whitmarsh by the name of Hector Shaw. The events are that during that afternoon, Shaw was taken to a part of the hospital for an MRI Scan. He was accompanied by one of the guards and taken by a porter to the MRI suite, where he underwent the investigation. When it had finished and during the transfer back to the ward, the porter, who we now believe was known to Shaw, threatened the guard with a gun, tied him up and locked him in a storage room while Shaw escaped wearing scrubs and a white coat. We believe that he and the porter then got into a stolen vehicle, a black VW Passat, which then made its escape.'

Rainsford paused the TV. Anna kept looking at the screen for several seconds, blinking, trying to assimilate what she'd heard.

'But I was with him yesterday morning.'

Rainsford nodded.

'He looked sick. Really sick.'

Rainsford nodded again. 'I've spoken to the doctors. His anaemia, they think, was self-inflicted. He was bleeding himself. But the medics wanted to be sure by ruling out an internal source, hence the MRI. Yesterday, he waited until he had the transfusion before escaping.'

'Instant rejuvenation.' Anna nodded. *Just like a vampire,* she thought. Her brain was thumping. She hadn't thought to ask. Hadn't spoken to anyone in authority at the hospital about Shaw's illness.

'Have you any idea where he might have gone?'

Anna shook her head. 'None.' Rainsford kept looking at her, waiting for her to say something. 'What?'

'Come on, Anna, you're the obvious target.'

'Me? No way. He doesn't want to get to me, sir. He wants the people who killed his daughter.'

'She committed suicide.'

'He doesn't think so. And I'm beginning to agree with him on that one.'

'What do you mean?'

Anna was acutely aware of how keen Rainsford had been to point the team in the direction of the broader scope of the Black Squid suicides. Dawes had kept reminding her of that. But the picture was only now becoming clearer with the Dorells in the frame. Time to update him on what they had so far, even if it was still all conjecture.

She told him about the Dorells. About how Krastev was not just a facilitator but very likely an enforcer. About how King and the Dorells had watched Jamie Carson die, perhaps even at Krastev's hands. 'The Black Squid feeds on these kids' anxieties. And it's no good thinking it's too far-fetched to be true, because we have proof. They think they're in a game. But what they weren't expecting was the big monster waiting at the end of it in the shape of Krastev. Shaw was convinced that the same thing happened to Abbie.'

'But why would anyone want to...'

She sent Rainsford an almost pitying look. 'I don't know enough about the Dorells to answer that yet, sir. But what I do know is that there is no point trying to apply any logic to this.'

'I don't like it. I still think Shaw's too unpredictable.'

'What do you want me to do? Hide? Safe house?'

Rainsford narrowed his eyes. 'I'm going to put someone outside your flat for a few days. Until we catch this bugger.'

Anna shrugged. There didn't seem much point in arguing.

Rainsford got up from his seat. 'Where next?'

Anna sighed. 'We look for King. Look for the Dorells. Confirm the body in the amusement arcade is Norcott, though it's unlikely to be anyone else. He'd insulated it with old sleeping bags. Had enough food in there for a week. A Primus stove, a battery lamp, paper for his golems. We have CCTV footage of him using the walkway across the M5 to the services at Gordano. They have free showers there.'

'Do we have any more insight into why he was off-grid?'

Anna shook her head. 'Do we need one? The authorities treated him like an animal. His mother treated him worse than one. Why would he want to be a part of any kind of society? I may get more from Beth when she's fit enough for reinterview.'

'OK, I think we have plenty to be going on with. The Dorells may be the breakthrough in the Black Squid business we've been looking for. It's good work, Anna.' Rainsford nodded, his gaze never wavering from Anna's face. 'You look awful. Take the afternoon off.'

'So I can sit at home and think about what I bumped into in that amusement arcade in the dark and the wet?'

Rainsford said nothing and they both knew his offer was half-hearted. He needed her locked and loaded.

'Someone is still sending messages to troubled kids, sir. The Black Squid… We need to stop it.'

'I'm still putting a car outside your flat.'

'Tell them not to expect tea and biscuits.'

CHAPTER FIFTY-SIX

They had Norcott's dental records at Ryegrove. Gupta used them to confirm that the body from the amusement arcade was him. Beth might well have been able to ID the body but Anna quashed that idea without a second thought.

The investigation was now firmly centred around finding King. There were other people in the office now. Faces she recognised but didn't really know. Her team were all there, but Dawes seemed to know everyone, and she realised some of these officers were his colleagues from the Major Crimes Unit. Dawes was on the phone, but he held up a finger, which she interpreted as him wanting to speak to her as she ducked into her room. Anna answered some emails for ten minutes until Dawes ended his call, crossed the room and walked in, closing the door behind him.

'Gupta's prelim report shows Norcott also had a skull fracture.'

Anna squeezed her eyes shut for two long seconds, trying and failing to ward off some inner pain. 'That ties in with what Beth Farlow told us.'

Dawes' response was silent. The grim line that was his mouth was enough.

They held vespers late that afternoon, Rainsford in attendance. Anna leaned against one of the desks, and it was she who kicked things off.

'The toxicity report on Norcott said he had haloperidol in his system but that he died from a heroin overdose. Someone had added caustic soda to the mix to make absolutely sure.'

'Heroin? We didn't find any evidence of that sort of stuff in his mother's house in Wales. I didn't know he was a user,' Dawes said.

'That's because he wasn't,' Anna said. 'Beth Farlow said she saw King inject Norcott several times.'

'The last reported sighting of King was the day he got back from the hospital,' Holder said. 'The patrol car dropped him off and duty officers can confirm he went into the building.'

'What's the CCTV coverage like?'

Dawes shook his head. 'Not brilliant. He lives on a quiet avenue. Nice little ground-floor apartment. School opposite. They have cameras covering the street but that's about it. We're having a look, but if he didn't go in that direction, then…'

'What about neighbours?'

'No one saw him come or go after he got dropped off.' Dawes shrugged. It was his turn to point a remote at the screen in the corner, and he mirrored it with the screen on his desktop.

'This is St Boswell's Court.' It was daytime onscreen, and the camera flowed through the stone pillars at the pavement entrance, panned up over the three storeys and then down into the basement flats before swivelling back around to show the road and the buildings opposite. Big, solid-looking Georgian stone structures adapted now for non-residential use such as clinics and schools. It zeroed in on a camera mounted high on the wall of Clifton High School Prep opposite. Then the POV shifted and led them along a wall separating the apartment complex from the church next to it, right through to a garden area behind and the back entrance to Christchurch Road. The rear garden was communal. Lots of windows looking out into the neat little space. 'Difficult to see how he could slip away without being seen, isn't it?'

'Not if he knew the other owners' movements. Could he have slipped over the wall into the church next door?' Holder said.

'Maybe.' Dawes paused the video. 'I'm not going to show you inside because there's nothing to see. It's clean and tidy. No laptop or phone and, last I heard, no passport either.'

'What about other properties?' Anna asked.

Khosa said, 'I've spoken to his ex. She doesn't know of anything. We're getting bank statements now and phone records, of course.'

'Did his ex say anything else?'

Khosa smiled a wry little smile. 'She was surprised and upset, obviously. Worried about how King being involved in a police investigation might impact the children. They have a boy and a girl. Both in their twenties and living in London. But it was more what she didn't say, ma'am.'

'As in?'

'As in, "No you're wrong, it couldn't be him." She didn't say anything like that.'

Anna nodded. You needed to separate an estranged spouse's possible vindictiveness from sheer surprise in these situations. If the divorce had been acrimonious, there might be an element of Mrs King seeing some hateful pigeons coming home to roost. On the other hand, there was probably no one who knew King better.

'I'll need to talk to her at some point,' Anna said.

'Any more about Shaw, ma'am?' Holder asked.

She turned towards Rainsford, who shrugged. 'Nothing yet. They've had several sightings, all spurious. One of the hazards of going to the press, of course.'

'Talking of the press, they're going to want to know who the USU dragged out of that amusement arcade,' Dawes said.

Rainsford nodded. 'I'll handle it. As of this moment we're still waiting for formal confirmation of identity. That's all they're getting.'

Anna pushed away from the desk and went to the images still up on the whiteboard. She stood next to Alison Johnson's, staring up at it as she spoke.

'I think we can be certain Krastev had a hand in Jamie Carson's murder, and I'd put money on him having something to do with Alison's too. But King's up to his neck in this as well.' She turned to Khosa. 'Tell me where we are with regard to the Dorells.'

Khosa's expression crumpled. 'Down a blind alley so far.'

Anna shook her head. 'OK, let's just keep chasing up everything we have on King and the Dorells and see where it gets us.'

'So how do you see it, ma'am?' Holder asked.

She turned back and faced the team. 'Let's imagine Alison Johnson knew Norcott had seen something. Perhaps she told him not to say anything until she found out what it was. What if, like Beth Farlow did, she went to see someone she trusted. Someone who knew Norcott.'

'King,' said Khosa.

'Exactly.'

'But wouldn't Norcott have told her that King was one of the people at the fence?'

'Maybe, probably. But then Norcott was a patient. Perhaps Alison wanted King to explain it to her so she could reassure Norcott that what he'd seen was not what he thought it was. She was hardly likely to take everything Norcott said to her at face value.'

'Doesn't explain why she's buried next to the railway line,' Dawes said.

Anna nodded. He was right. There were still big pieces of this jigsaw missing. Key pieces that meant they couldn't progress until they'd been found and slotted into place. It was now well after six. She told the team to go home and get some rest.

Rainsford ordered her to do the same. 'Give me ten minutes, I'll get a car to follow you home and check out the flat with you.'

'Shaw's not stupid enough to be waiting for me at home,' Anna said.

'No. But he might be bright enough.'

That left her wondering.

CHAPTER FIFTY-SEVEN

The two uniforms escorting Anna back to her flat were a young woman called Sue Watson and her partner, a stocky, grizzly haired sergeant called Ewan Back. They made her open her front door and wait outside while they checked the premises. Inside, the first thing Anna did was give them tea and biscuits before she went to fetch Lexi, who, on their return, instantly made friends with the two officers and got half a biscuit for her trouble.

'Will you be taking the dog out later, ma'am?' Back asked.

'No, she's been walked. Might let her out into the garden, that's all.'

'OK. We'll be circling back every hour or so. After eleven, there'll be someone here on and off.'

'Talk about overkill,' Anna said.

Back nodded. 'Thanks for the tea.' He gave Lexi one last fondle as he left.

As soon as they'd gone, she switched on the TV and scanned the news channels for information on Shaw's escape. Sky had a reporter, hair blowing in the breeze, outside the entrance to Worcester Royal. As if geographic authenticity lent credence to their 'on-the-spot' reporting. But despite spending ten minutes listening to another speculative run-down of what had happened, spun in terms of patient security and threat to the public, she was no wiser than after hearing Rainsford's blunt report.

She picked up her phone and toyed with it. There was someone she could ring. It meant jumping way over Rainsford's head, but

Anna didn't think he'd mind too much. In fact, she suspected he might be disappointed if she didn't.

The number she had was George Calhoun's, governor of Whitmarsh prison. He'd provided it through Rainsford as an emergency fallback should anything happen during one of Shaw's awaydays to the various burial sites he'd insisted on taking Anna to. She'd never used it. She did now.

Calhoun answered after four rings, his Scottish burr gravelly and raw from fielding calls from various government agencies and the press, Anna surmised.

'George Calhoun.'

'Sir, this is DI Anna Gwynne.'

Calhoun exhaled loudly. With the air went much of the aggression she'd heard in his barked greeting. 'Inspector Gwynne. Are you well?'

'I am, sir. I hope you'll excuse this call. I probably shouldn't, but—'

'Of course you bloody well should. I hope they've got someone watching over you?'

Anna went to the curtains and peeked through. Back and Watson were still there. 'Yes, they do.'

'Good. I suppose you want to know what happened?'

'Superintendent Rainsford has filled me in and I've seen the press interviews but I daresay there's another story.'

'Hmm,' Calhoun said. It sounded like one of his trademarks. 'The porter knew his way around. Knew where the MRI scanner was. When they'd finished and before Shaw could be manacled, the porter pulled a gun on the guard in an anteroom and threatened him. There was no one else there. Two to one. I don't blame the guard. I'd have done the same, no questions asked. Shaw was dressed in scrubs. He nabbed a white coat, wore a surgeon's cap, and they walked out through the main entrance. We suspect his accomplice was parked off-site.'

'And the guard?'

'Unharmed. Trussed up like a turkey and left in a storage room. They found him two hours later.'

'Two hours is a long time.'

'It is.'

'But Shaw was ill. I saw him.'

'Shaw had lost weight and was anaemic. Not eating did the former, and as for the latter, we think he bled himself. Kept bleeding himself like a bloody leech. There were track marks hidden in a tattoo on his forearm. The doctors assumed he'd done drugs in hospital and he fed them some rubbish about being a user. But Shaw was not an addict. His blood work was clean. Must have used the needles like a medieval apothecary to stick himself.'

Anna knew how easy it was to get drugs in prison. It was common currency. Needles too.

'Do you have any idea who the accomplice was?'

'Hmm. CCTV isn't helping. He was male, wore a hat and dark glasses. That's about it. He was taller than Shaw, that's all we know.'

'Still have no idea where he went?'

'None. What about you?'

'Me? I have no idea either.'

'He may try and contact you,' Calhoun said. 'You know how he thinks.'

She did. What Shaw thought about most of the time was the death of his daughter and who was responsible for it.

'I don't think he would want to harm me. But he may want some information.'

'Yeah. And we both know how he goes about getting that. I'd be on my guard, Inspector.'

After Calhoun rang off, she phoned Ben, knowing he was at work. They'd texted during the day, but now she wanted to hear his voice.

'Hey, are you OK?'

'I am being guarded by two uniforms in a patrol car who are providing a presence. And by a fierce dog.'

'Lexi not there, then?'

Anna smiled. The Hawley sense of humour finding its mark again.

'Are you worried?' Ben asked.

'No, funnily enough.'

'You and he had a thing, didn't you?'

She thought about it. Ben of course knew about Shaw. Knew why he was in prison and how dangerous he was. '"Thing" is just about the right word.'

'I mean you passed his tests. Didn't you say you even thought he trusted you?'

The tests Ben was talking about had been Shaw's probing of her ability as a detective. A little game he'd played that almost got her killed in the process of hunting down a killer the press named the Woodsman. But there was no doubt that after she'd survived and proved herself, Shaw had been much more cooperative in his own way when it came to revealing the whereabouts of Black Squid victims.

'He fooled me, Ben. He fooled everyone. He'd been bleeding himself to induce anaemia. That's how he got himself to hospital.'

The other end of the phone went quiet for a moment.

'We'd better put tonight's tapas on hold then.'

'That's why I rang,' Anna sighed. 'Much as I'd love to, there's no point. They'll probably want me where they can keep an eye on me. I'm exhausted and I have to go in tomorrow so I'll be up early needing a clear head. There's too much happening to sit on this all weekend. Sorry to mess you about.'

She listened for something in his voice, something that told her he was getting tired of her work commitments. But he was a doctor, he knew all about commitment.

'You're right. No point going Spanish and drinking lemonade. I'll ring and cancel. Let me know tomorrow how you're fixed, and I'll be here if you need me. Stay safe, Anna,' Ben said.

'I will.'

The day was rapidly catching up with her, but before giving in to tiredness, she poured herself half a glass of wine and sat. She needed to distract herself, try and trick her head into relaxing. Let all the dancing dots of information line up, ready to be joined. She knew there was a great deal of knowledge available to her and the team in this case, but they had not made the right connections. Not yet.

And it didn't happen that evening. There was too much background noise. Too many images from the day and the night before. She tried to filter. To find the thread which, when she pulled it, might unravel the knot. But which one to pull?

When the glass she was holding slipped in her hand and she jerked awake from a half-slumber too late to prevent wine from slopping on to the carpet, she gave up and went to bed, falling into an exhausted sleep almost immediately. She dreamed of Norcott walking the streets, stalking her as she waded through a dark cavern, then rising from the water ahead of her to accuse her with a pointing finger.

CHAPTER FIFTY-EIGHT

SATURDAY

She was up again before dawn with a headache, the nightmare still fresh, an uneasy echo in her head. Norcott, the outcast. Misunderstood and shunned by his bitter mother, held captive in Ryegrove by a powerful, vindictive King. He had not deserved any of that. He'd killed, but she wondered what his life might have been like if he'd been shown some understanding, or love, when he'd most needed it, instead of being treated like some sick animal by his feckless mother.

Those echoes brought other images to mind. Her great-aunt Mary in Talgarth having her synapses fried. Her own mother, trying to scare her into 'normal behaviour' by subjecting her to the example of the locked-away family member.

Anna sat in her front room with some tea and looked through her notes, waving to a different patrol car when it slid along the street outside a little after five thirty. By seven she was showered and dressed. She called Lexi to her, clipped on her lead and frowned as her fingers met with something unfamiliar.

Anna stared. There was something attached to Lexi's collar.

Anna kneeled and grabbed the buckle. Lexi, thrilled by all the close attention, wriggled and shifted her head in an attempt to reciprocate. Eventually, Anna got her to sit and rotated the collar so she could get a good look. What she saw was a small, dark oblong on the brown leather, secured by a tightly wrapped black cable tie.

She hadn't put it there. Lexi certainly hadn't put it there. So, who…

A whirl of swirling pinpoints suddenly lit up in her head and made the breath seize in her throat. She got up, told the dog to stay and rushed out through her front door.

Maggie, in a shapeless sweatshirt and a fur-strewn skirt, was full of surprise and disappointment when Anna turned up without Lexi. Bruce bounced around excitedly as she followed them through to Maggie's lived-in kitchen.

'Where's Lexi? Is she all right?' Maggie asked.

'She's fine, but as I was about to bring her over, I noticed something attached to her collar.'

'Yes, the plastic tag thingy.'

Anna's eyebrows shot up. 'Did you put it there?'

Maggie laughed. 'Me? No, I thought you had.'

'Why did you think that, Maggie?'

'It was there when I took her lead off after our walk yesterday afternoon. I assumed I hadn't noticed it earlier but that you must have put it on that morning. Some kind of new ID tag, I thought. Or an exercise monitor. I've seen those advertised.'

'I hadn't put anything on her collar.'

Maggie frowned. 'But if you didn't put it on, who did?'

It was an excellent question. One that Anna's brain was doing its best to answer. Unfortunately, none of the ideas she came up with were making the lurching anxiety in her gut calm down.

'Yesterday, on your walk, did you see anyone? Did anyone touch Lexi?'

Maggie blinked, frowning and looking down at the lino at her feet as she thought. 'I let her off the lead on the common. You know her, she's a live wire. Very sociable.'

Makes up for me, thought Anna.

'She says hello to dozens of dogs, and their owners usually make a fuss. You know what dog people are like.'

Anna smiled. It took a lot of effort.

Maggie said, 'I remember seeing a Jack Russell, a couple of setters, three labradoodles.'

'What about their owners?'

'I don't really take much notice, not unless they're close by and wanting to exchange a word.' Maggie looked away, thinking. 'Mostly women. One man on his own with a springer spaniel.'

'Can you describe him?'

'Not really, he was too far away.' Maggie's eyes strayed to Anna's face. 'Lexi's OK, isn't she?'

'Yes, she's fine. No problem. I'm just going to make a call.' Anna was already turning away, wanting to get back to the dog, speed-dialling Dawes as she walked.

'That thing on her collar. It isn't anything nasty, is it?' Maggie called after her.

Anna swivelled and exhaled. 'That's a good question, Maggie. And I really wish I knew the answer.'

Dawes took twenty minutes to get to her. Twenty minutes during which Anna sat on her hands to stop herself from taking off Lexi's collar. When the doorbell finally rang, the first thing Dawes did on the very threshold of Anna's doorstep was hold out a pair of gloves. 'By rights, we ought to have CSI over here. But we don't know what this is yet. That's our justification. Even so, I reckon we should be professional about it.'

Anna nodded and slid on the gloves. Lexi was still in the lounge, delighted to see Dawes, even though they'd never met. Anna calmed her down while Dawes ran his fingers around the inside of the collar.

'There doesn't seem to be anything attached. No wires. Nothing to suggest a trigger on removal.'

Anna nodded, hearing Dawes' words but finding them far from consoling. She hadn't even thought to look. She fondled the dog, constantly reassuring her. 'Good girl, Lexi. Good girl.'

'Right,' said Dawes. 'Let's get the thing off.'

'I'll do it,' Anna said.

Dawes put out an arm to stop Anna. 'Let me. You're in no state.'

Anna stood up and back, wondering why her legs were shaking so badly. Dawes examined the collar carefully, noting the cable ties and peering at the dark shape they'd been looped around.

'There's writing on it,' Dawes said eventually. 'A diamond logo and "16gb". I'd say that means sixteen gigabytes. A thumb drive would be my guess.'

Relief flooded through Anna like a cold shower. She pushed all the terrible thoughts of what it could have been into the corner of her mind for later introspection. Anthrax had been on that list; a horrible disease with spores that stayed active for years in powder form. As had a plastic explosive like Semtex that would have severed Lexi's neck if it had been set off.

Dawes undid the clip and, with an extra set of wags from Lexi as he stood, put the collar on the table.

'Looks like someone has left you a message,' Dawes muttered, and then said, 'Got any scissors?'

Anna passed her kitchen scissors to him; he snipped the ties and placed them, together with the freed USB stick, on the worktop.

'So, how do you want to play this?' Dawes asked.

'I want to know what's on it.'

'We could get it to Hi-Tech.'

Anna nodded. 'And God knows how long it'll be before we have a report done. Varga might help, but she's snowed under. No. It was attached to my dog so it's fair game. I'll get my laptop.'

'Any idea who did this?'

She threw him a glance that spoke volumes in its implication.

Come on, Phil, thought Anna. *We both know who this is likely to be. Someone who knew I'd be watched but that Lexi would not. Someone smart and devious who knows where I live, my patterns, my habits.*

Dawes nodded and glanced at the kettle.

Anna nodded. 'Yes, a cup of tea is definitely in order. Sugar's in the bowl next to the caddy.'

Five minutes later they were in Anna's small lounge, laptop set up on the coffee table in front of them. Anna was on the sofa; Dawes preferred to stand behind. Prowl behind would have been a better description since he seemed incapable of standing still. Anna'd kept her latex gloves on as she slotted the USB stick into its port and saw a little grey avatar appear on the desktop labelled 'DIAMOND'. She double-clicked and saw one file appear in the index. An MP4 file labelled "BS".

'I hope that doesn't mean bullshit,' Dawes said.

'It's a video,' said Anna. 'And I'd put my money on BS for "Black Squid".' She double-clicked the file and watched the screen fill with a static image, her eyes narrowing as a wall of rough stone appeared. The image was steady, the camera, she guessed, mounted on a stable surface. Light illuminated from the right. A window, perhaps?

And then the camera panned around. A face appeared. King's face. Grey and moist with a sheen of sweat. He sat, arms tied behind him, duct tape wrapped around his chest and the chair back. Very much like Beth Farlow had been.

But unlike Beth, his mouth was not taped over, nor were his eyes. And his eyes were what drew Anna's. Ragged with fear, they looked up above the camera lens at whoever had placed him in that chair as the video ran.

CHAPTER FIFTY-NINE

King shivered. A muffled voice from behind the microphone spoke.

'Do it.'

King didn't respond.

'DO IT.' Louder.

King flinched so badly the chair he was sitting in jerked. 'OK, OK,' he said. Quickly, wanting to reassure for fear of reprisal, like a child might. His head shook, his voice cracked and dry.

'I am Martin King. I work… worked at Ryegrove Hospital, a medium and low secure unit, part of the North Bristol Mental Health Trust. In 1999, we admitted a girl by the name of Miranda Dorell. She was very disturbed, diagnosed with schizo-affective disorder, resistant to treatment. To accepting any form of treatment. Eventually, she began to respond. It isn't unusual for such patients, bipolar patients with schizophrenic tendencies, to avoid treating their bipolar disease. They yo-yo. Miranda Dorell did not want to be at Ryegrove, but she'd been sectioned from the courts. She had a brother. They were very close. I might even say pathologically close.'

Something changed in King's expression then. It might even have been a rueful smile dragged up by a fleeting memory.

'She was attractive. The sort of looks that turned heads, and she was very aware of that fact. She flirted outrageously with some of the other inmates. We, as staff, were all on our guard, as we always were with manipulative young women. The unit was going through renovations at the time. It was difficult, sometimes, to keep track of exactly what was going on with a new perimeter fence, closure of old buildings,

construction of newer ones.' King hesitated, looked up again at the person behind the camera, dropped his eyes and continued.

'It's no excuse for what happened, I know. One evening, Miranda wanted to talk. We arranged to walk in the garden. The two of us. She said she liked to look at the railway line, see the trains passing. I agreed. It was summer, and I said we'd be out for twenty minutes. We were out for fifty and if I could take that fifty minutes back from my life I would…' King blew air out of his mouth, as if there was a lit candle in front of him he was trying to extinguish. But all he was doing was composing himself before continuing. 'There was a spot near the fence next to some woods where you could to see the railway. When we got there, she became very excited. She thought she'd seen a rabbit in the woods and ran in after it. I followed. But it wasn't a rabbit in the woods. It was two men. One of them was her brother. I'd met him on visits' King shook his head. 'Joshua Dorell was… is a very sick person. Sick in all senses of the word. I am certain he has a mental disorder, but he is also high-functioning. An intelligent mind behind a very dark, sociopathic persona. The other man, Krastev, had a shotgun. A sawn-off, stubby thing. They made me do things… with Miranda. She was a willing accomplice. Insurance, Joshua Dorell called it. They took photographs of me naked with her. But I swear it was at gunpoint, I swear it. They wanted me to get Miranda released and said that if I didn't, they'd show the photographs to the press and my wife. I had young children—'

A noise, sudden and very loud, erupted on the video. Something metallic being banged down on a hard surface. It made Anna jump. It made King almost fall backwards in the chair he was tied to.

'Stop lying,' said a voice in a tooth-grinding growl. 'You slimy shit. You weren't forced into anything and you know it. Either tell me the truth now or tell me with a knife between your pathetic coward's ribs.'

King's eyes were round, white-rimmed orbs, locked on to something at about waist level off-camera. About the level someone might hold a knife.

'All right, all right!' King's protestations were shrill and desperate. 'They didn't make me do anything. I had sex with Miranda. She was very physical. She did all the running. Her brother…' King shook his head. 'They weren't normal. They were… are unique. A sibling folie à deux. *They shared everything. Had no empathy. I was fascinated by them, I admit that. But I swear I didn't know what they were planning that night.' King's eyes dropped, and when he looked up again, it was as if they had sunk deeper into his face.*

'They took me to the fence. They were laughing. It was like a show to them. Joshua had brought the circus to his sister. Krastev disappeared into the woods through the tunnel they'd built. When he got to the other side of the fence, he walked across to the railway line. There was someone else there. Smaller, a boy. He argued with Krastev, tried to get away, but he was already tied and easily overpowered.' King's voice dropped low. 'I saw the train coming. Saw its lights. It wasn't dark, but dusk was falling. I watched from inside the fence as Krastev dragged the boy out from behind a stack of sleepers and threw him under the train.' King's breathing became suddenly ragged. Sucking in air as if he'd been running.

'I watched the Dorells as it happened. I watched them smile, watched them hold hands as the train smashed into that poor kid. Joshua Dorell said that what I'd seen made me special. That they'd given a tormented soul a release. Then he said I was going to be a part of it. That I already was.'

King's head fell. He was crying. It went on for thirty seconds before a muffled growl was followed by a plastic bottle full of water hitting King in the chest, thrown by the person controlling the camera. King jerked up, fear overtaking his self-pity again in a flash. He sucked in another lungful of air, composed himself and spoke.

'I fixed it for Miranda Dorell to get an early release. I lied, cajoled colleagues. Got her out after a few more months. I never went for a walk with her again. But on the night this happened I was in a state.

A real state. I couldn't go home. I didn't know what to do.' He paused, looking into the camera as if asking for understanding.

'You could have reported it, you shit,' Dawes muttered. But King couldn't hear him.

'I was in my office when Alison Johnson came to see me. She was concerned about another patient. Colin Norcott. He claimed to have seen something at the fence. Saw people staring out at the railway line. Thought he'd seen something happen there. Alison was worried.'

King's mouth made ugly shapes, as if he was disgusted at hearing himself speak these words. 'I lied to her. I said that I'd seen something as well and that I was about to go and investigate, drive around to the railway line in case an animal had been injured. Alison said she'd come with me. She had a thing about animals. I had Dorell's contact number. He wanted constant updates on his sister's progress. Before we left Ryegrove that night, I sent him a message.

'There was blood all over the tracks. Then Alison found a severed hand. She became hysterical, wanted to call the police. I tried to stop her, to explain. That's when Krastev came out of the bushes.' King's voice was calm now. His delivery dead. 'He didn't hesitate. He knocked her down. Hit her twice on the head, then strangled her. God help me, I… I helped him bury her. I went to see Norcott. I told him he'd been seeing things. That Alison had gone away and if he told anyone else, they'd go away, too. I modified his treatment so his symptoms were not completely controlled. His own psychopathy took care of the rest. By the time of his release he'd suppressed everything. Buried it silently inside. Or so I thought. But then the police found the bodies by the railway tracks. Norcott was always a little unstable. He was following Beth Farlow, a nurse he'd become attached to. When he saw reports of the bodies being discovered near the tracks, it opened the old wound.

He took the discovery as a sign that he could now tell someone what he'd really seen at the fence that night all those years ago. Beth told me she'd seen him. Signs of him. I went to her house, saw Norcott go in. I had to do something. I'd managed to hide everything so well… I… I knocked on Beth's door, pretended I was there to help.' King hesitated, licked his dry lips before going on. 'Norcott attacked me.'

Behind Anna, Dawes reared up. 'You bloody snake.'

King continued, 'He was wild. As wild as he was when he killed his neighbours. I've told the police the rest. I told them—'

More muffled sounds off-camera. Not easy to make out. But Anna thought she heard a few words she recognised. *'Fucking liar'* and *'squid'*.

King inhaled and then exhaled. Juddering noises. His voice rose again, became urgent.

'Dorell, Joshua Dorell, maybe Miranda too, used me to play their games. I know he used others; we were all part of the Black Squid network. The Dorells got their claws in you and they'd never let go. They made me an administrator. Made me lead these disturbed kids down a path of "deliverance". That was Dorell's choice of words. I did it. I'm not sure how many times I succeeded.'

King let his head drop.

'Krastev used to confirm the deaths. Though from what I saw on the railway tracks that night, I suspect he was instrumental. But after a couple of years he disappeared. Later, Dorell said we ought to make the players use their own phones, or drones even, to film their suicides.'

More voices off camera. King looked up.

'Sorry? Of course I'm sorry. I'm sorry for it all. But you don't know what it's like. You have no idea what it's like to have your family threatened—'

Sounds of movement, furniture scraping, the camera jolting, tilting on its side to show a different wall. Shouts, yells, a scream. Then the camera upright again, King bleeding from his nose, snivelling, staring back.

'My name is Martin King. I colluded in the killing of Alison Johnson. I am an administrator of the Black Squid. And I am sorry.'

A momentary edit, the screen blank and then a piece of paper. A line of numbers – GPS coordinates – and then a face, balaclava covering it, glasses beneath.

A new voice. Muffled through the covering. But Anna knew who it belonged to without any need of confirmation when it spoke.

'Come and get this bastard, Anna. He wanted you to see him as a victim. I reckon his knock on the head was self-inflicted. I went for him because he was the only one who knew all the players. The Dorells, Norcott, Alison Johnson and your missing nurse. He's lying about her, too, by the way. And he's lying about being made to do the things he's done. He and the other Black Squid fuckers do it because they get a sick kick out of it. But I don't trust myself. If I make him talk any more, I don't trust myself to stop. So I've stuffed a gag in his filthy mouth. He's all yours. You know he's in this up to his lying neck. Find something to put him away with.' Shaw held up a phone. 'This is his. I need it for a while. I'll post it back to you when I'm done.'

The video stopped.

Anna and Dawes sat in silence, looking at each other.

'Jesus,' Dawes muttered eventually. 'It was him, wasn't it? In the balaclava. Hector bloody Shaw.'

Anna opened up Google Maps and punched the coordinates into the search box. The map that came up was of Wiltshire. Anna recognised Warminster. But the map was centred on a place called Imber. Anna zoomed in towards lots of empty space and a few buildings.

'Doesn't look like there's much there.'

'There isn't,' said Dawes. 'Not now. But there used to be a village there. Farmhouses, pubs, a church. I think the church is still used, but the rest has been abandoned thanks to the MOD. It's on their training grounds on Salisbury Plain.'

'How do you know that?' Anna asked.

'Did a missing person search there once. Teenager. Never found anything. But I walked through it. It's a bloody creepy spot.'

Anna got up. 'So, what are we waiting for?'

'Might be a trap.'

Anna shook her head. 'Shaw doesn't want to harm me. He never has. He wants whoever killed his daughter and it looks like he's just caught one of the big fish.'

'The confession might not be worth much,' Dawes said. 'It's obviously under duress.'

Anna nodded. 'You're forgetting Beth Farlow. That's abduction and attempted manslaughter right there. Never mind what he did to Norcott.'

Dawes collected the mugs and Anna followed him to the kitchen, where he was washing up.

'You're well trained,' she said.

Dawes was looking out of the window into Anna's back garden. There was nothing there but dripping bushes and wet furniture. 'Does Lexi bite?' he asked.

'No.'

He upturned their cups and placed them on the drainer. When he turned his face towards Anna, she read a volcanic anger dancing behind his eyes. 'Pity. We could have sent her in to find King first.'

CHAPTER SIXTY

Anna rang Khosa and sent her and Holder to Southmead to speak to Beth Farlow. Someone needed to tell her Norcott was dead, but Anna knew it would soften the blow if she knew that King had been found.

Anna and Dawes went to Imber supported by an armed unit from Wiltshire Constabulary. They found King in an abandoned shed at Imber Court farm. He was still gagged and taped to the chair, dehydrated and weak, but otherwise unharmed. At least not in a physical way. The same could not be said of his psychological well-being. But then he'd spent some quality time with Shaw.

When he saw the police come through the door, he moaned with relief. They cut him loose and gave him some water. Dawes was all for reading him his rights and arresting him right away, but Anna shook her head, and while her Wiltshire colleagues searched the area for signs of Shaw, she switched her phone to record mode and put it on the little table where, she presumed, Shaw had placed the camera he'd used for recording King's confession.

King was beside himself with relief. 'Thank God. Thank God. Have you found him?'

'Who?' Dawes asked, his voice as terse as his expression.

'The maniac who took me.'

They put a blanket around King's shoulders and the paramedics cleaned up his cut face and were ready to take him to Salisbury District A and E for assessment. But Anna told them to wait outside.

King clutched the blanket around him as he spoke, head down, looking frail. 'He was waiting for me outside my door. I left the flat to get some provisions and he took me. Said he had a gun. I know he definitely had a knife because he held it to my throat more than once.'

Dawes was leaning against the stone wall to the left of King. 'We've seen a tape of you confessing,' he said.

'Of course I confessed.' King turned his face towards the sergeant and made a noise that might have been a laugh. 'I told him what he wanted to hear. I made it all up, you must see that?'

He was right, of course. His confession, delivered under extreme duress, would not be worth much in a court of law. It was why Anna had decided, on their journey over to Wiltshire, to be economical with the truth. Give King a little rope with which to tie a noose for his own neck.

Shaw had labelled him a liar and she wanted to see just how far he'd go to try and save his own skin.

Anna took the good cop role. 'It must have been awful for you. We know what Shaw's capable of.'

When King looked up, she read genuine fear there. She understood that. Anyone sitting within five yards of Shaw, knowing he was free to act, would be terrified. Equally terrified, having survived, just recalling it. But there was something else in King's face. A different fear. He couldn't hold Anna's gaze and his eyes slid away. A movement driven by some disingenuous calculation Anna had seen many times in the guilty, fed by a desperate hope that they might still have a way out.

'What about Beth Farlow, Martin?' Anna said, keeping her tone even, acting out the subterfuge she and Dawes concocted. 'Do you know where she might be?'

There was a moment, a fleeting couple of seconds where King might have considered telling them the truth. Anna wanted to believe she saw it in the widening of his eyes. But then it faded, his lids dropped back down, and he sat up, sensing – like some cornered animal seeing a crack in the wall it might squeeze through – a way out. 'I told you, Norcott took her. Did you search? Norcott's probably miles away from Severn Beach by now.'

Anna nodded, stood up and walked forward. 'What if I told you we have found Beth and Norcott?' She saw the words 'found them' form on King's lips as his brows crowded forward in confusion. 'Was it dark when you put the tape over her face, Martin? After you'd injected Norcott in as many veins as you could find to make it look like he was mainlining? Was that the plan? Make it look like Norcott had wrapped the tape around Beth Farlow's head and then rewarded himself with an extra shot of H conveniently laced with drain cleaner? Bad luck for him to have sourced a shitty batch, eh? By the time someone found them, those fresh needle marks would have looked old anyway, wouldn't they?'

Anna could see white sclera showing all around King's irises as he took in her words.

'I wondered about it being dark because it must have been difficult for you to see what you were doing. That would explain why you left a little gap. Somehow, Beth worked at it, made that half-inch slit big enough to breathe through. But breathe she did while the flood waters rose around her and Colin Norcott drowned, or choked on his own vomit at her feet. She had a lot to tell us when we found her in that amusement arcade.'

Desperation was a strange beast. It made people do the oddest things. Anna had seen grown men cry. Heard mourners wail as if the noise in their throats could bring back their dead children. She knew how shock worked. King, knowing finally that there was no way out, thrust himself up and tried to run for the door. Unfortunately for him, it was guarded by a very large constable. King seemed not to see him and tried to run straight through. There could only ever be one result. Dawes lent a hand in the restraining. Lent a couple.

King, mewling, screaming, spitting, was finally subdued.

When he was back in the chair, handcuffed and slumped forward, Dawes sent Anna a questioning look. She nodded.

He read King his rights and arrested him for the murder of Colin Norcott and the attempted murder of Beth Farlow. More than enough to be getting on with. They'd talk to him about the Black Squid later.

CHAPTER SIXTY-ONE

Anna wasn't one for big celebrations but even she felt like she needed to blow off a little steam when they got back to Bristol. They met at the Lantern late that Saturday afternoon and sat in a corner table well away from everyone else. Rainsford had wanted to come. He even stood them a round. While he was at the bar and Holder and Khosa were playing Who Wants to Be a Millionaire on a slot machine and out of earshot, Dawes looked unusually serious.

'Ma'am, I may not get a chance later, so I just wanted to say, thanks for letting me be a part of the squad.'

'It's me that should be thanking you, Phil,' Anna said. Dawes had been great for the team. His brand of tough love was something she knew the squad valued. And she would never forget him accompanying her to that amusement arcade.

Dawes nodded but he looked uncomfortable.

'Sounds like this is a goodbye,' Anna said.

'That's just it, ma'am.' Dawes turned again to make sure Khosa and Holder were out of earshot. 'The missus is always telling me I have the knack of choosing exactly the wrong moment, but it's been on my mind and I wanted it sorted.'

Anna held out her hand. 'OK. Well, it's been a pleasure. We...' She paused. 'I appreciate everything you've done.'

Dawes looked at the hand but didn't offer his own. 'Thing is, Superintendent Rainsford told me there's a vacancy in the squad, ma'am. This may not be the way to do things and there probably ought to be a formal interview, but I've really enjoyed working with you. They said the cold case squad could be a little quiet.' Dawes shook his head. 'I don't know many DIs who would have been prepared to walk through four feet of dirty water to find someone in a cyclone. In fact, bar you, I don't know any. So, if I applied for a transfer, do you think I'd be in with a shout?'

Anna stared at him. He was exactly the sort of sergeant they needed. She needed. Experienced, tough, a good example. And there wouldn't be an interview.

Dawes saw her face change, mistook it as hesitation and said, 'You don't have to say anything now, ma'am. Bad timing as usual.'

Anna's hand had dropped away but she held it back up now. 'The job's yours if you want it, Phil.'

Dawes grinned. This time he did shake her hand. He looked across at Rainsford, who was signalling for some help with the drinks, and got up to assist. Anna saw the men exchange a few words.

'Right,' Rainsford said when he got back to the table and Holder and Khosa had joined them. 'Congratulations to everyone involved for concluding a very complex investigation. We have King in custody and I suspect he'll be more than happy to give us information on the Black Squid ringleaders if we tempt him with a lesser sentence.'

'Don't tell me he's going to get any leeway for what he did to Colin Norcott,' Anna said quickly.

Rainsford shook his head. 'There are other ways. Killers like King don't do well inside. They get eaten up and spat out. Guaranteed separation from the general prison population tends to work well as a bargaining point. Let's see what he coughs up once that's on the table.' He held up his drink and said, 'Cheers.'

The other four members of the team did likewise.

Rainsford took a deep breath. 'But that's not all I have to tell you. There is good news and bad. First of all, funding for the MCRTF is taking a further significant cut. We can't justify continuing on the basis of cold cases only.'

Anna felt the blood drain from her face. Rainsford had warned her, but she hadn't expected it to be this soon.

'There was a budget meeting this morning. I've come straight here. Brutal stuff.' Rainsford gave little shake of his head but then looked up with a tight smile. 'However, given your expertise and results, it has been recognised that abandoning this task force completely would also be foolish. However, it means that as well as cold cases, you'll be working active major crimes. The MCU could do with the help. It was the only way I could swing it with the chief constable. And closing this case today did not do our prospects any harm.'

Holder and Khosa exchanged glances. Anna read excitement in that look. Working active major crimes was a big step up for them.

'So, we'll be expected to do what we do now and deal with ongoing cases?' Anna asked.

'Yes. More of the same and some. But the silver lining is a confirmation that Phils' presence on the team is now a permanent one. He'll bring MCU expertise.'

'What was that your wife said about your timing?' Anna said with a wry look at Dawes.

Holder grinned. 'Welcome to the madhouse, Sarge.'

Dawes, dry as ever, said, 'I see my role here primarily as a tool for affirmative action in attempting to get the average age of the team up a few notches.'

Anna nodded. 'There is that.'

'And to develop good policing habits like getting the tea on for everyone as soon as they arrive' – he turned pointedly towards Holder – 'Justin. So as well as expertise, I'll be bringing Hobnobs every Friday.'

Smiles all round.

Rainsford was good at his job. Good at engaging people in conversation. Even Anna. 'Plans for tomorrow, Anna?'

'Not much. I think the weather's dry and Ben's off, so we'll walk the dog. Go to my sister's for Sunday lunch probably. Normal, healthy things.'

Rainsford nodded. 'A welcome and much-needed antidote to the horror and the filth.'

While Dawes made Holder and Khosa laugh with one of his jokes, Anna leaned forward towards her boss. 'Any news on the Shaw front, sir?'

'No. He's nowhere.'

'He must be somewhere.'

'Do you know something, Anna? Any help would be greatly appreciated by our colleagues in West Mercia. They're like headless chickens up there at the moment.'

'He'll be going after the Dorells, sir. I have no doubt about that.'

'From what I know about them, it doesn't help us much.'

Anna nodded. It was becoming clear the Dorells had managed to conceal their whereabouts very successfully from every and all forms of bureaucracy and authority.

'I mean, are they even in the country?'

Anna considered this, knowing she had already. 'I'd say yes, sir. It's one thing to try and hide within the New Age community here, another thing altogether to try and get abroad. Not with their records.'

'They don't have credit cards or phone contracts.'

'They don't, but perhaps whoever it is they're pretending to be might. And if they're still responsible for Black Squid deaths, like Kimberley Williams', we have a duty to do something about it.'

Rainsford nodded. 'But that will be for another day.' He sipped his drink. Orange juice from the look of it. Anna plumped for the house white and wished she'd gone for the Riesling instead. But Rainsford's questions brought Shaw effortlessly back to her mind. She knew he'd be thinking exactly the same thoughts as she was. The Dorells and their sickening coercion were a pox that needed to be eradicated from the world. There would, she knew, be other cold cases for the team to investigate, but the Black Squid, until it was caught and laid out on a slab, would remain a thorn with the potential for turning poisonous at any moment.

The antidote, as Rainsford so aptly put it, was Ben and Lexi and Kate and her family. She was lucky to have them all. Lucky Ben convinced her that she needed to show patience and maybe even a little forgiveness towards her mother. She would try. And Kate's roasties were the treasure at the end of the booby-trapped path the Sunday visit would no doubt turn out to be. Ben kept telling her she should embrace the fact that she was different and not fret about it.

Fretting only led to unhappiness.

Dawes, who was having a lift back with Khosa, had already finished his pint and was now offering to buy a second round. Anna declined politely. Ben was on his way to pick her up. But Holder said yes to Dawes' offer while Khosa rolled her eyes and warned them she was leaving in half an hour.

'Half an hour,' said Dawes. 'That's four rounds, then.'

Khosa started to object but then she saw the teasing look on Dawes' face and threw a beer mat at him.

Anna smiled but was already detaching, doing this thing she did in company, becoming an observer, always the cold analyst. Someone shouted at the bar, the punchline of a joke. The words were incoherent but the accent caught her ear. Northern, Mancunian.

It wasn't him; the joke-teller was bigger, the wrong age at early forties, yet the noise pricked her consciousness and triggered the strangest thought.

Shaw was out there. Like her, he was now looking for scum, killers, monsters. He'd helped her on three occasions now. Helped her and played her as well. But when she raised the wine to her lips while the team laughed and joked around her, she felt herself saying his name in her head, knowing she could never say it out loud in polite company.

Not quite, but almost, a toast.

EPILOGUE

Oscar Louden had a bucket full of anxieties, but it was now a much smaller bucket.

Many of the ones that plagued him at his old school had disappeared after just four days. His new class accepted him as a quiet, average student with a bit of a thing for music. Marston's teachers were encouraging. Best of all, his parents – his father – relented and let him wear the designated uniform. No more blazer. He'd heard them arguing over it.

But the one, the biggest anxiety, would not go away.

He had not heard from the Black Squid in four days. The message would come, he knew it would. He wondered what would have happened if he'd slid off the church tower those few nights ago. Would he have ended up like the kids in wheelchairs he saw at school?

No, of course he wouldn't. The Black Squid wanted an end to things. But Oscar didn't. Not anymore. He'd been to some new lessons, subjects they hadn't offered properly in his old school. The music tech lab was brand new, and the teacher, Mrs Ingham, was nothing like the stroppy, discouraging, ponytailed man hiding in the studio of his old school. Mrs Ingham ran a lunchtime club for people who wanted to make music. And Oscar could make music from all sorts of things. She'd even given him some free software to play with at home on his old PC and he'd already decided to ask his parents for a combined Christmas and birthday present in the form of a new laptop.

There was also a science-fiction reading group run by one of the English teachers, Mr Bilton. Oscar had gone along and heard them discussing *Stranger Things*.

He loved *Stranger Things*. Sometimes he felt like he, too, had been stuck in the Upside Down for months. The book they were now reading was *The Illustrated Man*. Mr Bilton had even lent him a copy.

For the first time in years, perhaps even his life, Oscar Louden liked going to school. And what he did not want was for this to now end. But what he feared was the threat of the Black Squid exposing his weaknesses to his new classmates if he did not comply.

Sometimes, when he thought about it, he broke out in a sweat and had to sit down and pick at the skin on his arms where he'd cut himself before.

He'd been so stupid to play the Black Squid's game. So, so stupid. Occasionally he let himself believe that changing schools had also somehow pushed the Squid away; he'd not heard from it for days. But that wasn't how Oscar's life played out. Not if his past was anything to go by. He knew in his heart that his hopes would turn to fears.

The next day as he walked to school, they did just that with a single alert on his phone.

He glanced at the WhatsApp notification and his stomach dipped as a swooping nausea took hold. He stumbled to a shop doorway and leaned his head down to stop from throwing up. A passer-by saw him and asked if he was OK. He couldn't speak, only nod weakly. When the waves of nausea had gone, Oscar straightened up, walked on a few yards and stopped again, turning away from the street, wiping tears from his eyes with his knuckles.

His hands were shaking when he held the phone up and pressed the screen to call up the message.

Welcome to the Black Squid. Do exactly as instructed. Day 20. Your last day. Your day of liberation.

The Squid has been eaten by a bigger fish.

You have no more tasks.

Go in peace and LIVE.

Delete this contact.

Oscar read and reread the message, his heart hammering. He thought about texting back. Thought that perhaps this was part of the game, to make him think it had ended when it hadn't. But it ordered him to delete the contact. Delete the Black Squid!

Oscar tapped the screen, the contact, the address book and it was done. He pocketed his phone, walked to the bus stop and began to think about what instrument he could add to the drum track he'd laid down the day before.

Something good and upbeat, he reckoned. Someone from his new school called to him across the street. A girl from his class. Oscar raised his hand and ran across the road to join her. He did so quickly, a smile on his face.

He was too busy smiling to see the figure in the doorway of a shop opposite watching him. Too busy living to notice the figure, wearing a watch cap over a bald head, nod to himself and turn away to walk on towards a postbox.

Hector Shaw didn't need Martin King's phone anymore. It had done its job.

At the postbox he deposited a padded envelope addressed to DI Anna Gwynne, c/o Avon and Somerset MCRTF, Portishead, Bristol, and moved on, swiftly, into the belly of the city.

A LETTER FROM DYLAN

I want to say a huge thank you for choosing to read *Before She Falls*. If you did enjoy it and want to keep up to date with all my latest releases, just sign up at the following link. Your email address will never be shared and you can unsubscribe at any time.

www.bookouture.com/dylan-young

I'm pretty certain that Anna and Hector Shaw's 'relationship' has not quite ended yet. Especially now that he is out in the wide world. For those of you coming across them for the first time in *Before She Falls*, you might like to read more in *The Silent Girls* and *Blood Runs Cold*, the first two books in the Anna Gwynne series, also available from Bookouture.

As for the future, please sign up and I'll keep you posted.

I really hope you loved *Before She Falls*, and if you did I would be very grateful if you could write a review wherever it is you purchased the book. It's always fantastic to hear what you think, and it makes such a difference in helping new readers to discover one of my books for the first time.

You can get in touch on my Facebook page, through Twitter, Goodreads or my website.

Thanks again,
Dylan

ACKNOWLEDGEMENTS

Once again, my thanks to the team at Bookouture, who make the process of creating a book as easy as a difficult job can be.

Printed in Great Britain
by Amazon

40355397R00183